Presents

Duncan Ralston's

- *a Horror Collection* -

"Cuttings" first published in *The Black Room Manuscripts Vol. One* (The Sinister Horror Company), © 2014

"Chompers" first published in *Death by Chocolate* (KnightWatch Press), © 2015

"Sanctuary" first published in *The Sirens Call #21*, © 2015

"Stray" first published in *The Animal* (Edge), © 2015

"He Is Risen" first published in *Easter Eggs & Bunny Boilers* (Matt Shaw Publications), © 2016

"My Protector" first published in *The Devil's Guests* (Matt Shaw Publications), © 2016

"Squirm" first published in *VS* (Shadow Work Publishing), © 2016

Cover design by 77 Studios © 2017

ISBN-13: 978-1988819334
ISBN-10: 1988819334

HOW TO KILL A CELEBRITY

A HOT WIND swept up from the Mississippi as Annie Watkins entered Channel 5 through the employee entrance. Barely a year out of school, she hadn't expected to hear back from "NOLA's Favorite News" at all, let alone in the same week as her interview. The job hunt had been arduous, but with any luck it was finally over. Annie thought, and not for the first time, about destiny.

After a wait of a few minutes a man named Ray Smart met her in the foyer, introducing himself as her supervisor. She laughed aloud, elated by the news, before rushing to apologize for the outburst. After so long working at the City Park Muffuletta stand while looking for a job in her field, she could finally tell them she was done—unless, of course, she screwed it up acting crazy on her first day.

Ray gave her a tour of the station. She'd been to several TV facilities the past year, almost literally begging for unpaid work, but had never gotten the full tour. When Holly Weathers—a fitting name for a meteorologist or an adult film star—strode past them in the hall, beaming her sunny smile on them, Annie found herself a little star-struck, but she managed to conceal it well.

Ray was friendly in a business-like way, chatty about colleagues and staff, but never offering gossip. Annie, with a pad and pen, took notes of things he seemed to feel the need to stress. Rotating shifts, days and afternoons, with overtime as required.

Annie came back on Monday to meet the man who'd be training her. Scrawny, hunched-over, wearing prescription sunglasses, a Rush 2112 t-shirt and cargo shorts with gray tube socks pulled up to his virtually hairless shins, the man reminded her of a grimy '80s record producer. His brown hair was thick and wild, skin like tallowed leather and teeth so clean and straight they could only be dentures.

"I'm Burt Ellis," he said, offering a scrawny hand with too-long fingernails. Annie took it, zapping him with static. She pulled back, shaking out her hand in pain and embarrassment.

"Sorry," she told Burt, who stared, mouth agape, in something like horror. "Must be the carpet."

Burt's dentures clacked shut, and he gave her a measured look. "Musta been," he agreed. He didn't appear to be pleased to have her beside him in the cramped editing suite, but he did as Ray asked, showing her the ropes in a mechanical, droning way as they recut a digitized version of the Rod Serling obituary Burt had edited on 2-inch quadruplex videotape in 1975. Annie was too young to remember *The Twilight Zone,* but she recognized the theme song.

She found Burt's tobacco smell unpleasant, and his stolen half-smiling glances were vaguely disconcerting, but she learned a fair bit, and made copious notes. During lunch, the two of them sat side by side in the cafeteria, eating without conversation. After lunch, more of the same: a methodical recitation of information and demonstration, after which Annie showed him what she'd learned.

"Close enough for cable," Burt said at five minutes to six, pushing out of his chair. "That's enough for today. *Hasta mañana*. I need a fuckin' drink."

The following day, Annie returned to work to discover Burt Ellis had retired.

"You're on your own," Ray told her.

"But... but I'm not ready."

"Burt told me you have a gift. He said... what was it he said? Was it 'Practice makes perfect'? You'll do fine. It's just standbys." The telephone rang. Ray gave it a look of annoyance. "Let's touch base at the end of the week, huh?"

"Wait a minute, sir, what are—" The door closed behind him. "—standbys?" she finished with a resigned sigh.

"STANDBYS," KYRA NG told her over lunch. "Obituaries of famous people. Say the Queen dies, or, I dunno, Steven Tyler. You need an edited package for a live hit. You've seen them. The more famous the celebrity, the more unstable, the older or sicker they are, we've got their life stories on hand, ready to tweak the second the news of their deaths comes down the wire."

The cafeteria was noisy, every seat packed with techies, office workers, and on-air talent. The sports team took up the table next to them, chatting and guffawing in the phony-sounding way they did during color commentary. Annie found it difficult to hear.

"That's pretty morbid, don't you think?" she asked, leaning in close, taking the opportunity to spear a crouton from her colleague's Caesar salad.

Kyra raised her eyebrows by way of reaction while she chewed and swallowed. "Morbid?" She sipped from her water bottle. "Welcome to 24-hour news."

Annie and Kyra, who worked in the edit suite across the narrow hall, had made fast friends. A little older, a little more cynical, a few too many animal sweaters in her wardrobe, Kyra edited hard news pieces: terrorism, murders, arson, gang violence.

As for Burt, he had edited the standbys for as long as Kyra could remember, and she'd been at Channel 5 for twelve years. Word was he had started in the Telecine days, when they shot programs on film and transferred them to tape for air. "It was weird that he retired like that," she said. "He musta had his foot halfway out the door, just waiting for you to get here."

Annie nodded. "Maybe." She recalled his strange

sidelong glances. At the time she thought he'd been ogling her, but now she had to wonder.

"Anyway, you'll do fine."

"That's what Mr. Smart said."

Kyra laughed. "'*Mister* Smart'!" She shook her head. "It's Ray, hon. Just Ray."

After lunch, Annie sat in Burt's old editing suite—considering it as her own would jinx it, she felt—and waited for an assignment. The whole day long, no one had entered the room after Ray had left her with Burt. She hadn't thought anything of it then, but after hours of twiddling her thumbs in front of the identical wavy backgrounds on the two computer monitors, she started to wonder if she'd entered the Twilight Zone herself.

Peering across the hall, she waited until Kyra looked up from her work and caught her eye.

"What's wrong?"

"Should I be doing something? It feels like I should be doing something."

From down the hall a deep male voice Annie recognized as one of the *Live @ 5 News* anchors shouted, "Kyra, how's that ISIS piece coming?"

Kyra threw an annoyed look at the wall. "Keep your pants on, Phil!" She turned back to Annie, looking frazzled. "When they need you, they'll let you know."

"But what do I do until then?"

Kyra provided a brief look of sympathy. "You've got the internet, don't you?"

Annie faced the Mac's desktop, found the browser icon. "Uh-huh."

"Well, there's a whole world wide web there just waiting to be discovered," Kyra told her, and swiveled her chair back toward her desk.

Annie stared at the icon a moment, then clicked it. The browser opened. She watched the cursor blink in the search bar. She hadn't signed on for this. She craved action. She wanted hard deadlines, she wanted Phil Macready yelling at her for the ISIS piece. Sitting all day facing two monitors each with empty edit windows—they were *paying* her for this?

At six PM, after what seemed like endless hours surfing the internet, Annie grabbed her purse and stood up from the desk. "Close enough for cable," she muttered to herself, and stepped into the hall. "See you tomorrow, Kyra?"

Kyra looked up, still frazzled despite having handed off her piece. "You bet."

Annie made a weak attempt at a smile. "Have a good night."

Kyra saluted her, and returned to the screens.

IT WAS A week before Annie's first original standby obituary.

The second day on her own, a young blonde Production Assistant with hipster glasses and a wallet chain told her to update a few older standbys: a hip hop artist with a notoriously dangerous lifestyle, an actor with a degenerative disease, a famously inflammatory politician facing a handful of death threats.

Then… nothing.

Several days, staring at the monitors. On the fourth day, she brought in some home videos to practice cutting. Her father having passed two years prior, she thought she'd put together a little tribute to him for her parents' anniversary this year. Not sure if such a thing would be appropriate, she'd asked for her aunt's blessing before proceeding. It was difficult for her to watch, at first. Eventually, she grew accustomed to seeing her father's face again: the way his bright smile rose all the way to his eyes, the way he often swept a hand across the top of his head, as if brushing away non-existent dandruff from his close-cropped hair, how he'd sweep Annie and her mother up in giant hugs and twirl them from the kitchen, passing under the creaky bannister, to the front room.

Orville Watkins had been a defense attorney before taking up the gavel, though his closest friends had been calling him "Judge" since grade school. He'd been a good father, had called Annie from the office when putting in extra hours, and when he finally attained the chair he'd been born to fill, he'd spent long evenings in the backyard, tooling in the garden while the sun sank over the lake. She'd bring out a tall glass of bitter iced tea, the way he liked it, and he would beam his big smile up at her.

All the while, all those years, an invisible noose

had dangled over his head, poised for the right moment to tighten.

At noon, with a good amount of footage digitized and some clips dragged in a rough edit on the timeline, Annie broke for lunch.

How did Burt deal with so much boredom? she wondered, slinking off alone to the cafeteria. With Kyra on days off, she had no one to sit with. Other people in her department were pleasant enough but seemed to be too busy or too into their own cliques to offer much more than a nod and smile.

"This seat taken?"

Startled, Annie looked up to see the creepy old Camera Operator from *Live @ 5*, though she'd already identified him by the aura of cheap Scotch. He stuffed an apple in his mouth like a cooked pig as he sat, setting his cafeteria tray down on the table. She thought his name was Walt or Wilt, though it didn't matter. She wasn't so desperate for company as to consider making conversation with a career alcoholic.

"Burt asked how you're doing," he said, crunching the apple between words.

She wasn't sure if he was talking to her or the news anchor across from them, but the newscaster — a term Annie always liked, as if they created the news through magic—dressed in a pinstriped suit, didn't look up from the sports pages.

"Excuse me?"

"Burt Ellis," Walt—it was Walt, she remembered,

Walt Brenner—said. "The guy whose shoes you filled?"

"Oh." Some people thought Burt had come into money, but it didn't look to Annie like the guy had ever seen real money in his life. He'd retired early, apparently. No golden handshake, just a reduced pension. And no one knew why.

"Never did occur to you why they let you jump the book to get that position, did it?"

"'Jump the book'?"

"Whole ass-load of union members lookin for editing gigs," he said by way of explaining, "not to mention freeloaders—I mean free*lancers*, excuse me—and they give the job to you, fresh out of college." He crunched his apple, breathing loudly through his nose. "You couldn't *give* that job away, sugar. Then here you come, fresh-faced and innocent, ready to take on the whole goddamn world." He swallowed just as noisily as he breathed. "Burt knew right away, you were the one."

Annie sipped her vegetable cocktail, playing nonchalant. "What does that mean, 'the one'?"

"He woulda felt a whole lot better if it'd gone to someone who deserved it, you know? *Really* deserved it. Like that little twerp who does Chyron I'd love to smack that kid in the chops."

Walt gnawed off a chunk of apple, looking off while he chewed, likely imagining how the scene would play out. "I don't want you to blame Burt in this, okay? He didn't choose you any more than he was chosen. Just bad luck, I guess. Some of that N'awlins juju. But he asked me to tell you, the burden is yours now. And practice makes perfect." He set the apple core down, already beginning to go brown. "I'm real sorry this had to happen to you, kiddo. That's me saying that part, not him."

The last bite of chocolate croissant stuck in her throat and wouldn't go down. She took a big gulp of juice, swallowing hard to dislodge it. "Sorry for what?" She tried not to gasp for breath. "There's nothing to be sorry about. I love my job."

Walt Brenner gave her a look, his tired gray eyes jittery. "Suit yourself." He shrugged up his skinny shoulders and slid his tray away from her, moving himself to the next seat.

A half hour later Annie returned from the tape library with an armload of yellow Betacam boxes. Not sure what she was hunting for, Annie came across a movie she hadn't seen since she was a kid, which started her on a hunt for more of Eddie Bing's comedies, talk show appearances, and standup specials. She made herself stop at the seven tapes she could carry without mishap, hoping to find more footage in the digital archives.

Kyra stopped what she was doing to give Annie a funny look.

"Anyone come by while I was gone?"

"Just some tumbleweed." Kyra smirked. "Looks like you got your work cut out for you."

Annie shuffled the tapes awkwardly. "Yup.

That'll be the time someone gives me an assignment, right?"

"Don't count on it."

She stacked the boxes beside the old VTR, and, one by one, began racking through the tapes, looking for the best clips to digitize. With headphones on, her laughter at Bing's antics drew the attention of Kyra.

"You all right in there?"

"Remember that movie *Cool Feet*?"

Kyra sneered. "Ugh! I hate Eddie Bing. So corny."

Annie shrugged. "I like it." She caught Bing hamming it up as he tried to remove his foot from a toilet, and laughed a little quieter, self-conscious. Kyra shook her head, while Bing ended up slipping out of his shoe and fishing it out of the toilet, only to be caught by his fiancée's father with the dripping loafer in his hand.

Annie cut the footage together into what felt like a fitting tribute, a good mix of Bing's comedy performances and dramatic roles, with sound-ups in all the right places, ending on a slow-mo clip of his famously awkward smile, and fade to black.

Something jingled down the hall toward the edit suites. Shuffling feet on the carpet stopped at her doorway. The P.A.'s wallet chain jingled once more, then quieted as she stopped in the doorway.

"We need a new standby, ASAP."

Annie rose in her chair, brightening… It took her a moment to realize a more respectful expression was required. This was, after all, someone's life. "Who is it?"

The P.A.—Hilary, Annie recalled from her first-day notes—caught a look at the monitors and staggered back a step. "*God*—" She gave Annie a look of horror. "How did you…?"

Annie followed her wide-eyed gaze. "What? It isn't…?"

"It's Eddie Bing." Hilary shook her head in incredulity. Behind her Kyra peered out of her suite with concern. "Suicide, they think. Dead in a hotel room, that's all I know." She tore her eyes off the screens to look at Annie again. "How did you *know*?"

Annie felt accused. "Me? I didn't know. It's just a coincidence."

The P.A. took another step out of the room, shaking her head. "Just… I'll get a reporter… for the voiceover." She backed away until the doorway was empty. Her jingle-shuffle disappeared back down the hall. Kyra remained in the door to her own suite, eyeing her queerly.

"Annie? You okay?"

"Yeah." Annie was shaken by the coincidence—at least she *hoped* that was all it was. She felt like she'd stepped on a live wire plugged directly into the macabre machinery of the universe. "Yeah," she said. "Just a little weirded out, that's all."

"No doubt." Kyra was clearly a little freaked herself. "Let's get a drink tonight, huh? Just you and me."

Annie nodded, turning back to Bing in the dual

monitors. Looking at it now, she recognized how haunted it appeared. Unlike her father's, the smile never reached Bing's eyes.

"I think that would be good."

THEY SAT AT the bar, drinking too-sweet Sazeracs, watching KBNO's sister 24-hour news channel. Annie's pony tail had come undone, sticking out from the purple elastic like frayed wires. Beside her perspiring Old Fashioned glass, she'd ground a small pile of peanuts into the scuffed, dark wood. She plucked another nut from the bowl, cracked it open, and smashed its insides under her glass.

Eddie Bing's death occurred two weeks before the theater premiere of his latest comedy special. A dramatic series had just been greenlit with him in the lead role, he'd been reuniting with his ex-wife, and communicating with his estranged children again. All signs pointed toward a renaissance in Bing's career, in his life, until—

"*Suicide.*" Kyra shook her head at the big screen TV over the bar. "No one could have predicted that. Just a whole lot of bad luck, Annie."

"It happened at the *same time...*"

A troubled look crossed Kyra's face before settling on a sympathetic smile. "Coincidence."

"Hung himself, just like—"

"Like?"

Annie simply shook her head and crushed another peanut. The anchor repeated that more would be revealed about Eddie Bing as it was discovered, then threw to the 11P.M. news. Annie's standby was the first piece.

"Turn this up," Kyra told the muscular bartender. When the segment ended, she turned to Annie, their faces washed in blue light from the TVs. "No matter how you feel about it, that's a hell of a package you cut." Annie said nothing, merely sipped her drink. "Hey, it took me eight years to make the top story," Kyra told her. "You did it in *six days*."

"Are you trying to make me feel better, or worse?"

Kyra shrugged. "Little of both, maybe. I'm totally jelly."

Annie allowed herself a grin. Her companion nudged her with an elbow.

"There's that smile." She turned toward the bartender's gleaming bald head. "Bartender!" When he turned, she shook her glass. "Another two Sazeracs, *por favor*."

"It really is good, isn't it?" Annie asked when her companion's attention wandered back from the bartender's tight jeans.

"*Too* good," Kyra agreed with narrowed eyes. "I better watch out. You might make a standby of me, and take *my* job."

Annie slugged her in the shoulder. Kyra cackled, rubbing her arm.

"I'm totally kidding!"

"It's *not* funny." Dead serious, Annie scowled until Kyra could no longer keep a straight face, and the two of them busted out laughing. The bartender gave them a peculiar look, only making them laugh harder.

ANNIE CAME IN hungover the next morning, the licorice taste of absinthe still on her tongue.

She stood in the doorway to her edit suite—it was *hers* now, no denying it—and peered in at the equipment. Green lights flickered in the dim room, lighted by the overheads in the hall. Nothing particularly menacing about anything. And yet...

A groan from behind shook her from the edge of psychic distress. Krya shambled toward her, baggy eyes and hair a mess. "I am so tired."

"Me too."

Kyra stepped past her into the dim room and flopped down in Annie's chair. Annie imagined latches clamping down on Kyra's wrists, the chair swooping her toward the desk, the twin monitors turning themselves on like the eyes of a malevolent animal rousing from sleep. But the monitors remained dark. Kyra looked up at her in mild curiosity. "Whatcha doin'?" she asked, drawing out the words in singsong.

Annie shook her head, temples throbbing. "Nothing."

She following Annie's gaze toward the monitors. "Annie, it was a *coincidence*. It's just a bunch of—" She plucked the mouse off the table, set it back down. "—*harmless* junk." She flicked on the monitors, one after another. They brightened to their wavy backgrounds and tiny icons, not malicious eyes, not a cackling malevolent demon trapped behind the twin screens.

Annie nodded. Of course it was a coincidence. *Of course.* She hummed the *Twilight Zone* theme. Kyra squeezed her aching temples while the two of them laughed.

A metallic jingle moved toward them. They both turned with identical looks of dulled shock.

"Annie, we need a standby for Eleanor Harrison," Hillary said, not daring to meet Annie's eyes. "You guys look like shit."

"What happened?" This was Kyra. Annie couldn't speak.

"You guys didn't hear? She's on the news right now."

Kyra changed the input on the small monitor beside the VTR. Without sound, all they saw was a black man in his mid- to late-fifties speaking somberly from behind a podium. Behind him was Eleanor herself, fifty-three, a tad overweight but otherwise healthy, hugging her grown children, who in turn hugged her grandkids. The story swept along the bottom of the screen: **PASTOR AND CIVIL RIGHTS LEADER ELEANOR HARRISON CANCER DIAGNOSIS SHOCKS FAMILY AND FRIENDS, CELEBRITIES LEND SUPPORT…**

Shocked into action, Annie got to work, scouring old library tapes for clips of Harrison in sermons, interviews and debates, protesting another black youth gunned down by white police officers, shaking hands with Maya Angelou and Queen Elizabeth. Watching the highlights of this uncompromising woman's life, Annie couldn't help but feel genuine sorrow. Harrison was one of her parents' heroes and her own. She cut a suitable tribute for the woman, "sweetened" it with somber music, and had Phil Macready sit for a voiceover, all the while bothered by the look on Hilary the P.A.'s face when Annie handed the Bing standby to her.

After work, she puttered around the apartment for hours, trying to get the Harrison standby off her mind. *Couldn't happen twice*, she told herself, a mantra on repeat. Inevitably, she ended up opening one of a stack of photo albums. A photo of her parents made her smile, young and in love in the '80s, Orville with his short jheri curl, her mother's blonde hair in Bo Derek cornrows that dangled over her dashiki dress. Exhausted, Annie finally fell asleep on the sofa with the book in her hands, missing the 11P.M. news by eleven minutes.

She woke early the next morning, but still had to rush to get to work on time. Driving in dense traffic with the news on and a cool breeze coming from the open windows, the words "Eleanor Harrison was found dead..." shocked her so badly she stepped on the brakes in the middle of the road. Horns bleated by on either side, vehicles swerving to avoid collision. Annie sat rigid behind the wheel, breathing shallowly, unable to think beyond those terrible words—*found dead*—let alone make the movements required to signal and pull off onto the soft shoulder of the road.

She couldn't go back to work. Couldn't face that room, those monitors. Fear got her moving again. She pulled into the Raising Cane's lot, told the on-call scheduler she was ill and wouldn't be able to make it in for her shift the next day, then speed-dialed Kyra's cell.

"Hey, sweetie." There was compassion Kyra's in her voice. Still at work, she'd obviously heard the news. "You okay?"

"I'm fine," Annie said. "You wouldn't happen to know Burt Ellis's home address, would you?"

"That old creepazoid? Oh yeah, me and him were tight."

"Kyra, I'm serious."

A moment's silence. "There's a master list in Scheduling. Let me go see if he's still on it."

"Call me back."

"I *will*," Kyra said, responding to the urgency in Annie's voice. "Are you coming in today?" Annie told her she wasn't. "Probably a good idea. People are really creeped out about that standby, especially after Bing's. Although I think most of them are just jealous you made top story twice in two days."

Annie sat in the car, peering out at the red and white blur of passing traffic. *Twice could still be a coincidence,* she told herself. *Couldn't happen again.*

Her ringtone startled her. "Got it." Kyra rhymed

off Burt's address. "Be careful, Annie. He's one odd duck. I'm not entirely sure he's not a serial killer."

I'm not entirely sure I'm *not one*, Annie thought. She offered thanks instead of voicing her concern.

Burt Ellis lived in a boathouse in the West End. The next morning, Annie parked beside his truck in the small lot up the road, gold metallic paint with a cap on the bed and a bumper sticker declaring EDITORS DO IT NON-LINEARLY.

Burt's twiggy mail-order and/or stripper girlfriend answered the door in a kimono. She shouted into the dim house in a thick eastern European accent—as if the couple lived in a multi-story house rather than what was essentially a double-wide trailer on the water—then lit a cigarette and slinked away inside, but not before shooting Annie a scathing look.

Burt came to the door in a grimy robe he was still tying over boxer shorts and scrawny, hairless legs, blinking rapidly before putting on his prescription sunglasses. "Well, I can't say I'm surprised to see you, except for maybe that it took you so long to show up."

Dishes clanged in the sink inside, deliberately loud. Burt peered toward the kitchenette. Annie couldn't see from where she stood, but she could imagine his girlfriend or wife doing the dishes in a fit of jealousy. "Guess we should pro'ly take this outside. Let me get some pants on."

A few minutes later they sat down at a picnic bench in Breakwater Park, overlooking Lake

Pontchartrain. The dark scudding clouds from earlier had moved off toward the east without rain. In hurricane season, the city would surely have felt their wrath. Nearby, children shouted and scurried while their mothers gabbed.

"You're scared, aren't you?" He stuck an unlit smoke between his lips with a sheepish grin.

"Why did you leave so suddenly?"

"I take it you're not ready to talk about this."

Annie held her tongue while Burt lit his smoke. "It was the '70s when I started at Channel 5," Burt told her, "back before all that *Five Means Live* bullshit, when we still called it KBNO. We were still smoking in the studios, and everybody, I mean *everybody*, was on coke." He dragged on his smoke. "That's what I passed it off as, at first: some paranoid dope fantasy."

Annie didn't ask what he meant. There seemed to be no point in pretending she wasn't scared out of her wits.

"The Serling standby, the one we worked on last week? That's the one that really got under my skin. The first handful, it was easy enough to pass them off as coincidence. With Serling's, I couldn't shake that feeling—"

"Like standing on a live wire," Annie said.

Burt agreed with a solemn nod, blowing smoke as he squinted out at the clear, flat water. "How are you sleeping? Any nightmares?"

"I don't sleep well."

"No, I wouldn't imagine. That'll change. You'll get

00:28;00

used to it."

"I don't want to get used to it." Annie watched a little girl in a polka-dot dress chase two boys around the swing set. "I keep thinking it can't be real, it couldn't be me causing this to happen..."

"Except for that feeling." Burt butted out his cigarette on the picnic table. "I used to think the film caused it. When Serling died, KBNO still had a lot of old footage on film. We had to transfer to video with a process called Telecine before we could cut it for air. They probably taught you about it in school. They did? Good. I thought maybe it was the silver gelatin—you know, silver's been thought to have magical properties for centuries. Personally, I think it's a bunch of bullshit, but back then I was grasping at straws. And hell, this was *Rod Serling* we're talking about. The guy practically *invented* shit like this.

"June 26th I cut that obituary. Serling was my third standby. We knew he had heart troubles. By then he was already in the hospital. Docs were talking about open heart surgery. These days that's nothing, but in those days, it was a huge risk. It took him two days to die from that last heart attack on the operating table, but I knew... I mean I *knew*...that last one was because of me."

"But you must have done hundreds of obituaries since then. Every one of them died?"

"Only the completed standbys seem to do it. Think of it like casting a spell. It ain't gonna work without reading the last few words, will it?"

"But you did it again?"

Burt raised his t-shirt—Meatloaf's *Bat Out of Hell*—to reveal a long white scar from his right hip to the middle rib on his left side.

"*Ouch.*"

"You said it. I flew the coop after Serling died." He mimed a plane taking off with his right hand, an unlit cigarette poised between his fingers. "I wanted to get as far away from the Big Easy as possible, but I knew I couldn't stand those New England winters. Miami seemed like a good start. Took the Airlift flight from New Orl'ns International—this was long before they changed the name—on a rickety old DC-8."

Annie didn't know where to begin. She couldn't imagine why he would have come back, burdened with the curse she now bore herself, and told him so.

He grinned. "Guess you never heard about Airlift International Flight 208."

Annie admitted she hadn't, but she was starting to feel as though she knew what happened.

"I swore to myself I wouldn't do another standby. Not a single one. I mean I quit without a day's notice, just up and left. Packed a bag, hightailed it. I got on that plane feeling... *blessed relief.* About as close to whatever you want to call a religious experience as I'd ever felt. I mean, I was twenty years old. I didn't know shit about God. But when that plane took off, I felt like I could join the seminary and be perfectly content for the rest of my life."

He lit the cigarette. Took a long drag, long

enough for the ash to curl. "Weren't up in the air ten minutes before the trouble started. There was this loud *boom*, and suddenly the plane is leaning on its side. Not just women and children screaming but grown men. Hell, *I* was screaming. Those of us who hadn't fell into the lap of their neighbor or into the aisle were hangin from our seat belts. They told us later that an engine blew. But I knew different." He narrowed his eyes at her. "*It* was pulling me back. *It* wouldn't let me leave until I was done."

Annie merely shook her head.

"I prayed, I mean I *prayed* like I never have in my life. I promised I'd go right back to work if whoever was in charge of all this would spare my life. I meant it, too. And just about the time I'd finished promising, the pilot managed to get that bastard horizontal again by some force of sheer luck, and we water-landed in the Gulf just past Chandeleur Sound. If we'd been any closer to shore, no doubt the gators woulda been eatin leftovers for weeks. Out of a hundred and twenty-seven passengers fifty-three of us made it, including two stewardesses, without whom we all woulda drowned. Everyone in the cockpit died. Everyone in the front of the plane died. Miserable, groveling excuse for a sack of shit me made it out alive to kill again. And God help me if I didn't think that someone like me had already cut the story for the late news. That someone had, through the same sort of magic or what-have-you that made me cut the Serling obituary, caused that DC-8 to drop out of the sky."

"That's..." Annie didn't know how to describe what he'd told her so she merely said, "*Wow*."

Burt uttered a morose chuckle. "Honey, that is the understatement of the goddamn century. And you know, there isn't a day goes by I don't wish I'd died in that crash. That it ended, whatever the hell it is, with me on that plane in 1975."

"Cut to forty years later," Annie said sardonically.

"More like a long cross-dissolve. All told I've killed thirty-eight people. I wish like hell I'd had the guts to kill *myself*."

Annie's father might have *Amen*-ed to that. Of course having sent an innocent man to the chair in 1990, and having later discovered the deceased's innocence through DNA evidence linking the murder-rapes to a man already doing time for aggravated assault, Judge Orville Watkins had hung himself from the bannister in the Watkins family home.

Executioner was her family legacy.

"Why me, Burt? Why did it have to be me?"

"It's a dirty job, but someone's gotta do it." He favored her with a dour smile, crushing another smelly butt on the table. "I wish I knew. I'm sorry, but I didn't choose you anymore than I was chosen."

"That's what Walt said. I think there's more to it than that."

Burt shifted uncomfortably, wiping away bits of cut grass that had blown up onto the table. "It wasn't a choice, you gotta understand that. You ever see someone for the first time and swear you've met before? It's like that. First time I saw you, day you brought in your resume, I passed you in the foyer and knew—*I knew*—you were the one. I gave my notice that same day. Then when we shook hands…"

"The spark."

"Passing on the torch. Old Jewish fella by the name of Ham Gottlieb ended up blowing his brains out with an antique Ruger after passing on the hex or whatever it is to me. I mean this guy survived the Holocaust, and he couldn't hold another week with what he'd done."

"You think it's a curse?"

"Annie, I wish I knew. This is powerful shit you're dealing with. I mean, this thing survived film, videotape, all the way into the digital age. Who knows, it could have existed before film, maybe the guy who passed it on to Gottlieb wrote obits for the *Times-Picayune*. All I know for sure is you don't just quit on it. I learned that the hard way."

He slipped the end of a cigarette out of the pack.

"Not another one," Annie said. "Please."

Burt shrugged, tapping the butt back inside. She thanked him. Her *lungs* thanked him.

"I still don't get how you knew they'd pick me. They could've picked anybody for the job."

"Same way I knew my time was up, and for the same reason old Ham Gottlieb picked me out of every kid who put in an application, I suppose." He traced out the symbol for infinity with a finger on the table. After a moment, he looked up at Annie again. "Way I figure, they don't know they're doing it. Probably think the decision was theirs, when they hired you. When they hired *me*. But it's not. They're just playing into the hands of fate."

Annie shook her head. "So there's nothing I can do. I just have to—what? Wait thirty years for that feeling to hit *me*? Pass it on to the next poor kid who drops off her resume?"

"I honestly don't know." Burt smoothed his mustache. "I feel for you, kid, sincerely, I do. But… and this might sound insensitive… but have you considered keeping the balance?"

"Like what? Yoga? Fucking *meditation*?"

Burt snickered. "Hell no! I mean, you make a standby for someone who might actually deserve it. Maybe get some serial killer's death penalty put on the fast-track." He shrugged. "Make some scumbag scam-artist like Madoff get his just desserts."

She thought of her father's gray face. The noose. The creak of the bannister. Annie had been the first one home that night. If Lydia Watkins hadn't stopped for groceries on the way from work, she might have spared her daughter a lifetime of questions, of *nightmares*. "I couldn't do that," she said, her voice weak. "Play God like that."

"Aren't you already? I mean, I don't know if you noticed, but it seems to me like God's been on extended sick leave, don't it, sugar?"

00:34;00

"Don't call me that. All you old-timers call me *sweetie* and *sugar* and it drives me up the fucking wall."

"Annie it is." Burt grinned sarcastically, holding up his hands in mock surrender. "Wouldn't want to upset you. You might wind up making a standby for *me*."

"That's not fucking funny. And I wouldn't. I *can't*. I can't do it again. Not ever."

"Suit yourself," Burt said. "Sooner or later fate or destiny or whatever it is makes you and me and Gottlieb do what we've done is gonna force your hand. All I know is, when I hated my job, my *life*, I did everything I could to make it as painless as possible."

He plucked the twisted butts off the table, and pushed himself up with a groan, both from himself and the aging wood. "I wish you all the best, Annie Watkins. Sincerely, I do. But if I spend any longer out here shooting the breeze with you, the wife'll be fixin' to Bobbit my ass."

Annie watched him go, shrinking into the distance across the long expanse of grass, the weight of helplessness pressing down on her, stopping her from chasing after him and screaming at him until her throat was raw.

The table creaked as she stood herself, creaking like the bannister, like the noose around her father's neck. She wondered, and not for the first time, if suicide was her legacy, too.

II

MAXINE WATKINS KEPT shop in Bywater, selling Central African-inspired art and sculpture out of her home. Fat little terra cotta heads with bug eyes and fish-like mouths were her biggest seller—one even graced the Contemporary Louisiana Art exhibit at NOMA. As a child, they'd always reminded Annie of the illustration from the books of Roald Dahl.

Maxine poured her niece a glass of iced tea, then sat on a small stool at the worktable. She did good business with her art, good enough to move into a larger home in Algiers or the Garden District, but she'd lived in the "Sliver by the River" long before her name became known in the local scene. She had her studio, her kiln out back, and a small living quarters in the camelback upstairs, and that was all she required.

Annie sipped her tea. Bitter, the way she liked it.

"What's on your mind, child?" Maxine asked, kneading a large hunk of clay. "You didn't come all the way out here to drink my tea."

A ghost of a smile crossed Annie's lips. "No, I didn't. But I would, you know. It's that good."

Maxine waved the compliment away. "Is this about your job? I never did congratulate you, did I?"

"No. Thank you, Auntie Maxie."

"Well? Are you going to tell me or would you have me drag it out of you?"

Maxine wore her hair in a scarf, and her

overlarge, brightly colored shirt couldn't hide the many paint stains and smudges of dried clay. Annie had always admired her aunt's artistic abilities, but she'd never envied her wardrobe. In snug blue jeans and a white t-shirt, Annie felt underdressed. She told Maxine everything.

"Well that's quite the tale," Maxine said, pushing aside another fat little head ready for the kiln. "If you weren't your father's daughter, I wouldn't believe a word of it."

"You believe me?"

"I've never known you to lie, even when you should have. You didn't come to tell me a story, though, now did you? You came to see if I could speak to the Loa on your behalf."

Maxine was the only family member who practiced what Annie thought of as "authentic Louisiana Voodoo." Annie's father had disavowed it, ashamed of the commercialization and skeptical of the religious aspects, although her grandparents had been traditionalists, like Maxine. Annie had loved Maxie's sculptures and paintings, but the Hoodoo charms, the dolls and Gris-Gris in her aunt's bedroom, had always intrigued her most. She'd often wondered if they were merely decorative, or if Maxie had ever used them.

Tears stood in Annie's eyes. "*Please,*" she said. They fell, moistening the clay in two spots on the table. "I can't live like this."

Maxine took her niece's hands. The dried clay felt

chalky against Annie's skin. Maxine held them firmly, glittering green eyes fixed on the deep brown of Annie's. "Though it works through modern tools, this evil is *old*, Annie. Make no mistake."

Annie shivered. Despite the late-spring heat, the warmth from her aunt's hands was just about the only place she didn't feel cold. "Can you help me…?"

Maxine kissed her fingertips. The warmth spread to Annie's wrists.

"I can try."

THE HALLS OF Channel 5 were virtually empty when Annie brought Maxine through. The security guard on duty looked up from whatever he was watching behind the big desk and gave them a nod. Annie used her card on the door, and held it open for her aunt.

"He's cute," Maxine said once they were safely behind the door. "For you, I mean."

Annie shook her head, proceeding down the main hall. Maxine followed, lugging the cloth bag onto her shoulder, glass clinking inside. A spiral staircase took them down toward the newsroom. As short as the two of them were, they still had to duck under the ceiling. The overheads came on as they entered the carpeted hall leading toward the edit suites, startling them both into an embrace.

Maxine clucked her tongue. "Look at us. Scared of the lights."

They chuckled nervously and let go of each other. Annie continued to her suite, flicking on the light before entering. Maxine settled her bag on the chair.

"I expected something more ominous. This…"

"Is it cursed?" Annie wondered.

"We'll find out, won't we?" Auntie Maxie opened up her bag of tricks. She brought out the candles first, white and black, a half dozen of each. "To send the evil back from where it came," she'd said while taking them off the shelf and packing them into the bag. Next came the checkered cloth in red and white, which she laid on the chair, setting the fat candles atop it. "Red and white. Those are Papa Legba's colors," she explained.

Annie repeated the name as a question.

"You'll see, Annie-dear." Maxine began marking out a large circle on the carpet, a cross in the circle. "Can't do this without the cosmogram," Maxine explained, reacting to Annie's mortified gasp. She laid the cloth over the center of the cross, placed candles at the ends of each line. She removed two tall wine glasses from the bag, a bottle of water, a bottle of white rum, and a clay pot painted red, then placed them on the cloth. She poured water into one glass and stood it in one of the pie-shaped areas she'd chalked, and the contents of the rum bottle into the second. Into the bowl, she placed a handful of salt water taffy, a cigar and a tea candle. She scattered some coins beside it.

"For the offering," she explained.

Maxine poured water into a rag, and held it out to her niece. "You might want to cover the smoke detector." Annie did so, wrapping it with the dampened fabric. The two of them lit the candles together, then Maxine stood in the circle, holding out a hand to Annie.

Annie took it. Stepped into the circle.

In the silence, the hall lights went out. They turned to each other, momentarily frightened. "Somebody ought to do something about those lights," Maxine said. Annie agreed with a nod.

Maxine led Annie in reciting The Lord's Prayer, Hail Mary, and the Apostle's Creed. Once finished, she let go of Annie's hand, got down to her haunches, and raised the bowl. "Odu Legba!" she cried, holding out the bowl to the four directions. "Papa Legba, open the door! Open the door for me, so that I may pass!"

Annie listened to the dull hum of electricity, watched their flickering shadows on the wall. There was no live wire feeling tonight, senses dulled by too much crying, too much worrying.

"Open the door, your children await!"

The monitors flickered on. Annie sucked in a nervous breath.

"We wish to speak with the Loa! We wish to speak to Baron Cimetière!"

Video was already playing in on the twin monitors. Watkins family home movies. The two women shared an anxious look. "That wasn't you, was it?" Maxine asked, an edge of fear in her voice. Annie merely shook her head. Something about the videos troubled her. Something was different, but she couldn't put her finger on what it was.

The hall lights buzzed on.

Both women turned, expecting the Baron's dark figure to enter the room.

Suddenly it hit her: Orville and Lydia Watkins weren't present in the video. All the time she'd spent cutting it, making it just right, and someone had removed all the clips of her parents, leaving only herself and Aunt Maxine.

Boots clomped down the hall toward them. Maxine clasped Annie's hands tightly in her own as a tall figure stepped into the doorway, candlelight flickering over the figure's brute features. She recognized him immediately. Not a supernatural presence, but the night security guard, the one Auntie Maxie called "cute."

"You ladies can't be burning candles in here," he said, eyes wide to take in everything. "You can't be doing Voodoo in here, neither."

"*Hoodoo,*" Maxine corrected, before apologizing and hurriedly blowing out the candles. Annie joined her, fear still gnawing at her like animals chewing on electrical cables. The videos had played by themselves, for one. For another, they seemed only to feature herself and her aunt.

The security guard stood out in the hall while Annie and her aunt gathered everything back up into the bag. "You know, you could get into a lot of trouble bringing alcohol onto the premises," he warned Annie.

"We'll keep that in mind," Maxine said for her. "Have a good night."

A light rain had slicked the pavement as they made their way to the car. "You felt it in there, didn't you?" Maxine asked. "An evil presence... reaching out from beyond?"

"I don't know."

"Those videos... playing by themselves... Did you make those?"

Annie got in behind the wheel. "It was the video for Mom."

"I thought you said it was a tribute. I didn't see your father in them at all. Didn't see your mother, either, come to think of it."

Annie started the car, drove out of the empty lot, her mind still on the videos. She pulled out into oncoming traffic without looking—

"Watch out!"

Annie jerked the wheel, swerving a hair too late to avoid the oncoming car. The sedan clipped the driver's side and Annie's car spun out, skidding over the slick street, leaping over the opposite sidewalk. It struck a tall hydrant head on.

Shattered glass silenced Maxine's rising scream. The air bag exploded in a cloud of talcum, bursting Annie's nose, the pain dulled by the agony in her lower back as the seat belt jerked her backward. Stars flooded her vision. The horn bleated out into the night.

She came around a moment or minutes later. No

one had come across the accident yet, so she assumed it was the former. The airbag had deflated. Blood smeared over its silver surface, her own blood. The windshield lay in pieces on the crumpled hood.

What she at first took for rain pattered on the roof and fell in through the window frame. Even in her semiconscious state, she understood the collision had popped the hydrant.

With immense strain, she turned toward Maxine.

Rain fell into her eyes. Her vision blurred, went pink, as she stared at the empty passenger seat. Blinking away blood, it struck her: Auntie Maxie had gone through the windshield.

Please, she thought, as a queasy wave of oblivion washed over her. *I'll do whatever you want... just please... don't let us die...*

The promise echoed in her ears as her world faded to black.

GETTING BACK TO health took time. She'd suffered fractured discs, had broken two ribs and fractured two more. The surgeons had straightened her nose, stitched gashes in her forehead and cheeks. After weeks of healing and physiotherapy, Annie once again sat in front of the editing monitors in her eight-by ten cell, a sentence she would serve forty hours a week until her time came to pass the torch.

Ray Smart welcomed her back, told her he'd "touch base" with her at the end of the week. For the constant pain in her back, he'd brought her an orthopedic chair.

Maxine had survived the crash with extensive internal injuries. Blood was drained from her skull, her punctured spleen removed. Due to compound fractures in her left leg, she walked with a cane. Walt Brenner, drunk and speeding toward an overtime shift, had passed away in the second ambulance.

Annie eased into her new chair, gazed for a moment down at the indistinct chalk marks left on the carpet between her feet. The pain wasn't so bad with her pills. She'd been taking too many, but the haze was navigable. She settled in behind the monitors, and got back to work.

On the streetcar ride to work, she'd read about Congressman Lassiter, a staunch homophobe and segregationist currently suffering from heart troubles. When the P.A. jingled down the hall, dragging her feet on the carpet, Annie was ready.

"How did you—?" Hilary began. But of course she knew. *They all* knew.

"Just keeping the balance," Annie said with a morose chuckle, handing it over.

Kyra peered over from across the hall, and for a moment, their eyes locked. She turned away quickly without expression, and the P.A. crept out of the room, standby in hand, glancing back at Annie until she was gone.

CHOMPERS

DR. BARRERA—IF he was a real doctor—worked out of an abandoned warehouse in the factory district. Shipping containers stood empty amid slats of dust-swirling lamplight, scattered like broken teeth after a bar fight. Dim light poured in through holes in its painted-over windows. Shreds of wiring hung loose from high catwalks, where metal staircases had rusted and toppled. Somewhere deep inside, a generator grumbled.

At the far end of the warehouse, one shipping container had been set up with a dentist's chair, a small sink, a white cabinet, and an instruments table. Long orange cables snaked from its insides to the rattling power supply. A garden hose led off into the darkness beyond the container, toward a source of water. The contents of the container were pristine white and shimmering steel under large halogen lamps strung from its corrugated top. A mid-fifties Hispanic man dressed in white, dark hair with silver-gray wings at the sides, and an older woman with curly hair and large tinted glasses on a lanyard—clearly his assistant, possibly also his *madre*—stood on either side of the dentist's chair. They both smiled, showing off perfect white teeth in their tanned brown faces.

Ray Havers thought of a tropical spa in the desert.

How Ray had ended up here was simple: his teeth hurt like heck. Several wiggled painfully when he ate, and his gums had months ago turned an angry crimson. Since he couldn't afford the insurance, he'd already put off going to the dentist for several years. With a wedding to pay for, with a fiancée too timid to get a job, and a temperamental diabetic cat who required two daily shots of insulin, he just couldn't afford to get any sort of dental work done on his meager salary working night security at the West Midland Mall... especially so close to Christmas.

Ray turned to his friend and coworker Santiago Tinto. The older, slimmer security guard had suggested visiting Dr. Barrera—a possibly illegal dentist he'd heard spoken of through friends of friends—but now that they stood here, he seemed to think better of it. Ray shrugged, and Santiago said something in Spanish to the dentist. Dr. Barrera replied with a single word Ray recognized: "*Si.*"

"*Bueno,*" Santiago said, and to Ray: "Go on."

Pausing at the heavy steel doors, thoughts of cartel death squads and organ harvesting squirmed through the spongy gray tissue of Ray's brain. He knew Santiago would never have deliberately led him into a trap, but his entire adult life until this moment had taught him to expect the worst.

00:46;00

He might actually have turned and gone back the way they'd come, sparing himself the trouble that followed, had his teeth not suddenly felt like the keys of a badly tuned piano slammed discordantly by an angry student. The agony doubled him over, grasping at his jaw before quickly withdrawing his hand with a wince. In that moment, he made up his mind to do whatever Dr. Barrera said, no matter where the man had received his diploma… if he'd gotten one at all.

Ray's hard soles made hollow clanking sounds as he staggered into the container. "What? No magazines?" he said, joking to cover his nervousness.

The dentist gave Santiago a quizzical look. Santiago translated, but neither the dentist nor his assistant appeared to get it.

"You have money?" Dr. Barrera struggled with his English. "Jes?"

"Yeah, I've got money."

"Show me."

Slightly irritated, Ray pulled out a wad of bills, a good chunk of his wedding fund. He displayed them for the dentist and his assistant with his eyebrows raised challengingly.

"Hokay. Seet. Please."

Ray stuffed the money back in his wallet, and sat in the chair. The assistant put a bib around his neck with an ingratiating smile, and Dr. Barrera leaned over him. The man's breath smelled like cinnamon and cigars when he said, "Ahhhhh," sticking out his tongue like a wizened brown lizard.

Ray mimicked the action, opening his jaw until it hurt.

Dr. Barrera picked up the scraper and pressed it into a molar. Pain erupted on the lower right side of Ray's mouth, white explosions blooming behind his eyes. When the dentist removed the instrument, Ray felt a tackiness, as if the molar itself were gummy. Spanish was muttered to his assistant. Out of the corner of his eye, Ray saw Santiago recoil at whatever Dr. Barrera had said. The dentist did the same with ten more teeth, poking them and—Ray assumed—naming them to his assistant, who scrawled them in a chart while Ray tried not to squirm in the chair.

Finally, Dr. Barrera withdrew from Ray's open mouth. He lowered his green facemask with a sour look, and shook his head.

"What? What does that mean?"

Santiago repeated the question to the dentist. Dr. Barrera spoke hurriedly.

"What? *What did he say?*"

"He says that you're gonna need *denturadas.* Dentures."

"Dentures?"

"He says your gums have receded, and the nerves of many teeth are very dead. Either you can get dentures—"

Dr. Barrera spoke again. His assistant agreed with a solemn nod.

"—or transplants, he says."

"I can't afford transplants. Heck, Santiago, I can't afford *dentures*."

Santiago said something to the dentist (Ray recognized the word *dinero*), and the dentist replied, animatedly waving his hands.

"He says it won't cost much. Five-hundred dollars."

"Five-hundred—!"

Dr. Barrera spat out a reply.

"He says he could do it for three-hundred and fifty."

Ray considered it. Not much to lose, just some rotten teeth. If he cheaped-out and went for the dentures, he'd have to clean them in a glass of Polident at night, and Nora would wonder where he'd gotten the money. "Can I look at the teeth?"

Santiago translated. The dentist nodded, and the old woman opened one of the low cabinet doors. Inside were an array of teeth set in molded gray plastic gums. Oddly, not a single pair looked the same. Tiny square teeth, and long straight teeth. Teeth with too-long incisors, and teeth that all ended in a neat, straight row like a movie star's. Even a set of snaggleteeth lay on the bottommost shelf, though Ray found it difficult to believe anyone would choose them, let alone that any company would have manufactured them. He supposed they might have been defective, pulled from the production line to end up here, in a storage container doubling as a dentist's office.

Dr. Barrera spoke.

"Dr. Barrera… he says he wants you to choose," Santiago began translating.

The dentist spoke again, insistent. Santiago squinted, as if he didn't quite understand.

"He says… 'You must choose the teeth which *sing* to you.'" He shrugged. "That's creepy, right? That's kinda creepy."

"That *sing* to me, huh?" Ray looked them over again. Aside from the ugly ones, nothing really jumped out at him, not at first—certainly, nothing *sang*. It felt like when he tried to pick scratch tickets at the bodega, going by juju, hoping something would call out to him *Pick me!*

And then he found them: the perfect set. They didn't quite *sing*, but Ray had always admired his grandfather's long, straight teeth, so he chose the teeth on the top right. Dr. Barrera's assistant took them down for him to inspect. Ray thought they looked handsome. Distinguished. They also looked very realistic. Not quite what he'd expected implants to look like at all, although they were shorter than real teeth, ending in a smooth semicircle, without roots.

Dr. Barrera spoke to Santiago. "Okay, he says they're going to give you the gas, and then they'll put in your new teeth. You'll be…" He listened to the dentist. "He says you'll be good as new."

Ray nodded.

Santiago said, "I'll be right here if you need me."

00:50;00

"Thanks, Saint. You're a good friend."

Santiago waved the compliment away, going red in the cheeks. "Aw, shush."

The assistant brought over the nasal mask. She pointed at Ray's head, clearly embarrassed by her lack of English. "I need…" she began.

Ray lifted his head. The woman gave him a grateful smile, and tugged the strap over, settling the mask snugly on his nose. Before she could bend to turn on the nitrous, he said, "Wait!"

Startled, Santiago and the dentist turned to look quizzically at Ray.

"Will I… dream?" Ray asked, a little embarrassed by the question.

Santiago passed the question on to the dentist. In stilted English Dr. Barrera said, "No. No dreams."

"Okay." Ray nodded. "I'm ready."

The dental assistant twisted the nozzle.

Squeak. Squeeeak —

WHEN THEY ASK Mickey what he wants for his last meal, he says, "Chocolate. Lots of it."

The two hacks look at each other like it's the strangest request they've ever gotten, but Mickey Dunn knows the last guy they gassed in cell block C asked for pussy, and rumor has it the guy before him asked for world fucking peace. They bring Mickey his chocolate without question, just some stuff one or the other of them picked up at the Safeway on break: a box of maraschinos, a couple of Charleston Chews, a 3 Musketeers and a Butterfinger. He eats them all, relishing the sweet chocolate liquor oozing down his throat, and when they strap him down on the gurney two hours later, he's still licking bits of it out of his long, straight teeth.

Here in Oklahoma they use nitrogen asphyxiation instead of lethal injection. They call it "killing with kindness," and Mickey figures it must beat the shit out of riding the lightning. Killing with kindness is a far cry from how he'd cut up those girls in Tulsa, and Stillwater and Broken Arrow, and the irony of it makes him chuckle.

The pastor asks if he has any lasts words, and Mickey says, "Yeah. I wish I ate more of 'em," meaning the chocolate, but he realizes the victims' families probably think he means their daughters and sisters and wives, and even though it wasn't what he meant, he smiles at the memory of their blood on his tongue and oozing through his teeth, and the taste is far sweeter than chocolate. As the pastor does his little pantomime, the nurse reaches out to draws a clear plastic mask over Mickey's head—he sees the glint of the pretty young thing's wedding ring and snaps out at her fingers with a snarl, but the strap across his chest prevents him from rising, and his teeth miss her by mere inches. He laughs as she hesitates, and one of the hacks— Mickey can't see which one—holds him back by his hair so she can secure the mask over his nose and clenched smile.

Mickey says, "Gas me, Doc," and the doctor does, turning it on with a prolonged squeeeak.

It's not long before Mickey's head feels like a partially deflated birthday balloon some kid rubbed against his corduroys and stuck to the wall. The faces of his victims' *families swim beyond the safety glass in the gallery. He can't make out their expressions, but he feels their bitterness, their rage. He gets drunk on it.*

"Shit, man, I'm high as a kite," he laughs, but the mask makes his words sound hollow, even to his own ears.

He struggles to keep his eyes open, to remain conscious. He knows if he closes them, he'll never wake up. If he drifts off now, it'll be into death, and his limbs are numb, and he can't feel himself breathing, and the numbness is crawling up his chest to his neck, to his mouth, he can't even smile, show them he's still cool as Hell, he's still fuckin' invincible, but soon the cold gray numbness will reach his eyes and they'll shut on him whether he lets them or not, like the steel door to the cell he'd spent the last six years of his—

WHEN RAY SWAM up out of the darkness, the entire lower half of his face felt like it was missing. He had to reach up and touch it to make sure it was still there.

Numb.

He felt dislocated, like waking up in a strange hotel. Blinking at the harsh light, he searched his surroundings: the shiny steel, the pristine white. Santiago stood nearby with worry in his eyes and crumbs in his black beard. Sometime during the operation, he'd obviously gone to get his sandwich from the car. The dentist stood looking over Santiago's shoulder. Behind the two men, the assistant cleaned what looked like blood off the porcelain sink.

00:53;00

"Heyyy, man." Santiago smiled. "How you feelin'?"

"Could be better," Ray tried to say, but his tongue couldn't quite form the words. "How do I look?"

"'Ow ooh…'? Oh, how do you *look*? Great, man. Never better. I mean, you've got a little Bell's palsy thing going on there, but Dr. Barrera says that'll clear up once the freezing wears off." He flashed Ray a wan smile, then gave him a queer look.

"What?"

"Nothing, man. Nothing. Hey, let's give him a look at those chompers, huh, Doc?"

Dr. Barrera handed Santiago the mirror. Santiago held it out for Ray to have a look, and Ray saw what he'd meant: the right side of his face hung entirely slack. He couldn't quite get the hang of moving his lips, and when he tried to smile, they peeled back from his new teeth like a dog bearing fangs, startling himself. He looked the same, only the teeth were different… but the teeth changed everything. It was as if his face had always been waiting for them. Like the last piece of a complicated jigsaw, Ray's new teeth completed his face.

Gradually, his lips formed a smile.

STILL UNDER THE effects of the gas, Ray got a lift home from Santiago. The bungalow he and Nora shared with a nice elderly couple was dark, aside from the small basement window out front, where the blue light of the television flickered. Nora had likely fallen asleep on the couch with Mr. Muggins in her lap, as she often did when he worked. Since he'd told her he was working a half shift tonight (as opposed to telling her the truth, which he had to admit he might not have believed himself), she'd just gone with the routine, waiting for him to come home and tuck her into bed.

Drifting in and out of consciousness, Ray had noticed Santiago giving him weird looks a couple of times on the way to the house. As he opened the door and the dome light came on, he decided to ask what in the hell was wrong.

"That was some really sick shit watching Dr. Barrera drill into your jawbone. I never seen anyone get so many teeth pulled before. Probably won't ever be able to eat again."

"You got some crumbs in your beard."

Santiago ran a hand over his salt-and-pepper facial hair. "I mean, I was hungry, so…" He shrugged up his shoulders. "Hey, don't forget to drop by Stanford's office this afternoon. Pick up your bonus."

"Oh crap, I would've forgotten. Thanks, Santiago. And thanks again. You know, for everything. I owe you one."

"No worries. You got your pills?"

Ray shook his jacket pocket, rattling the pills in their container. The Oxis had cost him a little extra, but he thought he might regret not having them if his new teeth started singing—wasn't that what Dr. Barrera had said? —like the old ones had.

Surprisingly, though his gums were a little sore now the freezing had mostly worn off, his new teeth didn't hurt at all. He supposed it made sense, since the teeth themselves weren't connected to any nerves, just abutments screwed into his jaw.

Ray said his goodbyes and crept down the stairs. The sound was off, but the TV still flickered. He turned it off, and knelt in front of Nora. Mr. Muggins, resting on the bunched-up afghan in her lap, opened a single green eye to glare at him, then stumbled off to the floor.

Nora woke. She blinked at him, her own green eyes looking dark in the gloom. "Mmmhi, honey. What time is it?"

"It's late."

She held out her hand for him to kiss, something he'd done the day they met, a dorky sort of accident that became one of those "cute couple things," as Santiago called it. He pressed his lips against her knuckles just below the small diamond he'd saved six months to buy. She'd told him she loved it the night he'd slipped it onto her finger, but he'd always felt she deserved better.

"How was work?"

"It was okay. You ready for bed?"

"Mm-hmm."

Ray helped her off the couch and into bed. Before he followed her, he stood in front of the bedroom mirror, admiring his new teeth. Already it felt like his gums were less angry. The pain was minimal when he bit down, just a dull ache—a memory of pain. He considered brushing them, but since he hadn't had anything to eat since the procedure, he thought it might be a little redundant, maybe even vain. Instead, he turned out the light, and crept into bed. He kissed Nora on the forehead, and drifted off to sleep.

IN THE KITCHEN the electric can opener buzzed. "Hon, where's the cat?"

Ray stood in front of the bathroom mirror, waiting for the shower to heat up. "Huh?"

"Mr. Muggins?" Nora said sleepily. "He didn't come to bed last night."

Ray wiped a circle of steam off the mirror and bared his teeth at his reflection. They looked better in the light of day. A little pink he assumed was blood had stained the white, but no sign of infection Dr. Barrera had warned about. They felt better than they had in years—like finally being able to scratch an itch after months of being in a cast.

"That's weird," Ray called over the running water. He sniffed his armpits. Still smelled relatively clean, although he supposed he wouldn't have sweated much since he hadn't actually gone to work last night. He drew the curtain and stepped in.

Once he'd given his hair a good lather, he turned to rinse out the shampoo. Blinking water out of his eyes, he saw the bloody handprint caked on the tiles. Worried, he checked himself for wounds, thinking the cat might have clawed him while he slept. Finding his skin without injury, he splashed and scrubbed the handprint off the wall. Pink water ran into the drain.

Nora's scream startled him. He dried himself hastily, enough so he wouldn't track on the carpet, and hurried toward where she stood calling his name. "What? What's the matter?"

"Look," she said sullenly, pointing at a dark stain behind the furnace.

"Flooding again?"

"That's not water…"

Ray took a step closer, barefoot on the cold cement. The smell hit him then—cat urine. His watering eyes adjusted to the dimness and he realized Mr. Muggins lay in a pool of coagulated blood, his innards spilling out, his little pink tongue lolled between his fangs, his big green eyes already turning milky white.

"Oh, jeez," he muttered.

Nora threw herself on him, weeping. He took her hand, brought it to his lips to kiss, but the idea overcame him to bite the finger that held her ring—and not just nibble it but tear the goddamn thing off with his new teeth. He pictured separating flesh from bone, suckling on the gnawed end like a kitten at its mother's teat, and the image disgusted him so thoroughly he thrust her hand back at her. It struck her in the chest, and she staggered back in shock, looking up at him with tears in her eyes.

00:58;00

"I'm sorry," he choked, suddenly nauseous. "I feel sick..."

Ray stumbled off to the toilet, and fell to his knees, a violent red torrent splashing against the toilet lid, chunks of undigested meat splattering in the bowl. His mind processed what he saw, and another torrent of red and purple chunks came hurtling up from his gullet, tearing his throat as he groaned.

"Ray...?"

Nora stood in the doorway, her face ghostly white, eyes bulging at what he'd unleashed into the toilet. *"Go away!"* he cried, kicking the door shut in her face. He spat a thick string of syrupy red into the bowl, and slammed the lid, flushing the contents out of sight—

The bloody handprint. Blood in his teeth. Could he have sleepwalked?

Had he just thrown up everything the dentist's suction tool hadn't managed to slurp up from the procedure... or had he done that terrible thing to poor Mr. Muggins, their diabetic cat? Had he done it with his *teeth*?

His gums itched, crawling under the skin like insects. He shook a pill from the container, staring at his pallid face in the mirror, a streak of blood staining lip to chin. He chewed the pill dry, bitter, numbing. Shook out two more and did the same.

MR. STANFORD'S OFFICE door was open when Ray

headed into the back of the mall in a drugged-out haze. The water and air conditioning pipes hummed and rattled pleasantly. Kitchen sounds echoed from the opened back doors of food court restaurants, and the smells made his stomach growl, despite his earlier bout of vomiting. A day shift security guard Ray knew only as Dino stepped out of Stanford's office, tearing open an envelope. He blew into it, then pulled out the contents.

"Shit, man... A Midland Mall gift card."

Ray parsed the comment. "How much?" he asked, feeling his words vibrate his teeth.

"Fifty bucks. But you gotta spend a hundred bucks to get it. Can't even use it in the food court. I mean, shit, they coulda just mailed the fuckin thing."

"Yeah. Guess I should've just stayed in bed."

"Story of my life, bro," Dino huffed. "See ya on the flipside."

Ray knocked lightly, then entered. Mr. Stanford had wedged himself in between his desk and the wall, where his diploma in Business Management hung askew beside a picture of his pudgy, apple-cheeked self with the late Ronald Reagan.

"Ray, come on in."

"Hey, hi, Mr. Stanford," Ray said, too mellow from the Oxi to feel his normal awkward self in the presence of his boss's boss.

"Have a seat."

Ray plunked down into the offered chair.

"Ray, in the ten years I've known you, you've

been an exemplary employee. A real credit to the West Midland Mall, and to your uniform. But times are tight. I'd love to say the old gal is doing better, but the fact is, our profits are far lower than in Q3, and it's almost Christmas."

Ray wasn't sure what to say. Odd, this talk of money concerns, considering the "old gal" was currently elbow-to-elbow with shoppers.

"What I mean to say is, if there were more in the coffers, I'd be happy to offer you a better bonus. As it is, please accept this gift certificate, and a sincere thank you from myself on behalf of Terrace Green Holdings and W.M.M. LLC."

"Thank you, Mr. Stanford," Ray said, pocketing the envelope. "Sir, you're not obligated to give a bonus, are you?"

Stanford's eyes narrowed. Ray hadn't ever dared question him before, but the pills had numbed his fear—and the teeth were pulsing, making his jaw open and shut, a motion he felt the need to fill with words. *Singing* to him, he supposed, like the dentist had said. Ray plucked a pencil off the table and put it between his teeth to stop their restless movement. Heard the wood crunch between his grinding teeth.

"The company offers bonuses this time of year as a gratuity for its employees," Stanford said. The phrase sounded more like a question as he stared in mildly angered bafflement at his pencil between Ray's teeth.

"Right," Ray said, "but if times are tight, like you

say, why not just do away with the bonus, instead of giving us the same gift certificates you offer customers?"

"I don't—" Stanford's mouth hung open. Ray felt his teeth wanting to gnaw off the man's plump lower lip. "*What?*"

A rap on the door startled Mr. Stanford from his stunned gaze. "What is it?" he demanded.

One of Santa's elves, a pretty young blonde, leaned half through the door. Ray's gaze flashed on the shiny crucifix swinging between her small breasts and the pencil snapped between his teeth.

"Mr. Ellison just puked all over Santa's Village," the girl said.

"Who in the hell is Mr. Ellison?"

"*Santa*, sir."

"Oh, jeez..." Tapping his plump fingers meditatively on the desk, he caught Ray's narrow-eyed gaze at his hand and stopped, withdrawing it, hiding it under his desk. "Get one of the food court janitors in to clean up the puke. Where's Santa now?"

"Mrs. Claus sent him home."

"Christ, you gotta be kidding me! It's nearly Christmas and we've got no Santa Claus..." His gaze fell on Ray. "Did—Ellison, was it? Did he puke on the suit?"

"There's a little on the lapel. Should clean up easy."

"Good. Ray, what are you doing this afternoon?"

Ray looked from Stanford to the elf and back.

"Mr. Stanford, I can't play Santa Claus…"

"It pays a hundred an hour."

He did need the money. Refill the coffers, as Mr. Stanford might say. "But, sir, I really don't do well with children."

"Don't like 'em?"

"More like they don't like me."

Stanford laughed, his belly jostling like the jolly old fat man's. "*Nobody* doesn't like Santa Claus."

RAY PLOPPED DOWN in Santa's chair. Already the beard was itching, the extra stuffing inside the bright red coat made him sweat, and the line outside Santa's house was mind-bogglingly long. Kids crying, pulling each other's hair, tugging on their mothers' sleeves. He nodded to Kelly, who opened the gate, and he waved the first kid up. Kelly lifted the child onto his lap.

"Hel-*low*, little boy," Ray said, making his voice deep, thanking God for the Oxis. "What would you like for Christmas?"

"Um, um… I want um, a nucular weapond so I can blow up my sister!"

Ray couldn't help but laugh. "That's very naughty… but I suppose we all want to blow someone up every once in a while. I could use one of those to blow up my boss, come to think of it—*ho ho ho!*"

Kelly gave him a queer look, and Ray lifted the boy off his lap.

"Merry Christmas!" he bellowed, already certain it was going to be a long day.

A dozen kids later, he'd been peed on, gotten a sucked-on candy cane stuck in his beard—which Kelly had patiently trimmed out with scissors—and a child's size shoe in the balls twice. His patience beginning to wear thin and the drugs wearing off, the urge to tear off the whole costume and spoil the mystery of Santa Claus for everyone was pretty strong. Kelly hoisted a skinny kid with brown smears on his freckled face onto Ray's lap. The boy was sucking on the end of a chocolate Santa. Ray's stomach growled. He'd never much liked chocolate... but the kid kept waving it in his face when Ray asked what he wanted for Christmas.

All Ray ever wanted was a mouth full of teeth that didn't feel like shards of glass. He'd been granted his wish, but it seemed like every treat he'd ever gotten in life came with a trick.

The kid leaned in to whisper in Ray's ear, breath sweet. The Santa, its head sucked to a round brown nub, hovered close to Ray's bushy beard as the boy's hot breath tickled his ear. "I want my mommy and daddy to be nice to each other." Not the first time he'd heard something like that in the hour or so since Ellison left sick, but Ray's hunger overcame him, and he leaned forward to bite the top off the kid's treat.

"What are you doing?" his mother screeched.

"What?" Ray said, mouth full.

"I saw what you did! You ate his chocolate!"

The boy saw the demolished treat, and his face twisted up in misery. Before he could start bawling, his mother yanked him off Ray's lap by the arm. The damn busted then, tears virtually squirting out of the kid's eyes. Ray used the moment to chew. The sugary liquor oozed between his teeth and down his throat, so sweet it made him gag.

"Santa wouldn't do that, ma'am," Kelly assured the woman, but her eyes showed she knew the truth.

"I *saw* him do it!" The boy's mother pushed her son behind her back to approach Santa's chair. "Spit it out," she told him, holding out her hand palm-up like a school teacher to a loud gum-chewer.

Ray wanted nothing more than to spit the excessively sweet saliva into her waiting palm. But the teeth gnashed out, as they'd nearly done to Nora that morning, and his mouth filled with the salty tang of her blood.

The woman screamed blue murder. Ray spit the meaty part of her palm into her hand before she closed it into a quivering fist. A shower of red ran down his beard and spattered the coat's white fur trim as she hugged her injured hand to her breast. Kids began crying, screaming, parents shielding their eyes and drawing them away from Santa's Village. Kelly hugged the freckled boy, who stood in stunned silence with tears rolling down his cheeks while his mother caterwauled, blood painting her fur jacket like an animal rights protest.

Ray fell back against the chair, stunned at what

he'd done. The chair toppled, smashing into Santa's gingerbread house, splitting the wall and breaking the plastic "icing" window frame. He lurched off, tripping over the Rudolph and the candy cane fence, and ran headlong, the stuffing shaking loose from inside his blood-stained coat, pushing through the crowd of sudden goggle-eyed onlookers. He barreled through the hardware store turnstile, rushing past a slack-jawed greeter, knocking the flyers from his hands.

"Sir! Sir!"

Ray recognized the voice: Dino, the day security guard. Someone had radioed him. Now he was at Ray's heels. But Ray had one more thing he needed to do. Tearing off the beard as he ran down the tool aisle, he scoured the shelves, hunting, hunting—there! He grabbed the plastic packaging and hurried to the back of the store as Dino rounded the corner, the former football player's beefy shoulder slamming into the shelf, rattling tools and shaking screwdrivers and hammers and wrenches to the floor.

Ray tore the clear plastic open with his teeth, amazed by their strength, their sturdiness. He pulled the tool from the wreckage and slammed into the men's room. Wheeling round, he pushed the door shut against Dino's football tackle, and locked it.

"*What the hell*, Ray?" Dino said as Ray brought the pliers to the mirror. "I'm mad about the gift certificate too, but you don't have to go nuts."

Ray stared himself down, looking like a

demented elf with the baggy red velvet pants and big brass belt buckle. This was going to hurt like hell…

He opened his mouth wide, and reached inside with the pliers. The teeth bit down on it, clacking hard against the metal, pain reverberating in his jaw. "Huck!" he cursed, his tongue depressed by the cold metal, and yanked it free, the bolt scraping against the two front teeth. They clacked shut on each other, refusing to open.

"C'mon, Ray, open the door. You won't like it if I have to bust it down…"

"You don't want to come in here, Dino," Ray said through clenched teeth, then squeezed his eyes shut and swung the pliers at his mouth. The tool rattled off them, bolts of pain shooting up into his temples and exploding behind his eyes. When he flashed his gums in the mirror, the teeth remained unharmed. He yanked on his lower jaw, trying to pry open his mouth, but the teeth held fast.

"You goha be hucking kidding ee…"

Seizing on an idea, he grabbed a fistful of hair and yanked his head back. His mouth opened involuntarily, and before the teeth could shut again he dove in with the pliers, attacking a molar. He yanked. At first he felt no give, was merely pulling his head along by the metal grips, painfully stretching out the tendons in his neck. He would have killed for those Oxis now, possibly *literally*. And suddenly the tooth tore free from his gums. Blood streaked the mirror, and the tooth rattled into the sink.

Ray dropped the pliers, staring down at the *thing* in the porcelain bowl.

The tooth had grown *roots*.

Even more inexplicably, tiny red nerves wriggled and trashed like the tentacles of a dying squid. Ray had a moment to realize the other teeth lining his gums had likely grown similar appendages—that they'd laid down roots, making themselves a home in his unsuspecting mouth.

Behind him, the door frame splintered inward.

Ray saw Dino's eyes widen as the Taser came out. He cried out, "Wait!" through gritted teeth, throwing up a hand as the larger man pulled the trigger. One dart struck Ray in the chest. The other hit him in the jaw. His whole body seized as the electricity passed through him.

Falling unconscious to the floor, his mouth fell slack.

TWO OFFICERS THREW Ray into a small, dank cell. His whole body ached from the Taser and the beating Dino had laid upon him before the cops showed up, when he saw what Ray had done to the poor woman at Santa's Village—all but his teeth, which felt, aside from the constant squirming beneath his gums, perfectly fine.

In the silence that followed the heavy metal bars clanking shut, Ray sat on the bunk, and thought he could finally hear his teeth singing.

00:68;00

He stood, and went to the window. Grasped the bars and pulled himself up. Not a far drop to the ground below. Two stories. Maybe three.

Ray stood on the seatless toilet and twisted his head to bite down on a cold steel bar. He ground his teeth against it, moving them forward and back like a saw, tasting flecks of metal shavings on his tongue.

Oh, the teeth were singing, all right. And they wanted two things: *blood* and *chocolate*.

MENTAL

I CAN TELL they're getting close by the ringing in my ears.

They'll find me soon. Find me and lock me up in a small white room with a hard white bed and stark white walls. I know because I've been there. Nothing to look at, nothing to do but submit myself to their experiments, their mind games. Poking me with needles, pushing me to exhaustion, forcing me to my limits, *beyond* my limits, clouding my conscious mind with experimental drugs to tap into the basement levels, the subconscious… where the killer lies sleeping.

I have to leave this room. If they've sent a low-level Empath, hoping to get the drop on me, I'm already caught. I doubt they'd risk it. They know how powerful I've become. Their training made me the Mental I am now. In a duel of minds, I'd pop a low-level Empath's neural net like frying a circuit board and be out of here before the trench coats have even gotten close.

Still, I shouldn't stay. Just leave this message, and

go. I know where that ringing in the ears leads. I've seen it. I've *caused* it.

They can't use me anymore. I'm a liability. I understand that. They'd happily erase me from the world. Redact me.

I just need to think.

Think about what to do next.

Think about what came before, and how it can help me now…

AS A KID, all I knew about my power was that people didn't want to be around me for very long.

My parents abandoned me at the hospital. The other kids at my foster home never wanted me to play with them. Nobody ever picked me for anything. In a big old farmhouse with eleven kids all under the age of sixteen, I was lonely but rarely alone. Our foster mother hated the others, was only keeping us for the monthly checks, and I suppose it's why she took a special liking to me. While she beat and scolded the other children, she taught me how to read and write. She taught me to be strong. To conceal my emotions. To guard my thoughts. She was a cold woman, and she was vengeful. She never married, and to my knowledge, she'd never been in a relationship of any kind.

Mary O'Shaughnessy loathed people. And since people had always taken an unconscious disliking to me, I suppose she must have felt we were somehow similar. Kindred spirits.

The night everything came crashing down around me—the night Billy died—I was up in my room in the attic, the only bedroom not shared by more than one dirty, underfed and undereducated child. I was reading Orwell's *Nineteen Eighty-Four*, and I'd just gotten to the scene where Big Brother's agents capture Winston and Julia when little Billy came bolting into my room, torn shirt, dull brown eyes wide with fear, his face red from crying.

Ms. O'Shaughnessy shouted up after him. By the sound, her voice slightly tinny from echoing off metal pots and pans hung above the stove, she was still in the kitchen. Billy locked eyes with me. I could almost feel his fear turn to calculation, like flicking on a table saw, the blade cold and sharp. In an instant he was scurrying over on his hands and knees so our foster mother wouldn't hear his footsteps. Those dull eyes never left me, his little red mouth twisted into a snarl.

Billy was two years younger than me. Small, but vicious. Even the older boys, like Parker and Jeb, were wary of him. He could slip out of their chokeholds. He could climb onto their backs and jam his thumbs into their eyes while pummeling their kidneys with his dirty little feet. I saw him do it a dozen times. Nobody messed with Billy, and by luck of being in the spot Billy had chosen to hide, I'd stumbled onto his bad side.

Without a word of warning, he leaped onto my bed, swatting the book from my hands, and before I could scream for help, a wiry arm slipped painfully around my neck while his other hand, smelling like sweat and chicken grease, slapped hard over my mouth.

We stayed that way for what seemed like forever, but I knew from the clock on the wall had been no more than a few minutes. During that time, Billy kept whispering to me, "It wasn't my fault. I didn't do it on purpose. Always picking on me. Not fair, is what it is. Anyway, it wasn't my—"

My heart beat sluggishly, as if time had slowed. My imagination still swarming with Orwell's Thought Crimes and doublespeak, I thought if I could get inside Billy's head somehow, I just might be able to *make* him let me go. Even then I knew it was a silly thought, but fear had its cold claws in me, and I was grasping at straws.

I thought of myself as a small insect, an earwig— no, a *spider*—and I crawled into the warm, fleshy shell of Billy's ear. My weightless legs navigated daintily through the dark, smelly maze of tiny hairs and brown wax until I reached his ear drum. My abdomen distended, I pushed and pushed until the pale pink orb squeezed out of my shimmering black carapace. I danced over the egg sac, spinning my wriggling, squirming children into a silken cocoon, and scurried out of Billy's ear just moments before he dug a finger into it, feeling nothing but a slight itch.

"—didn't do it on purpose. Always picking on m—"

A low-pitched drone rose to a crescendo in my

ears—you know how kids used to say if you hear a ringing in your ears, it means someone is talking about you? Like that, only stronger. *Louder.* The whole time I imagined myself as an evil little spider crawling into Billy's ear, my own ears burned.

In my imagination the egg sac split open, spilling hundreds of little versions of me into his ear. We broke through the barrier into the spongey, wet tissue of his brain, and *bit.*

"Ow," Billy groaned. "*Ow OW!*"

His hand slipped from my neck. I heard it slap against his head. The other came free of my lips and I fell off the bed onto the floor, rolling and crab-walking back until my head struck a rafter. Billy had been holding his head, but his arms fell slack to his sides as the pain at the back of my skull rattled him from my thoughts.

"*My ears—*" he cried, and that's when blood started spilling down his cheeks from those smelly orifices, as if the imaginary bugs I'd filled his head with had gobbled up all the meat inside. Billy's eyes rolled back to the whites and he slumped over, flopping like a fish onto my bedspread—arms flailing, legs kicking out spastically. I watched him in growing horror, certain he was dying, unable to move from where I sat with my back against the wall. Finally, he rolled off the bed onto the floor, where his head struck a raised nail, and he stopped moving.

Blood trickled into his eyes and he still didn't blink. His body remained motionless. Not even a breath. Somehow, my thoughts had done that to him. Somehow, I'd killed him with my mind.

Ms. O'Shaughnessy's head rose through the attic opening in that same moment. I suppose the first thing she saw was Billy lying there dead, blood oozing from his ears onto the oval rug. She looked up at me and held my gaze.

"You did this to him." It wasn't a question. She could always tell when I was lying, so I nodded.

"He came up here, and you—what? Hit him with something?"

I shook my head.

"You made it so he couldn't hurt you."

I agreed with a tearful nod.

With a nod of her own, very business-like, she came up the rest of the way. She pulled the folding stairs up, the coils *twang-twang-twang*ing against my nerves. Already it seemed like what I'd done wasn't real—but the evidence still lay on the floor, bleeding into the multicolored wool. Hunched so she wouldn't hit the ceiling, she approached me cautiously, like I was a wild animal trapped in the attic, and she seemed to be undecided on what to do next.

"Whatever you did, we'll tell them he fell."

She nodded as if to solidify the notion, and held out her hand. I took it reluctantly. She gripped mine tight, her fingers dead cold.

"Promise me," she said. "Whatever it is you've done, promise me you'll never do it again."

I promised her. She'd never really meant much to

me, our foster mother, and I understood she was not a good person, even though she'd treated me well for the most part. But the promise wasn't for her, it was for myself. Watching Billy squirm, even though just moments before I'd hated him to the core of me, with every firing synapse, even though when he'd had me trapped I'd wanted him dead more than anything I'd ever prayed for in my short, miserable existence, I could never forgive myself for what I'd done. I never wanted to do something like that again.

But it was a promise I wouldn't keep. Not because I couldn't, not because I ever wanted to harm another person after that night…

Because *they* made me.

The police never arrived. Two men came in their place. Men with sharp, smooth faces, wearing gray trench coats. The other children gathered around in the front hall—their hatred made my skin crawl. My foster mother spoke with the men in hushed tones, then turned to me with wet fear in her eyes. She addressed the others with a forced smile.

"Your sister has been invited to join a gifted program. These men will be taking her with them."

The others, my "brothers" and "sisters" (though Ms. O'Shaughnessy had never referred to us as siblings before), looked at me with pure malice. I'd been chosen. They hadn't. There was always the possibility one of us would be chosen before the rest, but none of them would ever have imagined it would be me.

00:76:00

It was Parker who offered me the tiniest of smiles as the men led me away. He'd never shown me kindness before, unless ignoring me when it came time to dole out punishments toward his younger "siblings" could be considered compassion, but I would remember that smile fondly, until the men and women in white coats warped even that memory into something terrible.

The men were pleasant as they led me to their car, not forceful. They wouldn't answer questions: I suppose they didn't know much themselves. I discovered, much later, these men had found me because of the ringing, reported by dozens of households for several blocks around our foster home. For over a decade, they'd passed it off as electromagnetic hypersensitivity caused by the nearby power lines, but they never stopped watching, hoping to pinpoint it with an incident like what I'd done to Billy.

"The cause is *you*, Marigold," the man I knew only as Lex told me in my cold white room the following morning. The men and women in white coats became my new family, the white room my home and my prison for the next five years.

THEY'RE GETTING CLOSER. Can you feel it?

The ringing in the ears is just the first sign. It's how you can tell one of them—one of *us*—is thinking about you. This is not a good thing, to be thought about by a Mental. Even a low-level Empath could scramble your emotions enough to give you a nervous breakdown.

Next comes a sensation of being very close to powerful electricity. You've probably felt it. Your hair might stand on end, like you've just rubbed it against a balloon. If you hear ringing and static electricity snaps your fingers when you touch something—doesn't matter what it is, metal, plastic, fabric, whatever. The best thing for you to do is run. Don't hesitate, don't pick a direction, just go, as fast as you can. If the ringing gets louder, that feeling of electricity so strong your teeth start to feel like you've just stuck a battery against an old silver filling, turn around and run faster.

Don't stop until the ringing goes away. Even then, keep running if you can.

Because it means we're thinking about you.

One of us. A Mental.

Please trust me when I tell you: *you do not want to be in our thoughts.*

I WAS THIRTEEN when they brought me to The Eye, their secret compound. One of the White Coats, a woman with a long scar down the side of her face, told me abilities such as mine often presented themselves during puberty. I had my first period in that room, in the white pajamas they'd given me—as if getting my period in front of a bunch of strange adults watching me via closed-circuit cameras wasn't embarrassing enough in a room as white as a detergent commercial T-shirt. They must have had other girls there concurrent to me, since maxi-pads had been readily available. The scarred woman, whose name I never learned during my time at The Eye, taught me how to use them.

It was Lex who taught me how to harness my powers.

On the afternoon of the first day, he brought me *Nineteen-Eighty Four*, still marked where I'd hastily dog-eared the page when Billy stormed into my room. He was skinny and pale, shaved bald, with thick, wormy veins at his temples. "You're just about at my favorite part," Lex told me, grinning as he placed electrodes on my temples. "Room 101 terrified me when I was your age."

"It scared you?"

He nodded. "Will you raise your shirt for me, please?"

Dutifully, I pulled the back of my shirt up. I had no reason not to trust them at that point. They had been nothing but pleasant. In that first night, aside from the oddness of the accommodations, I felt as though I'd been treated to a stay at a luxury hotel. The food—chicken Kiev with scalloped potatoes and crunchy green string beans—was better than I'd had in all my years living under our foster mother's roof. They'd even rolled in a television and let me watch *The Craft* on the VCR, and made microwave popcorn for me to snack on. Ms. O'Shaughnessy never would have let us watch a movie like that, with curse words and witchcraft. She certainly never let us have treats like popcorn or candy, confiscating them if she'd caught us with them in our rooms.

Lex reached over my shoulder and stuck two electrodes already cold with lubricant to my skin under the shoulder blades.

"But you still like it?" I asked him, referring to the book.

"Mm-hmm," he said. When he stood before me again, he wore an earnest smile. "It's good to be scared, Marigold. Fear reminds us of the importance of life."

I thought about that as Lex left the room. A moment later, his voice boomed over the loudspeaker set up in a high corner of the room.

"Marigold, I want to ask you about William."

"William?" The question confused me.

"Billy," he clarified. "I want you to tell me what you did."

I shut my mouth tight. My lower lip quivered as the image of blood dripping into his vacant, unblinking eyes flashed in my mind.

"Marigold…?"

A tear tracked an itchy trail down my cheek.

"I know it's difficult to talk about, Marigold. But the reason we've brought you here to stay with us is to find out a little bit about why you are what you are."

The word stung me, calling me a *what* as opposed to a *who*. I suppose I must have flinched, because I heard a bassy rattle followed by a flurry of muffled, hollow-sounding voices, like listening through the inside of a shell, and I guessed that Lex had cupped the microphone with his hand. After a moment, the voices ceased, and the rattle of Lex removing his hand brought crispness back to his voice.

"Marigold… you are not like other children. You are special. Your parents saw that in you, but they lacked the strength to raise someone as special as you. Your siblings at Ms. O'Shaughnessy's home saw it, but it made them scared, and jealous. We see it, too. We want to help you live up to your potential, Marigold. We only want what's best for you.

"Nobody here will judge you for what happened. You may think what happened to Billy was your fault, but it wasn't. It *wasn't*. If Superman tried to open a jar and he didn't know his own strength, no one could blame him if the jar broke. What happened to Billy…" He paused briefly. "What happened to Billy is the same thing. You didn't know what would happen, and you broke the jar. But it was an *accident*, Marigold. We forgive you."

Tears had been streaming throughout his monologue, but something in his words reached me. I suppose I must have been seeking forgiveness. Or maybe it was what he'd said about my parents. Whatever the reason, I told them everything then: the fear, the spider, the egg sac, the fall. They asked me about my relationship with the other children, and I unburdened myself. I'd had no one to talk to for so long, aside from Ms. O'Shaughnessy, who mostly just lectured, it felt good to be able to talk to a sympathetic ear. I told them about my loneliness, how I somehow both loved my parents and hated them for abandoning me, how I escaped into books, how the only one who'd ever shown me kindness was my older "brother" Parker.

I had no idea I had offered up every little detail they required to shape me into a killer.

The following week, they brought in two gerbils and told me they were to be my new friends. I asked Lex why they hadn't brought me rats, and he grinned slyly. He nodded at the book on my nightstand. "Did you like the part in Room 101?"

"Uh-huh. Only…"

"Only what?"

"Well, I didn't so much like it when he told them to torture Julia instead. He loved her, so why would he want her to get hurt? It really wasn't very nice."

Lex thought about it. "I don't think Winston wanted her to get hurt. He only knew he didn't want to be hurt himself. Do you remember, earlier in the book, how they say Room 101 is 'the worst thing in the world'?"

I nodded.

"Well, the way I see it, the worst thing in the world wasn't the rats chewing off his face," Lex said. "The worst thing in the world was that Big Brother made him betray the only person he ever loved."

I nodded again, thinking I understood it. "You

were right, though. The scary parts made me glad I wasn't in Room 101, too."

His smile was halfhearted. Changing the subject quickly, he pointed to the little tawny gerbil. "This is Nibbles. And this is Chewie," he said of the dark brown one. "You can do whatever you like with them."

Hesitantly, I asked, "I can take them out of the cage?"

"Uh-huh. If you want to."

"I can feed them?"

His eyes flashed with an emotion I couldn't make out, but something about it disturbed me. I understood later that he must have known the outcome of their little experiment long before they even knew who I was. I supposed they must have gone through many gerbils with silly names from the other boys and girls living at The Eye before they'd found me.

"Yes, you can feed them, too," he said, and left the room.

I stood over the gerbil cage as soon as the door closed behind Lex. It smelled like sawdust and the slightly acidic tang of urine. Aside from the wood shavings covering the floor, the dish filled with little greenish brown food pellets and a bottle of water attached to the metal bars, it looked like a child's playground, with colored plastic tubes to run through, a slide, and a translucent blue den where Nibbles cowered, chewing his paws. Chewie got into the wheel and started it spinning. It rattled lightly as he scurried up and down, up and down.

I wanted to take them out and pet them, but I didn't find the courage to do so for a few hours. The only rodents I'd known were the rats and mice that chewed our cereal boxes and left turds on the counters and next to our beds. After lunch, I removed the lid and reached out to Nibbles.

His sharp little teeth snagged onto the end of my finger, and he hung on tight as I pulled my finger from the cage. Nibbles plopped down onto the floor, and I managed to grab him before he could scurry under the bed. I held him cupped in my palms, and sat cross-legged on the floor.

"No wonder they call you Nibbles." The gerbil had curled into itself, chewing on its paws, peering up at me with little black dewdrop eyes. "Aw, you're just scared, aren't you? You didn't mean to hurt—"

Suddenly, I understood why they'd given me the gerbils, or at least thought I did. They wanted me to know that even innocent little animals will fight back anyway they knew how when frightened enough.

I stroked his soft fur, and put him back into the cage. Immediately he scurried over to his den, and dug a pit into the wood shavings. Chewie had grown bored with the wheel and was eating from the dish. I watched them a while longer, then picked up a book Lex had left for me, *We Have Always Lived in the Castle* by Shirley Jackson. The book had a sort of hypnotic hold on me. I felt bad for the girl, Merricat, because she was ostracized like I was, but also because she was so strange and seemed to have no idea how odd her behavior was.

Over the next two days, I read and ate and watched my new pets play. In the afternoon of the second day, after waiting patiently with a kibble between my thumb and forefinger for several minutes, I got Nibbles to finally scurry out of his den and approach my hand to take the food. His little claws pawed delicately on my fingertips. He didn't even bite me. It made me smile. We'd become friends.

I'd almost finished the whole book by the time I noticed supper had gone by without a visit from Lex. My stomach growled. Nibbles had emerged from his den again to gnaw on a kibble. I assumed they must have just been late with it, and I read the end of the book. I remember taking away a lot from it, but mostly the idea that change is a good thing. Merricat and her sister had always lived in the castle, and they would always live there, in its crumbling, dirty, waterlogged rooms, because they refused to change. The castle was a ruin, and they were its ghosts.

I'm still not sure if Lex was trying to tell me something by giving me the book, but I suppose he must have been. He'd always been subtly manipulating me, even though I didn't know it at the time. I would find out soon enough.

There was no clock in my room, no windows to judge whether it was day or night. I knew it was late because my stomach hurt from hunger, and the nocturnal gerbils skittered restlessly around their cage. I flicked off the light, pulled the covers over myself, and tried to sleep. I woke up sometime later, shivering from hunger. I flicked on the light, padded barefoot to the camera in the upper corner near the door, and waved my hands at it.

"Hello! I'm hungry!"

Nothing. Not even the telltale rattle of Lex's microphone.

"Hey! *Hey!* I'm starving in here!"

I felt a bit like when I used to pray for my parents to come and rescue me from Ms. O'Shaughnessy's house. Just like God, the White Coats ignored my appeals.

I returned to my bed. I watched Chewie eat a kibble, feeling a twinge of jealousy as sharp as the pangs in my stomach. Finally, I drifted off to sleep again. When I awoke, I was drenched in sweat and felt feverish. The tip of my finger where Nibbles had bit me two days prior had swelled to an angry white welt surrounded by red. I was convinced he'd given me rabies.

I spent the next several hours alternately shivering under the covers, and pacing my cage. I shouted to my captors that I needed food, that I was sick, but they didn't respond. I cursed them. Begged for Lex to save me. For the first time in my life, I swore aloud, calling them every rotten thing I'd ever heard the boys call each other.

I was lucky to have a bathroom attached to my

little cell, where I could at least satisfy my thirst and cool my sweltering head under the tap. I considered eating the soap, trying to decide if filling my gut would be worth suffering through its awful taste. Eventually I settled down on my bed again, and tried to sleep. The pain in my stomach was too much to bear.

The hollow clatter of hard pellets against ceramic and tinny rattle of ceramic against metal wire drew my attention to the gerbil cage. Nibbles was eating from the overstuff dish. I wondered what gerbil food tasted like.

I couldn't read. I couldn't *think*. I was angry. Frightened. I wondered what would happen to me if they'd all just gone home, and left me in my room. If they'd forgotten about me, I knew I would die.

I tore the blankets off my bed. I threw my pillow at the camera. I began to shred the sheet in strips, desperately hoping that if I acted out they could no longer ignore me.

The gerbil wheel rattled. Chewie ran, up and down, up and down, while Nibbles stuffed his furry fat face with food.

I was a parasite living in the kibble. Nibbles chewed up my home and swallowed me, unaware of my presence in his food. I sat in his guts, gestating, then burrowed into his bloodstream, like a gerbil in a plastic tunnel. I swam the tight canals of his veins, passing through into his little gerbil head and gnawing into his pea-sized brain.

A high-pitched whine in my ears built in intensity during all this until Nibbles squeaked. He dropped his food and tumbled into the wood shavings. His back legs twitched, his tail squirmed. Then he stopped moving altogether, and the whine in my ears stopped.

When I broke down in tears, it wasn't for Nibbles and it certainly wasn't for Billy. I cried for myself. For everything I'd been neglected throughout my worthless life, for all the pain and suffering at the hands of bullies and careless social workers. For all the times people threw me away, my parents especially.

Exhausted, I collapsed on the bare mattress.

The door came open with a heavy clunk, waking me. I had no idea how long I'd been passed out. It could have been minutes or hours. Lex stepped in with a tray of food in Styrofoam dishes. I smelled chicken noodle soup and sweet tea. My stomach churned with hunger, but for a moment, I thought I'd dreamed the whole thing. That I hadn't torn up the bed and poor innocent Nibbles was still alive.

I sat up groggily. Nibbles remained in the wood shavings beside the bowl, stiffened. Chewie spun the wheel, oblivious. My bedding lay on the floor, scattered and torn.

Lex smiled at me as he laid my food on the nightstand.

"What the heck are you smiling about?" I snapped at him.

00:88:00

"You passed your first test, Marigold. You got an A."

Ignoring him, I dove for the food before he could take it away from me. Lex paid me no mind, just removed the gerbil cage from my room and locked the door behind him. I ate until my stomach began to hurt again, then soothed it with tea.

I slept again. When I woke it must have been morning, because Lex had left breakfast for me where the gerbil cage had been. I ate the scrambled eggs and buttered toast, the cantaloupe wedge and grapes. I guzzled down the carton of milk, and the plastic cup of orange juice. When I finished I burped pleasingly.

"Good morning, Marigold," Lex said over the loudspeaker. "Did you enjoy your breakfast?"

I sat down on my bed, crossed my legs, and folded my arms across my chest.

"I'm sorry about Nibbles. You understand I have superiors. If it were up to me, none of that unpleasant business would have happened."

I picked up my book and pretended to read.

"So... what did you think of Merricat? Did you feel sorry for her?"

I flipped a page, trying my best to ignore him, though it was getting difficult, his voice penetrating my thoughts.

"If you like that book, I could bring you more. You're old enough for a real scary book, I think."

I glanced up at the speaker and became electricity, surging through the wires and out the other end. As Lex reached out to touch the microphone, I jolted him with a shock. The thousand-watt charge traveled up his arm to his heart, cooking it like a frog in a pot.

"I think you'd like that, wouldn't you?" Lex said, his voice unwavering, seemingly impervious to the murderous effects of my imagination. I gave him nothing back, though his books were all I had. Without them, I was alone.

"I don't *have* to bring you books, you know," he whined. "Maybe I'll just take them all back to the library."

"No," I blurted out, my voice very small. "Please. I want you to."

"Mm, nah. It doesn't sound like you *really* want them."

I got up out of bed and stood under the camera, looking up. Wearing my biggest pout. I clasped my hands tightly against my chest like some kid beseeching the angels to bring her father back safe from the war. "Please, Lex? I'm really sorry. I didn't mean to get mad. It was just… it was dumb. *I* was dumb. Please, bring me more books."

The microphone muffled voices in the background. A moment later, Lex came back on, clear as day. "Okay, Marigold. You've convinced me."

I smiled, much wider than if it had been all about the books. Because even though I apparently couldn't harm Lex while he was outside of my room, he was no longer the only one manipulating people around here. I didn't need his books, but I did need him to *believe* I needed them, to think he held this power over me.

What I took away from the Gerbil Test was that the White Coats, Lex included, and whoever he was accountable to, they would push me to the brink of death to get what they wanted from me. They might even kill me, if I refused them.

So I would give them what they wanted. I would betray myself and the promise I'd made. But I wouldn't let them get inside my head.

This was *my* Room 101 now but I wouldn't be their victim, not any longer.

I'd be the rat.

THEY PUSHED ME to limits and beyond over the next few months. During that time, my "brother" Parker had always been a ghost in my thoughts, whispering in the halls of my mind, smiling at me from darkening recesses of memory. I dreamed about him often. Aside from Ms. O'Shaughnessy, he was the only real person I ever dreamed of—unless you counted my parents, who sometimes showed up in my dreams in various incarnations even though I didn't know what they looked like. I suppose those dreams of Parker, where he would show me kindness, where we would hold hands and sometimes kiss, had solidified our relationship long before I ever saw him again. I often woke up wondering if he dreamed of me the same nights I'd dreamt of him. If somehow we had shared the experience.

One day the scarred woman injected me with something that made me groggy and giggly before she brought me to a room so tall it could have been an old missile silo. At the center of the tall white room was a school desk, the kind made of chrome and orange fiberglass and wood laminate. It stood under a great big skylight, with a view of the perfect blue sky way, way up top.

"This is The Eye," the woman told me, and left me there to wander. We'd passed no one in the halls as we traveled there. It seemed as though, aside from Lex and me and the woman with the scar, the place was deserted.

I ran a hand along the smooth, circular wall, feeling cold where it must have been its outer edge, on the opposite curve of the wide room from the door we'd entered. Seeing the sky above got me really thinking of escape, though I'd been vaguely plotting it since the Gerbil Test. I wanted to work on a map in my head of what places might potentially lead outside, and how I might get out there. Aside from the single door and skylight, The Eye itself seemed to be impenetrable.

"Hello, Marigold," Lex said over a loudspeaker, his voice strained. He cleared his throat. I heard a small squeak I assumed to be his chair as he situated himself.

"Hiya, Lex," I replied brightly, feeling what I

would later discover was very similar to drunkenness.

He chuckled. "You're sounding very chipper today."

"Why wouldn't I be? It's a beautiful day."

I heard the smile in his voice. "It is, isn't it? Marigold, why don't you have a seat at the desk so we can begin our lesson."

I sat obediently. He thanked me.

On the desktop were several sheets of blank beige drawing paper and three black Crayola crayons.

"Do you like to draw, Marigold?"

I shrugged. "I kinda suck at drawing."

"Well, that's not really the point of drawing, now is it?"

"I don't know." I was deliberately argumentative at that point. I couldn't let them have everything they wanted without a fight, or it would look suspicious.

"Could you do me a favor?"

I nodded.

"Pick up a crayon and just start drawing. Whatever pops into your head. A tree, a pony—"

"A pony?" I said, rolling my eyes.

"Right, you're too old for ponies. Well, why don't you draw something you dream about?"

Immediately Parker came to mind, and my cheeks flushed red. The camera pointing at my face buzzed. I felt their eyes on me, and it only made my face and neck hotter.

"Marigold?"

I cleared my throat. "Mm-hmm, yes?"

"Might be better to draw something you've never seen before, okay?"

I picked up a crayon, put the tip to the paper, no idea what I would draw, certain it would all end up looking like stick figures even if I force my imagination to play nice.

The walls began to rumble, as if the air conditioning had come on. The temperature didn't change, but I did feel a rising vibration in the legs of the desk. I hummed along with it, trying to find the right pitch, until my voice melded with the sound of the walls.

Feeling a tremendous pressure just to start something, whether from the White Coats or myself, I just started scribbling. The scribbles came together, darker in places, lighter in others. Eventually almond-shaped eyes begin to take shape. A sharp nose. A narrow mouth with tight lips. The crayon snapped and I kept going, wearing it down to a nub. Small ears with slight elfish upper curves. Angled eyebrows, one raised slightly higher in a look of suspicion. A square jaw and dimpled chin.

Finally, I set the crayon nub down on the page and looked at the woman I'd drawn. My own skill surprised me. I'd never drawn anything as realistic in my life. Whoever she was, I was certain I'd never seen her before.

The air conditioning died down, the hum giving way to silence.

00:94:00

"You're finished?" Lex's voice startled me. I held it up for him to see. I heard clapping in the background before he covered the mic. "That's good, Marigold. That's *very* good."

"Who is she?"

"I'm sure I don't know that. She came from your imagination, I suspect."

The woman with no name came to collect me and my drawing, and brought me back to my room. They gave me a chocolate popsicle with lunch, and we never spoke of the woman I drew again.

Over the next few months they asked me to draw more things, like men I'd never met, whose faces seemed to jump into my head full-born like the woman with the dimpled chin had the first time, and a bus, and black stretch limousines. During the second session I noticed the air conditioning or whatever it was began to hum again just before I started to draw, only it was a different tone from the first. I drew an angry-looking man with a small head, narrow eyes and a curled goatee. Again, he looked like no one I knew or had even dreamed.

Over the months, I began to see the pattern. The hum, the seemingly automatic drawing, the praise from Lex and the nameless woman. I never really got any better. All of my drawings remained scribbles, only vague impressions of what I supposed they were meant to be. And the tone of the hum changed every time. I began to understand it wasn't air conditioning at all. *They* were making the walls vibrate, controlling the sound. And something about that sound was connected to the scribbly people I drew for them.

One day the woman and I entered The Eye to find a standup piano set up where the desk used to be, its back to the door. Lex stood beside it, smiling, a hand on its gleaming wood surface. He was dressed in his typical white jumper, but I half-expected him to be wearing a topcoat and tails.

"Good morning, Mary."

"Morning," I said as I approached him. "I hope you don't expect me to play that thing."

A smile crept onto his lips. He sat down behind it, an old red chestnut-stained Steinway, and ruffled the cuffs of his white coat before playing the high notes of "Heart and Soul"—and not very well.

"You *stink*," I told him.

"It's really a duet." He shifted on the seat, and patted its surface. Reluctantly, I sat with him. I noticed in the interim the nameless woman had made her exit.

Lex shifted his knees toward me. "I thought maybe you were ready to know a little bit about why you're here."

"Okay…"

He pressed down on what I now know was Middle C, but then I just saw it as a white key near the middle. The note rang out in the wide, tall room. "I'm sure you know what we hear as notes are actually vibrations. The way we perceive pitch or frequency is through the oscillation of thousands of tiny hairs on our tympanic membrane, or ear drum. They convert the sound to electrical impulses that travel directly to our brains. You know this, right?"

I shrugged. I don't recall Ms. O'Shaughnessy ever teaching me that, but it seemed to make sense.

"What if I told you, each of our brains works on its own frequency? And that frequency is as unique to us as our fingerprints."

I folded my arms across my chest. "That sounds a little farfetched, honestly."

Lex laughed. "Well, for the sake of argument, let's say it's true. Now, you can see the piano has a wide range of notes, or frequencies..." He thumbed the lowest key, which rumbled out into the spacious room. For some reason those low notes on the piano have always given me the creeps, and I was glad when the sound faded away. He did the same with the highest key, reaching over me. His elbow brushed against my left breast, which was still no more than a nub, but it made my cheeks feel hot. Lex didn't seem to notice. The note he'd played was so high it didn't resonate long.

"But it doesn't have quite the same range as the human ear, or the human brain, which can *sense* far more frequencies than the ears can perceive. Those lower frequency vibrations, lower than 20Hz, are practically *ghosts* of sounds. And anything higher than about 20,000Hz can damage our ears even if they don't perceive it. There are studies now that are looking into ultrasound—higher than the human range—and *infra*sound—lower—that are producing excellent results which may lead in the future to acoustic weaponry."

"Great," I said sarcastically.

Lex flashed a grin. "Anyway, as you can tell, the human limit of hearing is not anywhere near the limit of sounds that can be produced. Even just within the range of human perception, there are nineteen-thousand nine-hundred and eighty different frequencies *that we know of*. There may even be frequencies *in between* those frequencies that we've yet to discover!"

His eyes twinkled at the thought of it. "I can see your eyes are glazing over. To the point then. Think of these frequencies as radio waves. On a simple radio, you have your FM band and your AM band. There are millions of stations around the world, but since these waves travel over the air, we're only able to hear a certain number of them in any one place, and the rest of the dial is filled with static. Now think of each radio station as a person, or more specifically, a person's thoughts. That's seven billion radio stations! Instead of the latest Beyoncé chart-topper, or the local weather in Kazakhstan, as you turn the dial you're hearing *thoughts*. There's absolutely no static on the dial, because there's barely enough room to contain the stations we've got. Some children can tap into those thoughts like they're listening to the radio. We call them Psychs, which is short for psychic.

Others can tap into only the emotions. Here at The Eye we call them Empaths.

"You, Mary—" He'd started calling me Mary a few months into our drawing sessions. While I didn't so much like the name, it meant he was feeling more familiar with me, which was to my advantage. "—we don't have a name for children like you yet, because there *are* no children like you. You've been able to mimic just about every frequency we've thrown at you, with or without your drawings. And when you tap into the frequency of someone's thoughts, you tap into their *mind*. You may not be able to hear their thoughts, or sense their emotions..." His eyes twinkled with unknown possibilities. "But you can tinker with their brains, and that's *far* more powerful. Those other abilities are parlor tricks compared to what you can do—especially when we boost your signal here in The Eye."

I considered this. Somewhere along the line I'd figured out what they had me doing here was far less innocent than mere doodling. But the exact nature of their experiments, considering I hadn't been able to "tap" into Lex's mind when he was sitting in the next room from me, didn't quite fall into place. Now it all clicked. I felt a hollowness in the pit of my chest, and swallowed hard.

"All those people you had me draw..."

"Criminals, gangsters, killers," he said. "Evil men and women, every one of them."

My head was spinning, but I struggled to gain

control of myself, on the verge of blacking out. I stood up from the chair, needing air. The faces I'd drawn over the months and days rose in my rapidly grayed-out vision. I grabbed the piano to stay upright, heard the wires hum discordantly at my touch.

"I never wanted to hurt anyone," I choked out.

Lex had stood up and took my shoulder, but I shrugged it off violently. He stepped away, looking wounded. I paced the room, getting my sight back, gaining more control with each step away from the piano and Lex.

I thought of the limousine. The bus. How many people…? Surely I couldn't have crashed a *whole bus* to kill a single victim?

I wiped tears and snot from my face, and looked up clearly, as fiercely as I could, at Lex. He shrank from my gaze. The walls began to hum at a very low frequency.

"Marigold…" Lex pressed a finger against his right ear. "Mary, you don't want to do that now—"

The walls rumbled. The piano began to match its resonance with a deep twang.

I had found Lex's frequency: a very low minor chord.

He stood and staggered to the door. I saw blood trickling down from his ear as he pushed past me.

The sound ceased immediately as the door slammed behind him. I sat cross legged on the floor, staring up at the camera.

Eventually, I began to laugh.

00:100;00

❚❚

I FIRST NOTICED Lex's lingering looks—jeepers, there's a mouthful—the year I turned sixteen. That was the year the girl I saw in the mirror begin to change into the woman she would become. My button nose straightened out. I lost the baby fat in my cheeks, my cheekbones becoming more prominent. My blonde eyebrows darkened, and my lips grew plump. I wouldn't exactly say I was pretty, but I was definitely not what people would consider ugly.

At first I thought it was fear in his eyes from our encounter in The Eye, but soon I realized I was mistaken. The day I found Lex's frequency—not to kill him, I don't think, just to assure them I wasn't quite as helpless as they might've imagined I was, that I still held some power in our arrangement—that happened so long ago I could barely recall what had started it by then, but the consequences of that day remained. Lex never entered The Eye with me again, and I never saw the woman again. I suspect she must have quit, thinking her life might be in danger. Lex came to my room to present me with food and clear the tray, but we never talked like we had. From that day on, we only spoke with the loudspeaker and camera between us. On those brief visits, and while he walked me to the silo, I noticed an addition to his wardrobe: a small black earpiece.

They were jamming my signal.

The day I discovered Lex's feelings for me, I'd just

gotten out of the shower as he brought me my lunch. I'd put on the T-shirt I'd worn the day before, and was changing into a fresh one when the door opened. I turned to find Lex's mouth agape, the tray of food just about forgotten in his hand. When he closed his mouth his teeth clacked together.

I stood there with my not-so-small-anymore breasts exposed beneath the rumpled shirt, my elbows still in the air, marveling at his reaction.

"I… sorry, Mary, I… here's your lunch." He set the tray down and scurried out, his cheeks revealing the embarrassment if his stammering hadn't already.

He waited until I'd sat down to eat before addressing me again, but by then a vague plan was in motion. He'd pulled the lever himself, and the rats had moved into the front compartment. With a little bit of coaxing from me, I would chew off his face.

"Mary." He cleared his throat. "I've got a special surprise for you."

I chewed silently, not reacting until I'd swallowed. Then I looked up at the camera. "Oh?" I said.

"You have a visitor."

The news caused me to drop the spoon into my tomato soup, tipping the bowl. A splatter of red stained my white shirt as I stood abruptly, rattling the kitchenware.

"You've spoken quite a bit about this person recently, I thought maybe you might like to see him."

I scurried to my drawers and put on a second

fresh T-shirt, thinking it could be only one person. In all the years I'd thought about meeting him, I'd never thought it would be here. I'd expected to be out in the world by then, living on my own somewhere in a nice-sized condo, working a job I didn't care about just to pay the rent while I… well, that was where the fantasy ended. I had no idea what I would do out in the Big World, aside from be relatively free and *live*.

I didn't know then I would end up running for my life.

We met outside in the yard, which was just a long stretch of concrete that may have once been a runway. Lex hung back at the door, within earshot. Parker stood under the silo's shadow, and when he turned to me I saw just how much he'd changed since I last saw him at Ms. O'Shaughnessy's.

"Hello, Marigold." Parker twiddled his fingers in a wave. He wore a tweed jacket and tight blue jeans, not skinny like people wear them these days, but form-fitting enough that I got a good look at the shape of his ass.

"Parker," I said, trying my best to play it cool. The teenage scruff he'd had on his chin had spread, thickening to a dark day's growth of stubble. His blue eyes took me in with intense curiosity.

"So… this is where you live?"

I looked back at the enormous, windowless facility and shrugged. "Beats Ms. O'Shaughnessy's."

Parker laughed. "Yeah, I suppose it does." He scowled, the sun in his eyes. "Are you happy here?"

"Is anybody really happy these days?"

This got another chuckle out of him, before he looked at me seriously. "They say you're doing good work here. That you're helping the government with a top secret project."

I glanced back at Lex, who shook his head so subtly I might have imagined it.

"Yeah. It's interesting work," I said. "Experiments and stuff. Mostly I just spend my time reading."

"Same old Mary." He smirked. The diminutive didn't bother me so much when Parker said it.

I asked the question that had been on my mind since Lex had told me about my visitor. "What are you doing here, Parker?"

"It's funny." He laughed awkwardly. "You probably wouldn't believe me if I told you."

"You'd be surprised at what I can believe."

"Well, okay," he said. "Can we walk and talk?"

I looked over my shoulder. Lex nodded. We walked, Parker and I side by side. He was taller than me and when I looked up, once we got out from under the silo's shadow, his face was silhouetted by the sun. Lex followed a little ways behind us, always within earshot.

"I've thought about you a fair bit since you left the house," he began. "I know that sounds weird, you were only twelve—"

"Thirteen."

"Which would make you, what now?"

"I turned sixteen in September" I told him,

desperately wishing I was older.

He nodded soberly. "Right. But... but it wasn't like I thought of you that way, you know? At first I think I was just happy for you. And I wished you would do great things, because it was hope for the rest of us. Or me, at least. Do you ever think about m—" He stopped himself, squinting off at the buildings on the horizon. "—about *us*? The other foster kids?"

I nodded, unable to stop my cheeks from turning red. A sly grin briefly crossed his lips.

"Okay. Okay, good. But here's the weird thing: I started to notice every time I thought about you, my ears would start ringing. You know how they say 'your ears are burning,' and it's supposed to mean someone's talking trash about you?"

"I kind of always thought it meant you were thinking about each other at the same time," I told him. "Like when you go to call someone and they're already on the other end."

Parker smiled. "I like that. Let's go with that." The smile faded. "Well, after a while I started to notice the ringing in my ears would be louder, and sometimes it would be quieter, like that game you play where you're looking for something and they tell you whether you're hot or cold? I'd be on my way to work on the subway and the ringing would get so intense I couldn't hear the music on my phone. It kinda drove me nuts," he said, chuckling a little. "But eventually I realized it always happened when I passed this place.

So this morning I rode my bike out here, and the ringing all of the sudden just stopped. I went up to the security booth and the security guard told me to go away, but when I told him what happened, you know, why I was here, pretty much desperate for someone to believe me, he didn't laugh at me like I expected. He called up to the main building, and your friend Lex came to talk to me." We both looked back at Lex, who pretended to be studying the clouds. "I thought he was going to send me home, but when he asked me where I grew up and I told him about Ms. O'Shaughnessy, he brought me inside."

"I'm glad you came," I said, not knowing quite how to respond, since he obviously hadn't known he'd been drawn here by me, nor who or what he would find when he got here. He hadn't come here to visit, in other words, which was what I'd been hoping to hear.

"I'm not disappointed, if that's what you were wondering. It's real good to see you, Mary." When he put a hand on my shoulder I felt warmth spread from his fingers and radiate through my body. "I'm glad you're okay." He offered a smile, and in that moment I truly was okay.

Lex had approached us from behind, spoiling the moment. Parker withdrew his hand from me, as if embarrassed. "Marigold, it's time for your lessons," Lex said.

Parker nodded. "I guess this is goodbye."

"I guess," I nodded.

00:106;00

He leaned down and kissed my cheek. "Stay well."

I said, "Mm-hmm," and frankly it was all I could say. To have him swirl into my life only to be whisked away so quickly, it was startling, to say the least. But as Lex led him back to the door and came to collect me, standing in the sunshine, I thought I understood why they had let me see him.

"Well, that was a nice visit."

"Strange," I agreed.

"How do you think that happened?"

I shrugged. I had a theory but I wasn't about to let Lex in on it. I wanted Parker out there in the world, to live for both of us. If they'd realized what I had, that Parker must have had some vague empathic abilities even he was unaware of, I was certain they would have locked him up, too. Lex had assumed I'd called him to me somehow, I thought, but his next words made me wonder.

"You know you can't think about him anymore, don't you." Not a question—it was an imperative. "I don't have to remind you of the danger in that."

I nodded, glad Lex had his own theory. Let him believe Parker was merely picking up my signal if it spared him from harm. "He won't come back again," I assured him.

"He'd better not." Lex gave me a dark look. "But just to be sure, I've told Garrison to give him a ride home."

"That was nice of you," I said, painfully aware the

sentiment was far from "nice." They would learn where Parker lived, and I would be forced to do whatever they told me to do from then on, no matter how grievous.

That afternoon in The Eye, before I knew what I was doing and could stop myself, I'd drawn an airliner. The terrified faces of passengers stared out at me from hastily scribbled windows.

THE RINGING STOPPED. I know you can't hear it, not over the webcam, but it's gone now. Maybe I was wrong. Maybe I've got time after all. Maybe they haven't found me.

It's stupid to hope I've gotten away. I know that. All the months I've spent running, they've been so close behind me all along, like shadows. Like an echo.

I'll never get away from them. With all that I've done, maybe I don't deserve to be free. I am a killer. I've *killed*. And I will do it again, without hesitation. Nibbles the gerbil bit me because he was cornered. All of their training at The Eye taught me how to bite so hard no one would be stupid enough to bite back.

But they have to contain me. Not because they're worried I'll go to the papers, not because I'd reveal everything they did to me at The Eye. They have to contain me now because I'm a danger. I'm a wolf in the henhouse. A terror cell in a hoodie and black jeans.

The government distanced themselves when Project Blue Sky became declassified. You probably heard about it on the news. "A modern-day MK Ultra," CNN said. "Our Nation's children subjected to Guantanamo-like conditions," the headline said in the Washington Post. And my personal favorite, "An Orwellian nightmare," from some newspaper in Canada. The other kids were released back into the world, like domesticated animals into the wild. I read an article recently about one of the older boys having committed suicide, and another who'd tried to kill the couple who'd adopted her. She's currently locked up in a mental hospital. Post-traumatic stress, her court-appointed psychologist claimed.

Lex disappeared. I'd love to believe he's given up on me but I've felt his frequency too close and far too often not to know he's still on my trail.

Project Blue Sky didn't end, it just went underground. Off the grid. It's a science experiment beyond the petty concerns of limitations and government sanctions.

If I hadn't escaped, if I'd waited it out a few more months—and honestly, what's a few months when you've been locked up for five years?—they might have let me go. My participation in Blue Sky might have been explained away as another attempt to awaken dormant psychic and/or empathic abilities in children. They might have forced me to sign non-disclosure agreement in exchange for a massive payoff. They might have threatened my life, and the lives of everyone I cared about—a list growing smaller by the minute.

But Lex made waiting it out impossible, and I ran the first chance I got. Those black lines in the declassified documents, they're hiding *me*. I've been redacted.

I'm just an inconvenient mess to sweep under the rug.

ON NEW YEAR'S Eve, 2013, Lex staggered into my room after dinner holding a bottle of champagne. I'd just turned eighteen years old.

"Maaaaary," he sang, and flopped down drunkenly on my squeaky mattress. Unconsciously, he'd managed to replicate his own frequency on the low note. Or maybe he knew. Another game. Another tease.

"The girl already collected my tray," I told him.

"I'm not here to clean up after you," he said with a long, heaved sigh. He took a pull from the bottle. The sound of his lips withdrawing from the rim reminded me of when he used to muffle the microphone, back when the White Coats weren't quite sure how to deal with me yet. Some of the champagne spattered on my pillow.

"Celebrating all by yourself?" I asked, standing by the door. I sensed something was wrong, more than just Lex's unrestrained drunkenness, and it made me wary, like a wolf when the zookeeper's come to clean its cage.

"I'm not by myself," he slurred. "*You're* here."

"But I'm not drinking."

00:110;00

Lex rose groggily from the dampened pillow. He squinted at me drunkenly, and made a come-here gesture with his index finger.

I glanced up at the camera then. Lex followed my look and grinned stupidly.

It came to me then, what was wrong. The camera's ever-present whine I'd grown so accustomed to in all the years I'd spent in my small white room—it wasn't there.

Lex had turned the camera off.

He studied the soft rise of my belly beneath my T-shirt, visible because I'd taken to cutting the midriffs out of them, mimicking a style I'd grown up seeing on television and in movies. His ogling made me tug at the frayed edge, pulling it down to the waistband of my pants.

"You're a shy one, aren't you? Coy." I shrugged, feeling suddenly very vulnerable. With the camera off and the door mag-locked, I was at his mercy. He swung his feet over the edge of the bed. "The government's cut our funding, you know. We're done here. Finished. *Kaputnik.*"

"Where is everyone?"

"Big party in the silo," he said, flashing me a cruel look. "One last hurrah on the government's dime."

He caught my look back at the card reader lock, and laughed. "Cheer up, Marigold. It's New Year's Eve!" Slowly, he staggered to his feet, champagne sloshing in the bottle. "Oh, and guess what. I've made a resolution..." He swallowed an apparently sour

burp as he approached me. "Mary. I've decided…
that I'm going to kiss you."

I crossed my arms over my breasts. "What if I
don't want to be kissed?"

"You're a tease," he said, his smile twisting down
in a grimace. "You think I don't see you putting on a
show for me in front of the camera? You think I don't
know when you've been naughty?"

His implication made me sick. I fell back against
the door, reaching back to prop myself up. Lex
stopped barely a foot from me, and took another swig
from the bottle before offering it to me. "C'mon,
Mary. Be *nice* for me. It's just you and me here.
Nobody has to know."

"They won't see?" I asked, as innocently as I could
muster.

The stupid grin returned. "I shut off the camera."

I smiled and took the bottle from him. Swigging
from it, I let most of the sour, fizzy liquid spill down
my chin. His greedy eyes followed the white froth
down my throat to my T-shirt, where it soaked to the
skin. While he stared at the nipple it revealed, I took
a deliberate step toward him.

My eyes lingered on his small, angry mouth, then
shot up to his eyes. His gaze moved from my chest to
my parted lips as I pressed myself against him. A
little moan escaped him. I felt him begin to stiffen in
his jumper, and that's when my teeth clamped down
hard on his nose.

Lex screamed, staggering back, stymieing the

flow of blood with his hands. Behind his fingers his eyes were wide with surprise, but anger quickly followed. "You bitch!" he said, his voice muffled by his hands, reminding me again of our first meeting, when he'd referred to me as a *what* instead of a *who*. I hoped my teeth had stung him as badly as he'd stung me that day. But just to make sure, I gave him back the bottle.

It struck him solidly above the ear, making a hollow note as it connected with his skull. The black earpiece fell to the floor and skittered over near the bathroom door. Stunned, bleeding now from his nose and the gash at his temple, Lex scrambled for it on his hands and knees, but I was quicker. I crushed it under my sole before he could snatch for it.

His eyes grew wide with fear.

No need to imagine anymore, no need to draw. I simply let the anger flow from me. For all the times he'd tricked me. For all the times he'd gotten the upper hand. For his leering. For Nibbles. For the people he'd made me kill. For the five years of my life he'd kept me locked up in that tiny room, a place I hope I'll never see again.

On the floor, the emptied bottle resonated a pitch-perfect match to Lex's frequency. The digital bedside clock flashed all 8s. The desk and bed began to rattle, the overhead lights flickering.

"Mary, don't—" he gasped, his lips drenched in blood from his nose.

I reached down and tore the keycard from the

lanyard around his neck. "What's the code?"

Lex fell over on his side, grasping at his ears.

"Tell me the code, or swear to God I'll fucking kill you!"

"Two-two-five," he sighed, squeezing his eyes tight as a wave of agony struck him. "Two-two-five."

I punched in the six digit code, giving him points for the reference.

"You know they won't let you get out of here," he groaned, looking up at me from the floor. "Even if you do make it, you'll be looking over your shoulder the rest of your short, miserable life."

"Maybe," I said, swiping the card over the reader. The maglock clicked, and the door opened with a gasp of air. "But at least I'll never have to see your ugly face again."

I backed into the hall.

"Don't count on it!" he shouted after me as the door locked between us.

The hall was empty. As quiet as a museum. I ran, passing more doors like mine, wondering how many children like me were behind those doors, praying for escape. I thought about letting them all go, taking them with me… but the risk was too great. What if they drank the punch? What if they were perfect little obedient killers?

The rest happened in a blur. Doors flew by, corners, dead ends. The alarm began to blare, flashing red on white. My heart beat so heavily in my ears I could barely hear it. Finally I stood in front of a door, knowing this was the end.

"GET ON THE GROUND!"

I turned, a cornered rat. A guard in full body armor had taken up a stance at the bend in the corridor, aiming a huge black machinegun at me. I found his frequency in seconds. The gun began to quiver, its parts rattling. He gritted his teeth, struggling to maintain his grip. Finally the resonance was too much for his tiny mind and his finger flew open, and the gun clattered to the floor as he brought his hands to his ears with a cry of agony, falling to his knees with a heavy thud of armor and gear.

I swiped the card. The maglock clicked.

The door opened with a sigh of fresh air.

I took one last look at those white walls, and stepped out into the clear, crisp night.

I'VE BEEN RUNNING ever since. For the first few days, I was terrified of being caught. For about a week after that, when no one seemed to be following me, I was sure I'd gotten away.

The news broke during the second week. The President came on TV to address the scandal, claiming Project Blue Sky had been officially terminated. The children were freed, some sent back to their parents, others to foster homes. No one seemed to be aware of my participation. He revealed nothing about assassinations, bus accidents or plane crashes.

Those first few weeks were the most difficult. I'd

never lived on my own. I'd never had to fend for myself. I spent two nights on the street, shivering in an ATM vestibule under a blanket I'd salvaged from a dumpster. Once I'd decided I didn't have to worry about Lex anymore, I moved to a women's shelter. I told them I was an orphan, that my husband was abusive and probably looking for me, that he was in law enforcement so I couldn't tell the police. The woman in charge of The Healing Place, a shelter run out of her rambling ranch-style home, was sympathetic when I said I hadn't been able to get at my ID before I ran. She assured me no information would be shared with the police or the public. My "husband" would never find me, she said, despite the resources he would have at his disposal as an officer of the law.

Unfortunately, Lex had been granted far greater power to find me.

I was provided clean clothes and the basics: toothbrush, toothpaste, hair brush, shower gel. They cooked for us and we kept our own small rooms clean. It was The Eye all over again, in that respect. All of these women were running from someone. They had all been through horrific trauma. But none of them had suffered quite the same experience I had. Once again I found myself lonely but never alone. I listened to their stories, and kept tightlipped about mine, only offering a few fake details when it felt necessary to maintain someone's trust. I felt more kinship with their children, and spent much of my time there reading stories to them, babysitting when they weren't in school or daycare and while their mothers attended group sessions, counselling, and social assistance appointments.

The night the news showed the remaining children escorted by police from The Eye, their faces blurred, I was reading *Where the Wild Things Are* to the little wide-eyed survivors of abuse and addiction, acting out the voices the way I thought a mother might have to her children. I stopped to listen to the broadcast.

"Those poor kids," a woman named Elana said, her prematurely gray hair a reminder of the years of physical and mental abuse she'd suffered at the hands of her husband. I saw tears standing in the eyes of some of the other women. It amazed me how much they could feel for someone they didn't know, when their own lives were in such disarray.

I'd read somewhere that suffering breeds compassion. A Buddhist thing, maybe. I thought about my own life, how selfish I'd been when I'd lived at Ms. O'Shaughnessy's, how all I'd ever cared about was my own little interior world, and whether or not I would ever find someone to love me, to accept me for who—not *what*—I am.

At The Eye, all of Lex's training had backfired. I'd actually learned how to care about others while they forced me to kill. Without compassion, I wouldn't have spared his life the night I escaped, to the detriment of my own. As my eyes filled with tears watching the other kids being led out of The Eye with coats and blankets covering their identities from the press, I thought that was something, at least.

I think I'd finally learned my lesson.

ME AGAIN. I'M back.

Did you think about me when I was gone? No, of course you didn't. I'd know it if you had.

Sorry I took so long, but a lot has happened since that first message. A few minutes after I stopped recording the last video, someone knocked on my door. My first thought was to run, but I knew if I did it would be just like Lex said, I'd have to keep looking over my shoulder for the rest of my life.

I'd had enough of running.

So I made a choice. I opened the door.

It wasn't Lex. It was her: the woman with the scarred face. The woman from The Eye.

But it wasn't *just* her. Behind her, the hallway was filled with children, teenagers, and young adults. Their faces showed fatigue, but they didn't have the malnourished look of Ms. O'Shaughnessy's kids. I wasn't sure how to react until the young crowd parted, and Parker stepped out from among them.

"Hello, Mary," he said.

They all smiled then, as if on cue, mimicking his words like hopeful students addressing their new teacher.

"Hello again, Marigold. I'm Dr. Nadine Maven," the woman without a name introduced herself, and stuck out her hand.

I shook it.

She told me we had very little time. We were going underground. Off the grid. Project Blue Sky was meant to be about understanding the limits of the human mind, but Lex—she called him Dr. Lexington, which I thought was funny—and the military higher-ups had warped it into a killing machine. He'd lied to me when he said there was no one like me. There were others. Dr. Maven needed my help to round them up.

We had work to do, she told me. I packed up the few pairs of shirts and pants I'd gotten from The Healing Place, my laptop, and a copy of *Nineteen Eighty-Four*, both stolen from the public library a few blocks from my motel room, and followed them outside.

In the yellow school bus with tinted windows that drove us toward our final destination, an old Victorian asylum somewhere deep in the woods, Parker sat down beside me.

"Bet you thought you'd never see me again."

"I had a feeling," I told him with a grin.

"You were thinking about me."

I shook my head. "We were thinking about each other."

I put my hand on Parker's knee. He smiled, covering my hand with his. I tucked my head into the hollow of his shoulder and we sat that way in silence, watching the world flit past in the windows.

We each have our own rooms. We're free to come and go as we please, and the people in the small town nearby think we're students and teachers at a special school, which I suppose we are, but not the same kind of special they believe. Some of us provide therapy for drug addicts, veterans, people suffering from mental illness, and victims of abuse. Some help authorities track down murderers and missing persons. Others teach new recruits how to harness their own gifts.

The truth is I finally feel accepted. I finally feel like I'm a part of something bigger than myself. We are the children of The Eye. We can manipulate your thoughts and emotions. We can make you reveal your darkest secrets. We can cook your brain like a microwaved potato, but we can heal it if it's broken.

We use our powers for the Greater Good.

We are the Mentals.

DEAD MEN WALKING

PALOMINO WORKED THE night shift for the peace and quiet.

There were only two problems with this: one was his work partner, Jim Friedkin, just about the biggest class-A asshole you'd be likely to meet. The other was that executions at Alamosa County—or "Alamo," as they called it around here—were scheduled for the break of dawn, a tradition dating back to its early days.

According to a handful of old-timers Palomino talked to—those who *would* talk—when they used to fry Death Row prisoners at midnight the breakers would trip pretty regular, poor wiring being the likeliest culprit, plunging the entire prison into a Hell of pitchest black, subjecting anyone present to a horrific display of light and *smells* and *sounds* as the remaining electricity in the condemned's body made him dance a jig that would haunt any sane individual until his dying day.

Those same old-timers told Palomino about an inmate who'd caught fire in the chair back in 1921 or '22. It happened a handful of times but this particular instance had been the worst, according to consensus. The man's name was Harvey Jessop, a farmer convicted of killing half a dozen migrant farmhands in a rampage with a pitchfork.

Because Jessop was a pig farmer, the press had bestowed upon him the unfortunate nickname "The Pig-Man," though less imaginative writers had called him "The Pitchfork Killer," and less often, the more esoteric "Devil's Hand." They could have called Jessop "mud" for all the difference it made once the fire started, his agonized screams filling the execution chamber as thick as the black, choking stench of his charring flesh. According to Jeb Watson, a CO during those days, the human body smelled a lot like salted pork when it burned, and Harvey Jessop, aka the Pig-Man, had been no exception. It was an anecdote Palomino tried not to remember on the mornings Jenny cooked bacon and eggs for him and the kids.

With the lights out, civilians and officials scurried and screamed, trampling and vomiting on each other and themselves in their combined revulsion and panic, unable to escape the putrid-smelling smoke until someone managed to get to the breaker and the overhead lights were restored. Those old-timers said that had been the last straw. A few men had even quit over it and Palomino couldn't say he blamed them. From that day on, Retired Navy Col. Hap Shetland, the warden at the time, decided it would be best to wait until sunrise to fry up some cons.

Most of Alamo's people thought the Warden's decision had been purely practical. Citizens and politicians failed to appreciate the macabre, and it was in Warden Col. Shetland's best interest to play the game, his position being elected. Some claimed superstition: that Shetland believed killing a man so close to the witching hour was bound to create angry and vengeful spirits—and Alamo already had enough of these among the living. Whatever the reason, this new tradition stuck long after Alamosa County and the rest of the state gave up the electric chair in favor of lethal injection.

They called it a more humane death. George Palomino hadn't been around in those days, but he'd seen a few men ride Old Sparky. And since not one single prisoner in Florida (where electrocution was still on the menu) had chosen to ride the lightning since 2000, when the State had switched to the three-drug protocol, Palomino had to figure they believed it, too.

Given the choice, Palomino had to agree. At least that was how he'd felt before the execution of José Vasquez, when just about everything changed.

JOSÉ VASQUEZ WAS a lifelong sinner who met Jesus Christ somewhere between two consecutive life sentences and the death penalty. Corrections Officers Jim Friedkin and George Palomino led the three-time murderer from his Death Watch cell through Z Block—where José's old cell remained empty, until the new prisoner was scheduled to arrive, not long after José shuffled off his mortal coil—and to the death chamber.

Palomino's peace and quiet had come and gone. Though the inmates watched quietly from their bunks, painfully aware they would soon be walking bowlegged in these same shackles toward their own end, it was difficult to stay Zen leading a man to his death, be he cold-blooded killer or not.

Seemed a little like overkill giving José The Ride the way things were going on the outside, at least to Palomino: the war, the economy in the shitter, the various epidemics, famine and AIDS and all our heroes caught doping or cheating on their wives. Sending José back to Jesus felt like more of a mercy these days than any sort of justice. José's Biblical horsemen were saddled up and ready to ride, and they would all face their own judgment soon enough. They were all dead men walking on Z Block (that was the reason for the name, after all—the signage and forms were labeled "BLOCK C"), whether they'd come to terms with the fact or not. It was only a matter of time.

Palomino didn't believe in the Rapture but he did believe in the law, and as an officer of said same his duty was to uphold it, no matter what his own morality said about them on a case-per-case basis. José's God required an eye for an eye, a life for a life. The good people at Alamosa County Prison were happy enough to oblige.

00:124;00

A shadow leapt up from the bunk in cell 7B and grabbed the bars with the speed of an animal in a cage. It was Mozey. His dark skin, lined with tattoos even on his shaved skull, glistened under the halogen lamps. "Hey, Vasquez," he hissed, "pass dis along to Jesus when you see him, uh?"

José, rail-skinny and so pale his skin just about looked yellow—he'd sicked up Red Vines all night, puking and shitting the color of fresh blood—cocked his bowed head to an angle as they passed. Mozey's horker caught him right between his dazed eyes.

That old dog Friedkin was unnaturally quick with a baton despite, or because of, his age. The hollow *thock* and crunch startled Palomino. Friedkin had freed the baton and slammed it across the fingers of Mozey's left hand before Palomino saw it coming. Mozey yelped and fell back into the darkness of his cell.

"That'll teach ya to blaspheme, faggot," Friedkin growled.

Mozey held his hand in his lap, rocking back and forth on his mattress. "Broke my fingers, cocksucker," he whimpered. With Mozey's accent it sounded more like *Coke-suckah*, which wasn't an insult as far as Friedkin was concerned. The veteran CO was a sugar junkie as much as some of these cons were just plain junkies, and he sucked down two medium-sized bottles of cola per shift.

Palomino—known to some as "Pal-o-mine"—knew a fair bit about most of the men on the Block and Mozey was no exception. Mozey wasn't his real name, for one: it was short for Mozambique, where his family had emigrated from when he was a child, since his real name was unpronounceable to most— Hell, *Mozambique* was a tongue twister to some of these halfwits. Mozey'd been caught stealing a car when he was fourteen. He'd killed the cop, and because he'd killed one of their own, the State had tried him as an adult. He claimed self-defense, that Officer Mike Daniels, a rookie cop with a wife and two kids at home, had used excessive force. Mozey had beaten Officer Daniels into a coma with the steering wheel lock, what they used to sell on TV as "The Club." The charge of aggravated assault became Murder One when Officer Daniels died in the hospital a few weeks later. When they'd transferred Mozey here, his skin was so thoroughly cut and bruised he looked like an extra from *Roots*, aside from the tattoos.

Same old story. Whether it was sad or a fine example of the law protecting upstanding citizens from harm was up to the individual. Palomino figured it lay in the gray area between: as a law enforcement officer, he thought it was in his best interest to give the good guys the benefit of the doubt.

Still, he didn't think Mozey deserved to have his hand broken for what amounted to a minor beef, and he planned to tell Friedkin so as soon as they were done shift. A power struggle between two hacks still on the Block would only make one or the other of them look weak in front of the inmates, and that was never a good idea.

"What's the hold-up?" Captain Jepson said, leaning her head out the guard station window.

Rather than answer, Palomino nudged Vasquez along, and Friedkin followed with a final snarl at Mozey's cell that told of more coming if Mozey dared made a stink to the higher-ups.

The three of them reached the gate, and Donna Jepson buzzed them through. She was heavyset with short-cropped hair, skin as dark as most of the men on the Block. Palomino had always thought it must be tough for her being a woman in this job, tougher still being African-American knowing what she must about the skewed correctional system. It was hard not to admire her, particularly with the way she was treated by the inmates, as a piece of meat for masturbation material despite—or because of—her reputation as a hardass. Married, no kids. Kids or not, Palomino couldn't imagine letting his own wife work here. This was no job for a woman. No job for a man, really, short of options. Palomino himself had pretty much been railroaded into it. In Jasper, FLA, without a college degree, it was either work the prison or in the steel mill, and his asthma had ixnayed that.

Z Block's gate slammed closed behind them. Palomino and Friedkin turned Vasquez to face that long, dim hallway in which he had spent much of the last thirteen years of his life. He didn't appear to be homesick. His expression was entirely blank. Made his peace, Palomino guessed. Either that or his mind had shut down from fear. It did that to some of them: their eyes just glazed over, their faces slack and devoid of emotion, like deer caught in a set of onrushing headlights.

Donna came out of the station to give José a thorough pat-down, her duty as Death Watch Supervisor for Vasquez. Some of the COs on Z Block figured it was a PR move by Warden Cole, putting a woman in charge. It wasn't like she was any more or less capable than the rest of them. Palomino and Friedkin had already checked José before removing him from his cell, but this was procedure. *Measure twice, cut once*, Palomino's dad used to say. The last thing the Warden needed was a prisoner slashing his own throat with a sharpened toothbrush or a knife fashioned out of reinforced glass that he'd somehow managed to hoop up his ass crack, especially in front of a live studio audience.

Palomino considered José Vasquez's pitiful life as they strapped him onto the gurney. Grown up dirt poor, seventh child of migrant workers, never knowing a home for longer than a season at a time. He told Palomino he'd lived in Alamosa longer than anywhere, making it the closest thing he'd ever had to a home. At the time it had struck Palomino as one of the saddest things he'd ever heard. He'd been a rookie then, and had heard a lot of sob stories since, not many of them sadder than that. For some reason the men on Z Block felt they could confide in him. It was why they called him "Pal-o-mine." Dale McKittrick, the closest CO George had to a friend, said it was because Palomino had an honest face. Friedkin told him it was more likely they knew how to spot a sucker.

Even José's last meal was pitiful: three McRib sandwiches, two super-sized French fries, a large Pibb Xtra, and a big bag of Red Vines. He'd eaten the entire meal, sucking a finger to stick to the grains of salt at the bottom of the fry box, licking the leftover barbeque sauce straight off the greasy cardboard. It had cost more than the twenty dollars allotted for the condemned's last meal—the delivery charge was five bucks, plus a buck for a tip—but Palomino had paid the extra three dollars and fifty-eight cents out of pocket. Maybe he was a sucker after all, but the way Palomino figured, if he was about to be put to death he would have wanted someone to do the same for him.

He and Friedkin wheeled José into the execution chamber, Donna walking heavily just steps behind. Once inside, a pleasant-looking female EMT and a grim specter of a man in doctor's whites went about the business of unbuttoning José's pale blue shirt and attaching electrodes to his smooth, jaundiced chest. They found a fat juicy vein in the crook of José's left elbow—Palomino'd always considered that a strange phrase, *the crook of the elbow*, up there in the category of Strange Phrasings with *a murder of crows* and *bite the bullet*—which the nurse swabbed with alcohol.

José stared at the ceiling while they worked on him, never once looking at his executioners. He didn't so much as flinch as the needle penetrated his flesh. Was he still too dazed by his approaching death to notice, Palomino wondered, or did the pain of a little prick pale in comparison to whatever bug had hit him during the night, making him puke up his last meal, and giving his skin that waxy yellowish appearance, like a man carved from margarine?

Palomino didn't know. What he did know was the sight of blood filling the flash chamber had always made him queasy. He looked away, accidentally catching the eye of Deputy Warden Adams. The nasty little pissant had dressed him down for a minor uniform violation last week, and of course he'd had to stand there and take it, Friedkin snickering to Donna in the guard station and Donna staring at her feet, just waiting for the situation to end. Palomino couldn't afford to lose this job, not with the way things were on the outside, not with Jenny and the boys to take care of and a baby on the way, but he didn't have to *like* it.

Adams gave him a slight, expressionless nod. Palomino looked off, pretended he didn't see, a snub that would likely put him further in the doghouse. Fuck it. All he had to do was win this week's lottery and he'd be free and clear. No more taking orders from self-important prigs like Adams, no more making excuses for mean little tyrants like Jim

Friedkin.

How did that jingle go? *Just Six Little Numbers Could Change Your Life?*

Where the hell was the Warden anyhow, leaving Adams in charge? Most likely Vasquez's case wasn't enough of a PR win for him to show. Nobody cared whether José lived or died except the usual die-hard Liberal zealots, the witnesses, and the few illegals who'd heard about the case on the six o'clock news. Palomino had arrived last night expecting the usual picketing that came with these events, but he'd driven through without any trouble.

Deputy Warden Adams checked the restraints, dress shirt buttoned so tight around his throat Palomino could see the arteries throbbing under the stubble on his neck. He nodded to the doctor, to Donna, then went and opened the blinds to the witness room.

Behind the window men and women sat muttering to each other, sweating through their clothes and fanning themselves even though the sun had just barely risen. The air conditioning in this part of the building always seemed to be on the fritz, the whole damn wing as hot as the Devil's nutsack. As the blinds rose a reverent sort of silence fell over the room, as before a sermon.

The faces he met once the blind went up had always bothered Palomino. The stabbing looks of hatred had never troubled him, they were expected. It wasn't the keen interest of the morbidly curious (the ghouls), or the press, either. It was the *hope* on the faces of family and friends of the victims, hope that bearing witness as the murderer of their loved one was put to death would offer a sense that *justice had been done,* a closure this monster's imprisonment had failed to bring. Yet more often than not they would leave disappointed, disillusioned, heads hung low, ashamed of their own desperate hunger for vengeance.

Hope is the slowest poison, Palomino had always thought. Pessimism isn't the antidote, but a healthy dose did the heart a lot of good.

In the execution chamber José said something to the Chaplain, and the young priest—far too young to have acquired much life experience outside the three years he'd spent at Alamosa County—smiled beatifically, offered the Sign of the Cross, and began his prayer.

"My Jesus, by the sorrows Thou didst suffer in Thine agony in the Garden, in Thy scourging and crowning with thorns..."

While the others in the execution chamber bowed their heads for the Chaplain's benedictions, Palomino scanned their faces. He saw the EMT turn to whisper something into the doctor's ear. The doctor nodded but not before throwing a worried glance at Deputy Adams, who was closest them. Palomino saw all of this, and wondered what she'd said that Doctor Death was concerned Adams would overhear? Had she noticed the subtle quiver of the doctor's hands as they went about their business, as Palomino had, and the sweat glistening on his brow? Or had she declared she couldn't wait to get this execution in the bucket so she could put his limp uncircumcised dick between her lips?

Palomino sneered at the idea. Thoughts like this were Friedkin's influence. He'd worked side-by-side with the racist, sexist bully far too long. Captain Milton was stepping down in a month, and Palomino had talked with Jenny about putting his name in for the position. It would get him off the night shift (he would miss those early morning Zen moments, but he could live without them), and allow him more time with Jenny and the boys, the new baby they hoped would be a girl. It would also get him away from Friedkin, and nothing bad could come of that. Of course it would put him closer to Adams, but he supposed kissing a little pucker was the price one had to pay for ambition.

Deputy Warden Adams spoke briefly to the Commissioner, voice hushed. He nodded once, and cradled the phone. "José Vasquez," he announced, and at the sound of his name being spoken José rolled his eyes in the Deputy Warden's direction. "You have been condemned to die by lethal injection by a jury of your peers, a sentence imposed by a judge of good standing in the State of Florida, and to be carried out by the staff and officials of Alamosa County Prison. Do you have anything you wish to say before the sentence is carried out?"

José's eyes rolled toward the witness room window, regarded the people sitting there for a moment. Palomino expected a final dramatic statement, a *May God have mercy on your souls* to turn the table on his executioners, or something more befitting of his newly Christianized state of mind, like the confession he'd never offered. A turning of the other cheek. Tears. Blubbering. Christ, *anything* really.

What José Vasquez did was shake his head and lay back to await his fate, a pitiful end to a pitiful life.

Adams covered his surprise well. If nothing else, the man was a PR machine. "Very well." He tipped a nod toward the executioner's room, where the doctor stood alongside Donna Jepson, soundproof, bullet-resistant glass between themselves and the condemned.

Doctor Death opened the IV clamp. Sodium chloride began to drip down the tube. Palomino imagined its ice-cold fingers creeping through José's veins. The doctor then administered the Nembutal into the IV port. This was a slow, methodical process that in reality Palomino had only seen a handful of times in his seven years on Z Block. There were eleven syringes in all: four 50cc injections of pentobarbital to put the convict to sleep, followed by a saline flush to clear the line; two 50cc injections of pancuronium bromide to paralyze the inmate, so as to prevent any inconvenient muscle twitches or dancing limbs during the final set of injections, and a second saline flush; two syringes of potassium chloride, 50cc in each, to stop the heart.

Another saline flush would be administered, but by then the inmate would already be dead. This last injection was simply to clear the poison from the tubes.

It was during the second flush that Palomino grew concerned. He'd been staring at the fluid bubbling its way down the tubing when he spotted the pinky finger on Vasquez's left hand twitch once, twice. The self-inflicted tattoo on its first knuckle was a crooked cross of tiny dark blue pinpricks.

Palomino studied the faces in the death room to see if anyone else had noticed. He met only impassive looks, expressions they'd practiced once a month in Day Four simulations with volunteers in place of inmate and physician. Friedkin caught his eye and gave him a brief scowl, and Palomino was suddenly sure.

Not a single soul had noticed the movement but him.

Well, so what? he thought, hoping to calm the strange cold creeping into his own veins. The worst that could happen was José might do a little hop and jiggle on the table when the potassium chloride hit his heart, a Mexican hat dance without the hat. And anyway, it was too late to stop the process now. The final chemicals were already coursing down the tube toward José's prostrate body.

The only thing Palomino could do now was wait

and watch, both things he was being paid to do anyhow.

Watch the fingers for twitches. Watch the eyelids for a flutter. Watch the chest for a slow rise and fall.

Palomino's heart beat heavily against his uniform shirt.

Nothing.

Thirty seconds passed without movement, and he finally allowed himself to breathe a hushed sigh of relief. Involuntary muscle spasm, he figured, and the moment he thought this, the heart monitor began its steady drone, signifying José Vasquez's life had ended.

The doctor gave a somber nod to Adams.

"The sentence of José Vasquez has been carried out." Deputy Warden Adams adopted a suitably gloomy tone. "Thank you for your attendance, and please ex—"

The creak and pop of the restraints stopped him from finishing, from saying *exit*, but that final word would not be necessary. Somehow José's right arm had come free. The dead man lashed out with it, untrimmed fingernails slashing across the Deputy Warden's cheek, tearing it open, before anyone could react.

In the witness room, a woman shrieked: high-pitched and tremulous, as if she were consciously trying to break the glass separating herself from the horror show.

José was still attached to the heart monitor—he

was still *flatlining*—but somehow, despite the poison they'd filled him with, his left hand snapped from the second restraint and he sat up, arms pin-wheeling, clawing out mindlessly at his captors as a long, rattling cry of rage arose from his snarled lips, his eyes rolling wildly like an animal at the slaughterhouse, feet kicking at the restraints like a child crying out for a toy.

Palomino thought: *Something's wrong with the monitor.*

Friedkin's hand went to his baton. He fumbled with the clasp and couldn't manage to free it for probably the first time in his twenty-eight years on the job. The Deputy Warden had fallen to his knees in the corner, holding a blood-soaked handkerchief to his cheek, probably some sort of Italian silk, as he wept. In the witness room a mass exodus had begun with the scream: chairs overturned, purses forgotten, hats knocked off. A behemoth of a man wearing khaki shorts up over his belly button and a fat woman in a sundress had lodged themselves in the doorway, and neither would back down. The rest of them pressed these two through the doorway until finally they popped out into the hallway, the others spilling out behind them, a human levee breaking.

Behind the soundproof glass, Donna had the doctor in a headlock. The execution hadn't gone very well, and Death Watch Supervisor Donna Jepson was far from pleased. José Vasquez wasn't dead—or *was* dead, but his body refused to admit it. Dead/not-dead José had nearly beheaded Deputy Warden Adams with his fingernails. He had the nurse by the hair while she screamed for help, running in place, the soft soles of her Crocs squeaking on linoleum, her head wrenched back as she struggled to flee the monster's grip, her lime green scrunchie unraveling.

Palomino was in shock. His limbs refused to move, as if he, instead of José, had been given the near-lethal dose of pancuronium bromide.

Thankfully, Friedkin got his baton free and brought it down in a swift arc onto José's forehead. The flesh split open like a ripe melon. Blood spilled down into the maniac's white eyes, and the pain didn't even cause him to flinch.

"Kill it!" Adams shouted, still on the floor. "For God's sake, *kill it!*"

Palomino watched impassively as Friedkin gave it his best shot, strike after strike on the dead man's skull, neck, spine—*thock, thud, thump.* And though it was probably a slip of the tongue, Adams was right. José was no longer a *he.* This mindless creature, still strapped at the ankles to the gurney, was officially a *thing,* no more conscious of its own life than an insect. A man suffered no moral quandaries putting an insect to death. He just smashed and smashed and smashed until the goddamned thing was dead.

And Friedkin would have, except the thing on the gurney unexpectedly struck back. It let go of the nurse and grabbed the baton in the same motion. The poor woman, still running full-tilt away from José and screaming at the top of her lungs, slammed headfirst into the witness room window.

Whatever mindless instinct controlled José's body, it was fine-tuned. The dead man's hand fought with Friedkin's grip for only a moment. What Friedkin had with his baton was speed, and the element of surprise. The José-thing had *ferocity*. It wrenched the baton from Friedkin's hands and tossed it casually aside before turning José's face and rage toward its tormentor. José's pupils were no longer visible at all, trying to get a look at its own prefrontal lobe.

Friedkin's head twisted between José's hands with a kind of *pop! pop!* like bubble wrap, and in the moment before the CO realized he was dead, he looked straight at Palomino with a strange muddle of shock and anger. Then he fell to the floor.

It was only after his long-time partner was dead that Palomino noticed the electrodes were no longer attached to José's chest. They'd come detached when he'd torn out of the straps. He was *still alive*. He *wasn't dead*, let alone *undead*. Once this sunk in, Palomino found himself able to move again. A shotgun was racked on the wall for just such moments. Not moments *exactly* like this—moments like this didn't come up often, if at all. Palomino figured—but it would do. He ran for it.

Behind him, José lurched off the gurney. Still strapped in at the legs, the condemned toppled with a clang and a crash, his hips twisted sharply. The slap of his palms on the floor, the metallic drag of the gurney across the execution chamber's chipped tile floor.

Palomino fumbled with the shotgun, tried to pull it from the wall.

The nurse screamed again, waking from unconsciousness, and in the same instant as Palomino felt José's cold grip on his ankle, the latch opened and the shotgun all but fell into his hand. The thing was loaded, but still required cocking.

José clawed at his leg. Palomino's white sock, red stripes mismatched from the left's blue, slipped down to his boot as he turned to look into the whites of José's eyes. His hand, icy with fear, somehow managed to squeeze the forestock and jerk it back. *Clack-clack! Body's gon' stack!* as the "gangstas" in George Jr.'s rap songs said.

It was not customary for the executioner to speak. Palomino knew that. But José clawed at his leg with inhuman strength, threatening to pull Palomino to the floor, where the condemned could easily perform a repeat of Friedkin's fate on him, or something even more gruesome, and he found himself shouting—

"*GAH!*"

—as he pulled the trigger.

José's head exploded like chunky, wet red streamers, splashing on Palomino's uniform. A chunk of something, brain or bone or cartilage, struck his throat and unstuck when he swallowed, spattering on the linoleum floor by the gloppy, stringy remains of José's head. What was left looked a lot like what José had puked up overnight. Vasquez slumped to the floor. He did not move again.

Tendrils of cobalt gray smoke issued from the shotgun barrel.

Palomino stood for a moment, regarding the scene. That perfect dead quiet had fallen over Z Block again. His guts turned over suddenly, spoiling it. His dinner, a Tupperware of Jenny's leftover chili, came up on his shoes, fitting quite nicely with what was leftover of José.

The door to the executioner's room opened and Donna Jepson charged in, Doctor Death—*Doctor Fuckup, more like*, Palomino thought, and he liked that so much he laughed—running in on her heels.

"Oh shit," Donna said, wide-eyed, surveying the carnage. "What the fuck, George? What the *fuck*?"

Instead of replying—did she even *want* an answer?—Palomino looked through his tears, past José's headless corpse and Friedkin's twisted remains, beyond the upturned gurney, and several feet above the Deputy Warden still cradling his face with his bloodied handkerchief was the clock on the wall, showing a quarter to seven. Fifteen minutes until shift change. Gina Stavros was probably toweling off in the change rooms right about now, maybe having one last smoke before she came in to relieve him for the day.

I better get overtime for this, Palomino thought, tossing the shotgun aside. Donna knelt down beside the Deputy Warden, and while she helped him to his feet, Doctor Dipshit stood looking over the corpse of José Vasquez.

Palomino knew that look. He'd seen it from coworkers, when the punishment for some minor violation of the rules had somehow spiraled out of control. When a prisoner lay unconscious and swollen, bloody and bruised. Or dead, like José. The look on the doctor's face mirrored Donna Jepson's words. The look said *Oh shit*.

Regarding the gooey chunks of José he wiped from himself, Palomino decided this would be his final execution. José Vasquez had been a model prisoner, it was a shame for him to die like this. (Jim Friedkin, however, wasn't likely to be missed.) He would put in his name in for Captain by the end of the week. The way the Deputy Warden was looking at him, with a combination of amazement and fear, he'd be likely to get whatever goddamn job he wanted.

Even if he didn't—if Donna got it instead, though after today's debacle her chance of seeing any career advancement was about as likely as Jenny being able to get the bloodstains out of this goddamn shirt— he'd make sure he was out before the next con was hauled down to the Death Watch cell. He'd transfer off the goddamn Block if that was what it would take.

Who was next, anyhow? Mozey? That chickenhawk creep, Jim Lee Allen?

It didn't matter. They were all dead men on Z

Block. Even Palomino would someday be a wet splat on a funeral director's shirt, he figured.

Just a matter of time, really.

In the meantime, there was the lottery. He decided to buy two tickets tonight, instead of the usual one. After today's shift, he felt like his luck just might be heading for a change.

THE EYE AT THE DOOR

TODD PENDLETON HAD always felt like a poseur in the world of PR consulting, and the thought of his colleagues at Savvicorp knowing how he felt gave him stomach troubles.

While the Big Dogs power-lunched at Hy's Steakhouse or Canoe, at the top of the TD Centre, Todd would wolf down what he half-jokingly called a "powerless lunch" at one of the cheaper places in the mall. He and Darlene had just bought a house, and he'd always said it paid to save where he could. Darlene had offered plenty of times to pack up a lunch of leftovers, but Todd wasn't about to eat from a Tupperware container at his desk.

"Why not just put a big old sign on my head?" he'd asked her, miming the flashing sign by splaying his fingers out from his forehead. "*Loser! Loser! Not meant to be here!*"

Darlene had smiled patiently. After seven years of marriage she knew when her husband was just blowing off steam. Todd knew that she knew, and was glad when she permitted it. He kissed her on the forehead. "Sorry, Apple." He'd been calling her *Apple* for years now, and neither of them could remember why. "You're just looking out for me. And you know I love your cooking. But they're gunning for me down there, that's something *I* know. So far as they're concerned I've been meeting you for lunch, and while it's not optimal—what kind of weirdo meets his wife every day for lunch?—it's *worked*. At least the women around the office respect me for it."

Today was Casual Friday. Some of the others wore jeans, but Todd wore his favored suit—one of two he'd picked up at Tom's Place. They fit nice and looked twice as expensive as they'd been—afraid that if the others saw him in jeans, they'd spot how out of place he felt right away. Todd was rarely, if ever, casual at the office. Casual implied comfort, an easement with one's surroundings. Todd Pendleton was perpetually aware of the eyes at his back. A man like that was only ever comfortable with a door closed firmly behind him.

Kenneth Pratchett, the office wildcard, shot finger guns and/or winked at everyone as they stepped into the boardroom for their big Friday morning meeting. When Todd sauntered in, taking up the rear as usual, Kenneth simply nodded. "Todd," he said, not meeting his eyes.

The meeting didn't go well. The boss was as irritable as Todd's bowels. Work on the Raleigh's account was a slog, but it *was* progressing. The problem was they'd undershot the amount of time required to complete the job to guarantee they'd be the ones handling it.

Then they pawned it off on me, Todd thought miserably, sitting at his desk. *Raleigh's Industrial Lubricant. Sheesh.* What the heck was he supposed to do with a company that sells petroleum-based oils for machinery? If it was cooking oil, he could slap a pretty face on it. Hell, if it was *sex oils* he could do something with it. *Raleigh's Personal Lubricant: perfect for lubing up and taking it in the old poop chute from your superiors!*

He sighed heavily and glanced at the clock beside his framed photo of Darl. Looking at her picture always made him smile, but the smile would quickly fade. He didn't deserve to be with someone so perfect. Not that she would make a man jealous of him. She was, he hated to admit it, awfully plain (he wasn't so hot in the looks department either, particularly in recent years, with the growing paunch and his once magnificent auburn hair retreating from his eyebrows like Allied soldiers during the Battle of Mons). But intelligence and personality radiated from her. The two of them had married straight out of high school—"plucked her right off the vine," as his dad had once described their pairing—and as a result, he often thought she must have felt like she'd missed out on some of the more exciting aspects of life.

Lunchtime came, though he wasn't very hungry. He'd eat, of course. He *always* ate, even when he didn't feel like eating. He opened his briefcase, gathered a few things from the Raleigh's account—the pretense was that he and his wife worked together over lunch, Darlene grading papers—and tucked them in neatly with the Pepto Bismol and antacids, perfect companions for the National Post he kept for bathroom excursions.

Vic Reagan peeked around the cubicle wall, startling Todd, who snatched up his briefcase and held it against his chest protectively.

"Ted," the boss always called him *Ted*, not Todd, "lemme see you in my office after lunch, 'kay, Big Guy?"

Big Guy. Was that a crack on his weight? Todd wondered. Sure he'd put on a few pounds since he'd started five years ago, but he was by no means heavy, and most of that weight gain was stress-related.

The rest, he supposed, was related to lunches at the food court in the mall.

Todd felt the eyes of the whole office on his back as he lowered his briefcase. He made sure to plaster on a smile before turning to face them, saw Kenneth Pratchett leering, savoring his humiliation. Guys like Pratchett would always be at the top of the food chain, unlike Todd, who swam in the wake of the apex predators.

Todd had read that the unattractive earned significantly less than conventionally good-looking people. They called it the *plainness penalty*. Todd had been seated on that bench for most of his life.

"Sure thing, sir," Todd said, as Vic Reagan—who

prided himself on his namesake as if he'd been the one to tell Gorbachev to tear down the Wall—breezed past without awaiting his reply.

Todd's mind reeled with awful uncertainties. Office after lunch. On a Friday. Vic Reagan was notorious for firing off little Friday hand-slap emails to the entire office, not blaming anyone in particular, but referencing a specific incident so the intended target would still know they were being blamed, albeit unofficially. Then the coward would head out early for the weekend before anyone could offer their two cents. Seeing someone *in his office* on a Friday... that was an entirely different beast, and in Todd's imagination, the beast had horns and shark's teeth still pink with its previous meal.

They terminated people on Fridays. Todd had once read that if they fired someone earlier in the week there was a statistically higher chance of an "incident." What the incident might be was never specifically stated, but he'd seen enough movies to hazard a guess.

TODD WAS ON his way to the mall parking lot after lunch when the basket of deep fried calamari hit his colon like a freight train heading for the end of a long, dark tunnel. *Good God, not now!* The stomach cramps had been getting worse over the past few months, with the mortgage, the bills, the guys at work eyeballing him, and Darl hoping to conceive.

The wolf wasn't exactly at the door, but he was

getting his pipes ready to blow down *Chez Petit Cochon.*

Todd squeezed his cheeks and power-walked back to the washrooms, head swimming with the nausea pushing at the back of his throat. He knew exactly where they were and he should, considering he'd passed them five afternoons a week. The problem was that he hated—absolutely *loathed*—using public toilets. The few times he'd had to go to the john at work, after one coffee too many, or a particularly heavy dinner the night before, he'd try to use the washrooms on another floor, in another office. And still he'd startled with every squeak of a fart, pinched his legs closed around the space above the bowl where his meager genitals dangled over the filthy water, courtesy flushing to waft away the smell before wiping.

Insanely enough, he'd feared his colleagues, Big Dogs that they were, would sniff out his fear of them in his excrement.

If he thought he could have made it home, he would have. At home, the bathroom was a refuge from his daily stresses. It was his castle, as his father used to say—as in, "A man's crapper is his castle." It was where he came up with his best pitches, like the one that had landed him the job he held now, and the campaign that had gotten he and Darlene out of the sticks and into a nice new semi-detached in High Park.

But he had no choice in the matter. It felt like

everything he'd eaten over the past two days was about to drop out of him like the flush of an airplane toilet, whether he was hovering uncomfortably over the well-used bowl or still hurrying on his way to it.

A toilet flushed behind the closed door, and a man stepped out of one of the stalls just as Todd stepped in. He pressed past Todd, eyes on the floor—surprisingly clean for a public restroom—and on through the door. Todd watched him go, then glanced at the unused sinks, shaking his head in slight disgust. Some people.

With a quick scan of his surroundings, he saw no feet under any of the three stalls. No one stood at the urinals, either. At 12:30 on a Friday, this was about as close to a miracle as Todd had ever experienced.

Sweat beading on his brow, he slipped off his pants and cotton Jockeys just in time—Darlene had pressured him to wear boxers in order to increase his sperm production, but they just didn't keep the boys together the way he liked, and sperm production was the opposite of what he needed now—booting the stall door closed behind him.

Wouldn't that have been great, he thought, *shitting my pants before a meeting with Reagan*. He supposed he would have been all right, seeing as he was already at the mall. Just throw his crappy underwear in the trash and buy a few new pairs at the cheapest department store he could find. But the stink wouldn't wash off. He'd feel it sticking between his cheeks, itching, while sitting across the big desk from his tormentor. *What's that aroma, Big Guy?*

Someone was peering in at him, through the half-inch crack between the post and the door.

At first, Todd thought he'd imagined it. He hadn't even *heard anyone come in*. But someone *was* there: a single silver-gray eye scrutinized the place where Todd's legs came together. A blistered, pink tongue poked out to lick whitened, cracked lips. Wiry facial hair sprouted from nostrils like a tangled mass of tentacles, spreading out in a full mustache and beard. Under the door, Todd saw the dirty, paint-spattered coveralls and scuffed work boots that left a black rubber streak on the tiles.

Todd had a moment to think, *It's my imagination. No one's looking in, he's just waiting to use the toilet. Bad calamari, that's all. I'm sick and I'm seeing things.*

He tried to blink it away, to forget about the fact that there were *three* stalls, and all of them had been free when he'd come in. It wasn't even as though he'd gone into the wheelchair access stall by mistake. Whoever this person was, he was deliberately standing outside the door to the throne Todd occupied. This was no minor, excusable invasion of privacy, like taking the seat right next to someone on the train when there were dozens of empty seats. This wasn't just a minor violation of social convention. This was an infringement on a *basic human right*, to be able to shit without fear of harassment. If public toilets had been around in Moses's day, *Thou shalt not loiter outside the toilet while thy neighbor is shitting* would surely have been carved on one of those tablets.

Todd focused again on the crack in the door.

The pitch black pupil in the center of the silver-gray eye constricted. Todd had once read that pupils were sphincters. He pushed the useless thought away, noticing with rising horror a faint movement at the man's mid-section, but he couldn't see (nor did he want to imagine) what the man was doing to himself. It was all too much for his fragile mind to handle... that he was being spied on while defecating, and worse, that the voyeur might be *pleasuring himself* to the sight (smell?). Todd pulled his legs together tightly and cupped his hands over his genitals, unsure how he should respond to this violation... what he should say, if anything.

Please, God, make him go away!

Todd made to say, *Excuse me,* but immediately knew how it would sound. It was a problem he'd experienced often with colleagues: sounding meek. They'd swing their big dicks around the office—"Vaginas, with the women," he'd add for the benefit of Darlene—and Todd would still be scrabbling at his zipper like a nervous kid on Prom Night.

It was only then that he noticed the graffiti on the walls. There were the usual tags, the crude jokes and drawings. What commanded Todd's attention had been etched in rigid letters with a key or, he supposed, a jackknife:

See "ReSULtS" BeLOW

But Todd didn't want to see *anything* below. In fact, he'd already seen a lot more "below" than he'd ever wanted.

The man's breath came quicker, in tandem with the rustling at his crotch, the metallic clack of his zipper, and Todd felt suddenly sicker than he had after eating the calamari. What kind of man would do such a thing, in plain sight of anyone?

What kind of man *allowed it to happen*?

But he was completely vulnerable. He'd realized it the moment this perverse dance had begun. His pants were loose around his ankles, his privates exposed, excrement smeared between his buttocks. If he did say something—if he was to shout at this pervert to *Leave me alone*, to *Let me shit in piece for Christ's sake!*—he could neither prevent an attack nor make an escape should the fecophiliac take offence and stop pleasuring himself just long enough to kick in the door.

What could he do to defend himself if the silver-eyed man *attacked* him? If the smell was no longer enough, and the freak wanted a *taste*? What if he wanted to *play with it*, like a rotten little boy plunging his fists into his dirty diaper, to smear it over the walls and on himself and on its maker? What could he do besides sit there and let the terrible man do whatever terrible things he wanted, to wait until the man had finished with him—with him and his *shit*—

then pull up his pants and wash off his shame in the sink?

Todd considered in that long, excruciating moment—with his helpless brown eyes pinned in place by the single scrutinizing gray one—that he was a sitting duck, one which had been stripped of its feathers and splayed out naked, about to get its most private of orifices crammed with a fistful of bread and onions.

The man was grunting now, a vile, ululating groan of pain or pleasure—*uh-ruh-ruggh! uh-ruh-ruggh! uh-ruh-ruggh!*—as though he'd already rubbed himself raw in a prior affront and was gritting his teeth through the discomfort. The eye opened wider, the tongue sliding back and forth like a blind, desiccated worm feeling its way along dried concrete after a storm. One work boot shuddered and kicked out, the way a dog's leg might jerk when scratched in just the right place, thudding softly against the post.

Todd realized, as he watched the boot kick out, that it wasn't *paint* on the man's pants at all. Or, if it was, it was the thickest paint he'd ever seen, great globs of it like giant white slugs.

Oh, please, Todd thought pitifully, *why don't you leave me alone?!*

Todd heard the *clack* of someone pushing at a locked door, and his heart leapt. The relief that it wasn't the door before him was short-lived upon realizing it was the *outside* door, the door separating them from the food court. Somebody had tried to enter the bathroom and was foiled by the lock. Someone who could have potentially spared him further indignity at the hands of this maniac.

His thwarted savior.

Todd Pendleton was locked in and alone, trapped by the nasty silver-eyed man.

Why does this have to happen to me? Todd wanted to scream. But he knew why. It was the perfect metaphor for his impotence: both figurative and literal. He'd bitten off more than he could chew with the Raleigh's account, and everyone knew it. Meanwhile, Darlene wanted a baby—preferably a boy, but she'd be happy with either sex "just as long as it's healthy"—and Todd didn't have the guts, so to speak, to tell her he wasn't ready for such responsibility. His unrequited need to talk her out of it, at least temporarily, had just last week presented itself in erectile difficulty.

The man at the door had no trouble achieving an erection, unfortunately. All at once the silver eye widened, and the man began to sputter out breath after breath like a braying horse, sucking in through snot-sticky nostrils, the hairs in there writhing like tentacles—*Goddamn you, vile food court calamari!*—after each stinking discharge of cabbage and sulfur and a sickeningly sweet smell—*Maple syrup?*—from his lungs. It brought with it thoughts of death and rot and the fiery cauldrons of Hell and childhood trips to Pioneer Village where Todd had invariably gotten his face pushed into the snow by one of the Big Kids.

A gob of the man's cold, wet spunk landed on Todd's knee. Todd cried out. It was the first sound he'd made since he'd seen the man in the crack of the door, and its echo in his tiny metal death chamber startled him further. He wanted so desperately to wipe the sperm from his leg, but the libertine's cold, silver eye held him in place, daring him to move. Another spurt struck between the door and post, and oozed its way to the floor like a gleaming, pearly snail.

Then, as if Todd had nothing more to show him, the scatologist let out a pained grunt—*uuurrruunnghh!*—and shambled off, dragging his feet with each belabored step. Hunching down over his naked midsection, Todd watched the dirty boots scuffle away. The bathroom door unlatched and creaked open. The boots stepped out. The door hung silently in space for a moment, then slammed shut.

Todd heard himself whimper with relief. He wiped his ass and the jism from his knee—there was toilet paper at least, thank God for small mercies— and left the stall, grimacing in disgust as the man's semen plunked to the scuffed tile at his feet. He washed his hands, peering at himself in the mirror. His face was ghostly pale, sickeningly gaunt. His were the haunted eyes of a victim.

What he wondered was: had the man been lying in wait for just anyone to enter the toilets? Or had he picked out something in Todd, a vulnerability he could exploit? Todd sometimes used this toilet, so it was likely the man had seen him in this stall before. And the idea that the man had chosen *him*, of all people—*For what? Because I look like a wimp? A sucker? Someone who would sit there and take it and wouldn't make a peep in his own defense, exactly like I just did?*—made him more angry than the assault itself.

Strangely, the anger was not directed at his assailant but at the mortified face staring back at him in the mirror.

The door creaked open. Todd startled, watching its reflection as it swung open. A teenage boy in a black toque and a tight, ribbed undershirt stepped up beside him, began primping himself, swiping his hands through the scruffy hair above his ears and slicking back his eyebrows with the index and little finger of a single hand—the Devil's sign, Todd noted—all before spotting Todd standing beside him. The kid took one look, pulled a disturbed face, and walked out.

As Todd rubbed his hands together under the dryer, he glanced at the stall he'd been sitting in, indistinguishable from the others except for a pearly splotch still trickling down the door handle. He had an impulse to wipe it off, to spare the next person from the indignity of getting it smeared it on their palm, but an insidious, selfish little thought wormed its way into his head, surprising him into sudden, delirious laughter:

Fuck 'em.

He stood in front of the row of mirrors, laughing,

cackling at his own reflection.

What would someone say, he thought, *if they walked in and caught me guffawing like this—like a genuine nutjob?*

The laughter died in his throat.

He went back to the stall, wound a good bunch of toilet paper around his hand, then tentatively wiped away the spunk from the door. He did the same with the spot on the floor, glistening under the fluorescents, then chucked the sticky wad into the bowl and flushed it away. Todd had been raised to clean up after himself, and though it hadn't been him who'd made this gloppy mess, he felt at least partly responsible.

It occurred to him that feeling personal responsibility for being victimized was unhealthy, but he pushed it out of his mind. He wasn't a victim. He'd just been in the wrong place at the wrong time. It could have happened to anyone.

Yes, but would anyone have let it go on *happening?*

Again, he pushed the thought away.

He washed his hands a second time before leaving the washroom for good.

As he scurried through the food court, he scanned the patrons surreptitiously, looking for the man in the white-stained coveralls. Not to confront him—*Heavens,* no—but to *avoid* him. To identify him, so he could steer clear of him in the future.

A few customers caught his furtive looks. A teenager scowled over her taco salad and cell phone and an elderly gentleman smiled and ruffled his newspaper. There were no coveralls, there was no man with a beard and silver-gray eyes. If not for the mess he'd cleaned from the door, he might have been able to convince himself he'd imagined the entire ordeal.

Whether imagined or incredibly, horribly real, Todd never wanted to see those silver-gray eyes again in his life, if he could help it. And he'd certainly never go into that bathroom again, not even to wash his hands before eating. Maybe he'd drive to another mall on Monday, a little further if need be, to get his lunch.

If I've still got a job come Monday, he thought, launching into the parking lot elevator just as the doors began to close.

TODD DUCKED UNDER the scaffolding and back into the lobby of 323 Bay Street. They'd been doing renovations on the building for months now, caulking around the exteriors of the windows, painting the halls, and the inconvenience was bordering on intrusive. The living wall they'd installed when the renos began trickled pleasantly as always, but today it reminded Todd of urination, and urination reminded him of the washroom at the mall.

He hurried by to the elevators.

Hurrying to my own execution, he thought, and pushed the thought away. As a skill, he thought he'd just about gotten the hang of it.

All eyes fell on him when he stepped into the office, like wolves on their prey. Kenneth Pratchett nodded up at him from his chair as Todd passed by toward Reagan's corner office, the kind of nod you gave people at a funeral, with slightly downcast eyes.

Todd gave a hesitant knock on the door, opened just a crack so Vic Reagan could say "My door's always open" and mean it literally as well as figuratively. "*Come*," Reagan shouted, which had always reminded Todd of Captain Jean-Luc Picard of the Starship Enterprise (he and Darlene were closet Trekkers), but today made him think of the eye between the crack in the door, the silver-gray iris jerking up and down as he—

Todd pushed the thought away. In a way, ignoring the truth was an inherent component of working in PR.

"You wanted to see me, sir?" He cursed himself silently, remembering the promise he'd made to himself not to phrase everything as a question around his superiors. He'd read once that it made the speaker sound weak.

"Have a seat, Ted."

Todd, he thought but did not say. It was much too late to correct Reagan on that. He made to close the door.

"Leave it open," the boss said. Todd sighed inwardly, imagining Kenneth Pratchett pressing his ear against the crack, giving a hushed play-by-play to the rest of the office. Imagining the silver-gray eye at the office door, and its grunting, self-pleasuring possessor.

He sat. Vic Reagan lingered by the windows, taking in the impressive penthouse view of the city, the Harbourfront. His masculine figure, maintained at his personal gym by a fitness trainer who worked with visiting celebrities, silhouetted by the empty sky over the lake. "Ted, I've worked here fifteen years," he said, not turning. "I used to do copy when I started, did you know that?" Todd had heard it countless times, like everyone else in the office, but Reagan pressed on, not requiring a response. "In all my years at Savvicorp, I have never seen such potential as you had when you started here... just *squandered*."

Todd felt his cheeks flushing, and could do nothing. He shifted uncomfortably in his chair and glanced in the direction of the door.

"I took a chance when I hired you." Reagan finally turned. His silver gray hair shone in a halo of sunlight. "I looked past your cheap suits, both of them, and your not-quite-close shave, and that *cologne*," he pulled a face, "do you know what people say about your cologne, Ted? Look, I don't mean to sound like I'm berating you—"

Oh no? Todd thought but would never dare say. *You could've fooled me.*

"—honestly, Big Guy, I was pulling for you. I wanted you to succeed. Sincerely, I did."

Sincerely. The same complimentary close Reagan

used in all of his emails, as if he were writing a personal letter. With Vic Reagan, sincerity was the equivalent of a liar saying *Trust me*. About as genuine as a politician in the midst of a sex scandal.

If you wanted me to succeed, he thought, *you wouldn't have stuck me with the damn Raleigh's account.*

Todd said nothing.

At the window behind Reagan, while the man pontificated—sincerely—a work platform lowered into view.

"I mean, we're a *consulting firm*, Ted," Vic Reagan was saying, "we're certainly not being paid to consult with our wives over Big Macs at the mall."

Behind him, the platform blotted out the sun.

Todd watched as the worker shuffled his feet, his legs the only part of him in view, silhouetted against the sky. Could Todd push away the thought that those were work boots scuffling on the platform? Could he push away the thought that those were *coveralls*?

The ability escaped him.

Caulking, he thought. *The little white slugs were* caulking.

Todd considered how apropos it was that the sicko had caulk on his pants as the boss continued his spiel. "It's a dog-eat-dog world, Big Guy. Either you're the dog," Vic Reagan said, "or you're the bone."

Bone... Like the one the pervert at the mall tried to give me.

The sun highlighted straggly whiskers below the man's chin and on his cheeks. The caulking gun held in both hands at his groin. The silver-gray eyes staring with hunger, the shriveled tongue dragging across sun-chapped lips.

Todd could hold his tongue no longer.

"*AHHHYEEEAAGGHHHH!*" he shouted, leaping from his chair. He lifted it into the air, all sixty pounds of it, while Vic Reagan, he of the mixed metaphor, sat flabbergasted.

"Ted? What the heck are you doing, Big Guy?"

Todd rushed headlong at the window like a Spartan with a battering ram. He launched the chair, all sixty pounds of it, at the tempered glass.

Vic Reagan said "*Shit!*" as he leaped from his chair, shielding his immaculate salt-and-pepper hairdo from the imminent explosion.

The window shattered outward in a million tiny pieces. Todd stepped back, hit by the shock of impact, the *sound* of it, like a depressurizing airplane cabin at 32,000-feet. Recycled air rushed past him, ruffling his hair and the panels of his six-hundred-dollar suit, sucking out papers from Reagan's desk—his pink slip along with them, Todd hoped—which fluttered like doves into the pure blue sky as a rain of glass pattered against the polished hardwood floor.

Todd took another step back, sucking in a gasp like a man waking from sleepwalking, and surveyed the damage he'd done. A golf ball rattled to the edge and over, where the entire pane from floor to ceiling had disappeared.

So had the work platform.

Oh no, Todd thought. *Oh God no, please.*

He put a hand on the frame and peered over the edge of slick wooden flooring. Wind whipped his suit, his tie fluttering, slapping at his chin and cheeks.

Todd craned his neck upward first, certain the silver-eyed man from the bathroom had pulled the apparatus up in time to avoid the chair that would certainly have killed him. His gaze found nothing but glass and sky. Above them the rooftop was green, an innovative addition that had garnered them national attention at the time. There were no wires, nor anything to suspend them with. Anyone looking up would see the mirrored surface of 323 Bay, the reflection of the buildings along the Harbourfront, the blue of sky and water, unmarred but for the single black gap where a man stood, his mouth agape, his tie flickering in the wind.

They would assume he'd be soon to follow the chair out the window. It was just the sort of incident managers strived to avoid by firing on Fridays.

His first instinct was to apologize, to beg for Vic Reagan's forgiveness. But his boss had hidden behind the big desk. And anyway, he should at least see what sort of damage he'd done before he made his excuses. He might be better off saving his apologies for the jury.

Beneath the scuffed tips of his orthopedic dress shoes, colorful ants scurried about, huddling around a bright orange taxi in the street where Todd's chair had landed. The miniature cab driver stepped out of the car. It was difficult to tell whether or not he'd been injured. From the way the cabbie was moving, it appeared as though Todd had dodged a bullet.

"Whoops," Todd said, and cackled madly.

Behind him came a brief knock at the door and Kenneth Pratchett's smug voice saying "Everything okay in here, Vic—? *Ho*-lee *shit!*"

Todd turned and met Pratchett's eye. They stood in silence, the spacious room separating them. Todd on the other side of the desk now, Pratchett peering in with a look of shock, like a frightened animal caught in the headlights of Todd's wild-eyed gaze. Todd could think of nothing to do but shoot Pratchett with his own trademarked finger gun. Startled by the implication, the handsome weasel slinked back out of the room.

Todd stretched around, his right hand still on the window frame, to look for his boss.

Vic Reagan was kneeling alongside his desk like a kid practicing Duck and Cover during the Cold War. There were tiny square chunks of glass in his hair and on the shoulders of his Gucci double-breasted suit. He shook them off and stared at Todd with fearful fascination for a long moment. He didn't get up off the floor.

Todd held his gaze, until his so-called superior looked past him at the gaping mouth of the window.

"Todd? You know, you could have killed

someone down there, Big Guy."

He knew it. And although it must surely have been his intention to kill someone at the time, he hoped—*sincerely*—nobody was hurt now.

"Maybe you should take a vacation," Vic Reagan suggested. "Relax for a bit, come back with a fresh outlook."

Come back? How could he come back? These people would think he was a crazy man. You don't "come back" from an assumed nervous breakdown.

"That's a good idea, Vic," Todd said, looking at the open space where the window had once been. Had he imagined the man in the window? He was certainly nowhere in sight—which was good, Todd considered, because if he *had* been in the window when the chair went out, Todd would be worrying about how to shit in the toilet of a two-man prison cell instead of considering a vacation.

"A *very* good idea. But what about the Raleigh's account?"

"The lubricant guys? Oh Christ, Kenneth can handle that," Vic said with a dismissive wave of his manicured, unnaturally tanned hand.

That was good. Kenneth deserved it. That handsome little weasel deserved everything his good looks would afford him.

The telephone rang. Vic stood to answer it, still eyeing Todd cautiously. "Vic Reagan." As he spoke he never took his eyes off of Todd, until Todd turned his way. Then, blessedly, he lowered them. "Is anyone hurt? Oh thank God. Yes, it was an accident. The damn thing just slipped out from under my ass." Todd had to hand it to him. The man knew how to spin. Not the best maybe, but he could sell a line of bull with a straight face. Vic squinted at the window. "Okay, thank you very much. Yeah, bye."

Todd stepped away from the window. "I'm going to go now," he said.

Vic's face told him it was a wonderful idea. "Sure thing, Big Guy. Whatever you like."

Whatever he liked. Todd thought about this as he strode through the cubicles, everyone watching him until he turned to face them, then looking away, to their desks, to their computers, to their feet, anywhere but *at* him. It seemed as though looking at Todd Pendleton as he beamed through the office had suddenly become like looking directly at the sun.

They were seeing him for the first time. Oh, they'd looked a lot before, but they had never really *seen* him.

He was one of the Big Dogs now. Big Dogs did whatever they liked, and what he wanted right now was to go home, eat some supper, watch *Jeopardy!* and make love to his wife. He had a good feeling he'd see "results" below tonight... and an even stronger feeling he'd have the confidence to tell Darlene he wasn't ready to have kids just yet, particularly with a vacation in their future.

Maybe he'd swing by the mall first. Head into the men's room. See if the silver-eyed man with the bushy beard and filthy coveralls was in there, exposing himself to some other poor schmo. Todd wanted to thank him for inspiring his newfound courage.

Or smash his head into a door, he really hadn't decided yet.

CUTTINGS

KATIE WAS IN the kitchen when a low rumbling rattled the window. As she moved the curtain aside to peer out, a large off-white object filled her view, and the blast of a horn startled her away from the glass. Someone had pulled into the driveway.

Hanging half out the kitchen door, Katie took a cautious look at the back of an ugly old van spewing black exhaust into the carport. The tinted rear window was cracked, the bumper on a sharp cant, every inch covered in a layer of scum, even the small silver letters spelling out RAM.

"What the heck is this?"

The driver door opened as she spoke. Katie recognized her husband's designer jeans before he stepped down on the concrete slab, and she saw that he had clearly gone mad, because only a crazy person would have such a bright, goofy smile stepping out of such a filthy, run-down vehicle.

Gavin Leslie had only just recently lost his job and now he'd lost his mind.

"Honey, before you say it, I got a great deal."

"Unless you traded for magic beans, a great deal

is still too much."

"Honey," he said again, in the tone he used when he knew he was in the wrong, "you're gonna love this van. And she was only twelve-hundred dollars."

"*Twelve-hun*—" Katie let go of the doorjamb and stepped out onto the cement porch. She *had* to, for fear of keeling over in shock. "Jesus, you really have lost your mind."

Gavin threw open the back doors, his biggest surprise saved for last. In the back stood a bathroom cabinet papered with faux wood, alongside a soiled mattress. Katie gaped at them. Gavin took her surprise for a favorable reaction and the smile returned to his scruffy face. "You love her, right? I knew you'd love her."

"I know times are tough, Gavin, but surely you don't expect us to live in that van." Trying for patience, her tone sounded more like measured anger. Had he really just called it *her*?

"I'll take out the mattress," he assured her. "And the cabinet. I guess the previous owner must have camped in it." He squinted into the back, a forlorn quality to his look Katie didn't quite like. Then his eyes lit up. "I forgot the best part. It's got a tape deck! You remember cassettes."

"Honey, we're the same age. Of course I remember them."

"I found a whole bunch of old cassettes in the cabinet. It's got Mr. Big. You remember Mr. Big."

Katie rolled her eyes, and Gavin drew himself

away from the van to stand below her at the steps. "I bought her for us." He took her hand. "For the business."

"What business, Gavin?"

"The flower shop." Excitement crept back into his voice. "*Cuttings*," he added with a hopeful look, reminding her of the name he'd picked as a joke only the two of them and his dead stepmother would get.

Katie peered over her husband's newly balding head at the beaten-up van with its tape deck and '90s hair band cassettes and the moldering bedroom in the back. She knew what her sister would call it: she'd call it a rape van. Katie held a similar sentiment. Likely a previous owner had camped out of it, as Gavin suggested. *Or lived in it*, she thought uneasily.

But they could take out the mattress. They could take out the cabinet. The flower shop had been a pleasant dream when they'd first started dating, before bills and real life had gotten in the way. Before Gavin's stepmother, Deanie, who'd always filled the Leslie home with the colors and mingled fragrances of a hundred different blossoms, had passed away in a hospital room resembling a greenhouse with all the Get Well flowers.

"The flower shop," Katie said, warming to the idea. "I hate the name Cuttings, though. If we're going to go through with this, we really ought to call it Deanie's."

A smile crept onto Gavin's lips. He took her hand and kissed it gently.

II

SIX WEEKS LATER, Deanie's Flowers was a living, breathing thing eating up a good portion of their life. But it felt good to be doing something other than banging out her latest book, and even better to see Gavin working again. The layoff had been hard on him. Secretly, Katie thought he'd felt emasculated living off the meager royalties of his wife's crime novels.

With a view of the back gardens, the glassed-in conservatory made an excellent workshop. They'd removed all the furniture, filled the space with tables and covered them with asters and baby's breath and poinsettias and tulips. In the center of the room they'd erected a long counter with a stone finish where the two of them could work side-by-side.

Gavin was an expert with flowers, but arranging wasn't his strong point. Here, Katie discovered an untapped talent. So while he cut the flowers and groomed them, kept them fresh and vibrant, she performed magic with vases and pots and floral foam. While Katie placed orders and created the budgets, Gavin's experience in marketing gradually brought in new customers. He also drove the delivery van, which with its new paint job and Deanie's Flowers decal began to look somewhat respectable, despite its shabby past.

Together, Katie and Gavin Leslie made a perfect team, and as Deanie's Flowers began to bloom so did

Gavin's libido. His hunger for her had waned after the layoff but now it roared like the engine of his ugly old van. The day they cleared out the workshop, high from the news of their loan approval, they'd fucked on the cool ceramic tiles in the middle of the glassed-in room, oblivious to potential stares from over the back fence. Gavin devoured her with an enthusiasm he rarely showed, even during their courtship. Secretly, Katie had often thought he felt inadequate, despite her reassurances. But that night and every day since, he'd pushed her to orgasm multiple times until her own cries grew so loud she embarrassed herself, and the two of them lay their sweaty heads together on the cool slab floor, laughing and panting.

The Leslies were happy, healthy and growing more successful by the day.

GAVIN SNAPPED AWAKE. He'd been sleeping in an awkward position and his legs felt numb, belonging to someone else. His chest was constricted. His first instinct was to struggle, bound to a familiar chair, though his hands were unrestricted.

Where am I?

He blinked into the dark. As his vision adjusted, he saw the black rectangle before him, a glimmer of glass. He thought of the conservatory, of his chair at the worktable, but here the glass was too close. Moreover, he didn't smell flowers and damp earth but a familiar musty vinyl.

Yellow light flooded the backyard, triggered by

some creature of the night, and he recognized his surroundings: the van. The pressure on his chest was the belt in the driver's seat. Somehow he'd wandered out here in his underwear and buckled himself in behind the steering wheel.

The yard light dimmed, throwing him once again into darkness.

"How did I get out here?"

As he spoke he became aware of a presence at his side, the urge to turn both powerful and repellent. He unbuckled first, drawing his hand slowly across his lap, conspicuous of the erection tenting his boxers, the snap of the buckle like a dead twig to a prowler. When he was free, able to bolt if he needed to, Gavin stole a look at the pallid thing in the passenger seat.

The girl shivered in her flimsy bra and panties, bruised and beaten, rivers of mascara and saliva pooled in her sharp jugular notch. Someone— *Couldn't have been me*—had tied thick nylon rope under her conical breasts and around her ankles, the flesh red and angry beneath, as if she'd been struggling.

"Who—?" Gavin tried to ask, but the tape player came on abruptly with the dash lights, blaring the three-part harmony of Mr. Big's "To Be With You." At the sudden noise, the girl snapped her head toward him. Her eyes, dark brown and moist, bore the look of a beaten puppy.

She's afraid. Afraid of me.

Gripped by a fear of his own, Gavin snapped on

the dome light.

The phantom girl vanished under its harsh white glow. The music stopped and the dash lights dimmed like the picture in an old TV set.

Shaken, Gavin staggered out, bare feet on cool concrete, wondering what the hell he'd just seen.

Was it a dream? Never had a lucid one before. Never sleepwalked before, either…

Crickets chirped in the night. Otherwise, Dayton Street was silent. As loud as the music had been, it hadn't woken the neighbors. Gavin let out a small sigh. He crept into the house through the kitchen, aware of every creak.

Katie rustled in her sleep when he returned to bed, but she didn't wake. Gavin was glad for it, despite the persistence of his erection. He wouldn't have been able to explain where he'd been if she was awake. He couldn't explain to himself what had happened, let alone his wife of seven years. The image of the abused girl—*whatever* that had been— had disturbed him terribly.

Despite his worries, Gavin eventually drifted back to sleep. When he awoke in the morning, he found it easy enough to convince himself what had happened in the night was just a very bad dream.

THE WOMAN BANGED on the glass while Katie was at the grocery store. Gavin looked up from spritzing aphids off the primroses to see her dark figure standing at the door.

He let her in. "Welcome to Deanie's Flowers. You must be Madison."

"Yes." Dressed in black from her cloche hat to her shoes, she sniffled as she slipped inside. "Thank you."

Madison Davis had called in an order for her husband's funeral two days prior. Katie had taken the order and later told him, "If you died, I wouldn't have the strength to make that call." Gavin directed Madison toward long-stemmed flowers, bunched tightly among white carnations into several slim glass vases and wicker baskets.

"They're lovely," the woman said, wiping her nose with a tissue.

"You can thank my wife for that."

"I will."

"You know, callas aren't true lilies. They're from the genus *zantedeschia*. They're mildly toxic."

"Why do they call them lilies?"

Gavin shrugged. "A rose by any other name…"

"Well, my husband always loved them," the grieving widow said, almost apologetically, shifting so their elbows met for a brief moment. Gavin stole a sideways glance at her round face. Her green eyes shimmered with tears, plump lips pouty, her thick, lined neck with the visible blue slash of her jugular. Her heavy breasts rose and fell under a cinched black trench coat ending at a knee-length wool skirt and black pantyhose. Beneath a light woody perfume Gavin smelled the mingled aroma of sweat and baby powder, and he involuntarily stiffened in his work jeans. He stepped away from her, blushing.

She turned her dewy eyes to him, so sad and broken—and suddenly Gavin wanted to swat everything off the work table and throw her down on the space he'd made, slamming the breath out of her in a terrified gasp, her fat tits popping the top buttons of her jacket. He wanted to jerk up her skirt and tear down her panties, thrust his face between her smooth white cheeks and savor the fragrant bouquet of her cunt.

Madison seemed to sense something wrong. She took a step away.

Gavin flustered. *Not now*, he told himself. *Please, not now.* "I'm sorry for your loss," he said, hoping to cover whatever his face had revealed.

She thanked him again with a wary look at his dirty hands.

"Let's ring these up, shall we?" He crossed the workshop. Madison hesitated only a moment before following. The cash register stood beside the doorway to the hall, the master bedroom mere feet away. Gavin knew he could snatch her by the throat and the belt of her jacket and push her inside easily. He could throw her down on his marital bed and dry fuck the bitch while her tears dampened the comforter and she cried out for her dead husband—

STOP IT!

His hand shook. His head swam with her sweat and perfume and his balls felt heavy. He caught her eye. Again, she looked down at his hand. "Sorry," he said, and forced a cough. "I think I'm coming down with something."

"It's been going around," she murmured.

"If you'd like, I could send you the bill?"

Madison nodded a little too emphatically, her red-rimmed eyes on the door now, longing for escape. "That would be nice."

"I'll just bring them to your car then."

Gavin juggled two tribute arrangements through the door. Madison carried the third herself, eager to get away. Under the carport the air was in motion, her scent not as potent, and the sudden terrible urge to violate her disappeared. She wasn't his type to begin with, and worse: her tears reminded him of the phantom girl from the van.

He threw a look toward the van now, its fresh white paint job shimmering in the cool autumn air.

I'll go for a drive, he thought. *Play some tunes. Calm the nerves.*

He stood the tributes up on the floor in the back of her Audi. Madison held the third out to him with an uneasy look. *She wants me to do it*, he thought. *So she won't have to turn her back on me.*

Gavin took the vase, eager to get her going and get behind the wheel himself. In his haste, his still-quivering fingers brushed hers. The widow snatched her hand away with such a look of fright he might have thought she'd caught a glimpse of his twisted fantasies.

"I'll get the last of them." He placed vase with the

others and hurried back to the workshop.

Madison Davis was already in the driver's seat when Gavin returned. She'd started the car while he crouched for the last of the bouquets, a flower basket and the casket spray. He found the widow staring through the windshield at the back of the van, a troubled look in her eyes. Gavin loaded the last arrangements. She didn't acknowledge his presence until he said, "All done."

Only then did she shoot a brief, thin smile over her shoulder, flinching when he shut the door.

"Drive safe," he told her. The back tires squealed as she pulled out of the driveway.

The tape player blasted INXS when Gavin started the engine.

THE FIRST TIME he drove to Almond Street, Gavin met the van's previous owner.

He'd taken a circuitous route through town, clearing away the stress of the day, listening to the tunes he loved in high school. When he emerged from under the dirty graffitied overpass, he found himself in a seedy neighborhood of potholes and brick-faced warehouses.

The street sign out front of a run-down convenience store said ALMOND in white letters on green. Gavin made the realization as if in a dream. He knew the area by reputation only: it was said a man could get almost any kind of woman he wanted here, even underage ones. He hadn't meant to drive here, had only been going by the feel of the road, subtle vibrations in the steering wheel causing him to twist the wheel this way and that. He wouldn't have driven to Almond Street if he'd been aware of his destination—if he'd entered it into the GPS on the dash. It had been entirely unconscious, almost as if the van had driven *him*.

Women in impossibly short skirts and heels of equally improbable length trolled the grimy sidewalk. Gavin pulled up to the curb, meaning to make a U-turn and go back home, but pair of hands with black lacquered nails grasped the window sill before he could pull away, and a young woman peered in, chopped black bangs framing a pale, eager face and junkie's eyes.

"Hey, hot stuff," the girl said, before squinting at him uncertainly. "You're not Tony."

Another woman sauntered over, dark nipples like saucers protruding from a white tube top, cut-off blue jeans so short the frayed edges hugged her crotch and a waistband swallowed by her stomach. "How 'bout a threesome?" this woman suggested.

"Fuck off, Indica," the first girl said over her shoulder, ushering her competition away with a flick of her wrist. Indica stayed put, while the junkie hooker looked over the interior of the van. "Tone let you borrow his baby?" She gave him a dubious look, absently flicking the piercing under her lower lip against her teeth.

Gavin's entire being screamed for him to leave.

00:180;00

He jerked the wheel and stepped on the gas, peeling the girl's fingernails off the passenger window with a clack as the van squealed away from the curb. He drove home with his thoughts thudding in his ears as loud as his heartbeat. *What was I doing there? What the fuck is happening to me? I love Kate. I don't want anyone else. I love my wife. It wasn't my fault. I love her. I didn't mean to do it!*

But you didn't do anything, a stranger's voice assured him—a strangely *familiar* voice. *All you did was satisfy a little innocent male curiosity.*

The man's voice had a pleasant, gravely timber that felt like cinnamon candy melting in Gavin's head. As the van went over another pothole, the fuzzy dice Katie had begged him to throw out rustled from the rearview mirror.

Nothin wrong exercising your rights, the voice told him. *Nothin wrong with bein a man.*

"Nothing wrong at all," Gavin agreed. The voice seemed to come from everywhere, from the porous vinyl seats to the cold hard plastic of the dash. From the fuzzy dice. From the musty air. It was *the van* speaking to him, Gavin realized—and all this time he'd been calling it a "she."

"Who the fuck is Tony?" he wondered, recalling the look of recognition and confusion from the dark-haired prostitute.

At this, the van remained silent.

The owner of the storage facility, an old man by the name of Grosvenor, hadn't mentioned a Tony, a

Tone, an Anthony or Antonio. The Ram had been gathering dust in a storage shed for six or seven years. When Grosvenor's brother Barrett died, the old man liquidated his assets, but the owner of that particular shed couldn't be found. "Old number, I guess," Grosvenor said. When Gavin asked if the owner would be upset, the old man answered, "Fuck 'im. I'm getting outta Dodge, no pun intended. Gonna buy me one of them mobile homes. Get while the gettin's good."

Get while the gettin's good, the voice agreed. *That's some excellent advice. There's a reason they call marriage an institution—it's a correctional institution. Marriage is a prison, and that brainy little wifey of yours is the warden.*

"You're wrong," Gavin said. "She *saved* me."

Saved you? The van chuckled derisively. *From what? Gettin too much pussy?*

Gavin flicked on the radio, trying to tune the voice out. He sang along with Tom Petty until the dial changed on its own.

Can't get rid of me that easy, compadre, the van said, speaking from the static between stations. *We're takin the long way home, and you an me are gonna pow-wow.*

Gavin flicked off the radio. Relief washed over him in the silence that followed. *Is this what it's like to lose your mind?* he wondered.

Laughter as sharp as razor blades answered the unspoken query.

You really are pathetic, you know that? Sorry excuse

for a human being, let alone a man.

Gavin tried to turn at right at the next intersection, back toward home, and the wheel jerked out of his hands with a peel of tires. He tried to unbuckle, but the latch was stuck. "Why don't you leave me alone?" he cried. The man in the car beside them threw Gavin a queer look.

You an me are gonna get somethin straight. I'm runnin the show now, got it? So just shut up, sit back, and let the smooth grooves of WTNY All Tony All the Time wash over you.

The van drove straight. Gavin did as he was told — *Gonna hurt me more than it hurts you*, he thought inexplicably — but he didn't have to listen. So while Tony talked, driving him past ugly warehouses and rundown tenements, Gavin listed all the flower genera he could recall in his head: *Astragalus, Bulbophylium, Begonia, Centaurea...*

"...GAV?"

KATIE STOOD at the top of the stairs, a towel around her midsection, the smaller one from the set perched atop her head. She called down the stairs again. "Gavin?"

No answer.

"Where is he?"

She'd popped in for a quick shower before bed, and had been in there a little longer than expected: having realized her legs were bristly, she'd taken the extra time to shave. She emerged, toweled and moisturized, hoping to find Gavin primed and ready on the duvet cover, but instead it seemed as though he wasn't in the house at all.

With her deadline quickly approaching, Katie played catchup, moonlighting in the flower shop while writing her novel by day—barely any time to breathe, let alone play. Tonight during dinner, eaten at the workshop counter, Gavin casually mentioned it had been two weeks since they'd spent any time together. Katie promised to rectify the injustice tonight, deadline be damned, but Gavin was nowhere to be found.

"That son of a bitch," she muttered, suddenly sure where to find him. Holding the towel to her breasts, she hurried downstairs. "*Son of a bitch,*" she said again, bare feet stomping down the hall. She heard the engine rumbling even before she got to the kitchen door.

"Gavin!" Katie stepped out, moving toward the van while Mr. Big rattled its windows. She pounded on the back window before approaching the driver door.

Gavin sat in the driver's seat, staring off into the dark backyard. Several weeks back, he'd started going for long drives at night to God knows where while she worked on her novel. Secretly, Katie feared he was going through a midlife crisis, that the van's nostalgia had regressed him. Secretly, she worried he was having an affair.

He turned at the sound of her knuckles on the

window, fixed on a proper loving smile, and rolled it down. The twangy ballad spilled out into the carport, four overgrown boys longing to date the cool chick in school.

"Hi, honey," Gavin shouted over the music, oblivious. He looked her over, eyes lingering on the valley between her breasts where the towel pushed them up.

"Could you turn that off, please?"

Gavin gave the tape deck a queer look, as if he'd been unaware it was on. "Sure thing, hon." He flicked off the music. "We were supposed to be doing something, weren't we?"

"You were supposed to be doing *me.* Instead, you're doing… whatever this is."

"Just letting off some steam. You know — unwinding."

"Well, I'm going to bed. Are you gonna come, or not?"

His grin was half snarl. "Oh, I'll come," he growled, stepping out. He shut the door gently behind himself and turned, standing so close the hot breath from his nostrils warmed her forehead. "I'm sorry, babe," he said, smiling down at her. "I know you're stressed about your deadline. How 'bout I make you a drink? Give you a nice back rub?"

He was already hard. It throbbed against her stomach as he drew her into his arms and kissed the crook of her neck. His tongue slid into the divot below her trachea, flicking up, down. Katie leaned in

to him, getting wet. She wanted to be full of him—
needed it.

The moment the door closed behind them, Gavin snatched off her towel. She yelped in surprise, rushing naked into the darkened hall, and he laughed as he chased her to the stairs. She laughed with him, couldn't help herself, bounding up two by two.

In the bedroom, Gavin whipped her around and pushed her down on the bed. Katie spread her legs, felt his fingers wedge into her, out and in, felt them pull out entirely and heard him suck them before the velvet head of his cock spread her wider. Delicious pain in a thousand nerve endings of her scalp made her cry out as he grabbed a handful of her hair, pushing deeper inside her. His hip bones smacked her ass, warm vibrations spreading up her spine.

His thrusts grew frantic. Suddenly he jerked her up from the bed, wheeling her around by her hair and hip to stand her against the wall, pressing her face and tits against its cool surface. She cried out, unsure if she meant it in pleasure or fear.

Gavin grasped her shoulder, mashing her further into the wall with each thrust until her tits throbbed and cheekbone ached. Then his fingers slipped around her throat—

"*No*," she breathed.

But his fingers closed around her throat, dirty nails squeezing the thin veneer of flesh. Katie felt the airway close to a pinhole. Gasping now, she reached behind herself, throwing a blind fist at him, striking his thigh, his hip, feeling weak and very small. Gavin humped and humped until his body grew rigid, every muscle flexing but his fingers, which relaxed, a tender mercy. Before she had a chance to catch her breath he fell against her with a mighty groan, pinning her to the wall, cock spasming as it spewed his hot seed inside her.

Gavin drew away from her then, staggering back. She heard the springs creak as he flopped onto the bed, and stood there panting, feeling the dull ache of at least one skin tear in her vagina, maybe more, as his cold sperm trickled down the inside of her thigh. Gavin had never been like that before. *Never.* Katie couldn't begin to comprehend such a vast shift in behavior, so she didn't try. She merely held herself and wept against the wall until the pain and fear and confusion subsided and all she had left was anger.

When she finally turned, Gavin lay draped across the bed, staring up at the ceiling, still hard after several minutes untouched. "Never do that again," she told him. He turned to her with a look of wide-eyed innocence. "*Do you hear me?*" she said more forcefully.

Gavin nodded stupidly, looking like a hurt little boy.

This is going to hurt me more than it'll hurt you, Katie thought. *Isn't that what Deanie used to tell him?*

"I'm going to wash of." She gave him a measured look. "Sleep in the guest room, sleep on the couch, you can sleep in that fucking van of yours, if you want. But I don't want to see you in bed when I get out. You crossed a line. I don't want to look at you again tonight."

Again he nodded, lower lip pooched like a petulant child, impossible to tell if the words had sunk in. Katie held his gaze for a moment, then strode out of the room, to hell with the pain between her legs.

"I'm sorry!" he called after her, but she didn't return.

IN THE WEEKS since his first visit to Almond Street, Gavin and Tony's "pow-wows," which mainly consisted of Tony speaking and Gavin listening, became more frequent. Picturing the man behind the voice, Gavin saw Tony as the type of guy who sits at the bar swallowing two fingers of Jack Daniels, dressed well but all in black, spouting off about all the shit straight white males are forced to endure at the hands of the demon Political Correctness—and despite Gavin's innate loathing of conservative pundits, it troubled him how much truth he began to see under all of Tony's bullshit.

Gavin sang "Urgent" along with Foreigner on the way to Almond Street, beating his palms against the steering wheel, glad for Tony's conspicuous absence on this particular drive. The cassette collection old man Grosvenor discovered in the cabinet had sold him on the van. Gavin owned some albums on vinyl and many more on CD, but his first love had been

Memorex. As a kid, he would stay up late with a flashlight waiting for his latest favorite to play on the radio, RECORD and PLAY and PAUSE already pressed, just sitting on the floor with his legs crossed and a finger hovering over PAUSE, waiting for the DJ to announce his song coming up in the next row of hits, or to hear those first few telltale notes. Gavin had gotten so good at instant recognition he'd won a radio contest, although he hadn't been allowed to collect the prize because he'd been twelve.

"Those were the days, man," he told himself, wearing a goofy smile. He peered at his reflection in the rearview, brushing his dark hair out of his face. Crow's feet from his cold blue eyes betrayed his age, as did the lines on his forehead. Even the sides of his hair were starting to gray. Soon he'd be too old to fuck without taking a pill, and too ugly to find a decent piece of strange even if he did. Soon he'd be shitting and pissing in adult diapers, sucking all his meals through a straw.

Ain't that a bitch, Tony said. *Best to live while the living's good.*

Getting old *was* a bitch.

Katie could be a bitch, too, Gavin thought. The way she'd acted when he fucked her last night, after she practically *begged* him to fuck her, it was

Uncalled-for, that's what it was, Tony told him. *Hysterical. Just like a fuckin woman.*

"Just like a woman," Gavin repeated, feeling Tony's influence like a thick finger probing in the steaming meat of his brain. "Maybe she was right about crossing the line, though. I mean, maybe I was a little too rough."

You just took what was yours, Tony assured him, the dead lights of the dash peering into Gavin's soul. *She's your wife. You wanna break off a piece, that's your right as a man.*

"My right as a man."

That's the undeniable truth.

"Undeniable," Gavin said, pulling up to the grimy curb at Almond Street. The woman named Indica clicked over on high cork-heeled sandals. A violet vinyl skirt hugged her thick thighs tonight, her lower stomach fold obliterating its waistline. Jade jewelry dangled from a raw hole in her navel. A flimsy piece of leopard-print fabric barely concealed her tits.

Gavin shut off the van.

"Back again, huh, sexy? You musta got your GPS set on speed-dial."

Having a smoke a few paces behind Indica, a young Asian in latex thigh-highs chuckled as she exhaled.

"Do you know a guy named Tony?" Gavin asked. The girl by the wall raised her penciled-in eyebrows and dragged eagerly on her smoke a few times, remaining quiet.

Don't go asking questions you don't want the answer to, Tony warned.

"That some kind of innuendo?" Indica smirked. "Like 'If You Seek Amy'?"

Gavin had no clue what she meant, and didn't care. "Where's the dark-haired girl? The one with the lip piercing."

I'm telling you, man, you don't wanna go asking about me or that girl.

"It's called a labret," the other woman said on a breath of smoke.

Indica sucked her teeth and looked off. "You mean Lola. She ain't workin tonight." She turned her thick eyelashes toward Gavin. "But I can help you forget alllll about that skinny-ass bitch."

"Thanks for the offer. I'm just looking for some information. Maybe your friend knows something?" he asked, indicating the smoker.

Indica threw a dismissive look over her shoulder. "Got a taste for the Orient, huh? All right. I can tell when I'm not wanted." Gavin relaxed when she stepped out of the window. She sashayed toward another vehicle and another john who'd pulled up behind the van, while the smoker held up the wall, giving Gavin a sidelong glare.

"You know who Tony is, don't you?" he asked.

"Everyone knows Tony." She took a quick drag and exhaled. "That's why the other girls are avoiding your van like it's got genital warts."

"Listen, would you mind...? I have money." He took out his wallet. "I just want to know who he is. I *need* to know."

You aren't gonna like what you hear, compadre.

"Put your wallet away." She came over, leaned

her elbows on the window. Squinting into the darkened van, she saw the back filled with soil bags and hand tools and littered with dark earth. "You sure you don't know Tony? You aren't friends with him or anything?"

"I bought this van from an old guy at a storage facility. I swear I don't know anyone named Tony."

The girl nodded, still wary. "What's with all the dirt?"

"I'm a florist," he told her.

"I guess I shouldn't be afraid of a big bad flower man," she said, faux pouty, and opened the door. Sitting in the passenger seat, she flashed him a somewhat shy look, then held out her small right hand. "My name's Kitty."

Gavin shook it. "I'm sure you understand if I don't tell you mine."

Kitty smiled. She pushed Eject on the tape player and a cassette popped out. "Tom Petty and the Heartbreakers? What is that? Country music?"

Gavin started the van.

Well, hello, Kitty, Tony piped up a moment later. *You know, you're prob'ly just gonna get horny again in half an hour. You get it?*

Gavin ignored him.

"There's an alley where I take guys sometimes," Kitty said as they pulled away from the curb. "A few blocks over. It'll be more private there."

"I just want to talk," Gavin assured her.

Talk about the first thing that pops up, Tony

quipped, and laughed uproariously.

"Sure. Talk. Fuck. Long as you've got cash, I'll walk on all fours and bark like a dog if you want."

"Now there's an idea." The words came out before Gavin could stop himself, Tony's thoughts from his mouth.

Atta boy! Guess you got a pair, after all!

Gavin flashed Kitty an apologetic look. She merely smiled.

I love a woman who knows her place, Tony mused.

"Pull over in here." Kitty pointed to the dark steaming mouth of an alley. Gavin pulled in cautiously, worried he might tear off the passenger side mirror in the narrow passage. Kitty rose to peer out her window. Her ass, a perfect heart caressed by black leather, was a distraction to driving. It was a distraction to *rational thought*, though rational thought had pretty much flown out the window the moment Gavin met Tony.

"You're good," she told him, and Gavin eased the van through.

Oh no, sister, Tony replied for him. *I'm* far *from good.*

"You know, you kinda look like Tony," Kitty said, scrutinizing Gavin's face in the dim light once he'd parked the van. "Cuter, though Tony had a goatee."

Probably means a Van Dyke, Gavin thought. *Not many guys have true goatees these days*. He'd had a Van Dyke himself, in his younger days, but Katie had convinced him to shave it off a few months before the wedding. The clean-shaven look suited his face better, anyhow. Made him feel like a different man.

"You knew Tony well, did you?"

"We fucked a couple of times. Cheap asshole, though. Always trying to gyp me. Said I should be used to it since 'my people' bargain all the time. I'm third-generation American, I don't know what the fuck he was talking about." She flipped her sleek black hair with a hand. "He likes dark-haired girls. That chick you were asking about, with the labret? I haven't seen her around for a while."

"How long?"

"Like a month or so."

"And how long since you've seen Tony?"

"Six, maybe seven years." She shrugged. "Tony's the type of guy when he doesn't come around, you count yourself lucky. Why you wanna know so much about him, anyways? He owe you money or something?"

"I'm just curious who was in the driver's seat before me." Gavin patted the vinyl between his legs. Kitty took it for a cue and eased over onto his lap before he could stop her.

"You smell better than Tony did, too. I swear he must have bathed in Aqua Vulva." Straddling him, she leaned in to Gavin's ear. The heat of her breath prickled his spine as she nibbled on the lobe. "I'll call you Daddy," she told him, raising up on her knees and rubbing her small, hard tits over his dry lips. "I'll be your Mommy, if you want that, too," she whispered, tugging on his belt buckle.

The idea repulsed him, all of it, but when he searched his heart for a reason not to let her keep going he found it empty. *Already crossed the line*, he reasoned. *Katie said so herself.*

He helped her with his pants. His cock sprang up, and Kitty took him into her mouth. Her small, slender fingers matched the rhythm of her lips, mashing his balls against his bunched jeans. Kitty expertly reclined the seat without removing her lips from him and followed him down, taking him deep into her throat.

Gavin stretched out his limbs, ecstasy swallowing the whole world. But the feeling they were being watched nagged at him, and eventually he had to open his eyes. Tied up and gagged, the eyes of the dead girl in the passenger seat locked on his. She turned her gaze to the back where more bloodied, beaten women sat and kneeled, straight slash wounds festering on their skin, worms and beetles skittering and squirming in the moist earth.

Each woman was stripped to her panties and tied up with nylon rope. Each one as dead as Gavin's stepmother.

It was when he saw Madison Davis among them, the grieving widow, that everything fell into place.

Thaaaaat's right, the voice in his head purred—so obviously his own voice he wondered how he hadn't noticed until now. *You been tuned into WTNY longer than you care to admit. Now don't touch that dial, compadre. We're gonna play all your favorite hits tonight!*

Gavin stared into the bound girl's sorrowful eyes while the cold hands of the dead roamed his body, showing an eagerness no woman had ever displayed, not even Katie, and while Kitty sucked, a smile crept onto his lips. He grabbed the whore by the hair, thrusting her head down until she gagged, her eyes widening as he unburdened himself into her willing mouth.

His orgasm racking through him, Gavin felt free. He felt *powerful*. He felt like himself again, and he knew exactly what he had to do.

He didn't need his alter ego to tell him his next stop was home.

EARLIER THAT NIGHT, Katie acknowledged Gavin's emergence from the workshop with a nod from behind her computer desk. Her book was speeding along at a good clip. Gavin ordered a pizza, giving her a wide berth since what she referred to as "the incident" the night before, and went upstairs to shower. He came back down smelling of fresh soap and the new cologne she'd bought him, and while the scent awakened her urges, she couldn't help but feel an undercurrent of disgust.

Katie ate her usual two slices in front of the screen with a desk lamp illuminating her corner of the open concept living room. Gavin polished off the rest watching the final season of *The Sopranos*, belching loudly when he was full.

"Could you turn it down a little?" She didn't want to be a bother but it was hard to concentrate with all the macho bullshit onscreen. Instead, Gavin turned the TV off entirely and got up from the couch.

"I'm going for a drive."

Katie watched him go. He'd never been as aggressive as he'd been last night, and she'd already decided to forgive him. She knew he didn't have the balls to try it again after what she'd said. They needed to put an end to the subtle hostility, to spend some time hashing it out—all night, if that was what it took—but her deadline loomed, and she returned to the incessant blink of the cursor. In her current state of mind, Katie found it difficult not to make her protagonist seem too put-upon.

That sort of behavior doesn't just happen out of the blue, she thought, the words on the screen blurring as she chewed the ragged left temple of her glasses. *He must have been thinking about it for a long time.*

She thought of how gentle he'd been before, almost timid, and had to admit that until last night she preferred the new Gavin's assertiveness, at least in the bedroom. She could do without the mood swings, the late night drives, the blaring music from that awful van, and the all-around acting like a sullen, spoiled teenager.

I guess that would make me his mother, Katie thought dourly.

"That's not even the least bit funny," she told herself, and slipped her glasses back on, wondering what her editors would think if her straight-laced detective protagonist suddenly and brutally murdered her husband halfway through the book.

The words wouldn't come. The truth nagged at her. *Did he* rape *me? Was it* rape?

She'd said the word "no," that much was clear. She'd told him *no* and still he'd choked her until he finished, using her like a fuck doll and leaving her to clean herself off. It didn't sit well.

I can't sit well, she thought, shifting painfully in her chair. *I'm all cut up inside.*

Thinking this brought a conversation with Gavin's stepmother to mind, in which Deanie revealed a long-kept secret, describing Gavin's adoption in a florist's metaphor. "He's a cutting, dear," Deanie had told her. "Snipped from his birth mother's garden, and transplanted into wonderful new soil. You have to be delicate with a cutting. They take patience, and nurturing. They're more fragile. They have to grow new roots, you see. They have to *hold the soil.*" With this Deanie had leaned in, her breath smelling of the cinnamon candy she favored, which Katie had sneaked in to the hospital room. "But a hard wood cutting must be totally *submerged.* That's why Julian and I never told Gavin what I've told you today. And why he must *never* know, my dear…"

Naturally Katie had told Gavin soon after Deanie passed, and he hadn't seemed at all surprised. It had seemed to her that he'd already known, though he never seemed to show any interest in looking up his birth parents. He'd loved his stepparents dearly, but it was clear from what little he'd told her that they had been strict. When his mother was still living, he recalled phrases like "Spare the rod, spoil the child," and "This is going to hurt me more than it'll hurt you." After her death, it was easier to remember the good times, the loving times.

Why did I think of that just now? she wondered.

Katie eyed the photo of the two of them at Machu Picchu, snapped at the summit overlooking the ruins. Gavin's smile, partially obscured by that silly goatee he'd finally shaved off before the engagement photos, reminded her of better days, happier days. He told her she had saved him on that trip. She hadn't understood, and he'd never explained. She supposed she should have asked, but she'd assumed he had meant it metaphorically.

How could he hide so much anger?

She remembered thinking he seemed like a different person the night she'd sat on the cold floor of the workshop, the night his appetite became ravenous.

He was acting strange well before that, Katie reminded herself. *Ever since he brought home that fucking van.*

Katie flicked the word processor aside on a whim, and brought up the web browser. She typed in "vehicle registration lookup," and clicked the first link. She entered everything she knew about the van: make, model, year, license plates. When it asked for her credit card information, she provided it.

She drummed her fingers on the desk, awaiting the results.

What it revealed drew the breath out of her.

Before Gavin, the van was registered to a Tony Gleeson—but the address provided was 223 Dayton Street—*this* house, *their* house. Before that, Tony Gleeson had been living at the Leslies' bungalow with Gavin and Deanie and Julian, who had died when Gavin was twelve. The registry listed no prior owners.

"Who the hell is Tony?" she wondered. It didn't take long to realize Tony was a fake name, that her husband had been hiding a lot more than just the anger he'd shown in the bedroom the night before. That at one point in his life before her, he'd slept in a dirty van and from the look of that old, stained mattress had done a lot worse.

Headlights swept across the living room. A moment later the van rumbled into the driveway. Katie closed the browser hastily and brought up her manuscript. Minutes passed while she chewed her glasses, waiting for Gavin to come in through the kitchen door.

She got up, tired of waiting.

Katie called out his name as she stepped out into the carport. The van idled there, thick exhaust eddying around it like mist the color of graphite. Someone sat in the passenger seat, and though she could tell it wasn't Gavin, in the dim evening light and the haze of exhaust she couldn't make out who it was—but from the small, slim figure, Katie thought it was a woman.

She crept toward the van. "Gav?"

Cold metal struck the back of her head. Blinding white pain shot across her vision. Katie cried out and fell forward, darkness overtaking her as she reached out blindly toward the van to catch herself before she hit the concrete floor.

THE BITCH WOKE with blood clotted in her hair.

His cuttings had whispered a warning in his ear, pawing at his chest, groping him, running their hands through his hair: the bitch wanted to take them away from him, and they wanted to be with him forever. There had been many flowers before but these were his only *cuttings*, snipped from the hard soil of prostitution and drug abuse and transplanted into Tony's Eternal Garden. They were his for all eternity, freed from the burden of lives filled with nothing but pain and misery. His birth mother had named him Tony and they were his cuttings.

This was his van.

This was his legacy.

A seventh flower had joined their Garden tonight: Kitty's cooling remains still graced the passenger seat, the wimp's sperm congealed in her esophagus. Tony had been obliged to strangle her himself because the wimp still had cold feet, and the bound girl—not one of his victims but his birth mother, the young prostitute Julian and Deanie Leslie had adopted him from shortly before her untimely death—had howled in agony, but Tony had made the wimp silence the filthy cooze with the back of his hand.

Soon his Garden would welcome an eighth—but first, the bitch had to bend to his will. She had to *tremble* in fear of his power like a flower before the hurricane.

Gavin was kneeling before her when Katie's eyes snapped open. He looked insane, a wild man stripped down to nothing but a pair of argyle socks, fingernail scratches marking his chest and stomach. He was erect, the head of his cock crusted with dead sperm. In his left hand he held a pair of gardening shears. A small, olive-skinned hand and wrist dangled from the passenger seat, ugly jewelry and painted nails, the first two torn at the quick. Katie saw this and struggled against the ropes binding her bare arms to her ribs, wondering what had happened to the man she loved, wondering where her clothes were, crying out with all of her breath as she tried to tongue away the gag from her mouth.

Tony made Gavin's free hand pop in the cassette. A dark smile came over him as Mr. Big muted the bitch's cries. *Great fucking tune,* Gavin thought in Tony's voice, because he was Tony and Tony was him: he was turned on and tuned in: *WTNY, All Tony All the Time.*

Katie watched Gavin grasp the large shears in

both hands, his wild, incredibly vacant blue eyes burning holes in her. "This is going to hurt me more than it'll hurt you," he promised, chuckling softly, because that was what Deanie used to tell him when she gave him the belt. Katie shook her head wildly, screaming through the gag, praying for the neighbors to investigate the loud music. But they wouldn't. They'd had plenty of opportunity to complain in the months before and said nothing.

Gavin opened the shears. Had the music not been so loud, she would have heard a squeal of rust. She cringed away as he moved toward her on his knees. His dirty hands quivered. He hesitated, and for a moment the burning hatred fell away and he fixed her with a look of pure sympathy.

The rusted blades located his target—and *snipped*.

The vile things plopped to the floor before the explosion reached Gavin's pain receptors. The shears fell from his hands and he reeled, staring down at the wet, oozing cavity he'd made at his groin.

His still-hard prick lay like a fat, wet slug in the loose soil. His testicles had oozed out of his scrotum, a pair of glistening pink orbs beside it. But Tony's cuttings were free—*Gavin* was free. The station had changed, and Tony Gleeson had left the airwaves for good.

Gavin looked up at Katie, and through her tears she saw him laugh, causing blood to spurt from the raw red and yellow meat where his genitals had been.

"Tony's gone now," he said, before his eyes rolled back in his head, and he collapsed against the back of the driver's seat.

When the song ended, Katie's screams filled the silence.

BUS DRIVER MAN:
A DARK PINES STORY

THE LITTLE SHIT was at it again and Mr. McAllister figured someone oughta teach him a lesson.

Not me, though, he thought, pulling the big yellow bus away from the curb out front of Josie Stafford's house. *Hell if I'm gonna do jail time just so some lunkhead kid gets his just desserts. The world don't favor heroes.*

No, Mr. McAllister would play it by the book like he always did. He always followed bus routes outlined by the School Board, except during roadwork, in which case he'd notify them of any delay longer than ten minutes. He always kept his vehicle clean enough to cook a steak off the rad, and free of hazards, going so far as to file down sharp screw heads on the seats where the shop mechanic had stripped them. Always kept his class B driver's license up to date, and bathed and flossed daily. This last didn't matter so much to the School Board, but Mr. McAllister knew what it was like to sit for half an hour or more in someone else's stench, and so he made sure his breath was minty and his farts smelled like roses.

Mr. McAllister glanced in the rearview mirror. Only a few cars on the dirt road behind him. One of them, the maroon wagon, belonged to Dora Strathcomb. She followed behind the bus, and her son on it, every day. Crazy as a soup sandwich, but she had a tight little bod Mr. McAllister had taken pleasure in checking out once or twice. God only knew why she didn't drive the kid herself. Probably wanted to be sure he integrated well with the other kids, since the government had stepped in to stop her from home-schooling when they figured out he tested at a second grade level, a twelve-year-old kid. Not that slinking around while the kids took the bus to school helped get him situated among his peers. Probably got him beaten up more often than it didn't.

Somebody oughta teach Jessie Kinsmen a lesson, but it sure wasn't going to be Dora's son. *Pipsqueak* is what they used to call kids like him, and that was when they were playing *nice*.

"Oh, that little diaper-stain cocksucker Jessie Kinsmen," Mr. McAllister would tell the boys down at The Tap. "That little smoldering lunch sack of dogshit Jessie." He'd swallow a mouthful of Labatt's and add, "Did I say 'little'? That 'little' shit's bigger'n me. His poor mother must be looser than a landslide havin crapped that thing out her babymaker."

The boys knew this diatribe well enough not to interrupt. They'd just chuckle to themselves and nod their heads, sipping on their own wobbly pops. But there'd always be some bystander, some Tap tourist, who'd want to chime in with something like, "Yeah, but he's the *Mayor's* kid. So whaddaya gonna do?"

What am I gonna do? *Good question, Mr. Knowitall. Mr. Nosey-Parker, prob'ly hyphenated with your wife's last name 'cause you're so goddamn progressive.* He couldn't let that little—that *big*—dicksmear Jessie Kinsmen get away with the things he'd done just because he was the son of the most prominent person in town. *Hell, I didn't even* vote *for Kinsmen. He can suck my dirty dick if he thinks he can tell* me *what to do.*

Jessie Kinsmen was six-foot tall if he was an inch, and built like a fortified shitter. His fists were the size of ham hocks, and probably felt like it when they struck any kid on the back of the head who dared to sit in front of him. The one satisfaction Mr. McAllister got was when Jessie's big ginger melon would hit the roof of the bus going over the bigger bumps on Shiner and Dewlapp, the worst roads on their route with macadam older than Mr. McAllister himself. He'd slow down a little just so the big yellow bus wouldn't glide smoothly over the potholes, and grin wide in the rearview, savoring the sight of that big ginger head getting a solid thwack on the aluminum, Jessie himself screwing his eyes up against the pain so the other kids wouldn't get the idea he wasn't invincible and maybe they could defeat the giant.

Mr. McAllister would chuckle satisfactorily to himself, seeing that. But it was hardly enough.

Now Jessie was ragging on Mrs. Plimpton, the bus chaperone. Sure, she smelled a bit like baby powder and cat pee, and she dressed like a nurse on night duty with all those loose, flowery tops and her dirty yellow plastic shoes, the kind with the holes in them like peek-a-boo playground equipment, but she'd outlived probably everyone she would have seen in the early days of television, even plenty of folks she grew up hearing on the radio. She'd been around for the invention of nylons, and for the beginning of the Second World War. And this little—this *big*—heap of rat dumps scattered amongst little bitty grainy pellets of warfarin, who hadn't even been living when the goddamn digital watch was invented, thought he could shit all over her?

Huh-uh. No way, pal. Not on my Timex timepiece.

Problem was, you couldn't get away with anything these days. Last time Mr. McAllister had scolded a boy for kicking the back of the Freely kid's seat, one of the others had been videotaping with their phone (old Mrs. Plimpton had been alive when barely anyone had telephones in their *homes*, let alone their *pockets*), and had conveniently only caught Mr. McAllister's reaction to the abuse. He'd been written up for it, the School Board telling him they understood discipline had to be meted out, but if they didn't make an example of his, Mr. McAllister's, behavior, the PTA would shit a Brampton Brick.

That had been just fine with Mr. McAllister. The boys down at The Tap had joked he'd had to eat a hot bowl of shit, but what the hell did they know, working the pit—a *union* job. Sad fact of life is everyone wants to feed you shit, and you're gonna have to smile and choke it down at least some of the time.

And some Tap tourist, some nosey parker, had chimed in, "Why don't you do what that fella in Cleveland done? Kidnap the big dumb sumabitch and tour him around a few hours. Scare the pants off'm."

Of course, this had been before the "fella in Cleveland" was discovered to have been a mental fuckwit who kidnapped those poor girls. For a while there, Mr. McAllister had sort of looked up to the guy, being brave enough to attempt something so daring. Not that the kid likely deserved it, when you considered new evidence. But if any kid *did* deserve to be driven around against his will, it was Jessie Kinsmen. Hell, Mr. McAllister might be *applauded*.

But the incident with the Cleveland fella, who'd offed himself in prison since, had happened in the days before bus chaperones like Mrs. Plimpton, who was just now doing an admirable job ignoring that diaper-stain—*Oh fuck me, did I already use that one?*—that *fucktard* Jessie Kinsmen.

Mr. McAllister pulled the bus up to the corner of Groonie Road and Van de Meer, where the Freely kid waited, backpack in hand. Janey Freely was one of the good ones, which probably meant she took holy hell at school. "Good morning, Mr. McAllister," she said cheerily, with a wide smile that showed all of her braces.

"Ain't it, Janey?" Mr. McAllister said. She smiled again, a shining million-dollar smile, and took a seat near the front while Mr. McAllister closed the door and pulled away from the curb.

Mr. McAllister had no delusions any of these kids respected him. Not like they were taking up a chorus of "Hail to the Bus Driver" back there. But most of them were friendly, and that was something. He'd heard horror stories from other drivers at the annual NTSA meetings, stories about fruit kicked deliberately under pedals, about wads of spit-covered paper shot at the back of their heads while they made sharp turns on a road with poor visibility, about curses and pulled hair and snot rubbed into their clothes. *Jeezus Please-us lemon-squeeze-us,* Mr. McAllister thought, *if the kids on this bus tried to pull any of that bullpucky on me, I'da gone ballistic for sure.*

"Mrs. Plump-ton!" Jessie Kinsmen said in singsong, emphasizing both *plump* and *ton* to be sure she knew it was a measurement of weight. Some of the others giggled at that, with an edge of fear to their laughter. "Missus Plummmmpton!"

Christ! He's grating on my last nerve. Lord, grant me strength...

"Why'nchta stop picking on her?" said a kid near the back of the bus, a voice so meek at first Mr. McAllister thought he'd imagined it. He glanced at the rearview, saw the Strathcomb pipsqueak sitting up with his slender fingers gripping the back of the seat in front of him, and Jessie Kinsmen wrenched his big freckled neck around to fix the small blond boy with a look of death.

Aw, kid, you gone and done it now, Mr. McAllister thought, though he had to admire the kid's courage, even if he'd signed his own death warrant. He'd keep an eye on the two of them on the way in to school, but after that he couldn't do much for the kid aside from pray the fat shit-stain didn't thump him too hard. The world didn't fare well for heroes these days. There were policies and shareholders to think about, parents who refused to parent their own children to appease. Every action micromanaged and disciplined and Twittered about and shamed on the internet so you couldn't squeeze out a fart without having to issue an official fuckin apology.

The children all scurried off the bus, favoring the Strathcomb kid with looks of sympathy, and eyeing Kinsmen like a wild dog as they passed. Finally it was just the four of them left on the bus, Mr. McAllister, Mrs. Plumpto—*Plimp*ton—and Jessie Kinsmen and the Strathcomb boy, who both refused to leave until the other went first.

"You boys are gonna miss first bell if you don't skedaddle," Mr. McAllister warned them, trying to be as diplomatic as possible so as not to incur the wrath of the School Board.

When Jessie scowled, his fat face wrinkled up just like a sharpie dog, and Mr. McAllister had to wonder what sort of upbringing would make a Cujo like him. Probably got a good beating or two himself, with any luck. Ken Kinsmen looked like the type of guy who would beat a kid stupid, with his barrel chest and his perpetually rosy cheeks and his military-style hairdo.

"This isn't over," Jessie told the smaller boy.

Mrs. Plimpton harrumphed, watching the two boys through her thick, tinted spectacles, her whiskered lower lip eating the bottom half of her face.

"Go on to class, Jessie," Mr. McAllister said, causing Jessie Kinsmen's frown to deepen. He hauled himself out of his seat, shot another look of death at the boy in the back, then shuffled up the aisle toward the front. "What about *him*?"

"He'll be comin along soon enough, don't you worry." *And don't make me put my foot in your ass on the way down those steps*, Mr. McAllister thought, grinning wide at the notion. Jessie Kinsmen gave the smile a queer look, then he slumped down the stairs, one by one, the bus rocking slightly with each deliberately heavy step.

"Thanks, Mr. McAllister," the Strathcomb boy said, shuffling up with a hangdog expression.

"Thanks nothin. You lookin to get yourself killed, kiddo?"

The boy's eyes bugged out as if the idea hadn't even occurred to him. He peered out Mrs. Plimpton's window at Jessie, who threw one last baleful look at the bus before trudging up the cement steps to school. "I just couldn't take it anymore, is all. Why's he gotta be such a dick? Sorry, Mrs. Plimpton."

"Don't you worry yourself," Mrs. Plimpton said. "It was brave of you to stand up for me. Brave, and terribly stupid."

And wouldn't you know it, here was the widow Strathcomb, knocking on the folding door with a look of deep concern.

"Better not tell your mother," Mr. McAllister warned him. "Got a feelin she'll go ballistic."

The boy's eyes bugged out again, cobalt blue like his dad's had been.

Mr. McAllister put on his most charming smile and opened the door. "Why hello there, Dora. Aren't you a sight for sore eyes."

Dora Strathcomb stepped onto the bus without an invite. "Where's my son? Why isn't he in school?" She saw him then, her concern softening. "Dennie, sweetie, are you okay? What's the matter?"

Dennie Strathcomb gulped. "Nothing, Mom. We was just talking."

"*Were* talking," his mother said, then glanced at the two adults to see if they'd caught the mistake. After the government had forced her son out of home-schooling, Dora Strathcomb was very particular about how the two of them spoke in public. "He hasn't been any trouble, I hope," she said to Mr. McAllister, with a look that required a single answer Mr. McAllister was happy to supply.

"Go on to class now, Dennie," Mr. McAllister told him. "And don't you take any wooden pickles."

Dora gave him a weary smile before ushering her

son off the bus.

Mr. McAllister and Mrs. Plimpton watched Dora walk her son to the doors. Even after they closed behind him the distraught mother seemed undecided whether or not her boy was safe, whether or not she'd done enough. She took a hesitant step up the stairs, then back down again. Another half-step and down. Finally she scurried off to her station wagon.

"She can't watch him forever," Mrs. Plimpton remarked unhappily.

No, she couldn't. And Mr. McAllister sure as shit wasn't going to step in.

THE BUS PULLED up to the Gunny Street stop on another gorgeous day, the morning sun baking the black vinyl seats. Aaron Lesley, a gangly looking kid with a bad case of acne and the dirtiest, holiest t-shirt you ever saw on a kid outside of a PSA about Third World children, shuffled onto the bus with his head down like usual.

"Where's the Strathcomb kid?" Mr. McAllister said. "Where's Dennie?"

The tall boy shrugged, continuing on to his regular seat near the middle, far enough away from the front where the goodie-goods sat, and not too close to the back where the hotshots ruled their domain with an iron fist. Mr. McAllister decided to wait at the stop a minute. A peek in the rearview confirmed his suspicion: Dora Stathcomb's maroon wagon wasn't around, either.

"Maybe he's sick," Laura Engval suggested. What was funny about this kid was how close her name was to the woman who wrote *Little House*, which Mr. McAllister use to watch as a kid, and her resemblance to the little pig-tailed girl was pretty uncanny, too.

Maybe he *was* sick. That would explain why neither mother nor son were at the bus stop. Mr. McAllister glanced in the rearview again and happened to catch Jessie Kinsmen staring back at him with a big grin spread across his freckled face. Little piss squirt didn't even try to hide it.

Mrs. Plimpton raised a wrinkled arm to show Mr. McAllister her watch—digital, he noted—and Mr. McAllister nodded. He looked again at Jessie in the rear view, but Jessie was peering out his own window, aiming his smile at the sun.

"All right, then," Mr. McAllister grunted. "Can't wait forever." He dropped the transmission into gear and pulled the door shut, then drove on to the next stop and the next, greeting the kids with a smile as he always did, glancing every so often at Jessie Kinsmen's big ginger head in the mirror. But the boy never returned his look, only beamed his contented smile out the window, like a Buddhist.

Troubled by that smile, Mr. McAllister hurried home after he'd dropped Mrs. Plimpton safely back to the retirement castle (she said nothing on the ride home, merely gummed the bottom of her face to death), and checked in briefly on his father while he was there (still a vegetable? check). He skipped his usual Rueben sandwich and crinkle-cut fries at the Rodeo Diner (which the owner, Sara Chutley, strangely pronounced *Roh-DAY-Oh*, like the street in Beverly Hills), climbed on his computer even before he had his boots kicked off, and looked up Strathcomb in the White Pages.

"Nothin," he said to himself, leaning back in the old desk chair with a fart of faux leather.

Well, what the hell was he going to do, anyway? Place a call to the kid's mother? Ask her if her boy was doing all right or if he'd run into any doors lately? Maybe the kid really had gotten sick. Or maybe—and this was more likely—maybe the kid was *playing* sick to stay home from school, worried that if he'd attended today he might have had to contend with Jessie Kinsmen after school let out. The kid probably figured if he could wait it out a day or so, the big red-headed dummy would forget all about five-foot-nothin Dennie Strathcomb and set his sights on some other runny-nosed brat.

"Ah, hell," Mr. McAllister said, getting up from the chair with another fart of leather. He threw on his jacket, stepped into his boots, and went out to the car. The phone book might not have their number, but he knew their *address*. He could check out the house, at the very least. See if the boy was anywhere in sight. If he felt adventurous, he might even go knock on the door. It would be nice to see Dora outside of the school bus, anyhow.

Why do you care so much about this squirt all of a

sudden? he asked himself as he climbed behind the wheel of the old Datsun. *Why him?*

He thought about it for a moment. "'Cause the world don't favor a hero, for one," he answered aloud—but there was more to it than that, he just wasn't sure what it was. Maybe it was that the little pipsqueak reminded him of himself when he was a boy. Maybe he just wanted to get into Dora Strathcomb's pants.

Mr. McAllister silenced these thoughts by doing what he did best: he threw the transmission into drive and Christ-alive *drove*. Traffic was light, and he didn't hit a red all the way to Dark Pines Estates. Dora Strathcomb's maroon wagon wasn't in her gravel drive. The attendant, whom Mr. McAllister had gone to school with forty years ago, and whose better days were about that far behind her, looked up from reading *Better Homes and Gardens* and regarded him with suspicion.

"What c'n I do for ya, Pip?" she said, referring to him by his grade school nickname, Pip as in *Philip*, not Pip*squeak*, though he had surely been that. The silly sweater and bucket hat she wore—*Didn't she wear that style of hat when we were kids?* Mr. McAllister wondered—made her look even older than their fifty(-ish) years, and from her expression she would have preferred him to do something for her, and get the hell out of her mobile court.

Out among the trailers, a grungy fella in tighty whites and construction boots tromped through the muck from one trailer to the next with his hound on a leash, sucking down a tallboy. *There goes trouble*, Mr. McAllister thought, recognizing the guy's face from The Tap. "Dora Strathcomb around?" he said to Rosie Ferguson, whose attention had wandered back to her magazine.

Her suspicion grew as she looked up again. *Musta been hopin I'da disappeared*, he thought. "Now what business would you have with her?"

"Well, Rosie, I'd have to say that's nunya. As in *nunya* business." With this, Mr. McAllister showed her his teeth. Rosie flinched, as if she'd seen gristle in between them, though Mr. McAllister knew they were just as minty fresh as always.

"Well," she said, adding, "*Pip*," with emphasis, "tough titty said the kitty but the milk's still good. We haven't seen her since yesterday." When Rosie said we she meant *we at Dark Pines Estates*, not we as in her and a suckling tabby cat. "Dora blew out of here in a tizzy to take that boy of hers over to the hospital."

"Hospital?" That giant hemorrhoid pain-in-the-ass Jessie. That fat lump of yesterday's trash.

"Uh-huh." Rosie didn't look too concerned about it. "Poor kid had an eye black as the ace of spades, jaw all swelled up like a punkin. Not that that's *any-ya* business," she added, riffing on his earlier joke, but he was too annoyed to laugh.

"Thanks, Rosie." He patted the counter. "You always were a peach."

She gave him the bird as he got back in his car.

He drove the hour to Peterborough right away, figuring they would have had to take Dennie to Peterpatch Regional, being the closest hospital to Dark Pines. The nurse at the station directed him to the right room, and there was Dennie, his jaw wired shut, beaten and bruised as all get-out, the right eye closed up to a blood orange slit. Dora sat beside him, holding his hand. When Mr. McAllister stepped in she began to rise from her seat.

"Mr. McAllister?"

He held up a hand. "Don't get up. I just dropped by 'cause I heard what happened to Dennie. Jesus, I'm sorry, Dora. Is he gonna be okay?"

"The doctor said he'll be fine." Her eyes met his with suspicion.

"Why are you sorry?"

"That's good," he said, ignoring the question. *Can't a guy do something decent without everyone wondering what he's sellin?* Mr. McAllister wondered.

"Why are you sorry, Mr. McAllister?"

For a moment he considered telling her the truth, but he thought against it. "I'm just real sorry it had to happen, that's all. Nobody deserves that, not least of all your boy. Dennie's a good kid. He's—" He'd almost given himself away, about to call the boy a hero for standing up against Jessie when the fat asshole was ragging on Mrs. Plump—*Plimp*ton.

Goddamn it, now I'm callin her that, Mr. McAllister thought, and smiled down at Dora Strathcomb.

"Thank you." She smiled herself, her eyes damp,

and turned to her son, squeezing his small hand in hers. "And thank you for coming, Mr. McAllister."

"Phil," he said. "You can call me Phil."

"Thank you, Phil."

Mr. McAllister stood a moment longer, looking at mother and son—his face like mashed potatoes with the skin on—and began to feel like he'd overstayed his welcome. "Well, I'm glad he'll be okay. Lookin forward to seeing the two of you back in my rearview, Dora."

She nodded. Mr. McAllister crept out into the hall, feeling deceptive, wishing he'd had the guts to tell her what had gone down the other day. But the world didn't favor a hero—Jessie Kinsmen had proved that true when he broke Dennie Strathcomb's jaw. There were more Jessie Kinsmens in the world than Dennies, as far as Mr. McAllister saw it, and that was the real shame of the world. And those who were neither a Jessie nor a Dennie, most times they'd turn a blind eye when the shit hit the fan, when the Jessies of the world spat their poison and hate on all the Dennies and Mrs. Plimptons. They'd look away or hurry past, they'd turn up the music on their headphones or absorb themselves in their cell phones, pretending they saw nothing, hoping the "nothing" would end before they felt even more like a coward for ignoring it.

The world didn't favor a hero, but it didn't mean Mr. McAllister had to turn a blind eye. He vowed, as he left Dora and Dennie Strathcomb behind, to stop playing it by the book just this once, whether the School Board liked it or not. He was through towing the line. If standing up for what was good and right cost him his job, so be it. *Something* had to be done, once and for all, about that lousy scum-sucking Jessie Kinsmen and all the other Jessies of the world, and this time, Mr. McAllister would have to be the one to do it.

The question, as some Tap tourist might have asked, was *how*?

He found the answer later that night. There was a time, a few years back, when Mayor Kinsmen had petitioned to get peanut butter removed from the schools. Mr. McAllister looked it up, and sure enough, there were several articles in the Dark Pines *Signpost* about what had been considered a scandal at the time. Parents had been up in arms. How dare he tell them how to raise their children? What were they supposed to give their kids for lunch? *Sushi*? Not everyone in town could afford fifteen-dollar a pound steak like the kind Mayor Kinsmen bought to feed his Dobermans. Not everyone ran a chain—not one but a *half dozen* throughout Peterborough and Haliburton counties—of successful used car lots like Mayor Kinsmen.

Kinsmen's soapboxing had won out, as everyone had expected it would, and both schools in Dark Pines adopted the new nut-free policy. Mr. McAllister had joked, down at The Tap, that the School Board already had a nut-free policy, kowtowing to the PTA whenever an issue came up they were too chickenshit to fight over. "That's nuts as in co-*ho*-nays, fellas," he'd added with a grin, and the boys had chuckled genially and guzzled their beers. They never did appreciate the comedic genius in their midst.

The point of all his research was that he remembered hearing Kinsmen had only started the campaign because his son, Jessie, was an anaphylactic. Big old bully Jessie Kinsmen was afraid of an itty bitty peanut. If he'd ever met Jimmy Carter and shook the man's hand, he'd have swollen up worse than Dennie Strathcomb's jaw and had himself a popleptic seizure.

He might even die, Mr. McAllister thought, and strangely the notion didn't bother him much at all. *You don't feel sorry for a rabid dog when he bites,* he told himself. *You just pull up your big-boy pants and put the damn thing down.*

Jessie Kinsmen was a rabid dog. He'd just bit his last kid.

MONDAY CAME AND the trap was set. He'd spent the entire weekend mulling over the finer points, but the gist of it was simple. He'd leave a peanut butter sandwich under the seat, half-eaten (this proved to be the hardest part of the job, since Mr. McAllister thought peanut butter tasted like salted shit), and the epinephrine injector the School Board had made mandatory on all buses—after serious lobbying from the PTA—would have disappeared. "Couldn't say," Mr. McAllister practiced saying in front of the mirror, watching for the tell-tale facial tics of a liar, "I s'pose it musta fell and got trampled off the bus when the kids rushed off to school. You know how kids are with trash, always wanna kick it 'stead of puttin it where it belongs."

When he was satisfied with his confused yet tormented expression, he raided the cabinets at the old house on Greenbury Street. He'd had to put his father in the convalescent home recently, after the old man had fallen down the stairs and couldn't stop shitting himself. His visits to casa del McAllister, the old homestead, were far less frequent these days, mainly to make sure the roof hadn't caved in and the lawn wasn't going to pot. Having power of attorney, he could have sold it if he'd wanted. He just couldn't bear to get rid of the house he'd grown up in, not with all the photographs of his mother on the walls, who'd passed on when he was still quite young.

The peanut butter was in the cabinet. He opened the jar, sniffed it, and gagged. It was oily and smelled worse than normal—chemically. He'd bought a loaf of white at the Hometown Proud, aware there was a crusted jar of blueberry jam in the fridgerator he could use. He'd only have to take a few bites.

So he poured himself a tall, cold glass of milk, and he slathered the bread with salted shit and jam. Looking down at the sandwich, cut in half on a diagonal and laid out nice on a plate beside the milk, brought back memories of his mother. His dad had never been the same after she passed. Never cracked a smile or joked with him anymore. Never taught him how to ride a bike. Never spent a night without a six-pack in front of the boob tube. The shell of a man Mr. McAllister visited twice weekly, who pissed and shat in his semi-electric bed at the Castle, was just showing on the outside how he'd felt on the inside since Florence McAllister passed through the Pearly Gates in the summer of 1969.

He bit into the sickly sweet, gooey sandwich and chewed until it was doughy and gritty and swallowed it down before he could puke it with a big gulp of milk. Then he did it again, just so it would look authentic. He didn't even have to swallow, but it felt like eating a few bites of shit sandwich would be a minor penance for the crime he was about to commit. Even if the kid just got a small allergic reaction, it could still be considered assault in the court of public opinion. These days, that was just about the only court that mattered.

What happened, as far as he could figure, was that the mechanic who worked on the buses on weekends, idiot that he was, had been tightening the bolts under Jessie Kinsmen's seat while eating a PB&J. The sammie fell out of his hand, and forgot about the 5-second rule. He must have bumped his head or something, because he left it laying on the floor to rot instead of throwing it in the trash.

If the kid really was as allergic as they said and

not just faking it for attention, all the Dennie Strathcombs of the world might breathe a little easier knowing Jessie Kinsmen had a kryptonite.

He tried to hide his smile pulling up the curb in front of the Kinsmen house. The kid had the stop all to himself, that's how you could tell he was King Shit among all the little floaters. Other kids who lived closer to the Kinsmen stop walked several blocks out of their way to get on before or after Jessie, and Mr. McAllister couldn't blame them. What kid in their right mind would want to stand around without supervision in the company of a rabid dog?

"Jessie," Mr. McAllister said, biting his cheeks so he wouldn't grin, as the boy's weight depressed the right front shocks.

The kid wore a smile of his own, probably feeling pretty fine about the job he'd done to the Strathcomb boy, not seeing Dora's car idling behind the bus, nor the kid himself in his regular seat. The downcast eyes as Jessie passed made Mr. McAllister feel pretty good himself about the job he was about to do on Jessie Kinsmen's immune system.

But Jessie walked right past his seat, where he'd sat day after day for as long as Mr. McAllister could remember, right past his kryptonite, right past any chance Mr. McAllister had of getting even on the fat squirt.

Sweet fancy molasses! Where the shit is he going?

Jessie tromped on to the empty seat near the back, where Dennie Strathcomb would sit if it wasn't already occupied by one of the cool kids. The boy wedged himself into the seat and turned to face the front. He beamed his smile at Mr. McAllister, the proud smile of a boy who'd won a trophy, if only in his own mind.

Fuckity-fuck!

Mr. McAllister angrily threw the tranny into gear and pulled off from the curb, the whole plan foiled.

The whole plan! What now what NOW...

For a split second he considered slamming his foot on the accelerator, taking the corners at high speed in the desperate hope the sandwich in its plastic baggie would skitter across the dirty floor and somehow come to rest near Jessie's feet, a fucking *impossibility*, not fucking likely at all, Pip old chum, old chap, and even if it *was* possible he'd take hell from that, the PB&J wouldn't be the only shit sandwich he'd have to eat, and this time the School Board might just suspend him, or worse. He'd end up working the limestone pit with the boys from The Tap, choking up rock dust while sucking down their wobbly pops.

"Fuck that," Mr. McAllister said to himself. He looked in the rearview to see if anyone had caught it, but the only one looking at him was Jessie, his green eyes wide like he was gawping at a carnival freak.

Mr. McAllister squeezed the wheel and focused on his driving. It was all he could do to keep from pulling over to the side of the gravel road, stepping off the bus and just keep on walking all the way back to town, to The Tap, which hadn't even yet opened for breakfast, let alone for boozing. He'd sunk all of his hopes into this Hail Mary pass, a desperate clutch at his last scraps of humanity, and nobody was in the end zone to catch the damn ball.

Feeling more depressed than he'd ever felt in his life, except for those first few months after his mother passed, Mr. McAllister pulled the bus up to the corner of Groonie Road and Van de Meer, where Janey Freely stood, backpack in hand. "Good morning, Mr. McAllister," she said cheerily, as she always did, her braces glimmering in the sun.

"Ain't it, Janey?" Mr. McAllister managed to spit out. She smiled again, though she stopped suddenly as she turned toward her seat near the front, and her backpack slipped from her hand to the floor with a jangle of pencils and three-ring binders.

"What's the—?" Mr. McAllister turned as he spoke and caught sight of Jessie Kinsmen, his fat neck and round face much redder than normal, just about as red as a beet.

"…Mr. McAllister?" Janey said.

Jessie was choking, and not just on a sip of water that went down the wrong tube—Jessie Kinsmen choking *to death*.

"Cripes," Mr. McAllister gasped, looking around himself desperately. Mrs. Plimpton shifted in her seat to look back. She removed her glasses and held them out from her face like binoculars to get a good look.

"Somethin's wrong with Jessie," Barclay Robbins

shouted.

"He's not breathing," said a girl whose voice Mr. McAllister didn't recognize.

Everyone stood up in their seats, but nobody moved. No one made to help. They were frozen, transfixed, as Jessie's pink hands came up to claw at his throat.

"Christ Jesus," Mrs. Plimpton muttered, blinking hard with her beady chipmunk eyes. She turned to Mr. McAllister. "What do we do?"

"The EpiPen," Janey said, both she and Mr. McAllister turning to it at once. But it was gone, of course. He'd made sure of that this morning. The hope visibly drained from Janey's face.

Mr. McAllister hurried back to where Jessie sat, clawing at his own throat, eyes bugged out of his fat head. All the kids gawped. *What are they thinking?* Mr. McAllister had a moment to wonder. "Jessie," he said. Jessie stared straight ahead, his fingers clawing at his WWE t-shirt like they belonged to someone else. Mr. McAllister took hold of the boy's shoulder. "Jessie, look at me."

The boy's eyes rolled in the direction of Mr. McAllister's voice. "Jessie, have you got an inhaler? An EpiPen?"

Jessie shook his head more vehemently than it had already been shaking. Tears broke free from his eyes and streamed down his freckled cheeks. Pink froth began accruing in the creases between his lips. Pink froth. It brought back images of Mr. McAllister's father, dying slowly in a hospital bed. They'd asked him about pulling the plug last week. There wasn't much they could do for him, they'd said. He likely wasn't conscious at all, they'd assured him.

He said he'd think about it.

More pink froth spilled from Jessie's mouth, dripping down his chin and gathering on the collar of his shirt.

Think about it, Mr. McAllister told himself. Had he really *thought* about what would happen before he'd started this, or had he been moving on autopilot, as unconscious of what he was doing as his driving had always been? Did he even consider the fact that this was *murder*?

Mr. McAllister threw a look over his shoulder at Mrs. Plimpton, whose bug eyes looked even more insect-like with her glasses held out from her face. He caught the eye of Barclay Robbins, a handsome kid, like his father. The boy seemed to shake his head. Tanner Jones seemed to do the same. Even Janey, hugging herself at the front of the bus, seemed unsure.

They don't want *me to save him*, Mr. McAllister realized then, to his growing horror. *They've seen their chance. They'd let him die here, gladly, and that's on me. They'd smile and wave bye-bye but Christ-alive they'd regret it once he's gone. Can't put that on them. They're just mixed-up kids, they don't know what they want.*

"Fuck," he said, and nobody seemed to care. They just kept staring at him, at Jessie—who was just a boy, after all, not a rabid dog, not a monster—and praying for it to be over soon.

Mr. McAllister dropped to his knees before the dying boy. He peeked under the seat, pretending to look for the missing EpiPen. There was the sandwich, right where he'd left it. It hadn't moved an inch and still Jesse spazzed-out.

Guess he really is allergic, after all, Mr. McAllister mused as he surreptitiously slipped the EpiPen out of his pocket. "Found it," he shouted, popping up from the floor with the epinephrine in hand. He bit the top off and, hesitating for only a moment, jammed the needle into Jessie's leg.

Jessie began to cough immediately, his hands falling limp to his sides. His freckly pallor returned as he coughed and coughed. When he had the breath to speak, he said, "That hurt, you dick."

Then he allowed the ghost of a grateful smile to creep onto his lips.

Mr. McAllister patted the boy's back as a smattering of applause began in the back of the bus, Barclay Robbins furiously clapping, the others following suit, adding, "Way to go, Mr. McAllister," and "You da man," and slapping him genially on the shoulder as he made his way to the front of the bus.

"Atta boy!" Mrs. Plimpton said, her smile eating the bottom of her face.

Janey picked up her backpack, and looked up at him as he approached the front of the bus. "Where was it?"

"What's that, Janey?"

"Where was the EpiPen?"

The suspicion in her eyes made him flinch. "Well, Janey, I s'pose it musta fell and got trampled to the back of the bus when you kids rushed off to school."

"It was on the floor then?"

Mr. McAllister laughed. "Where else would it have been, Janey?"

She squinted past him, where Jessie was getting his own shoulder claps and praise, the boy smiling like a kid who'd won a trophy, as if he finally fit in. Janey's eyes softened, and she favored her bus driver with a brace-faced smile. She said nothing to him, only nodded, as if she understood exactly what had happened here, and she approved of the outcome, whatever he'd been planning.

Well, the world don't favor heroes, Mr. McAllister thought, driving the kids toward school just like he'd always done, *but liars seem to do okay.*

IN THE SHADOW
OF THE MASTERS

Be cursed, plunderers and imitators
of the work and talent of others.
- Albrecht Dürer

YANNICK TREMAINE HAD never seen a painting he couldn't copy, and Abrecht Dürer's *Self-Portrait* was no exception. Still, the forgery had troubled him since he'd begun it, and he often half-jokingly mused that the so-called Forger's Curse might be responsible, not that he believed in such things.

Tremaine's Kraków studio was quite large, with a spectacular view of the old synagogues and the flat, cool waters of the Vistula River, beyond which the Jewish Ghetto once stood. The apartment itself lay above a Turkish-run fabric store in a crumbling relic built long before the Great War, like most of the buildings surrounding it. With his considerable wealth, he'd converted his suite to suit his needs. Here, he painted Vermeers and Caravaggios and Monets—sometimes from memory, sometimes from books, often from stolen originals his benefactor kept hidden in temperature-controlled basement vaults, large humidors, and abandoned salt mines, like Göring had before him.

The day Mr. Ziminski came to check on his investment a final time, Tremaine snapped out of a trance at the sound of the doorbell, feeling like he'd run a marathon. Sweating, his mouth dry, eyes red from not blinking, from staring transfixed into Albrecht Dürer's haunting golden eyes, he blinked the haze from his own eyes and plopped the brush he'd been using into a Dripol fruit cocktail can he kept half-filled with linseed oil. Once again, he found it difficult to draw himself away from the long-dead painter's gaze. It troubled Tremaine how few people outside of the art community seem to know Dürer's *Self-Portrait*, also called *Self-Portrait at Twenty-Eight Years Old Wearing a Coat with Fur Collar*. Like many painters, he considered the piece worthy of the *Mona Lisa*'s fame. The stark interplay of light and dark, with a black void behind him, as if Dürer had deliberately painted himself adrift in time and space. A metaphor? Tremaine would leave it for the scholars to decide. Dürer's hand, slightly raised to handle the fur of his collar, thought to mirror portraits of Christ. But it was the eyes that held him in their sway always the eyes. He lit a cigarette from a pack of Sobieski Premiums with a quivering hand, and took a long drag, consciously avoiding eye contact with the painting.

The nicotine calmed him enough to chuckle at his foolishness. *Does anyone believe in curses anymore?* he wondered as he crossed his flat to the door.

Through the peephole he was greeted by the mashed nose of his benefactor's beefy Russian bodyguard. He muttered "*Fuck*" under his breath—quiet enough, he thought, but the ex-Spetsnaz raised his eyebrows and peered back into the dim hall.

"He hear hims," Vladimir said to his employer, lurking somewhere in the shadows beyond Tremaine's sight.

"I'm coming!" Tremaine called over his own shoulder, attempting to throw his voice. He unlocked the latch and chain barring the behemoth from entry, and Vladimir—Ziminski's very muscular, very ex-Russian paramilitary bodyguard—barged in. He eyeballed the large room with a hand held over the Desert Eagle Mark 1 carried in a leather sling holster over his black turtleneck, as if expecting a Navy Seal team crouched behind the kitchen counter, ready to get the drop on him.

"Is clear," he said to the open door.

Ziminski buzzed in then, his motorized wheelchair tracking dirt all over Tremaine's new floors, like the tracks of Nazi Panzers through the streets of Kraków. And like the city officials of the time, there wasn't much Tremaine could do but accept it.

Parked in the living room, his employer looked up with cold blue eyes, a colorful shawl holding in what little warmth his elderly body still created. "Well, Tremaine? Aren't you going to offer us a drink?" he asked, his accent faint—Americanized.

"Where are my manners?"

He would have offered Ziminski a can of turpentine if he hadn't switched to linseed oil to keep his brushes clean. Just looking at the old man's pale, yellowed-parchment skin always made his own flesh crawl… but Ziminski's money had paid for the flat and all its renovations. It kept the pimps from pounding down his door. And it was Ziminski's money that allowed Tremaine to paint for a living, which was all he'd ever wanted to do for as long as he could remember.

Reminding himself of this, he poured the evil man an American whiskey, and cracked a Tyskie for the Russian. Vladimir blew foam off the top of the can before taking a healthy swig.

"So what brings you here, Mr. Ziminski?"

"I've come to see my Dossi," Ziminski said, speaking of the reproduction Tremaine had been working on concurrent to the Dürer: Dosso Dossi's *Triumph of Bacchus*. "Coming along nicely, I hope?"

"It's getting there."

In truth, he hadn't been able to focus on it since he'd started the *Self-Portrait*. He'd been having trouble getting Dossi's depiction of the god Bacchus right, and he realized why just then: the nude minions hoisting him up in that throne, carrying him toward the endless after-party, reminded him too much of Vladimir lugging Ziminski and his wheelchair up the apartment stairs. He'd been subconsciously painting the youthful god as a decrepit old ghoul in effigy of his benefactor.

"Let's take a look, shall we?" Without waiting for his say-so, Ziminski zipped past him, over the fucking Berber shag—*mercifully* without dirtying it— and into the daylight bright studio.

"*Mój Boże…*" Ziminski breathed before Tremaine had even caught up, and he understood instantly the old man was looking at the Dürer and not the Dossi. He'd been so astounded by its likeness, he reverted to his mother tongue to say, *My God.*

When Tremaine laid a hand on the old man's bony shoulder, the bald, scabrous head jerked upward. The look of shame in his eyes—at least Tremaine *thought* it was shame—almost made him feel sorry for the old man. Ziminski brought his shawl up to his lips with a quivering hand and wiped away a runner of drool. Ice cubes tinkled in the glass in his other claw.

"Here's the Dossi," Tremaine said, directing his attention to the other painting.

"Lovely, lovely," Ziminski remarked dismissively. Then he clucked his tongue in disapproval, as something caught his eye—the Dürer forgotten now his critic's hat was on. "The breast is wrong. Too full. You've been sleeping with too many whores, Tremaine. Forgotten what a real tit looks like, hey?"

"It's still a work in progress," Tremaine said, barely hiding his annoyance. Worse than the insult, Ziminski had been able to see with his deteriorating eyesight what Tremaine himself couldn't, being too close to the work. The breast in Dossi's original was plump but not full, the nipple pointing downward. The breast Tremaine had painted could have belonged to an American stripper, a hard-rock thing with its nipple aimed toward the heavens.

Tremaine had always been a skilled technical painter. His teachers, back in art school, had said this of his work all the time. What he *lacked*, they had told him, was that creative spark the da Vincis and Picassos of the world seemed born with. A good painting drew you toward it, you could *feel* its meaning like an ache in your chest. You could *hear* it, whispering its untold secrets in your ear. An exceptional piece of art could move you to tears with its tale—it *lived*. A masterpiece, like Dürer's woefully underrated efforts, could make the work and its artist *immortal*.

Tremaine's own paintings had always been derivative of someone else's, even artists he'd never before seen, let alone glimpsed their body of work— this according to men and women whose own landscapes and portraits and bowls of fruit were so middle of the road they'd had to resort to teaching middle-class suburban children the Golden Ratio and color theory just to make a living. And how he could copy something he hadn't known existed had always eluded Tremaine, up until the day he'd taken their criticism to heart and decided to try his hand at forgery.

Eventually he became grateful for their criticism. Aside from having to paint at the literal barrel of a gun, he'd lived a decent life, and the thing he'd come to learn in his late-twenties that he hadn't been able to accept during school was that his teachers had been *right*. He'd never had that spark. Never would. His mind was a blank canvas, never to be filled with an image of his own design. Tremaine and his work would forever be left standing in the shadow of the Masters.

Ziminski had seen that in him. When Tremaine was still trying to make a name for himself, pimping his derivative art in as many galleries as would allow him, the old man saw a hunger in Tremaine's work, in *him*, that spoke of someone with big dreams—if only he hadn't lacked the "spark." And so Tremaine had appealed to Ziminski's vanity, as an artist must do with a potential patron. He professed admiration of the old man's appreciation and indisputable knowledge of art.

The first time he met Miłogost Ziminski, the old man had been standing with a group of glitterati, entertaining them with his critiques. This was before the wheelchair. Ziminski had once had dreams of his own to be a painter, in his youth. Even with the wealth he'd amassed since, he knew he couldn't sell a single watercolor, not without critics accusing him of using his money to buy acclaim. His skill had been middling at best long before the accident that had made his hands clumsy with a brush.

Ziminski liked to keep desirable things for himself, particularly, but not limited to, artwork. Back when he'd been married, Ziminski would only trot his wife Magda out during big gala occasions. This buxom blonde thing—and he'd criticized Tremaine's taste for whores—who wore furs and glittery dresses and offered her hand for strangers to kiss like she was royalty, Ziminski would parade her around at all the big parties, but when the event was over she'd vanish. He'd tuck her away in a closet somewhere in his hundred-room mansion. He'd lock her back up in her gilded cage.

Always wanting things he couldn't have, Tremaine had taken her in one of Ziminski's toilets during one of Ziminski's events. He'd fucked her again in the old man's vault, and had wondered more than a few times what had happened to her since the last time he'd seen her. He didn't have the nerve to ask the old man, knowing how easy it would have been to erase her from his life. Everyone would simply have assumed she'd left him for a younger man, gone to live on the French Riviera on the old man's dime.

Ziminski stroked his wispy Fu Manchu beard, admiring the texture of the Dürer. "Look at the *craquelure*," he marveled. "So much like the real thing."

Tremaine agreed the aging process was coming along nicely, despite having done most of it in a trance, applying layers of umber and water he'd snuffed cigarette butts out in to simulate centuries of wear.

Ziminski reached out to touch it with one shriveled, liver-spotted claw, causing Tremaine to shout "*Don't!*" The old man peered back with sullen ferocity, like a bad kid who'd had his hand slapped away from the cookie jar, and wetted his lips with his cankered tongue.

"It's still drying," Tremaine explained hastily, catching a darker disapproving glare from Vladimir, who cracked his knuckles in response. Cold sweat dripped from his armpits as he awaited Ziminski's reaction, imagining his ribs would make a similar sound caught in one of Vladimir's big Russian bear hugs.

The old man nodded at his monstrous companion. "Stand down, Igor," he said, blithely mocking a man who could crush him like a Soviet brand cigarette underfoot. "The man values his art more than his life. If that's not a quality worth admiring, I don't know what is."

Vladimir merely sipped his beer, eyeballing the artist over the rim.

"It will be ready in a week, I presume?"

"The Dürer? I thought the deadline was two?"

"The *dead*line—" Ziminski seemed to savor the word. "—is whenever I say it is. I've lined up another job for our technician in Munich a month from now. She'll need time to prepare."

"*I* need time, Mr. Ziminski."

"*Tosh*," the old man scoffed. "Fix the breast on the Dossi and keep up with that *craquelure*. Honestly, Tremaine, you're such a perfectionist. It doesn't have to fool them very long."

IN TREMAINE'S DREAM Dürer stepped out of the painting, his gaze unwavering, as undying as the colors in which he'd painted himself, his golden eyes focused on Tremaine through the darkened bedroom doorway. The man from the painting crept across the studio floor in the moonlight, bare feet padding over Tremaine's Berber shag, and entered the room.

Standing over the bed while Tremaine slept, fingering the fur of his collar, eyes glimmering in the gloomy abyss of night, Tremaine couldn't get a clear look at him in the darkness of his dream, but he was able to see Dürer whispering—staring at him and whispering. Cursing him in German. The Forger's Curse. Tremaine tried to wake up, to defend himself, to defend his work, but he couldn't move. Eventually, he woke up screaming: "I have to! It's all I can do!" Sweating, heart beating hard, he looked around, the sun already high above the Vistula, shimmering on its glassy surface.

Catching his breath, he padded out barefoot to the studio, following the path of Dürer's ghost, and found the dead painter still where he should be, still in the painting, those golden eyes challenging Tremaine to continue his day's work.

Fraud, they said. *Forger.*

Tremaine threw a drop cloth over the painter's head, and went to work on the Dossi. *Forger.* He could feel the young Master's stare through the fabric, couldn't fool himself into believing the eyes had closed, that they'd turned away. *Fraud.* Judging him. Watching him paint.

Tremaine dropped his brush in the Dripol can, threw on a jacket, and hurried out of the flat. He walked for miles, trying to clear his head. He ate brunch in the Rynek. Downed shots at a vodka bar in Old Town. When he returned, he was sufficiently drunk to finish the Dossi untroubled by thoughts of Dürer's judgment. The curse made him laugh aloud, and he eyed the pale drop cloth with reproach.

Returning to his Dossi, a little yelp escaped him, and he backed into the table, spilling his liquor and the contents of the Dripol can all over the floor. *Somehow* he'd painted the eyes of Bacchus to look like Dürer's. Tremaine got down on his knees to wipe up the spill, grabbing a cloth and patting the stain down, worried it would spread to his Berber shag rug. Finally satisfied he'd soaked it all up, he stood and turned to fix the Dossi—

His heart leapt. "*Where is it?*" The drop cloth was gone and Dürer stared into his soul. Tremaine scoured the studio, cursing himself, cursing the painting. Finally, he stopped moving around in angry endless circles, and found he'd used it to mop up the spill.

"Idiot!" He smacked himself on the forehead, hard enough to cause stars in front of his eyes. "Fucking *idiot!*"

Tremaine turned to the painting, his *curse*, throwing all of his anger and frustration toward it. Dürer returned the glare with a frozen smirk.

Burn it, he thought. *Burn it and be done with it.*

"And then what? Ziminski would have me killed."

Flee the country. Go back home.

"*Home…*" he said mockingly. "There's nothing for me there."

At least you'd be alive. Put the drop cloth back, and push it a scooch closer to the ashtray… you could say it was an accident. Left a cigarette burning.

"He'd never believe me."

It would buy you some time…

Tremaine gave Dürer a baleful look. The Master said nothing.

A perfect forgery. His *best*.

An idea occurred.

"I'm not going to burn you," he cooed, approaching the painting. He picked up his brush, dipped it into a brownish yellow blot of paint on his palette. It was the only way, his drunken mind told him. The only way to break the curse.

A counter-spell. An *incantation*.

By the time he'd blended the words into Dürer's

fur collar to be almost indistinguishable, it began to seem a little less crazy.

"YOU KNOW WHAT Dürer said about forgers, don't you?" the thief asked as they approached Wawel Castle from Kazimierz. In the distance Tremaine heard the *hejnał mariacki*, the historical call of a lone bugler atop St. Mary's Cathedral. The trumpeting stopped abruptly, as it always did, the same note left hanging in the cool night air as legend said it had during the Mongol invasion, when the bugler signaling the horde's approach had been shot in the throat by an arrow.

Tremaine wondered how the trumpeter must have felt, his life's work ended with a sudden realization his throat no longer held the breath to produce sound. He'd always believed his own need to create would only ever end with his death. Break his hands, and he would have found a way to paint without them, like Christy Brown, the painter born with cerebral palsy. Hell, he would have painted with his *cock* if it came down to it.

"Huh?" Tremaine said, only now realizing the woman he'd been walking with in silence for the last twenty minutes had finally spoken.

"Don't you ever worry about the Forger's Curse?" she asked him.

Tremaine sputtered. "Silly superstition."

The thief shrugged and carried on down the cobblestone street.

00:244;00

Wawel Castle, built for Casimir II the Great in the early-1300s, was even more beautiful at dusk, and Ziminski's "technician" stopped in the sidewalk on Dragon Street, gawking up at its lighted walls and turrets. Tourists milled below, snapping blurry evening photos and selfies. One of the largest museums in Kraków, Wawel housed an art gallery in rooms where 700 years of royalty ruled and prayed and fucked and shat, and its armories presented some of the finest examples of warfare, from the earliest broadswords to ship-mounted cannons. Tremaine had been many times, as new exhibits came and went between its walls, but he'd never grown immune to its beauty. Ziminski's technician, who'd just arrived from Sweden (a country not lacking in castles), managed to catch her breath before continuing on toward the front gate.

She stopped again in front of the bronze dragon. Some teenagers, drunk or high and chattering in Polish, had just sent it a text message that would cause it to breathe fire. When it finally did, the thief startled, her pale oval face blazing orange in the firelight, her choppy bangs as red as a Titian beauty's. Tremaine's initial loathing of her, for the simple fact that her presence required him to rush his work, lifted a little as the kids raised a cheer around them. In the firelight, under the hem of her black hoodie, he saw Vermeer's Girl with the Pearl Earring, Botticelli's Venus, Caravaggio's Salome.

Tremaine sneered at the fantasy. She reminded

him of America, that was all. Her Midwestern accent, rough around the edges, dredged up bittersweet memories of his wasted small town youth. Thinking of home made him remember snippets of his drunken evening spent painting the Dossi. He thought of the incantation he'd painted into the fur collar, and smiled again. No one would be the wiser until he'd gotten his money and left Poland.

The flames died. "C'mon, Tremaine," she said, calling him by his last name, the only name he or Ziminski had ever given her. He knew her as Archer, which made him think of the dead man and his trumpet. Ziminski had him meet her at the airport in one of his cars, like he wasn't the best fine art forger in the world but a common chauffeur. He'd claimed he wanted the first face Archer saw to be a pleasant one, but really it was to prove how thoroughly he owned Tremaine, so Tremaine drove the living hell out of Ziminski's Bentley like he'd rode Ziminski's estranged wife.

Holding up a sign he'd hastily penned "ARCHER" in the front seat of the car, he got more than a handful of smartasses miming a bow and arrow at him as they left baggage claim. Tremaine didn't even give her a second glance until she was standing right in front of him, telling him her name—or at least her *codename*—was Archer. His surprise must have been evident, because she'd said, "You were expecting Hudson Hawk?"

Tremaine was a regular visitor of the gallery. The

technician required time and silence to "case" the building, and with him at her side, her furtive glances at cameras and other security measures would likely go overlooked.

Tremaine enjoyed traveling to the galleries in other countries, as well. He loved to be steeped in art. But one of the great benefits of his job was being able to *touch* the works of the masters, not just gawk, once the technicians had swapped them for his forgeries.

"Imagine touching the *Mona Lisa*," he told Archer as they entered the castle. "Running your fingers over every brush stroke. Feeling the contours, the *impasto*, and understanding exactly what brush shape da Vinci used for each stroke, what type of bristle, which pigments he'd mixed to make each color and shade, what organic materials and metals and semi-precious stones were used to derive its natural pigments." He sensed her losing interest, as she gazed at gates and darkened, hidden recesses in the walls. "*Knowing* the secret in her smile and her eyes, that if she were able to move she would seal it with a finger placed upon her lips. Imagine, for a moment, stepping into the shoes of Munch as he composed *The Scream*, or van Gogh dotting his *Night* with stars. Imagine stretching up to the ceiling of the Sistine Chapel and touching the finger of God as He passes the gift of life to Adam. Imagine standing in front of the rough sketch of *Guernica* and choosing, with all of the colors in the spectrum at your disposal, to paint it instead in stark black and white monochrome."

Archer gave him a look then, as if he'd gone mad.

Thinking of the curse and his counter-spell, Tremaine believed maybe he had.

Upstairs in the State Rooms, the galleries, the halls quiet as a tomb, but the walls would not stay quieted. The chorus of a thousand voices followed them through chambers and antechambers, bedrooms and banquet halls, from tapestries and paintings on wood, on canvas, and directly on the wrought leather walls. The forger and the thief slipped silently past a thousand years of art history, and he suspected Archer cared little, if at all, about any of it. This was a job to her, nothing more. He saw it in her eyes, flitting past Madonnas and Sabine women, chubby cherubs, muscular angels and fussy royalty without a second look.

They moved into the Royal Audience Hall, where stone floors glimmered. Above, eyes met his gaze from Biblical scenes woven into tapestries, and from the coffered ceiling, where carved and painted wooden heads that once watched over Kraków's royalty watched over them, the art thief and the painter. The forger. The *fraud*. Never had a lick of talent. Never would amount to anything. Their gaze, with hollowed-out irises, full of silent reproach.

"Tremaine?"

Archer stood in the next room, a look of curiosity visible under her hood. Tremaine studied the faces above him a moment longer, then followed. She stood before two paintings hung side-by-side: Dossi's

Jupiter, Mercury and Virtue and Dürer's *Self-Portrait at Twenty-Eight Years Old Wearing a Coat with Fur Collar*, on loan from the Alte Pinakothek in Munich. *Jupiter* was a sort of painters' painting Tremaine had never particularly responded to, though he generally liked Dossi's work. But the Dürer had what art appreciators called "wall power." It drew the eye. It *spoke* to him, even more so than his own replica. It *commanded* his attention.

"*Jesus...*" Archer muttered. "Those *eyes...*"

Tremaine could tell she had no eye for art. Nothing had moved her to waver from her business, not a single painting had spoken to her until just then. If that didn't speak of the power of Dürer's painting, Tremaine thought, then nothing did.

While Archer stared, open-mouthed, Tremaine noted that aside from a few minor differences in brush strokes and *craquelure*, his forgery and the original were virtually identical. Even the best experts, the people Sotheby's called when there was a question of authenticity, or the agents who worked fine art forgery cases in the FBI and Scotland Yard, or conspiracy theorists who would spend hours poring over alleged ciphers in Dürer's work—even they would have been hard-pressed to tell the two paintings apart.

Only Tremaine knew about the flaw, his incantation warding against evil... just two simple words he hoped would protect him long enough to get far away from the painting and his forgery.

No matter what happened, this would be his last.

‖

TWO DAYS LATER, pleased the theft had gone unnoticed—or at least unreported—Ziminski and Tremaine shared a drink in the old man's study. Tremaine peered through the glass of amber liquid at a roaring fire, pleased Ziminski hadn't invited his bodyguard to drink with them. When a knot popped in the fire, he simply shifted in the large leather chair, and sipped his Scotch. With the Russian nearby, he might have flinched, or twisted round to make sure Vladimir wasn't looming over his shoulder, cracking the knuckles of his massive fingers.

"*Na zdrowie,*" Ziminski said, raising his glass in a toast. Tremaine sat up and clinked his glass against the old man's. Ziminski eyed him queerly over the glass as he drank, as Tremaine settled back into the groaning chair, sipping his Scotch. "Your work's improved these last few months. I've noticed a sense of pride not present in previous works, particularly in your Dossi, and of course, the Dürer."

"Thank you, Mr. Ziminski," Tremaine said. "As much as it's about the money, it really is a labor of love." The old man nodded thoughtfully. "Say, where's Vladimir tonight? You give him the night off?"

"The Mad Russian? He's making room in the vault. We have a new acquisition, as you know. It requires a place of prominence." Ziminski's thin lips curled in a smirk. "You've… never seen the vault, have you?"

"No sir," Tremaine lied. Magda had lured him there during a soiree, her breasts heaving as she dragged him through the house, and the both of them out of breath they'd proceeded to fuck on top of Ziminski's large antique safe. Since he hadn't had much of a chance to look at the paintings stored there, he felt the lie was more of a stretching of truth.

"Let's you and I go have a look at my Dürer, hey?"

Tremaine swallowed the last of his drink in one gulp. He leaned forward to place the glass on a coaster on Ziminski's black granite table. "I'd like that," he said.

Ziminski buzzed down the hall, turning left toward the east wing where the gallery lay, and beyond it, the vault. Inside, paintings much too valuable, not to mention illegally procured, to display to the general public lay. Tremaine had gotten a fleeting glance during his stolen moment with Magda, enough to know much of what lay inside had been painted long before he'd met the old man. There were paintings and statuettes long thought lost to looting and war. There were portions of frescos chipped and pulled from church walls, ornate capitals from the columns and pilasters of unprotected ruins, portraits of wealthy families thought stolen by jealous relatives excised from their wills.

Ziminski zipped into the gallery. Tremaine heard

grunting up ahead—only Vladimir hauling sculptures and display cases to make room for the Dürer, he knew, but it still unnerved him. He'd been feeling mellow, certain he'd gotten away with painting his little flaw into the forgery. As they approached the far room, the certainty dwindled.

"Do you mind if I use the loo before we…?"

"It can wait," Ziminski said over his shoulder, his wheels rumbling over bare wood buffed to a high sheen.

"I'd rather not," Tremaine said, lagging a bit. "My back teeth are floating."

Ahead of them, Vladimir stepped into the doorway. He wore a t-shirt and his shoulder holster, his hard muscles gleaming with sweat, his wide chest pounding from exhaustion. His brow furrowed as he looked up at Tremaine. The painter had no doubts even though Vladimir had tired himself, the Russian would outrun him before he could reach the stairs. Either that, or put a bullet between the shoulder blades.

Ziminski zipped around to face him. "If it hadn't been for Archer, I might never have noticed. She's got a good eye, that one."

"Noticed?" Tremaine tried hard to swallow. He'd misjudged Archer: she'd had an eye for art, after all.

"Don't play games, Tremaine. I always knew your ego would be your undoing. You couldn't just let it be. It's just like with Magda. You couldn't stand that an old man like me had a woman like her, and so you had to have her for yourself."

"I would never do that, Mr. Ziminski—"

"Oh, *tosh*. She told me everything." He smirked. "You're a scoundrel, Tremaine. I knew you couldn't keep it in your pants, but I had hoped you'd had enough pride of purpose to *not fuck with my painting*!"

Ziminski's words resounded off the silent walls. Vladimir cracked his knuckles, stepping out of the gallery and into the hall.

Tremaine threw up his hands, backing away. "Mr. Ziminski, Milo, please—"

"Oh, Milo nothing." The old man's face twisted into an approximation of disappointment. "You've failed me, boy. But worse than that, you *betrayed* me."

Much too late, Tremaine turned to run. Vladimir grabbed him fiercely by the shoulders and spun him round. Tremaine saw the old man look away in disgust as Vladimir slammed a fist into his face and painted the world black.

THUNDER ROARED IN Tremaine's skull.

He knew where he was from the smell before his eyes grew accustomed to the harsh light. Oil paint, dust, canvas, parchment. Tremaine blinked away a crust of blood and peered blearily at the empty insides of Miłogost Ziminski's vault.

Ziminski sat in the doorway. Vladimir stood over his shoulder, smiling darkly.

"You know, this vault is air-tight," Ziminski said. "I've thought a lot about what I would do with you when Archer pointed out your folly, and the solution was simple. What better place to kill you, than in the very place you first betrayed me."

"Milo, just listen to me," Tremaine groaned.

"Oh I think I've listened to you long enough. It's all bullshit, Tremaine. You're a fraud. Everything you do, everything you say, none of it *means* anything."

Tremaine said nothing.

"Funny thing." The old man licked spittle from the corner of his lips. "Magda gave me the same look you're fixing me with now, when she was where you are. It didn't take her quite as long to die as I suspect it will take you. You want to know why, Tremaine?"

Tremaine only looked at him.

"It's because you're full of hot air," Ziminski blurted with a laugh. "How long did it take, Vladimir? For Magda to die. Half an hour?"

"Forty-three minutes," the large man said.

"You see, after Magda told me about your little sexcapades, I installed a hidden camera in the vault."

Tremaine glanced at the bare steel walls.

"She never knew it was there, but Vladimir and I had a wonderful time watching her die. Gulping like a goldfish out of its bowl." The old man smiled at Tremaine. "We shared a bottle and toasted to the little slut's death."

Tremaine cleared his throat to speak.

"How long do you wager Tremaine will take to die? An hour?"

Vladimir shrugged. "Maybe less. If he's lucky."

Ziminski's smile grew wider. "'If he's lucky.' I rather like that." The old man backed up his wheelchair. His bodyguard grabbed the thick steel door. Behind them, the Dürer stood leaning against the wall. Tremaine locked eyes with the Master and chuckled morosely.

"Goodbye, Yannick," Ziminski said, as Vladimir slammed the door shut.

The painter threw himself to his feet, scouring the walls for indents, for loose screws, for seams. He fell to his knees and slid his palms along the floor, feeling for grooves, rivets, knocking and listening for hollow spots. The metal had bent in a small place on the edge of the door. He tore his fingernails on it, cursing, shouting at it, goading himself on through the pain, all to no avail. Exasperated, his raw fingers left a smear of blood on the door and he returned to where he'd started to begin again, his breath short, heart beating hard. After what felt like hours, he plopped down on the floor and wept with exhaustion. Nothing. All seams smoothed down. All rivets firmly in place. The vault solid and thick all the way through.

The air felt thick. Soupy. Difficult to breathe.

He thought of the trumpeter, bleating out his final note as the arrow pierced his throat. Dying doing what he did best. Not locked in a vault, breathing his own dead air, left with nothing to paint with and no canvas in sight.

Tremaine regarded his quivering hands, soiled

black with grease from the floor and red with blood from his fingertips. Hands that had forged so many masterpieces. Fingers that had spread and smeared and scraped. A thought occurred to him. He pushed himself raggedly to his feet, his head swimming, on the verge of unconsciousness. Not much time left, really. He vaguely wondered who would win the bet: Ziminski or Vladimir.

The painter staggered to the door.

Peeling the skin of his fingers on the sharp curl of metal. Carving into the pads of flesh. His hands dripped crimson as he turned to the wide, blank wall.

He began to paint, laughing wildly.

Drunk on creativity, Tremaine stepped back to admire his final masterpiece, his coda, his dying words. He'd painted a hand flipping the camera the middle finger and signed it with his name, a counter-spell painted in bold, bloody capitals:

YANNICK TREMAINE

Yannick stumbled out of the way, falling back against the door, hoping Ziminski and his bodyguard had an unimpeded view of his *pièce de résistance*.

Outside the vault, something toppled. Glass shattered.

Tremaine perked up, pressing his ear against the cold metal. Breathing shallow. Another great crash startled him, the sound of concrete or plaster crumbling. Heavy footsteps. Canvas tearing, wood splintering. For a moment, the painter thought he might be hallucinating the sounds. Wishful thinking, as the air grew thin and the last colors of his life bled away to white.

A horrific *BOOM* pierced the silence. Another. And again. Vladimir's Desert Eagle, firing at—*what?*

The man himself let out a blood-curdling shriek, cut off as it reached its crescendo like the final note of the trumpeter of St. Mary's.

Muffled, he heard Ziminski cry out, "No! *No, this can't be*—" before he was silenced, too.

In the quiet that followed, the world around Tremaine began to wash gray.

A squall of metal on metal drew him from soupy oblivion. Gears clattered, the door fell open, and Tremaine spilled out into the gallery. Sprawling face-first with his blood-smeared hands spread on the cool wood floor, he gasped for air. Slowly his vision returned, color bleeding back into the world. Blurry white snowflakes fell around him. He saw Ziminski's chair toppled, the man himself curled into a fetal ball, his head smashed on the floorboards like an overripe melon. What he'd thought was snow came into focus, shreds of parchment and canvas falling delicately around them.

Shakily, Tremaine rose on his hands and knees.

Behind Ziminski and his fallen wheelchair, the rest of the gallery was in ruin. Vladimir lay twisted and broken against the far wall. Paintings shredded, frames snapped into kindling, sculptures and idols smashed to sharp bits of gray and white and clay brown, display cases shattered into jagged, shimmering glints, wallpaper torn, floorboards splintered.

The only undamaged art in the room, Dürer's *Self-Portrait* regarded him without expression. In a loose pattern around it, three bullet holes still smoldered.

Tremaine held Dürer's gaze a moment longer, waiting. The air seemed electric, though he supposed it could have been his starved lungs. He watched for movement, and noticed the light from the vault had caused a dim shadow of himself to fall on the painting.

When nothing happened for several minutes, Tremaine decided it was time to go. He did not know why the Master's curse had spared him, although he recalled something Ziminski had said to the Mad Russian: *The man values his art more than his life. If that's not a quality worth admiring, I don't know what is.* Tremaine thought perhaps that might be the reason but he supposed he'd never know for sure.

He pushed himself to his feet, stumbled, righted himself, and staggered toward the door.

The Master's eyes remained fixed on the empty vault, and what his pupil had painted there. They did not follow Tremaine as he left the gallery.

MY PROTECTOR

"THE STATE OF those young boys..." the Principal lamented. "You understand, I'm sure, why it behooves me to have your daughter expelled."

Jenny's mother understood. The two boys outside Principal Villeneuve's office had been viciously attacked, barely able to sit in the hard plastic chairs without squirming for the pain. She turned to her little girl, whose eighth birthday they had recently celebrated with a tea party and pony rides. Jenny's green eyes, wet with shame, refused to leave her patent leather shoes, hovering inches above the gray carpet. Her freckled face twisted in a pout, her little red pigtails rested on the shoulders of a pale blue smock dress, Jenny might have looked the part of innocence were it not for the obvious spatters of blood. Whatever had happened, Mrs. Cooper couldn't imagine her little girl possessing the strength to do such horrid things to a single ten-year-old boy, let alone two of them—especially considering how much bigger they were. But shame had sealed the boys' split lips. And all Jenny seemed able to say was, "It wasn't me."

The shock of it, for Jenny's father, was dulled by a glimmer of pride. He fought to hold back a smile when he looked at his daughter, thinking she just might manage middle school all right on her own. The thought reminded him of the empty seat at the dinner table, of the room that would no longer carry loud music or laughter, only gather dust. He no longer felt the urge to smile.

"Mr. and Mrs. Cooper, I truly am sorry. But you see, I'm sure, how her actions left us with no choice. The parents have threatened to sue, and they have yet to see the damage she's done to their children!"

Jenny could no longer hold her peace. Her voice was so small, so meek, her father had to ask her to repeat it. "It wasn't me," she whimpered again, with a beseeching look toward her parents. "It was *Aaron*."

Jenny's mother and father shared an anxious look, and Principal Villeneuve's face lost all color. When Mr. Cooper looked at his daughter again, his heart nearly burst with compassion.

Only then did he notice she bore no wounds on her hands. They were, in fact, entirely free of blood: the boys' or her own.

WITH HEAVY HEARTS, Jenny's mother and father dropped her off at Camp Broken Wings. Bereavement camp was Principal Villeneuve's idea, and Jenny's parents had agreed spending time off school with other children of her age, who had suffered similar trauma, would be beneficial.

00:260;00

For her part, Jenny had been silent during the trip, and had yet to apologize for what she'd done. Her mother was still trying to wrap her mind around what Jenny had told them, that it hadn't been her who'd hurt the boys but her older brother. She tried to put herself in her daughter's shoes, to fathom why she would have made up such an obvious lie after doing something so despicable, when she could have simply blamed it on another student. She must have known no one would believe her. But the fact that she'd lied to them without a trace of guilt made Mrs. Cooper angry, particularly since it had been her brother she'd pointed to as a culprit, knowing full well it was impossible for Aaron to have hurt those boys. He'd protected her from bullies before the accident, but now…

Mrs. Cooper shied away from the thought. In the same moment, she looked up to catch her daughter's eye, and was surprised to find a glimmer of hatred behind the sullen pout. Hatred burning toward *her*.

The camp looked decent enough. Freshly-painted log cabins bordered the parking lot, surrounded on all sides by fragrant pines, spruce and cedars. Beyond them children laughed and squealed, and the faint smell of fresh water reminded her of the small lake, where boys and girls ages 8 – 16 could swim, paddle and play. Other activities included rope-climbing, scavenger hunts, soccer, and many more—at least according to the brochure Principal Villeneuve had given them.

Two counsellors dressed in red t-shirts and shorts approached from down a wooded trail, a teenaged boy and girl. Once they were nearer, Mrs. Cooper realized the white emblem on their shirts wasn't an ink blot—her first thought, and a peculiar one at that—but a bird with one wing twisted at an angle, the name of the camp spelled out in letters made to look like carved wood. She eyed the tanned, muscular thighs of the brunette, late teens, as the girl bent to address Jenny, pleased to note that her husband's eyes remained scanning the trees.

"Hi there. You must be Jennifer. I'm Brooke."

"Say 'hi,' honey," Mr. Cooper urged.

Jenny looked back at her father, then turned to face the counsellor with a sullen, "Hi."

"You're gonna have a lot of fun with us, Jennifer. Isn't she, Jonas?"

Jonas, the young man regarding Mrs. Cooper with his hands behind his back, snapped to and nodded. "Huh? Oh, you bet."

Jenny shifted her knapsack onto her shoulders. Above them, the red maple leaf strung from the end of the flagpole fluttered limply in a light breeze.

"You be good, okay?" Mr. Cooper told her with a hand placed gently on her head. His little girl nodded. "Your mother and I will be back to pick you up on Monday."

Jenny looked sullenly at her mother, who tried her damnedest to smile with tears welling in her eyes. This would be Jenny's first time away from home, and despite what had happened to bring them here, Mrs. Cooper couldn't help but feel a little saddened.

The tanned girl, Brooke, stood and held out a slender hand for Jenny. Reluctantly, Jenny took it. As the two counsellors led her away, she turned back in the direction of the car. Mrs. Cooper hitched a breath, waiting to meet her daughter's eyes, to leave her with one last hopeful smile. But Jenny seemed to find something interesting in the empty space between them and the car, and smiled anyhow.

JONAS AND BROOKE showed Jenny to her cabin, where she'd be spending the night with nine other girls of similar age, then introduced her to a group of young boys and girls on the soccer field. They played Red Rover. They paddled canoes. They made wallets out of duct tape, and friendship bracelets. They changed into swim trunks to play Marco Polo in the shallows of Lake Caribou. The counsellors tired the children out, and try as she might, Jenny couldn't manage to hold onto her sadness for long. She started to enjoy herself. She opened up to other kids. They found a baby turtle, and showed it to their counsellors. Brooke told them to wash their hands so they wouldn't get salmonella, and a little boy with a bowl-cut asked, "Don't you mean *turtle*-monella?" The children all laughed. The day wound down, the evening filling with cries of joy and laughter as they played tag and caught fireflies. For lunch, they'd had tacos. For dinner, it was chicken fingers and French fries. No bone-dry chicken and couscous like her mother made her eat at home. No cauliflower "steak" and Brussels sprouts.

After dinner when darkness fell, the children and counsellors all gathered on wooden pews circled around the big fire pit, reminding Jenny of paintings she'd seen about the mysterious Druids. Soon a tall fire crackled, and mosquitoes buzzed around their ears. Trees whose color had faded now glowed orange, their pointed tops stark black against a sky filled with more stars than Jenny, a city girl, had ever seen in her life. The counsellors roasted marshmallows for s'mores, and passed the finished treats around. Soon everyone's fingers were sticky, their mouths tingly from sugar, and their bellies full.

"Who has a story they'd like to share?"

Several children put up their hands. Jenny sat beside a chubby girl with short dark hair named Colleen. The girl, whose older sister had passed a few weeks before Jenny's brother had his accident, had given her a friendship bracelet. The two of them had stuck together during free time at the lake and had sat side by side at dinner. Neither girl put her hand up.

Darius, a bearded counsellor older than both Jonas and Brooke (and much too handsome to have a beard, in Jenny's opinion), pointed to a tween boy.

"W-what kind of story?" the boy asked, unfortunate enough to have both a lisp and braces which flashed with firelight when he spoke. "Like…

a ghost story?"

A ripple of excitement followed this. Darius motioned for the children to quiet down. "We don't tell ghost stories at Camp Broken Wings," he said. "You know that."

"Yeah, but why not?" a girl called out.

"Well, it's just our policy. Now does anyone have a story that's a little more pleasant? Maybe a story about something funny. Or heroic."

The children looked at each other. Nobody wanted to say anything, or had anything to say. Jenny felt frustrated. The suggestion of ghost story had stirred something in her and the others, but the camp's stupid "policy" wouldn't allow them to be told. But he had asked for a story of heroism, and the only hero she'd ever known was her big brother.

Jenny put up her hand.

"Yes." Darius pointed out a young boy in the front row he then called Timmy.

"My big brother tried to fart on my head once, but he pooped himself instead."

The kids all laughed, even the older ones. Everyone except Jenny, who wanted to tell her story and felt only anger toward the dull boy.

"I'm sure that wasn't funny for your brother, or your mom," the counsellor said, and scuffed his sandals in the dirt. "Anybody else have a story that doesn't involve poo?"

Jenny's hand fired up again. She twiddled her fingers so he'd see her first.

"Yes, uh…" Brooke leaned and whispered something to Darius. "Jennifer," he said.

"My brother is a hero," Jenny told him.

"Okay. That sounds like a nice story. Why don't you tell us a little bit about him?"

Jenny struggled to describe him, though his face was as clear as day, even at night. They both had the same freckles and red hair, the same green eyes. They both had dimples when they laughed, though presently he wore a scowl, shaking his head 'no.'

"Well… he's got one wonky ear and one normal one. My mom calls it his elf ear, but Aaron told me a while ago it was a defect he got in the womb. He's really really tall, but not as tall as my dad. Dad always said he'd grow up taller than him, but that was before. We don't talk about Aaron since the accident, an' if I forget and say something about him, Mom cries and Dad looks all worried."

"*Oh.*" The bearded counsellor turned to his fellow counsellors, who seemed at a loss. "Jennifer, I'm sorry, but we're not supposed to talk about… those who've passed."

Her nose wrinkled. "What's 'passed'?"

"He means died," Colleen explained in a whisper.

"Aaron's not dead." She turned to the empty seat between her and the small boy to her right, a cold place where the boy had first sat and then immediately shifted away from. "He's sitting right *beside* me."

Colleen reached out and clutched Jenny's arm.

The small boy looked at Jenny, fear registering on his face in the flicker of firelight. He hesitated a moment, scowling at Jenny, before pushing his friend over and scooching further away. Someone made a ghostly "*Woo-oo-ooh!*"

"Jennifer, that's not funny," Darius said.

Children craned their necks and stood up in their seats to get a look at her brother. An older boy sang the *Twilight Zone* theme tunelessly, and some of the children laughed.

Darius waited for the children to settle with a look of concern. "Your brother's not here, Jennifer. There's *no one* sitting beside you."

Jenny felt small and weak, her cheeks growing hot from all the attention suddenly focused on her, from the handsome counsellor with the stupid beard not believing her. She looked to the place where her brother had just been. "He *was*," she said, "until all your stupid jokes scared him away."

The children all tittered nervously, and the counsellors, apparently eager to change the subject, launched into a silly song about a camel named Alice and her many humps. Everyone seemed to know the words but Jenny, and her embarrassment deepened. She pretended to sing along to *On Top of Spaghetti* and *The Log Driver's Waltz*, but the counsellor had made her angry, and she was no longer enjoying herself.

Colleen turned to her as they all sang *Michael, Row Your Boat Ashore*, and whispered, "You can tell me about him, if you want. When we get back to the cabin."

Jenny turned to her, genuinely pleased. The two girls smiled conspiratorially, and began to sing along.

AFTER LIGHTS-OUT, the girls gathered at the foot of their bunks where they could see each other in the dim cone of light from a flashlight cupped in an older girl's hand. The oldest girl, Shondra, had directed them to tie their blankets around the beds to block the light from reaching the windows, "so the counsellors won't see we're awake." In the dark outside the cabin, frogs and night bugs chirped, but inside all was quiet.

"Nice one at the campfire, kid," Shondra said as she tucked the corner of a blanket into her bunk to act as the roof of the tent. "You broke the cardinal rule on your first day. Thou shalt not talk about the dead."

Jenny stirred on the bottom bunk closest the door, the word upsetting her. "I *told* you, Aaron's not dead. He got in a bike accident with a car on my street. When we got to the hop-spital, I heard the doctor say he died on the operating table but then they brought him back, an' after that, they let me in to see him. He had all these tubes and junk coming out of him, but I could tell he was still alive because sometimes he blinked. My mom said he's in a cona."

The older girls giggled. Jenny felt her cheeks grow red again. She didn't like to be laughed at.

"It's *coma*," Shondra told her, with the patience of a friendly older sibling. "So he's in a coma. You said he was sitting beside you at the fire."

"He… comes and visits me. Sometimes."

The other girls shared a look. Doubtful, worried—Jenny couldn't tell.

"V-visits?" Colleen asked.

"Uh-huh. Like the day before yesterday, these two boys were pickin' on me, pulling my hair and stuff when I was just trying to walk down the stairs, calling me 'ginger' and 'freckle-face,' so I told 'em to stop, but they didn't care." She shook her head, as if the boys should have known better. "They just kept on doing it. But I told them, 'I wouldn't do that if I were you,' because I knew what my brother would do to them if he found out."

Jenny took a deep breath. She saw the eager looks on their faces, wide eyes in deep shadow thrown by their cheeks from the flashlight. She hadn't been able to tell anyone what had happened that day. Nobody had wanted to hear the truth—not the principal, not her parents. But these girls were eager to listen. And technically, she wouldn't be doing wrong, since what she was telling them wasn't a ghost story.

"But they *still* didn't listen," she continued. "They kept teasing me even worse. They pinched my bum and stepped on the back of my shoes." The girls shook their heads in disgust. "And then after that they chased me under the stairs, but I bet they didn't expect my brother was gonna be waiting there. Right away, he hit 'em with a hammer from the art room. *Bop bop bop*." She made a striking gesture, the girls flinching as if she'd hit them. The flashlight beam flickered, causing their shadows to flutter on the blankets. "They ran crying to the Principal's office and lied and said I was the one that hit 'em."

Jenny looked at the others, saw the fear in their eyes mingled with delight, because the bad boys had been punished.

"But it was Aaron that did it," she finished. "Aaron's my protector."

In the shocked silence that followed the blanket closest to Jenny came down violently, and all the girls screamed, even Jenny herself. The girl called Delia who had a lazy eye dropped the flashlight, and when it settled on the dusty floorboards, the intruder's giant shadow fell on the wall by the open door, the blanket rumpled at his feet. They crawled to the ends of their beds, hugging their knees, eyes widened in fear of the man whose face still lay in darkness. But Jenny held her ground because she knew he wasn't her brother. This man was slimmer and wore sandals.

"I told you, *no ghost stories*," Darius said, bending into the light to grab her roughly by the wrist and yank her out of bed. "You're coming to the office."

Jenny allowed herself to be pulled along quietly, sullenly. Colleen reached out to her, and the other girls protested. Shondra merely shook her head.

"Wonder if her brother will protect her now," she muttered sarcastically.

DARIUS SAT ACROSS the desk from Jenny, who swung her feet from the tall chair. On the wall were photos of children at play, along with several framed newspaper articles touting the healing power of Broken Wings. A clock made from a flat piece of driftwood ticked away the seconds above two canoe paddles in the shape of an X.

The counsellor put his feet up on the desk, rattling a big metal flashlight with the words HEAVY METAL stenciled on its side, which rested beside a desk tray labelled IN and OUT, filled with various files. This was not Darius's office. The camp director, he'd informed Jenny, was away at a conference, and had put him in charge for the weekend.

"Whatever I say goes," he said with what looked like glee, "and I say we have to call your parents."

Jenny muttered something under her breath, her feet still swinging.

"Beg pardon?"

"I *said*," Jenny seethed, "'I wouldn't do that if I were you.'"

Darius's smile broadened. "Oh you wouldn't, would you?"

Jenny shook her head with a look of warning. Her feet stopped swinging.

The counsellor held her gaze a moment, then shook his head, chuckling derisively, and picked up the phone. He smirked at her while she stared daggers at him. In a moment, Jenny heard the dull sound of the telephone beginning to ring at his ear.

"Yes, hi, Mr. Cooper? I'm sorry to disrupt you so late in the evening. It's about your daughter." Darius stuck out his tongue at her. Jenny felt her brother's presence, very near. A sly smile crept onto her freckled face. The young man's smile vanished, and he swiveled his chair to face the wall. "Yes, that's right. I'm afraid she's been acting up. Well, we have a policy—"

Oh yes, Aaron was close now. She could feel him, and his presence emboldened her. Made her weakness solidify into raw animal strength. Made her grow armor. Made her *invincible*.

"Absolutely," Darius told her father on the phone. "No, that's no trouble. Tomorrow. That's fine. All right, see you then."

With a toothy grin, he swiveled back to cradle the phone. Surprise registered on his face when he saw Jenny standing over him.

"Pick on someone your own size!" She thrust the heavy flashlight down with both hands. "Pick on someone your own size!" The base struck his head with a metallic ping, stripping flesh from bone in a ragged flap. "Pick on someone your own size!" It obliterated his eye. Shattered finger bones when he raised his hand to protect his face. Cracked the top of his skull. Pulverized the gelatinous meat inside. He pitched forward, dropping the receiver, landing solidly on the floor.

Jenny panted heavily, standing over the counsellor's corpse as his blood soaked into the carpet. She dropped the flashlight beside him, then casually bent to pick up the phone.

"Dad…?"

The crackle of distance filled the long pause. "Jenny?"

She sighed heavily. "Can you come pick us up?"

Her father said nothing… but she knew he would come. He'd have to, if he'd heard what Aaron had done to the mean old camp counsellor. She cradled the phone then, and sat with her brother, who smiled silently from the seat beside her, waiting for their parents to arrive.

SANCTUARY

THE EAST TEXAS sun beat down on my head as I jogged the marsh trail through the animal sanctuary. Sweat poured down my back, matting my hair to my scalp. Togo, the four-year-old mutt my ex-wife stuck me with in the divorce, panted heavily as he ran along beside me.

The ex used to say—before the divorce made anything she'd said fall on deaf ears—I should exercise more. Exercise is fine, but the gravel crunching under my feet is a meditation thing for me, hypnotic. It cleared the head. The sanctuary was one of my favorite spots in the area, and just about the only place nearby you could go to get away from the trucks and bustle of the city.

A bird chirped high on an electrical pole, repetitive, trying to get my attention. "Robins are active today," I told Togo. He looked up at me, tongue lolling to one side—thirsty already, but we'd only just started running. I promised myself to stop once we got to the next intersection in the trails.

Up ahead, black smoke rose over the trees. A hunting cabin, most likely. The sound of rifle fire cut through the wind filling my ears, confirming my suspicion. Some yahoo gun nuts firing off automatic weapons. Something I hear a lot these days is, "Go big or go home." The expression doesn't just apply to pickups, or the portions at your local Tex-Mex.

Never was one for guns, particularly after having one pointed in my face where I tend bar. At least with open carry laws you know where you stand. It's the ones who've got them tucked into the back of their pants or under their jacket you have to worry about. When a fight breaks out in a bar where open carry is the norm, things either escalate quick—usually one dipshit or another ends up shooting himself in the foot trying to pry the thing out of its holster, Billy the Kid-style—or people calm down in a hurry, not wanting to be the object of some psycho's target practice.

Alligators lurk in the marsh out here. With Togo by my side, I had to keep an eye out that one of them hadn't slinked out of the muck to warm itself on the gravel trails. Part terrier, Togo would make a nice light snack.

I was in a sort of trance when he yelped behind me.

I spun around, still moving along the trail, running backward. Togo had gotten down on his haunches, quivering and looking up at the sky. Up in the haze of blue and white, a bird circled. As I looked, it dove toward us with a familiar cry.

The gull swooped down, its beady yellow eyes

locked right on mine. I ducked out of the way, but it was Togo the bird wanted. The poor little mutt rolled over backward as it landed in the dust, squawking at him, dancing toward him. Togo reared back and growled, but the bird kept coming, squalling, calling out for the feeding frenzy.

Scouring the tall grass where the marsh reached the ditch, wary of gators, I grabbed a fat black branch and hauled back with it to pitch at the gull before realizing my error. The stick wriggled in my hand, cool and fleshy to the touch.

Startled, I dropped the coachwhip, crying out in fear and disgust. I've seen those snakes eat mice whole before, but they're incredibly wary of humans. Rather than slither off into the brush though, the snake came right at me, and with a moment to react, I stomped down hard on the thing, feeling its insides crunch and squirt out from under my shoe.

Togo, meanwhile, bared his teeth at the gull. More cries came from nearby as two others landed near the first, the three birds menacing my poor dog. I moved to shoo them when something hard and sharp struck the back of my head.

I turned to a flutter of wings, a familiar chirp. As I rubbed the spot where the robin had hit me, feeling the wet warmth of blood, it dove in for another strike.

I ducked, swatting out blindly. The bird fluttered over my head. Somehow my wrist managed to penetrate its flapping wings and struck its fragile body. The bird chirped—whether in pain or out of anger, I had no idea, but I suspected the latter—then flew up to its perch on the pole.

Nature's gone haywire, I thought. *So much for sanctuary...*

Togo barked, frantic as the birds flanked him.

"Get the hell out of here, shithawks!" I shouted, kicking gravel at them. They stepped back, raising their wings defensively. Pleased, I stomped toward them, waving my arms like the biggest bird around. They waddled back, spreading out. Their yellow eyes, somewhat reptilian, watched me without betraying their intentions.

Togo screeched then, a tremulous sound that rattled my nerves. I wheeled, ready to kick some avian ass, but it was already too late. A gator had lurched up from the marsh, still shimmering, and had caught Togo in its jaws. Togo's front legs danced, his wet brown eyes looking up at me for assistance. I had none to offer. The gator snapped its head back, revealing a sickening glimpse of the steaming insides of my poor dog, and swallowed the rest of him whole.

I ran.

The birds parted for me, trilling cries. Out in the marsh, three fat gators splashed into the black water. The eyes of another rose from the reeds, locking on me. The one that had eaten Togo bypassed the gulls, as if unaware of them, and ran headlong at my heels. If you've never seen a gator run, be glad. It's probably the most terrifyingly hilarious thing you'll ever see, like a man-eating mudskipper.

As I thought it, glad I'd worn runners, glad to be in the best shape of my life after the divorce, the goddamn robin swooped into view and struck me on the bridge of my nose, shooting stars across my vision. I batted it out of the air, but the damage was done. The gator had gained precious feet. I was lunch.

Rifle fire made me jump. In the next moment, the alligator's head exploded in a shower of meat and gore. Its momentum kept propelling it forward, the legs still pumping, until the huge rugged beast slopped down at my feet, spilling its insides on my shoes.

It was then that I heard the growl of trucks. I'd never been so happy to hear axle-back exhaust and see a set of Bumper Nuts in my life.

A portly guy with mutton chops stood in the back, brandishing some sort of rifle. "Just about made yerself a horsie doover there, buddy!"

I looked back at the trail. The robin fluttered on the hot gravel. I'd somehow managed to break its wing. But the gulls were still coming, and more gators crept up from the marsh on either side.

The driver smacked the door. "Don't just stand there pissin' your panties. Hop on in!"

Another truck met the first, carrying two more guys I wouldn't want to meet in the woods on any other day, every one of them packing.

I didn't hesitate, just climbed into the passenger

seat.

Peeling away, we left the gators in a cloud of dust.

The driver turned to me, chewing on a mouthful of tobacco. "When the animals rise up against their masters, the whole G.D. world's gone snafu, ain't it?"

"Yeah," I said, peering in the rearview.

The fat guy in the bed had taken up a stance on one knee, the rifle sight at eye level. He squeezed off a round, a trail of gray smoke rising from the weapon. "Missed 'em!"

"No shit, you moron," the driver shouted over his shoulder, jumping up and down in his seat. "We're bouncin' all over the damn road. Save your ammo!" He spat a wad of tobacco juice out the open window.

"Gotta get to the city," I said, knowing the birds circling overhead would follow us, but at least we'd be safe from the gators, the snakes—for a while, anyhow. "Get to a high rise, and wait this out. Whatever it is."

The driver turned with a slimy brown grin. "You're in good hands, fella." He patted the Dirty Harry gun holstered on his hip. He was loving this, had probably been waiting for any excuse to kill every damned animal on the planet, and now he would get his chance.

Kill or be killed. Eat or be eaten.

I looked beyond the insane grin and out through the window. I saw the black smoke rising above the trees, and knew we were doomed. It wasn't a hunting cabin—I was wrong about that. The *city* was that way. We were too late.

When the animals rise up against their masters...

The driver yelped, and shielded his eyes, too late to even attempt to swerve out of the large buck's path.

The front end crumpled. The truck swerved, grinding hard into the gravel, and Mutton Chops standing in the truck bed pitched over the roof, crying out. The beast's head shattered the windshield, shards of glass pattering down around me, its antlers gouging up through the driver's throat and pinning him to the ceiling. His glassy eyes bugged out and his tobacco-browned tongue stuck out between his teeth.

The second truck braked, raising dust that swirled around us in a churning wind.

I sat there stunned, covered in glass. The buck snorted, breathing heavily, its face so close I could smell its rank breath and musky hide, see the feathered lashes on its glossy black eyes.

Slow as I could, I reached down for the belt buckle. The eye followed my progress. The animal was stunned, likely just as pinned as its victim. Its bulk had crushed the hood, and one leg was badly broken, jagged bone poking out through flesh.

The belt clicked, releasing me from the driver's chrome tomb.

The buck's head shifted. It blinked, moaning pitifully.

"Good," I said, and jerked the door handle,

propelling myself out into the road.

Mutton Chops rose from the dirt, groaning. His rifle had skittered away from him. I thought if I ran I could get to it before he could. Dog eat dog, and all that.

Poor fucking Togo...

Behind me, the other two had gotten out of their truck, rifles at the ready. "Jesus Pleasus! That's a twenty-point buck right there," the second driver remarked, dressed in full military camo.

"Like hell it is," his skinny partner shot back. "Eighteen at the most."

"When we tell the story, it's a twenty." Warning in the driver's eyes. "Teevo would have been honored to die by the hand of that sucker."

"Hoof," the other guy corrected him. "Bucks don't have hands."

"Would you shut the—" His eyes widened. "Oh, my shit..."

I looked where he was looking. A dozen gators had crawled out of the muck and stood poised to strike barely fifteen feet from the truck. Snakes had filled in their ranks, a battalion of Kings, pit vipers, coachwhips, corals and hognoses. Behind them, the rats, voles, moles, and hedgehogs clambered over each other to reach their next meal.

I ran.

Gunfire erupted behind me, and I bolted past Mutton Chops and his rifle. As the reports died out and the cries of immense pleasure became screams of intense fear, of agony, I kept on running. My lungs burning, my legs already beginning to tire, head swimming with thoughts of home, of a city teeming with killer animals, with nature gone amok, I sprinted down the sanctuary trail, evolution's last cruel joke clawing at my heels.

DO NOT SHAKE OR RATTLE

GRACE REALLY OUTDID herself this year, Donald thought from his armchair, looking at the heaping pile of shiny gift-wrapped boxes under the sparkling tree. *I told her, Mara and Donnie Junior's spoiled little brats'll tear up all that pretty wrapping of yours in oh, about 5.3 seconds, and it'll be my job to clean it up just like last year. Like every year. But does she listen? About as close as a deaf dog.*

A knot popped in the fireplace as Donald rocked in his chair, thinking about his wife of 46 years. Met after his first tour in Vietnam. *Gracie sure blew the doors off all the chicks the other fellas went home with that night. A real foxy mama. 'Course that was before that Viet Kong land mine took my leg. Before the job and the kids and the grandkids and Gracie's "many-paws," like she calls it. Now she's gone weird in the head, hot flashes and cold flashes and running around afraid of her own damn shadow.* Had Mara while he was in a rice paddy shooting zips for Uncle Sam, and Donnie Jr. once he'd got sent home in two pieces—*Well, they probably didn't keep the rest of my leg, lucky the damn thing was a dud*—just before he started work at the plant. Overall their marriage had been fine, when the kids were in the house, when he'd been working—*Worked my way up from lubing the machines to district manager*—but now that the kids had families of their own, and he'd retired—*Not that I wanted to, damn government*—she'd been grating on his nerves. Always checking up on him in the garage. Always peeking in while he sat reading the paper on the shitter. *Dunno what the hell's wrong with that woman. It's like she expects I'll drop dead any minute!*

A solitary green light flickered on the tree, spoiling his reverie, blinking like a dying star. The others—red, white and blue—shone uninterrupted. *Thank God I took those damn bulbs Grace got back to the store and traded 'em for parallels. Came with extra bulbs, too. A deal is a deal, but you don't go getting cheaply made China crap just because it's on sale. I told her, "You get what you pay for," but does she listen? Like a deaf dog.*

Donald eased himself out of the ratty chair, resting the bulk of his weight on his cane. Leaving the chair squeaking behind him like his Vaseline-greased stump in the new prosthetic Donnie Junior had gotten him made special last year, he made his way to the tree. He'd kept the extra bulbs in a baggie garbage-tied to the mass of plugs around back of it. He stopped a moment and warmed his hands in front of the fire—*Damn woman's got the temp so low I could freeze to death. Maybe that's what she wants*—then shuffled his weary bones to the big Scotch pine. Beautiful tree. Not spindly and sparse like the white pines Grace's Ma and Pop had in their house back when he and Gracie used to bring the kids to their place Christmas morning. Smelled good, too. Taking in a good strong whiff, Donald thought they should make bathroom deodorizers smell like this. *Make every poop smell like Christmas morn for just a dollar ninety-nine!*

Something caught Donald's eye as he reached around the tree. *Was that there before?* A new gift, about the size and shape of a shoebox. He squinted down at it. "To Donald from Grace'? I told her we're on a fixed income, she doesn't need to be getting me anything fancy."

Donald bent, leaning over his cane, to read the note taped to the side of the box.

DO NOT SHAKE OR RATTLE

"'Do not shake or rattle'? What does she think I am?"

After 46 years you think she doesn't have your number? Even when you were a kid you used to shake the gifts under the tree. Gotta give it a good rattle to figure out what's inside, right?

Donald peered over his shoulder. The house was pleasantly empty. Grace was at her sister's house, bringing her some "Christmas cheer." That meant more alcohol for the alcoholic. Donald could never stand Gracie's sister Diane, and the feeling was so evidently mutual. Never been married, just her alone with a fat tabby cat, Donald had a sneaking suspicion the woman was a card-carrying lesbo. *Flying the pink flag*, he thought amusedly.

He bent down over his cane, and picked up the box. "Oof!" He hadn't expected it to be heavy. *Damn woman nearly put out my back. What's she put in here? A brick?*

Turning it from side to side, Donald noted the usual meticulous Grace wrapping job. He watched her sometimes from his chair, where she sat at the dining room table. Everything just so. Tape here, bow there. The corners folded delicately like those easy peasy Japanesey paper swans. Fold and fold and fold. Watching her tear off just the right amount of Scotch tape, he could picture her wearing a jeweler's loupe around her neck like some Hebrew pawnbroker.

DO NOT SHAKE OR RATTLE

My ass, he thought, and gave it a good shake.

He heard a solid *CLICK!* and the sound was so familiar he might have been able to place it if the gift hadn't erupted in hand, bits of Grace's delicate wrapping paper burning to ash as shards of superheated metal threw him back into his ratty old chair, where he smoldered.

GRACE HEARD THE explosion from Diane's kitchen, two blocks south and one block east, where she sat drinking cold Baby Duck with her little sister. The antique land mine she'd purchased from the back of a van filled with an array of assault weapons, handguns and antiques, had worked as Buddy had promised. She would stay in Diane's spare bedroom until the crime scene folks finished cleaning bits of Donald off the living room furniture and walls. The house would require some repairs, of course. But with Donald's life insurance, the home insurance, she thought she'd make out just fine. And she would tell the police it was an antique. She would caterwaul. She would play the fragile housewife, the dotty senior citizen, the way she had for Donald.

"What was that?" Diane wondered. She placed the bottle of chilled sparkling wine—*So bubbly!*—on the table to go to the window. In her absence, Grace topped up her glass, then raised it in a mock cheer. After 46 years, she was finally free. No more bitter looks. No more complaining about her cooking, or his leg, or the government, immigrants, her sister, the "spoiled" grandkids, and all his ignorant racial stereotyping. This was a new world, and Grace wanted to be a part of it. There was no room for miserable old men like Donald.

"You get what you pay for, Donnie," she muttered, and downed the glass.

"Beg pardon?" Diane asked, still looking out the window.

"I said 'Merry Christmas.'"

Diane smiled, much too drunk. "Merry Christmas," she agreed.

STRAY

MAX AWOKE FROM an uncomfortable dream, vaguely aware of a wet, prickly thing sliming the palm of his left hand. He tore the hand away, shrinking back against the seat, clutching the duffel bag handle in his right.

A dog—a husky or malamute, Max couldn't tell which, and the breed didn't matter so much as the fact of its presence here at all—looked up at him with sad ice-blue eyes, peeling its lips back in a yawn or a snarl. Max couldn't decide which, and again, didn't care.

Looking up and down the car, hoping to find its owner, he found no one. The dog was on its own. *Max was alone with it.*

"Go on," he said, anxious. "Get out of here."

The animal didn't move, only panted, staring.

"Get lost!"

The dog whimpered, shrinking back, then sat on its haunches in front of the doors with a jingle—a sound signifying ownership, though Max saw no collar around its thick neck. Instead, a small loop of bathtub chain and silvery tags peeked out from its fur, reminiscent of another kind of dog tag. Its big pink tongue came out to lick its chops, as it eyeballed him with that *I-know-something* look.

Could it smell the rising fear in his sweat? Could it hear the increase in his heartbeat?

What was it doing on the train, anyway? Was it a stray?

Max had read an article once about abandoned dogs in Moscow that had learned to take the Metro into the city. Street dogs worked in packs there, using the smallest and cutest to beg for food and share amongst them. They stood behind people and barked, startling feckless humans into dropping their food so the dogs could eat it from the ground. The pack leaders were not the biggest and strongest, as in other species, but the *smartest*. The dogs with the most cunning.

What had occurred to Max from reading the article (and further research, including several videos) was that dogs, as a species, were growing smarter. But were they *evolving*, he'd wondered, or was it just a natural response to their environment, a "societal" change? Being a History major, Max wasn't scientifically inclined enough to say one way or the other, but history told him to be wary. And it was history—History *class*, in fact—that had put him on the train so early this morning, long before the other commuters. He'd needed to get to school before his fellow teachers, before Principal Anders, and before Don McTavish, the security officer. The janitors, who arrived early, would let him in without trouble, but Anders and the others would wonder what he was doing at school, and what exactly he had in his duffel bag.

"... CLAUBERG TOLD THE women he'd artificially inseminated them with animal sperm, and while it's unclear whether this is true or not, it's yet another example of the Nazis employing torture under the guise of scientific advancement."

Silence drew out in the small classroom. A few students fiddled with their cell phones, one or two girls twisted their hair around pencils or chewed it. Others doodled. The kids in the front row wore looks of disgust, which had been his intent. He'd wanted to shock them out of their apathy. What he hadn't known at the time was that this lesson would get him a six-week suspension. The school board would go on to cite some of his extra-curricular activities as being "red flags," in particular the small bit of enjoyment he got from playing General Custer in the Battle of Little Bighorn reenactments. They had wondered why he would "celebrate" such an atrocious period in America's history, acting as if he flew the Confederate flag and wore white sheets in the night. Even his brief tour of duty in the Iraq Conflict had raised suspicions at West Brinkley High. The fact that his left arm was barely functional due to shrapnel from an IED had been the subject of much speculation during his three years teaching History to students who for the most part couldn't remember beyond their last keg party.

One of the football players in the back shot up his hand. Max held his right hand palm-up toward him, as Principal Anders had deemed pointing "too confrontational."

"Yes, Michael."

"So, like, all that stuff happened a long time ago?"

"During the Second World War," Max said, nodding genially, though he suspected Michael had something tricky up his sleeve.

"So, like, I mean, why should I care about what happened before I was *born*?"

A handful of others nodded, muttering their agreement.

"Well, Michael, a wise person once wrote, 'Those who cannot remember the past are condemned to repeat it.'"

"And was that wise man you, Mr. Ellis?" Michael inquired with a shrewd smirk, garnering a few chuckles.

"No, Michael, it was George Santayana." He smiled as Michael's grin faded. "So what do you think it means?"

"Huh?"

"The phrase, Michael. Let me put it another way. When Churchill misquoted it, he said, 'Those who fail to learn from history are doomed to repeat it.' What do you think that means?"

Michael stared blankly for a moment, his mouth

hung open, his shaggy hair hanging in his face. "Like… you're gonna fail me if I can't answer the question?"

"No, Michael. You'll fail *life*. History is the most important subject."

"Not for me. I'm gonna go pro." Michael flashed his straight white teeth. "Gotta get *paid*," he said, and held his hand out so his friends could slap it.

"I'm going to be an entrepreneur," a girl in one of the middle seats said. "Why do I need to know all this gross stuff?"

Emphatic agreement met this. Even the burnouts perked up to join in.

These kids don't want to be teachers, or thinkers, or cure disease, Max despaired. *They all want to be Kardashians.*

"If you don't know this 'gross stuff,' you won't see the signs of it happening again under your nose, Larissa. Just as it's our responsibility to leave the environment in a good state for our children's children, we're also responsible for the state of *society*. We have to be wary, and *speak up* against what we feel is wrong, no matter the consequences. And when they come to silence you, when they force you into the shadows, remember what Edmund Burke said… 'The only thing necessary for the triumph of evil is for good men to do nothing.'"

This drew blank looks from almost half the class. The others appeared to ruminate on it, even the class entrepreneur, even a few of the burnouts.

Perhaps there's hope for the world after all, Max thought.

But someone had reported the lesson to their parents, and the parents had informed Principal Anders. Within a week, Max was out on his ass, his pleas for sanity unanswered. And during those first few weeks sitting alone in his apartment, pondering his place in the world, he wondered if he'd been wrong about there being any hope at all.

He began to think about the contents of his duffel bag.

HE'D PLANNED IT all out so carefully in the following weeks, allowing for several possible contingencies. Not even the greatest military strategists—Carl von Clausewitz, Hannibal Barca, Julian Corbett—could have foreseen the dog.

Max watched as the it splayed its legs and began licking its genitals, dispelling any myth of higher intelligence.

How many times did it do that before licking my hand? he wondered, letting himself relax against the seat back. Releasing the handle of his duffel bag from his white-knuckle grip, the zipper tab clinked against its metallic teeth. It was a comforting sound, like the tinkle of wind chimes he remembered from summer nights at his parents' farmhouse when he was a kid, drinking lemonade on the porch after a long day's work as cicadas droned in the fields.

The doors opened with a discordant chime,

sounding like an elevator arriving at the basement of Hell. A woman in a sharp business suit made to enter, looking up from her Blackberry just in time to see the dog. She leaped back, startled, then composed herself and scowled at Max, as if he owned the dog. When the doors closed, she was still glowering at him.

In the blink of an eye, the dog darted forward and bit his hand.

Pain splintered up Max's arm in hot waves. Crying out in surprise, he grasped his hand at the wrist, blood oozing from the jagged gash along the second and third knuckles, splashing against his work boots. Slashes of brilliant white bone peeked through the wounds on his numbing fingers. As he clenched his hand into a fist, tendons pulled taut in the exposed meat.

"Bit me!" he bellowed, incredulous. "You *bit* me!"

The dog reared back and bared its teeth, pink with blood. Max tucked into a quick roll as the dog charged again, slamming its full weight against the seatback he'd vacated. It staggered back, legs spread out to stop itself from slip 'n sliding across the slick tiles, then shook its head vigorously, spittle flying from its lips.

Max yanked the duffel bag off the seat and pulled it to his chest, using it as a shield as the dog attacked again, its powerful jaws tearing off a ragged swatch of oiled canvas.

With his left hand, Max tore at the zipper, shooting pain up his muscles from his old combat injury. The zipper slid easily partway, then caught. Momentarily fazed, he watched the dog spit out the grimy fabric, hacking at the taste. Grinning, Max reached into the bag and rummaged with his left hand. Pushing aside the Colt 1911—he'd trained himself to know each weapon by feel and weight, even with the backs of his fingers—he found the FN Five-SeveN easily, the same weapon used by Mexican drug cartels and the Fort Hood shooter. He jerked it free with a quick draw that would have made Cherokee Bill proud.

The dog registered almost human surprise as Max racked back the slide with the wrist of his injured hand, the hand itself still oozing crimson, and aimed with his left.

The dog bounded at him, snarling.

A deafening report filled in the cramped car. The Five-SeveN fired as smooth as—well, there really were no comparisons, in Max's mind, and if he'd done the firing with his right hand, it would have hit its mark. Instead, the bullet struck one of the safety glass windows and blew it outward. Hot morning wind blasted in, the sound of the elevated tracks clickety-clacking suddenly as loud as the gunshot.

The dog startled. Max fired a second shot, striking the dog in the leg, flipping the feral beast back with an arcing sprinkler spray of blood, Technicolor red under florescent lights. It rolled and slid all the way to the doors, where it slumped, eyes closed, bleeding on the shiny tiles.

Max stayed put, pressed against the seat, using the duffel in his lap to keep his aim steady. He wasn't stupid enough to think the thing was dead, to fall for that horror movie trick. Nor was he about to get up and check, like a kid approaching a firecracker that had fizzled out just before the explosion.

The dog shook its head, the chain around its muscular neck jingling. It lurched to its feet, eyeing him with its head lowered, and moved shakily toward him. A flap of grisly meat hung from its left hind leg, though the shot had merely grazed the flesh.

Max pulled the trigger, the kill shot, but the train began its herky-jerky entrance to the station and the small-caliber hollow-point went wild, carving a fist-sized hole in the ceiling that whistled as the train slowed to a jerky stop.

His right hand was scorched earth, the crotch of his jeans and the front of his plaid shirt black and gleaming with his blood. He could *smell* it, that acrid copper smell, and if *he* could smell his own blood, chances were pretty high the dog could, too.

Gravy Train makes real meat gravy, he thought humorlessly as the train stopped.

The shrill, unmusical chime stabbed his throbbing skull, and with the pain came a difficult decision. He could stay and fight, hoping he had it in him to go hand-to-teeth should the situation take a drastic turn—if the wounded dog managed to somehow gain the upper paw, ha ha so funny. Or...

he could get off this Helltrain right this fucking second.

A man has to choose his own path, someone who'd never made the history books once told him. *Courage comes not from following the path others have chosen for you, but by* straying *from it.*

Max hauled the bag into his arms and as the doors began to close, he heeded the advice of his father, a Montana wheat farmer, by bolting off the train into the empty station.

A sound somewhere between a bark and a snarl told him the blood-crazed dog had followed.

The doors shut. The train began to move. No chance to turn back.

Max considered jumping down onto the tracks, but he couldn't count on the dog not following him down there. And he worried about that third rail. The knowledge of it might give him the upper hand, but even if he was able to shove the dog onto the electrified rail, he didn't know enough about electric current to be sure he wouldn't fry along with it.

Running for the stairs with the sluggishness of a nightmare, the duffel bag weighed him down. If he tossed it, everything went with it. All of his planning. All of his goals.

He chanced a look back, saw the dog slobbering at his heels, and heaved the duffel at it. The mutt yelped and skittered off toward the edge of the platform—

A breadcrumb trail of blood led from where he'd

gotten off the train to the place he now stood, watching for a hopeful moment as the dog skittered and slid on the smooth tile. But the stubborn mutt struggled to its feet, undoing his attempt to make headway by throwing the bag in the first place. Now he was short a dozen magazines, the Colt 1911, a change of clothes—he would need it now, drenched as he was in his own blood—and he'd barely gotten a foot ahead.

Blasting off a few blind shots over his shoulder, he shortened the distance between himself and the stairs. Granite tile burst behind him in jagged gray clouds. The escalator stood not twenty feet ahead—blocked by a cage, CLOSED FOR REPAIRS. The stairs led down beside it. With a sudden burst of energy, like the last headlong rush to the toilet of the man who could hold it no longer, Max bolted ahead. He reached the stairs and bounded down two at a time. He hit the floor running in a bone-jarring crouch, saw the entrance, saw the fare collector sitting in his booth. Max got to his feet and waved his arms, running at full-speed.

"Help! *HELP!*"

But the man was asleep. *Oh, that's great! Hope you're having pleasant dreams, you asshole,* Max thought as his lungs grew tight and his muscles cramped. He dared a look over his shoulder, saw the dog still descending the stairs, squatting and moving down one step at a time, squatting and moving down, a look of fixed concentration in its wild blue eyes, its tongue lolled to one side.

"Ha!" Max cried ecstatically. "Ha-ha!"

Running for the turnstiles with renewed confidence, he smelled fresh air beyond them, summer rain and freedom just up the other set of stairs. Moist dirt and damp concrete. The sun would be up soon. All the little kiddies getting ready for school…

Behind him, all four of the dog's paws clacked down on the tiles. It had conquered the stairs, and now it would run full-bore toward him, treating the seat of his pants like a greyhound's rabbit.

Max used his gun hand to leap the turnstile.

"Hey! Hey, sir!"

Now the guy woke up. And he was concerned about the fare.

Max wanted to shout back at him, *Open your eyes, pal!* But he was short on breath and shorter on time. The dog skirted under the turnstile like a Marine under barbed wire, and now it was chasing, chasing, slobber dribbling back from its mouth, its fur rippling, and soon it would catch up to him...

"Hey, bud—" the fare collector said, then: "*Jesus!*" Max wasn't sure if the exclamation was about the bloodthirsty dog or the gun.

With a snarl, the dog bit into his Achilles tendon.

Max fell back, crying out in anguished surprise. He felt the flesh tear all the way up to the back of his knee, heard it tear like Velcro, yanking him back as the dog shook its monstrous jaws. His right foot slid forward on the newly buffed floor and the flesh tore free, like ripping off the world's largest Band-Aid, every nerve bursting, *pop-pop-popping* on his pain receptors, white-hot flecks of agony dancing in front of his eyes. The gun slipped from his grip and flew, clattering near the stairs to the outside, to freedom, and he lost his balance, arms pin-wheeling as he fell backward, slumping over the startled mutt.

The slashes on his hand had burst open, spraying fresh blood, and the back of his shin had been bitten entirely off, the torn scrap of flesh and tendon a joke-shop splat on the floor by the dog's hind paws.

The fare collector was on the phone. Max kicked the dog in the ribs with the boot heel of his uninjured right foot. It skittered back with a gurgling howl, teeth pink with his blood. Max pushed up onto his butt as the dog got to its feet and whipped around to snarl at him.

He snarled back, baring bloodied teeth of his own.

Max slipped the knife from his boot. The dog backpedaled, arching its back and lowering its head, watching as Max swished the blade back and forth, cutting the air, following the knife edge like a piece of meat.

Max darted forward with the Grohmann in hand. Its blade parted the fur on the dog's flank, slashing the grayish flesh beneath, finishing its arc bloodied.

The dog howled.

"Sir, the police have been called," came the fare

collector's jerky voice over the loudspeaker.

"Fuck the police, call Huckleberry Hound!" Max shouted back with a crazed laugh. He turned back to the dog just in time to see its tartar-stained teeth clamp down on his face. They tore through his left eyebrow and eyelid, pressing like sharpened vice grips against the eyeball itself. Max's nostrils filled with the smell of dog breath, his entire face clamped between the dog's strong jaws, and he screamed into the wet, ridged cavern of a mouth as the dog jerked his head back and forth in its teeth, the straining in his neck muscles less worrying now than the sound like a popped cork—virtually painless—and the trail of something cold slime oozing down the cheek below his obliterated eye.

Reaching up, he grasped through tufts of fur for the dog's throat and clamped his fingers around its esophagus. The dog reared back suddenly, pulling its fangs from his flesh with a sucking sound and a metallic snap. Max fell onto his back, gouts of blood splashing the faux granite tiles. He lay there stunned, gasping for breath as the torn shreds of his lips spilled over with his own blood. Alongside him, the dog had fallen, its face covered in his blood, its chest rose and fell slowly, as if it was unconscious.

Vaguely, he felt a cold hard shape in the palm of his left hand. He opened it to find the broken bathtub chain, looped through a military dog tag. Blinking away blood from his eyes, Max strained to turn his head and read it.

His bleeding lips opened wide in a laugh.

The dog's name was Custer.

Max laughed until the paramedics arrived to cart him away.

00:302;00

HE IS RISEN

FERTILE GREEN FIELDS rattled by the dirty window. Madison still hadn't gotten used to looking left out the passenger side as opposed to right. Thankfully, Colin had taken to seating himself on the right side of the car to drive quite quickly.

"Easy peasy lemon squeezy," he'd said as he downshifted with his left hand. They'd been in the English countryside a couple of days by then, sleeping overnight at quaint B&Bs, and Colin had already believed he'd picked up the lingo. Madison was sure the locals thought he was bananas, this silver-haired Canadian asking for a "cuppa" and "biscuits," but she supposed she should at least count herself lucky he hadn't started imitating the accent—*yet.*

The weather channel had called for rain this afternoon, but the sky had been blue since they'd arrived at Heathrow on Tuesday. Odd weather for April, the weatherman had mentioned, particularly considering the great dump of rain that had hammered most of the northern hemisphere during the winter. Madison was grateful for the respite. Rain depressed her, and the snow and "greige" in Toronto still hadn't let up by the time they'd left the city. When Colin suggested they travel up the Irish Sea coast to a fellow professor's country home near the Scottish border during break, she'd been leery, but anxious to spend some time with him off-campus. They'd only been dating since the beginning of first semester, and she thought this time together—away from the pressures of school and the prying eyes of the few students who knew of their pairing and found it questionable, Madison being Colin's T.A. (as opposed to his *T and A*, an insult she'd heard from several students)—just might push their relationship to the next level.

The weather had been a nice surprise. The sea air was crisp, but the sun felt good on her pale face. Colin was smiling at the road ahead, the small hatchback rumbling along a single lane of macadam carved out of the green as he slapped the wheel to an old Clash song on the radio.

"Hey, check it out," he said, his smile fading.

Madison followed his gaze. Among the green three—or was it *four*?—sharp gray stones jutted up from the earth like ancient claws. "Stonehenge?" she asked him.

Colin shook his head. "We're nowhere near there. The 'Henge is south of where we started. They've got standing stones all over the countryside out here, though. Nobody knows who left them, or why."

"*Nobody* knows?"

Colin gave her a curious look. "Well, I'm sure *somebody* knows. Spinal Tap, maybe."

He grinned at her, awaiting her reaction. Not getting the reference, Madison narrowed her eyes at him. The gap in their ages often showed itself in little things like this. She told her friends age didn't matter, and usually she tried not to let it get to her, but the more these differences piled on the more she felt the gap grow wider, until someday it would yawn like the mouth of a canyon, and one or both of them would stumble in reeling.

"Speaking of hard things..." Madison reached over with a grin and squeezed the crotch of his jeans. She felt for his cock, and began to massage it to life. Colin gave her an odd look. He took her hand, squeezed her cold fingers a moment, and placed it on her lap.

"Not while I'm driving, luv," he said.

Madison looked left out the window as they passed the standing stones, sulking for several minutes, as "London Calling" gave way to "A Whiter Shade of Pale," and the gray slabs of rock disappeared in the mirror. Colin began to whistle along to the organ. Though Madison liked many modern artists, and he enjoyed a fair bit of jazz—a genre completely lost on her—a love of classic rock was something they both shared. She turned to him and smiled, his shaggy silver hair riffling in the breeze from his window, open a crack.

A road sign caught her eye then, written in an

incomprehensible jumble of black letters she supposed must be Welsh or Gaelic:

DRWS MARWOLAETH

"Is that the name of a town?"

Colin squinted at the sign as they passed. "That, or one of the Elder Gods." He grinned at her and once again, the reference flew over her head.

Moments later, the town rose out of the fields. First there was nothing but green, and then pitched rooftops with smoking chimneys became visible, and windows bright with sunlight, and proper roads zigzagging, where people strolled cheerily and cars drove slowly, all seemingly moving toward the same place, the northern—if her directions were correct— end of town.

Colin followed the flow of traffic—not that he could have done otherwise even if they hadn't already been heading in that direction. Men and women walked hand-in-hand. Children scurried ahead, dressed in their Sunday best, some holding bunches of yellow flowers. Store owners flipped signs to CLOSED in the windows of stone shops, put on their caps and joined their fellow citizens marching down the main thoroughfare.

"It's Easter," Madison realized.

"Oh, right," Colin said, peering around edgily like a man in a shark cage. "Well, I guess that tells us where they're all heading."

A little girl wearing a pink bonnet waved at Madison, who smiled and waved back. The girl blew into a homemade pinwheel, making it spin. "What a friendly little town," Madison thought aloud.

"Too friendly, if you ask me."

"Why do you always have to be so suspicious of everything?"

"Comes with the territory," he said, grinning at her, and she managed to get that one: he'd meant because he was a philosophy professor. "You're a Catholic girl, aren't you? When's the last time you went to mass?"

"I'm a C & E Catholic." Colin raised an eyebrow at her. She grinned, having stumped him for once. "Christmas and Easter," she explained. "I totally forgot this year. Usually I'm at home over Easter, and my parents would take us."

"Doesn't say much for your devotion to the faith."

Madison scowled at him. Colin had often teased her about her religion. She'd never been devout, and didn't mind his jabs so much in the abstract, but in the midst of so many seemingly dedicated worshippers headed joyfully toward church, it irked her, felt somehow *profane.*

"How about we have a look at how Easter is celebrated in the picturesque town of Derwiss Marwo... *whatever?*"

"You just want to go so you can poke fun."

"No," he laughed. "I'm serious. I am honestly interested, Madison." Colin bit down a wicked smile, crossing his index and middle fingers. "Scout's honor."

Madison chuckled. "Who even says that anymore?"

Smirking out the window, Colin honked the horn, startling an old woman before waving innocently at her as she scowled down at him from under her frilly purple Derby.

"*Colin*," Madison scolded, grabbing him by the shoulder and swatting his leg.

"Just trying to get to get the giggles out before we enter the Holy Place."

"If you laugh in that church, you won't be seeing *my* Holy Place the rest of the trip."

Colin laughed. "That's what I love about you. You're not afraid to blackmail me with sex."

Madison's smile never faltered, though neither of them had ever spoken of love before, and she wasn't sure she felt it herself. She took a moment to ponder it, and by the time she'd settled on a response, Colin had already shifted focus to the massive church up the hill.

Hewn out of stone, like most of the edifices in town, the Gothic church towered over all that stood beneath it, casting its long shadow down the lush green hillside. The churches they'd seen here had dust older than most surviving parishes in Toronto, where few buildings predated the mid- to late-1800s. The sense of history in a place like this, of *life*, was far richer than in much of the Commonwealth.

00:308;00

Families left cars parked along the long gravel drive and in muddy tracks carved into the grass like at a rock concert, and ascended the rest of the way on foot. Colin pulled over into a tight space on the grass, muttering, "When in Rome," and the two of them climbed out together under the church's cool, dark shadow.

"Are you sure about this?"

"It's Easter," Colin said. "I'm sure God wouldn't approve of one of His children missing the day His only begotten Son rose from the dead," he added, rolling the *R* in *rose*.

"Don't start with the accents," she muttered, peering around to see if any of the townsfolk had heard him. "*Please.*"

"I shall make no promises," Colin said in passible posh English.

Madison elbowed him in the ribs, and he slipped his arm around hers. As she leaned into his shoulder, they caught up with the group.

"Welcome, welcome," a hunched elderly man with a shiny liver-spotted pate wheezed, his green jacket emblazoned with various medals.

"Did you see that?" Colin asked in hushed awe as they left him shuffling slowly behind them. "The two crossed swords. He was wearing a medal from World War II"

"Is that weird?"

"Well, considering the last World War I veteran died in 2012 or so, I'd say it's a bit weird, innit?"

Madison removed her head from Colin's shoulder to study the faces of those around them, hoping no one had heard his Britishism. Everyone seemed focused on themselves or each other, wearing smiles as they trudged the gravel drive to church. A little boy in black short pants with a jacket and tie wound his way between moving legs, somehow managing to not get trampled as he hurried to the front of the line.

"Maybe it's his father's," Madison said, having lost the old man in the crowd.

Colin shrugged up his shoulders. "I suppose you're right."

Hard soles hoofed up the church stairs toward the arched doors, opened on a gloomy vestibule. The line seemed to take forever to progress, and as she and Colin rose the stairs themselves, she saw the priest or pastor shaking the hands of every adult as they entered, and greeting the children warmly. A sign at the front announced it to be The Church of St. Francis.

"Not too late to change your mind," Colin offered.

"You're the one that should be worried. Just don't touch the baptismal water, you'll probably get scalded."

Colin showed his white teeth in a grin.

As the husband and wife ahead of them shook the pastor's hand, the pastor caught Madison's eye and smiled.

"Welcome, welcome," the pastor—preacher?—

said with a slight Welsh lilt to his voice. Tall and broad, dressed entirely in black save for the white collar, his pale face stood out starkly from under black, slicked-back hair. He held out a long-fingered hand, and Colin took it. The man rested his other hand on Colin's shoulder, which Colin glanced at without expression. "Welcome to our little church and our little town."

"Little?" Colin remarked. "I'd hate to see the big one."

The religious man smiled patiently, then focused his attention on Madison.

"We do so enjoy visitors." The reverend took her hand, his palm oddly cold. "But we'd love for you to stay a spell. Our little town has plenty to offer."

"Thank you, Reverend," Madison said as he let go of her hand.

"'Jack' is just fine." His gaze drifted to the people behind them, and she and Colin moved ahead.

"He seems nice," Madison whispered as they entered the knave.

"*Everyone* seems nice," Colin said. "It's a little eerie."

"You're so cynical, Colin." They sat in an empty pew near the back, Madison craning her neck to get a look at the vaulted ceiling high above, painted with scowling angels and morose saints, as more townsfolk piled in and took their seats. Finally, Reverend Jack entered and strode to the front. He took his place behind the pulpit, and the crowd quieted.

"Easter is a celebration of the Risen Christ… these days, it's difficult for some to believe in the Resurrection, and even more difficult to believe that Jesus brought a common man back from the dead, a man named Lazarus."

Murmurs rippled through the gatherers. Some shook their heads. "Of course, we here in Drws Marwolaeth know it to be true, as true as the rest of the Good Book. Jesus spent several days and nights in the earth—it's never quite clear how many days and nights He spent in His tomb, and nor does it matter. What matters is, crucifixion on Good Friday," he held out his right hand, palm up, "risen on Easter Monday," and he did the same with his left. "Jesus died to absolve us of our sins, and He rose again to prove that only He who created life has the power to *bring it back*."

His parishioners nodded. Colin turned to Madison with a quizzical frown, as if being used to this sort of rhetoric she might know where the reverend was leading.

"Man has always aspired to be like Him. It was our own St. Francis of Assisi who said, 'I want to *know* Christ—to know the power of His resurrection and participate in His sufferings, *becoming like Him in His death*,'" Reverend Jack emphasized, gaze sweeping from right to left. "Of course, there will always be doubters. Thomas couldn't believe the other Apostles when they told him—"

Several pews closer to the front, the little girl Madison had seen in the street turned and slumped her elbows over the chair. She raised the pinwheel and blew into it, its spokes reflecting bright colors as it spun. Madison waved, but the girl's mother tugged on her daughter's sleeve, and the little girl slumped back in her seat.

"And now," the reverend went on, "I'd like to ask that you all go outside, and join me in clipping our fair church, in the hopes that the Good Lord will bestow upon our church, and our town, new life."

The parishioners rose. Colin peered skeptically around at them. "That's it?" He shrugged. "I guess that's it."

"What's 'clipping'?" Madison wondered.

"Never heard of it. Likely just some folk tradition they trot out to creep out the heathens. And what was all that about the 'power of resurrection'?"

"Christ's Resurrection is very important to the church," Madison said, the two of them remaining seated for the time being while the parishioners marched outside. "Easter's much more important than Christmas for Catholics."

"Are these people Catholics, you think?"

Madison shrugged. "If they are, it's very different from what I grew up with. No bells and smells. Not even a Eucharist."

"Ah yes, the Holy Cracker," Colin jibed, and Madison elbowed him again. "You'd better stop doing that to me, or it'll become a fetish," he said, and kissed her neck below the ear. A chill ran up her spine and she giggled.

The little girl with the pinwheel passed by then, holding her mother's hand, and the girl waved timidly as Madison wriggled out of Colin's embrace to twiddle her fingers, feeling slightly ashamed.

"We would be honored if you would join us for the clipping," Reverend Jack said as he approached their pew.

Madison and Colin rose to their feet respectfully. "We'd love to join you, Rev — Jack," Colin said. "What is clipping, exactly?"

A smile flashed across the reverend's pale face. "Come and see." He ushered them into the aisle with an open palm. "We won't bite, I assure you."

Madison stepped out. Colin followed behind her, and the reverend led the two of them out into the gloomy vestibule.

"We use Easter as a time to reflect on our own mortality," Reverend Jack was saying. "And also to encourage a *renewal* of life. You've likely noticed there are many lovely young children in Drws Marwolaeth, but our hope is always for more children, to carry on our way a life." He smiled over his shoulder as they stepped out into the sunshine. "If I may be so bold, do you plan to have children?"

Madison and Colin shared a brief look, shielding the sun from their eyes. "We haven't discussed it yet, Jack," she said.

"I see. Well, plenty of time, I suppose. Time." He

smiled, seeming to reflect. "This is a very old town. Our traditions predate that of many communities in the North West. We're one of the only towns to continue the practice of clipping, a very old tradition—and certainly the only church to do it on Easter Monday, in honor of our namesake. Clipping derives from the Old English word *clyppan*, you see, which roughly translated means embrace, or circle."

He directed their attention to the townsfolk who had gathered outside, not in a group but in a line, each holding the hand of those on either side of them as the queue began to stretch around the church. It reminded Madison of "Ring Around the Rosie," and the image troubled her somewhat as she recalled a time where she'd played the game with her friends, and when they all fell *down*, the other girls had pretended to be dead. She'd gone around shaking them, trying to wake them up, but nobody moved or spoke until Loren Ainsley broke into giggles and the rest of them rose around her in a chorus of damning laughter.

"What we do," the reverend said, "as you see now, is we all join hands and circle the church. Once we've all linked hands and the circle is unbroken, we round the church once clockwise, and once anticlockwise. There must always be enough of us to completely encircle the church, otherwise the point is lost."

"And what *is* the point?" Colin asked.

The reverend squinted at him. "Like many rituals, its intended purpose has been lost to time. However, we like to believe it protects us, and protects our way of life. There's something to be said for a bit of mystery though, no?"

"Some might say it's the spice of life," Colin agreed, and slipped his arm around Madison's.

A woman approached the reverend, holding out something slate gray and globular. As Jack took it, Madison saw it was a rabbit mask, though it was far cry from the Easter Bunny, so devoid of cutesy as to be sinister. The reverend placed the mask on his head, tugged the strap behind it and turned to them, only his clear blue eyes and mouth visible. "For the benefit of the children," he explained, shrugging up his broad shoulders.

Reverend Jack the Bunny trotted down the stairs, chasing behind a few straggling boys and girls, who scurried to meet the end of the line. "Run!" he cried, laughing heartily. "Run, little children! We mustn't dally or the Easter Hare shan't leave his eggs!"

Colin turned to her. "Well, what do you think?"

Madison shrugged. "It's bizarre. But it's kind of sweet."

Colin embraced her and kissed her temple. She hugged him back, then started down the stairs to catch up to the others as the head of the line emerged around the other side of the church. Colin took the hand of a young dark-haired woman with high Irish cheekbones at the end of the clipping circle, and Madison took the hand left over. The old veteran took her free hand, smiling warmly at her from what had been the head of the line as they continued their stroll. Jealousy tweaked at Madison's nerves as the fair-skinned woman smiled back at Colin, but she trusted him. He could sleep with just about any woman in school, and he'd chosen her. If he'd been in the mood to sleep around, he'd have suggested it by now, and he certainly wouldn't have dragged her all the way out to the other side of the pond to do it.

She let the cheerful townsfolk merry-go-round her to the side of the church, where the crumbled, mossy gray stones of an old graveyard became visible on a green hill, the flat gray sea beyond it. Madison looked up at the steeple and bell tower, meeting the googly eyes of a gargoyle made to look like a monkey sticking out its tongue. Ahead of Colin and the dark-haired seductress, the pinwheel spun in the girl's limp pale hand as the wind took it, the girl herself hidden behind trudging legs.

Reverend Jack the Rabbit sprung from a doorway, throwing up his hands, and several people screamed, including the dark-haired woman, who smiled embarrassedly over her shoulder at Colin. They all laughed when the reverend raised the mask, and he smiled down on Madison as she passed.

"I hope we don't ruddy go 'round for very much longer," the old veteran said to Madison as they marched around the back of the church.

Madison smiled politely. She considered asking him about the medal Colin had pointed out earlier, but a woman's voice called out, "Now, round and round anticlockwise!" It took a bit of fumbling, laughter and apologies for people to get themselves turned around and traveling in the other direction. They passed the doorway where the reverend had jumped out and scared them, and for a moment, she felt Colin's hand slip from hers before snatching it again.

"Do you have the time?" the old man asked over his shoulder.

Madison twisted the hand he held to look at her watch. "It's quarter to two."

"Quarter of two, already? *Cor*, I'll need my kip in an hour!"

Madison didn't know what a "kip" was, but she smiled in sympathy. Colin's cold fingers grasped hers tighter, and she turned to smile back at him, startling when she saw a freckled young man with thick, dark eyebrows held her hand instead of Colin. "Where's my boyfriend?" The young man scowled at her. She called out Colin's name, prying her hand loose from the young man's, who held tight. "Have you seen my… my boyfriend?"

The young man continued forward, shoving her brusquely out of the way. Men and women gawked at her, suddenly not so friendly. The fields were empty. Gray clouds scudded across the sky. "Colin!" she cried, hurrying along in the other direction, disoriented by the blur of townsfolk trudging forward. "*COLIN!*"

The little girl's pinwheel stood alone in the grass,

spinning in the wind. A simian-like gargoyle stood on its perch displaying its genitals, mocking her.

Madison stopped running when she reached the doorway, a part of her already certain Colin had slipped off with the dark-haired woman into some dark corner of the church. Everyone was out here, mindlessly circling. Inside, they would have privacy. She had to get in. The queue kept moving forward, blank stares meeting her frightened eyes, no one kind enough to break the circle and let her through.

"Excuse me!" The townsfolk gave her bewildered looks. "Get out of my way!" she shouted, ducking to squeak in under the arms of an elderly couple, pulling their hands apart and temporarily breaking the circle. She stood in the alcove where the reverend had hidden, hugging the door in bewildered terror as the glowering eyes of the crowd still circled.

Nervous to turn her back on them, Madison kept an eye on the clipping circle and tried the doors. She spilled into a small dark vestibule as they opened. She closed them behind her, cold eyes peering in at her as the doors came together.

"*Colin!*" Her own voice echoed in reply. Madison pressed her palms against her eyes, adjusting them to the darkness. The small, round chamber contained a door and a winding set of stone stairs. She tried the door, found it locked. Upstairs then, or back outside with the insane people and their poor, oblivious little children.

Madison called out his name once more on the

stairs. The damp walls were cold to the touch, but the height made her nervous. She felt her way up to the top, where another door muffled voices in whatever room lay beyond. She pressed her ear against it, not ready to get caught by surprise, worried she might die if she saw Colin with another woman. Difficult to identify the sounds beyond the door: moaning or talking or some kind of rhythmic chanting.

Only one way to find out, she thought, and twisted the knob.

She saw Reverend Jack Rabbit first, standing at the far end of the bell tower, reading from a book he held out in one long-fingered hand. Candles burned and smoldered from crevasses in the walls. Below the old brass bell, Colin lay shirtless on a stone slab. The dark-haired woman lifted his head by his beautiful silver hair and before Madison could raise her voice in alarm, she dragged a curved blade across his throat.

The blood came in gouts, splashing the dark-haired woman's coat and showering Colin's chest as his tongue wriggled in strangled chokes, his warm brown eyes locked on Madison. She stumbled back, reaching out to grab hold of the arch, only vaguely aware of the steep drop behind her. Cold hands snatched her from behind and forced her roughly into the room.

The reverend pulled up his mask with a grin. "Ah… you've arrived just in time, my dear child, to bear witness to the conclusion of the ritual."

00:320;00

Madison struggled against the hands. "Let me go! *What the fuck is wrong with you people?*"

"Wrong?" He closed the book. "There is nothing *wrong* with us, dear. You see, this town is quite old and so are we. A handful of us are older than this church, aren't we, Carwen?"

Carwen, the dark-haired woman, winked and smiled, allowing Colin's head to strike the stone while his gurgling abruptly ceased. As the reverend crossed to Madison, Carwen unbuttoned her long red coat, revealing her pale, freckled body, small breasts with puffy, perky nipples, a triangle of dark hair in the crease below her jutting hipbones.

"What's she doing?" Madison wanted to know.

"Never mind her. Listen to me, my dear. If we're to prosper, this town needs children. You could live with us, the two of you."

Behind him, Carwen unzipped Colin's jeans and jerked them and his white briefs down to his knees. Colin's penis, slightly crooked in its thatch of salt-and-pepper pubic hair, sagged over his tightened balls while his lifeblood trickled down the slab to the cold stone floor, and his dead eyes stared vacantly at the interior of the bell above his head.

"You ki— you *killed* him…" Madison wept as the reality of it sunk in. "*You killed my Colin!*"

"Ah yes, but the power of resurrection!" Reverend Jack said. "St. Francis was right… it is possible to know the power of resurrection! To become like Him in death. He will *rise again,* my dear. We have *all* risen again."

"This is insane!" She struggled against the cold hands, hot tears streaming down her face. *"You're insane!"*

The reverend unbuttoned and removed his collar, revealing a jagged pink scar across his throat. "Do not doubt me, Thomas," he said to her calmly. He nodded to whomever still held her tight. "Show her."

The hands let her go, and she twisted round, face to face with the young man with thick eyebrows. He pulled up his shirt and she turned away, not wanting to see.

"Look at him, dear."

She didn't want to look, but the reverend wore the rabbit mask again, and Carwen had straddled Colin's body, crouching over his hips and thrusting herself back and forth on his limp cock, now glistening with her juices. She'd always thought she would die if she saw Colin with another woman, but here she was still alive and Colin dead. Reluctantly, Madison turned. The young man smiled at her, fingering a large open wound like a fish gill under his ribs.

"The same wound Pontius Pilate gave to Jesus," Reverend Jack said. "Do you still doubt?"

Madison shuddered. "What is this...?" she managed to groan.

"We need more children," the reverend told her. "Only the dead can impregnate the dead."

"But... but he's..." She turned to her lover, tears

filling her eyes, causing her vision to blur. She blinked them away, startling as Colin's prick began to stiffen, rising like a snake from the bushes. Carwen grasped it and slipped it into her dark, wet tomb.

"He is risen," the reverend said with a pleased smile, and as Colin's bloodied hands rose from the stone slab to grasp the woman's buttocks, Madison fainted dead away.

SQUIRM

THE SUN WAKES me, the sound of sparrows outside the open window. A summer breeze blows in, cooling the sweat on my bare skin where I've kicked off the sheet during the night.

I find it difficult to sleep in the summer. The heat makes me uncomfortable in my own skin. Erratic breeze from the fan startles me awake as it blows past, fluttering my hair in my face. Noises outside rouse me too easily with the window open: raccoons rattling garbage cans, distant sirens, drunken partiers. I've always been a light sleeper, but so much more so since the children came. Bill could sleep through the Apocalypse…

I lie there for half an hour, just listening to him breathe and watching the birds outside our window. I've always envied his ability to turn off his brain and recharge for eight hours a night. The boys don't wake him, creaking their way down the hall to pee or get a drink of water. When they were babies, it was always me who would wake first to shake Bill awake for his turn to change them or shush them back to sleep. Even now, I'd be lucky to get a few hours uninterrupted before my brain started circling around things that didn't bear thinking about so late at night.

I roll over to watch Bill sleep. In the dead of night, I may begrudge him, but watching him like this in the morning makes me smile. I think of how lucky I am to have such a perfect family, a perfect *life*, and the thought makes my heart swell with joy, bringing me close to tears. Few better ways to start the day.

The alarm clock on his side of the bed tells me it's still too early yet to wake him. I consider creeping out of bed and heading downstairs to read a little of my book, but a tiny twitch in Bill's cheek concerns me — something like a facial tic. I've never seen him do that before. He usually sleeps so peacefully, never shifting, eyelids barely fluttering, just lying there on his back like a man in his grave. The tic is something different. I don't do well with different.

He rouses a moment later to find me watching him. His lips upturn in a smile as he takes in a deep breath of morning air through his nose. "Mmm morning, honeybear."

"Morning," I say. He kisses my closed lips briefly, before I pull back, not wanting to give him a face full of morning breath.

Bill leans in again and kisses me deeper. Watching me. *Wanting* me. I let my lips part, despite my breath issues. I watch him as his eyes close, getting into it. I imagine him getting hard in his boxers, and the thought turns me on.

00:325;00

It's been weeks since we've had alone time (it's hard for me not to think of it as "Mommy-Daddy time," despite how fully it kills the mood), with the kids in bed, at their grandparents, or sleeping over at one of their friend's houses. I feel a deep urge to be with him, to have him inside me, his hands roaming over my skin. Then my mind starts circling. Stupid things. It's so hard for me to just be in the moment sometimes.

Should shower first. Brush my teeth. But then the kids will wake…

Bill's eyes open. A hand slips over my clavicle, down to my breast. All thoughts dissolve. His eyes follow the progress of his fingers, widening in hunger as the rough pad of his thumb circles my areola, bringing blood to the surface.

He blinks then, but his eyes don't close. He's too engrossed in his stroking, fingers tracing my freckles, the mole above my nipple. He blinks, but a translucent film closes over his eyes instead, shuttering over them from side to side, like an animal's, keeping them moist but wide open.

This is not my husband.

I tear my lips away from him, certain I must have imagined it. Pulling back in horror, I try to blink the image away, to look at him from a distance. To *study* him.

"What?" he whispers. "The kids won't be up for another half hour…"

Even if I knew what to say, I can't speak. It's

impossible. My lips won't form words.

Bill pouts like a little boy, his typical reaction when he feels scorned. No evidence of anything different in his eyes now. Of anything *other*. But I can't forget I'd seen it. The facial tic while he slept… had that been part of it? I'd been stressing myself out lately, looking for full-time work now that the boys were older, still doing my regular duties as a wife and mother. Trying to be the Supermom society expects of me. Compounded with the lack of good, solid sleep… is it possible I'd imagined it?

As I lie there considering how to reply, the boys come bursting into the room in their pajamas, all smiles, giving me the opportunity to separate from Bill without making it something to fight over.

"Mommydaddymommydaddymommydaddy!"

They leap onto the bed and climb in between us. Bill play-wrestles Dylan over his shoulder, making a monstrous growl. Dylan giggles uproariously, his laughter high-pitched, almost a squeal. Ryan climbs over Bill's legs and snuggles up between mine. Any other time I might have found the scene cute, but the image of Bill's eyes closing without closing has filled me with such confusion and dread I can't enjoy our morning routine like I normally would, his playful growl—the Mattress Monster, the kids call him—now vaguely sinister. Ryan crawls up my legs and cuddles into my lap, wrapping his little arms around my waist. He looks up at me with a wide smile.

"G'morning, Mommy," he says.

He sticks out his lower lip to blow shaggy brown hair out of his eyes, and translucent shutters close over them, just like his father's.

Ice cold fingers run up the nerves in my spine, despite the summer heat. I so desperately want to jump out of bed, to run screaming headlong down the hall and into the street, but then they'll know that I've seen them, that I know what they are. So I force myself to sit perfectly still, and it takes a concentrated effort of every nerve in my face to return the smile.

"Morning, honeybear," I say to the creature that used to be my youngest son.

NICTITATING—THAT'S WHAT it's called. Translucent membranes below the eyelids that protect the eyes and keep them moist. Birds have it, snakes have it. Some mammals. I spent most of the morning on the internet after dropping the kids off at school, looking it up, hoping it was possible for humans to have it. Some sort of vestigial thing. A holdover from our ancient ancestors.

After kissing Bill perfunctorily on the lips—with my eyes open to watch *his*—and whisking him out the door, I'd packed the boys' lunches into their backpacks and their backpacks over their shoulders, and hustled them off to the car. Driving behind the school bus with them sitting in the back seat, I found myself sneaking peeks in the rear view, worried they'd blink their membranes while I wasn't looking—or *worse*. I'd made sure they were buckled in tight, knowing I would hear the *click* if one or both of them decided to climb over the seat for a concerted attack while I had my hands on the wheel and couldn't defend myself without crashing the car.

I assured myself I was being crazy, a mantra I repeated in my head, one I hoped they couldn't somehow overhear. Thinking this, that they could possibly be able to hear my thoughts, I peered at them in the mirror again. Their brown eyes met mine instantly, as if they'd only been waiting for me to look. Their pale, gentle faces wore broad, innocent smiles. *Loving* smiles.

But when I looked away, I caught them turning their smiles on each other in my peripheral vision. And the smiles twisted into something menacing. *Knowing*. Their nictitating membranes flicked closed, and I swear I could almost hear a dry click, like a camera shutter.

It took all of my strength not to jerk the car into oncoming traffic.

I spent a lot of the day looking up postpartum psychosis, using terms like "delayed onset" and "late life" to narrow the search. Hoping desperately that what I'd seen was just a hallucination, something I could possibly suppress with pills or alcohol. I read that most sufferers experienced symptoms within the first six months after childbirth. Since Ryan, my youngest, was now five, postpartum didn't fit as a diagnosis.

Clearly I was hallucinating, though. You don't

just wake up one morning to find your husband and kids have been replaced by humanoid reptiles. Things like that don't happen. This isn't Kafka. This is reality. There are rules.

Humans don't have nictitating eyes. That's something I *know*.

I look at the clock on the computer, and realize I've spent the whole morning sitting here fretting. My coffee cold, a skim of clotted cream on the surface. I erase the browsing history, and close the laptop. It's time to pick up Ryan from school.

He kisses me on the cheek, and I buckle him in. No evidence of the creature I saw this morning, he's the perfect little angel he's always been. We drive in silence, while he holds a toy car up to the window, pretending to be driving alongside us. Shame twists my insides, making me queasy. How could I have ever believed he wasn't my son?

Ryan flops down and watches cartoons for an hour before I tell him to go out back and play. I can't think with the sound of the TV, and I need to think, to hold on to the notion that everything I'd seen wasn't real. My gaze falls upon an opened bottle of red on the counter while prepping for dinner.

Wine before dinner? Why not?

When Dylan arrives home, he looks at me sitting at the table in front of an empty bottle of wine and a stained wineglass, and scowls in confusion. I realize I haven't greeted him like usual, and smile. It's much easier to force a smile after two glasses of wine. "Hi, honeybear. How was school?"

He cocks his head, unsure of me. Then he shrugs. "School was school. Where's Ryan?"

"Out back."

He sets his bag down on the floor, and heads past me to the backyard. I watch the boys through billowing curtains. They stand very close together near the shed, speaking to each other. Then, as if they'd been talking about me, they turn to the window.

I wave cheerily. It's easier to cover my increasing sense of panic now that I'm slightly drunk.

The boys turn to each other, confused. As if *I'm* the one acting strangely, and they've been perfectly normal. Perfectly *themselves*. Then they separate and throw the ball back and forth.

BILL WATCHES ME floss through the bathroom mirror. I can tell he's been wanting to ask me about the wine all night, and I've been preparing myself for it.

"Are you all right?" he asks finally.

"Uh-huh," I say, running the dental pick between my incisors, putting too much force against the gums.

"It's just..." He hesitates, trying to think of the most delicate way to put it to avoid an argument. "You don't seem yourself today."

You don't seem yourself today either, honeybear.

"I'm fine. Maybe a little stressed. Job-hunting and all that."

Bill nods, seemingly understanding. He watches me a few seconds longer, then picks up his Robert Ludlum from the bedside table and opens it, settling into the pillows.

I spit a mouthful of blood into the sink. Looking at myself in the mirror, I stare until my eyes blur from dryness, until I can't hold them open any longer and involuntarily blink.

I look at the dental pick in my hand.

Eyeing Bill, I gently close then lock the door.

I return to the mirror, hold my left eye open with thumb and forefinger, and bring the sharp end of the pick toward it. I've never been able to touch my eyes. Can't even put in drops without blinking furiously like I've been splashed in the face with acid. Just watching someone else deal with their contact lenses makes me cringe.

The pick end blurs it's so close to my eyeball.

Ohgodohgodohgod—

The mint green plastic barely grazes the spongey lens of my eye and I blink it away hard. Feels like I've scratched the cornea, even though I know it wasn't enough pressure to injure me. Tears already streaming down my cheeks, I bend over the sink and splash warm water on my face. Blink blink blink away the pain.

All I wanted was to see the membrane. To see if I'm one of them.

Now I'm sure I'll never know.

II

MORNING. I'VE BEEN awake all night. I look a mess. I feel like a train wreck. I laid there beside Bill watching him sleep while the sirens wailed and the raccoons rummaged. He didn't move all night, but his skin did. The tic I'd noticed the previous morning had spread, his whole face suddenly doing the jitterbug. That's what I'd thought for the first hour or so as I lay there in the semi-dark, our bedroom illuminated by the fingernail moon. Over time, I realized it wasn't his skin moving at all, nor was it nerves. It was something *under the skin*. The flesh moved in ripples and waves, as if parasites were living inside him. Or an alien presence had dressed itself in his skin.

It *squirmed* under his face, flesh rippling.

Tentatively, my own heart beating so hard I could hardly breathe, I laid my head on his chest and I couldn't hear his heart. There was no heart to hear. I couldn't feel it, pulsing below his ribs. But I felt the creature under his flesh move, like snakes in a burlap sack. A living thing in a dead body.

I wondered what might happen if Bill's skin could no longer contain the thing beneath. If it suddenly split open and peeled back while I laid there, revealing its true form, blood and extraterrestrial goo soaking into the good sheets.

After a while, I realized I could smell him. Not his usual scent. Not the sharp tang of man sweat under a light breezy cologne, and the flat smell of clean hair. He reeked of cloves, like how I imagine a mummy might smell, and the salty smell of mucous as he breathed in and out deeply through his nose, so cloying it made me gag and I had to turn away.

I laid there beside that awful thing all night, knowing I'd have to kiss it in the morning. Knowing the creatures wearing my boys' skin would scurry in once the sun was up, and expect me to hug them and tell them good morning. Bizarre, once-impossible thoughts circled my mind like sharks, terrifyingly plausible now.

I slipped out of bed as the sun rose so I wouldn't have to reenact our morning routine. After the night I had, I knew I couldn't have possibly dealt with it.

I drank a vodka and cranberry juice before they came shuffling downstairs wearing my family's pajamas over my family's skin, appearing bewildered and even a little upset, hair a mess. The vodka took the edge off, but I'm still jittery. Jumping at any sudden movement.

Somehow I manage to get breakfast made. Pancakes. Still their favorite, though I'm certain the things they've become are only eating to appear normal. To avoid detection, conflict. I'm watching the two smaller creatures eat, cutting up the food I've made into bite-sized chunks with their forks and spooning it into their toothy orifices. I'm frozen with the milk jug extended in my hand, and when the thing wearing Bill's skin asks me to pass the syrup, I snap out of it, but I still can't seem to make my hand pour the milk.

My limp hand quivers, milk splashing against the inside of the jug.

"Honeybear?" it says.

The two smaller creatures look up at me, forks poised before their opened mouth-holes. Their eyes nictitate, unblinking. The creature wearing my husband's skin cocks its head to the side and watches me, as if I'm the one who's abnormal.

I can't take any more of this. This can't be my life. Only yesterday I was reflecting on how perfect it was, and now…

Now. Have to act fast.

Instead of the syrup, I calmly pick up the knife. I don't even excuse myself as I stand with it clenched in a fist and leave the table. The things wearing Bill and the kids stare up at me with their mouths open, not sure how to react. It's not until I've bypassed the counter and left the kitchen that the Bill-creature's concern becomes evident. I hear his chair squawk as he gets up quickly to follow me, but by then I'm already running down the hall.

I'm in the en suite bathroom with the door locked when the creature raps gently on the door.

"Hon, what are you doing?"

I need to know.

"Honeybear, why did you bring that knife into the bathroom?"

I wonder, if I was one of them, would I even

know it? Would I act any differently? Would I feel the same?

If my skin was a jacket, how could I be certain? If my insides squirmed, would I see it? *Feel* it?

He pounds on the door with his fist, but I know he's too cautious to break it down. I have time.

I need *to know.*

"I know what you are!" I shout at the door, moving in close to the mirror to study my reflection.

"*What?* Libby, what's *wrong* with you? What the hell are you *talking* about?

His fist on the door rattles the toothbrushes in their cup.

"Open the door!"

"Mom?" Dylan cries. "Mom, open the door!"

Ryan is weeping. I can picture the two of them, holding hands just outside the door. They sound so much like my family, but I know it's a trick. They're trying to lull me into a false sense of security, and when I open the door they'll spring their attack. They'll drag me back to their mothership or their underground lair to begin the change, to become one of them.

If I'm not already.

I grab my hair and pull it back, exposing my face to the naked white light of the vanity bulbs. I haven't looked at myself this closely in months, ever since I noticed the frown lines expanding between my eyebrows, and saw how large my pores looked in the makeup mirror. Aging is the least of my worries now.

I wonder if they age—the creatures? Do they mate? Procreate? Or do they just steal our bodies, using us like cuckoos use the nests of other birds?

I raise the knife to my face. Just below the scalp. This is where surgeons would cut me to erase the signs of having lived. Peel down the skin and sew it back together, tighter. The knife quivers in my hand, the edge of the blade resting against my forehead.

"Libby, open this goddamn door!"

It clatters against the jam. I've never heard Bill raise his voice like that before, and it startles me. I need to move fast. I need to finish this.

Cutting yourself deliberately takes much more force than you'd think. The first cut I make merely brings blood to the surface, leaving a raised pink welt that burns like a stinging swarm of bees. The second cut is deeper. The flesh blossoms open and blood trickles down my forehead, pain bursting in white stars before my eyes. The vodka I drank before preparing breakfast barely dulls it, but instead of making me stop, it's galvanizing. I cut deeper, dragging the blade, tracing an upside-down smile below my hairline, opening my flesh to the bone. I cry out in pain and frustration, finally allowing myself to grieve the loss of my family, blood spilling in rivers down my furrowed brow and into my wide, wet eyes. The creatures just outside the bathroom, faking tears, using Bill's fists to pound on the door.

"*Lib!*"

"*Leave me alone, you freaks!*" I scream at him, my

face painted red like a woman warrior. The blood-drenched knife clatters into the sink, and I reach up with both hands to grasp the ragged edge of flesh I've carved. It feels like warm, raw chicken, but the mental image makes it no easier to pull apart flesh from bone. I watch my fingers peel my skin, the pain so far beyond anything I've experienced that I'm now mentally detached from it, as if I'm watching it being done to someone else's body, through someone else's eyes. This flesh is no longer mine. This body is merely a vessel. A husk.

The door frame splinters.

I watch Bill's shoulder smash against the door through the wide, angled crack. Behind him, I catch glimpses of the little ones, the boys who were once mine. Then the flap of skin falls over my eyes with a wet slap like a damp hood.

For a moment, I see nothing, blinded by flesh. Fingers peel away the darkness to bright white. The lids pull away from my eyes with a terrible sucking sound.

I can see.

In the mirror I see a woman, thirty-five years old, blonde hair. The beginnings of laugh lines and crow's feet obscured by a jagged, curved flap of glistening, angry red flesh draped over her nose. The eyes now perpetually widened in horror or fascination. The mouth open, smiling, whitened teeth stained pink as she laughs.

Glimpsing bone amid the raw meat of her

forehead, she's unable to blink away the sight of her insides squirming as the door smashes inward and her husband stumbles in, his own eyes widening in revulsion, terror, stupefaction. The boys behind him, *her* boys, now screaming and huddling against each other.

Bill staggers back, a hand over his mouth. "Oh, dear God… *Libby!*"

A gauzy film draws over her eyes like curtains, moistening them. Nictitating.

I see the woman leave the mirror. She moves toward the creatures in the hall. No longer fearing them. She drops to one knee, and Bill and the children fall into her arms, weeping, afraid, relieved.

Creatures, like her, dressed in hand-me-down flesh.

"We are family," I say, and the body I wear hugs them tightly.

SHARP

A PARCEL TRUCK the color of dried blood crept through the neighborhood, the sunny suburban quiet pierced by the incessant ringing of its bell.

No children scurried from their houses to chase it down. The ring had more in common with a plague-cart driver's death knell than an ice cream truck's jaunty jingle, and this 1950 Ford Step-N-Serve with **JERRY'S GRINDING SERVICE** hand-lettered on the delivery door side provided no treats, only tricks.

Below the name, smaller block letters spelled out, **KNIVES SCISSORS GARDEN TOOLS MOWER BLADES.** Larger, and in the same font, the word **SHARPENING** caught a shard of sunlight, bright enough to stab the eyes of anyone unlucky enough to be caught looking. Every letter had peeled to the point of being nearly illegible. Metal corners bent up under rivets, jagged and rusted. Black smoke plumed from its exhaust and the holes in its sagging muffler. The interior smelled of oil and foul chemicals, the walls adorned with sharpened tools that rattled and swung from hooks.

This truck was a rolling machine of death. Fitting,

considering the man who sat behind its wheel ringing the bell was the man the newspapers had taken to calling "The Ken Doll Killer."

A diminutive man, Jerry drove with wooden blocks attached to the pedals so his feet could reach them. They hadn't called him "Ken Doll" because he was handsome. His victims had all been tall, slim and blonde, resembling the impossible standard of beauty set by Ken's sometime girlfriend, Barbie.

Without witnesses to his crimes, the papers weren't aware of his ugliness, which coupled with his lack of height made him self-conscious. Being called a "Doll" by the local news organizations gave him stabbing pains in his stomach that wouldn't go away with antacids.

"Sharp," Jerry muttered to himself, and tugged on the weathered string, clanging his bell.

Jerry eased the truck around the corner onto Hayworth Street, where he often idled to eat his lunch before turning in the cul-de-sac and weaving his way through streets named after dead celebrities. As he drove toward the end of the street, a woman in a bright sundress hurried down the steps of her colonial home. A look of disquiet pinched her attractive features as her heels clicked and clacked toward the sidewalk on the cobblestone path. The same sun that brightened the remnants of Jerry's sign shimmered in her springy cornsilk hair.

Jerry's instincts for spotting women in distress being nearly preternatural, he'd seen her long before she reached the street. She hadn't needed to wave her arms to flag him down, but he appreciated the glimpse of her jostled breasts as he slowed his already crawling truck to a stop.

"Ma'am?" He caught her eye for the briefest of moments before averting his gaze to the dirty floor of the truck and the wooden blocks he hoped she wouldn't notice. Always, Jerry outwardly deferred to women, while within the darkened, twisted caverns of his mind he stood before them tall and naked and proud—a *juggernaut*.

"Oh, thank God you're here," the blonde woman all but gasped. In his glance, Jerry had seen milky white flesh draped over her fine angular frame, and wondered fleetingly what her bones would sound like hollowed out and hung from his porch as wind chimes. He imagined their music might sound like Heaven.

"Thank God, indeed." He gave her an unforced smile. "What can I help you with today?"

"It's my good knives." The pout was audible in her voice. "The blades are too dull to cut butter, and I'm having a guest for dinner!"

"Just let me get my tools," he said in a tone he'd hoped sounded reassuring.

Rummaging in the back, Jerry attempted to control his breathing. He'd never seen this woman on Hayworth Street before. She must have kept herself busy inside the house, or in the backyard, during the many times he'd lunched here. Wherever she'd been, he felt grateful for his good luck finding her here today.

With his equipment gathered up, an awful certainty struck him: the woman had gone back inside and locked the door behind her, suddenly afraid of this small man with small fingers, small toes, and even smaller prick. Jerry hurried back out with his grinder, his breathing frantic again, only to find her still standing by the curb. The look of worry in her eyes became a strained smile when she saw his grinder: a hefty little thing with the look of a vacuum cleaner, the black grinding wheel cradled in its side like film on a projector.

"All set," he told her, leaping down onto the sidewalk, noticing as she lowered her chin to take in his small stature. Jerry didn't let it bother him. Now that he held his tools, he felt strong. When he got her in the house, his lack of height would not be an issue. When he stood over her prostrate body, breathing hard into the cleft of her bosom while hot, sticky blood oozed from her wounds, he would seem *enormous.*

"Follow me, please," she said, her sundress flipping up delightfully to reveal a muscular thigh as she turned on her heels. Jerry followed, taking small looks as her buttocks rose and fell, rose and fell like fleshy counterweights, well aware that anyone could be watching from their windows, wondering why the statuesque beauty next door would stoop to consort with such an ugly little man.

"That's quite an impressive tool you've got," the blonde woman said, peering over her shoulder. She might have caught his look at her sublime posterior had he not averted his gaze to the cobblestones.

Still, Jerry felt his cheeks grow red at the—possibly unintended?—double-entendre. "It was my f-father's," he choked out. His father had been the original Jerry, the man whose truck Jerry Jr. drove up and down nice, quiet residential streets like this one, day after day, in search of blades to sharpen. Jerry's father was long dead, as was his mother. She'd cut her wrists with the sharpest knife in the drawer when she'd learned, from the nice old lady next door, that her husband had been cheating on her with a tall, blonde woman named Sandra.

Another thing the papers got wrong: his victims weren't Barbies. They were *Sandras*.

"Sorry about the mess," this Sandra said as she opened the door.

"I-I'm sure it's fine," Jerry stammered, having focused most of his mental energy on stemming the flow of blood to his penis. However small his erection might be (and Sandra had made it plain how incredibly small it was), he didn't want the stubby protrusion alerting her to his intent before the woman let him into her home.

Stepping inside, her heels clicked on tile as Jerry followed, and he noticed what she'd meant by "the mess" right away. End tables and glass vases and the corners of walls had been smothered in bubble wrap and clear tape. The sofa, the fabric on the dining room chairs... it was almost as if she'd been attempting to seal off anything of value. To protect it from the incessant gnawing of some feral animal, maybe: a miniature hell hound in a fancy dog sweater. Or to spare them from being humped.

The woman ushered Jerry past all of this to the kitchen, where she indicated with an elegant swishing gesture the knives laid out on the counter. "You see?"

"Oh, they're dull, all right," Jerry said, clucking his disapproval. "I can help with that."

Jerry looked around himself at the counter island stools, the appliances, and the windows all taped over with bubble wrap. Even her fancy kitchen gadgets had been wrapped neatly in bloated clear plastic. It reminded Jerry of the padded cell they had put him in when he was still a boy. The hefty tool in his hands no longer made him feel strong. He felt uneasy. He felt that stabbing pain in his stomach again.

"Moving, are you?" he ventured, and licked the roof of his suddenly dry mouth.

The woman shook her head and offered nothing further.

Jerry gestured to a stool. "May I?"

"Be my guest," she said, then smirked as if her words had amused her.

Jerry dragged a stool to the counter, where he'd laid down his grinder. The layers of bubble wrap squeaked as he sat, the sound of a clown twisting balloons. He thought maybe the woman might not have wanted his sharpening equipment to damage anything in the kitchen, but it wouldn't explain why she'd wrapped the rest of the house. Thinking about it set his teeth grinding. Best to get this done, then—the whole nasty, messy business—and be out of here quickly.

But once Jerry got started, he savored the grinding and the sparks that were always a prelude to the work ahead. Gradually, his anxieties floated away. While he sharpened her knives, he drank little sips of the woman as she crossed and uncrossed her long legs from her perch on a second bubble-wrapped stool, smoothing down her lipstick-red nails with a pointed nail file.

Aside from her height and her hair color, this woman looked nothing like Sandra. Sandra had been street trash. Jerry's father had met her at a bar after a long day, and judging by the stories she'd told to anyone who would listen, Jerry Sr.'s truck had been bouncing on its springs in the back lot within the hour. This woman had an elegance about her. A fragility that Sandra, who chain-smoked and spat and scratched her genitals in public, never had. Sandra wore Press-On nails, much longer than anyone needed, and all of Sandra's clothes had been form-fitting, to show off her hips and the roundness of her buttocks. And while the eyes of both women were blue, Sandra's had been cold and calculating.

This woman's were soft. Kind. Sandra's whorishly painted lips had always twisted down, even when she'd been smiling. This woman's lips curled up at the corners, giving her the appearance of a smile even when she was frustrated.

Sandra was long dead now, murdered by Jerry's own hands. She'd moved into the house and into his father's bed barely a year after they had laid Jerry's mother in the ground. Sandra had toyed with young Jerry, both awakening and deterring his sexuality. The night she'd caught him masturbating at age twelve, Sandra had made him painfully aware of how small his penis was: "Stroking his little prick!" she'd called out to his father. Both father and son had been too mortified to look each other in the eye for days, though by then Jerry Sr. paid little attention to him anyhow, so enamored was he with his young new girlfriend.

And when he was thirteen, Jerry had heard his father grunting in the master bedroom. He had peeked in through a crack in the door to find his father lying face-down on the bed, his hairy ass in the air. The room smelled foul, like a soiled diaper. Sandra stood behind his father, her naked buttocks jiggling between the leather straps of some device, thrusting her hips toward Jerry Sr., grinding her hairy crotch—he could see the thick black thatch of her pubic hair between her legs—into his father's backside. Sandra's fleshy pink phallus—a dildo, Jerry knew now, though at the time he'd thought he understood why Sandra had mocked his penis, when her own penis was so large—plunged into his father's rectum and out, in and out, while his father grunted in pain and pleasure.

Cautiously, quietly, young Jerry had moved downstairs to the kitchen, ashamed by his erection, his young mind swimming with rage, jealousy, revenge. He opened the top drawer closest the sink, where the knife his mother had used to kill herself still lay, though cleaned, sharpened and unused since. He removed it from the drawer and crept back upstairs. He sneaked into the room as his father raised up on his knees and Sandra pulled on his father's hair like the reigns of a horse, his father's prick squirting milky fluid onto the fouled sheets.

Jerry Sr. had caught his eye just as Jerry brought the knife across Sandra's exposed throat. The mortification in his father's eyes could have been embarrassment of the act his son had caught him in as much as terror. Jerry would never know. As Sandra fell back, gurgling and clawing at her throat as gouts of blood spattered him and his father, the dildo popped out of his father's shit-smeared asshole with a wet plop and Jerry Sr. fell onto the soiled mattress.

Jerry had fallen upon him in an instant, the blade plunging in and out of him as the dildo had only moments before. His father's grunts were not of pleasure then, only pain. Sandra clawed the curtains down from the rod, the bright light of day cascading down on this grizzly scene. The smell of shit and blood had been so thick, Jerry's heart hammering so fast, that the world began to gray.

When Jerry awoke, he'd been in a padded off-white room. His father, dead. Sandra, dead. The police hadn't wanted to go into details of how they'd been found—the embarrassment had been as plain on their faces as it had on his father's—but it was clear they knew that he'd been the culprit. He'd spent the rest of his childhood in the institution, released to a halfway house the year he turned eighteen. With good behavior, he'd eventually been allowed to return home. Since his father had been good about paying his bills, the house and truck now belonged to Jerry.

Finally, Jerry completed his work. He wiped his greasy fingers on a handkerchief and took his receipt book from the deep front pocket of his coveralls.

"That was quick," the blonde woman said, something she might be moved to say again later, though by then she would have neither the strength nor the breath—perhaps not even the *lips*—to voice the remark.

Jerry smiled his practiced smile. "May I ask... what your name is?" He wouldn't look up at her, intent on the pen scrawling on his pad. "For the bill," he added hastily.

All he required was her signature. Proof that she wasn't Sandra, that more blades needed sharpening, more work required doing.

One day, when there were no more Sandras left to skewer, he would reveal his dark Other to the world. His shadow self was *gargantuan*—it stretched out dark and monstrous behind him, particularly in the late afternoon. Jerry preferred to kill a few hours after lunchtime, so his shadow would draw out long behind him when he left his victims, a dark mirror to the giant inside.

When there were no more Sandras, the world would see just how BIG he was, so BIG their minds would struggle to see him all… and in their fear, and in their desperation, they would put him away for the rest of his life, with no chance of parole.

Over the years, lonely women would write to him in prison. They would proclaim his innocence, profess their love, send him their silky underwear, fragrant with their scent. They would *worship* him. Jerry The Giant, his minions would call him. Jerry the *Juggernaut*.

"I'm Rose Stark," his next victim said, picking up one of the blades and admiring its shiny edge under the florescent lights. He wanted to suck the fluid from her windpipe and use it as a flute. He wanted to sever her pelvis and use it as a sex toy. But he wouldn't do these things. Even when fully absorbed in his Other self, Jerry was no animal. He would only cut her major arteries, slowly and methodically, and let her pumping hot lifeblood be the lubricant to their sexual congress as he worked his little prick into her anus.

Out in the street, the bell in his father's truck tinkled softly.

"Oh, this is perfect," the woman—*Rose*—said, rotating the shiny-edged blade in her hand.

"Sharp," Jerry agreed, nodding hypnotically.

Behind her back, Jerry tugged his mother's kitchen knife—not the same knife, that was in a moldering evidence box at the police station, but its double, the same heft and blade—out of the homemade sheath in his coveralls.

As he brought the knife up, its shiny blade shimmering under the recessed lighting, Rose shrugged the flimsy dress from her shoulders. Its fabric caught for one loving moment on her hips, and she shimmied slightly, her taut breasts jostling before she slipped free of it, and it finally cascaded down to her ankles. She turned to him, naked and proud, though her body was not without its flaws. Her flesh was blemished with dozens of scars, paler than the rest of her: little inch-long nicks crisscrossing her hips, her legs, her breasts, her arms. He hadn't noticed them in the daylight, and though they were certainly *odd*, it didn't diminish Jerry's lust for her.

He swallowed hard. Everything about him felt hard, suddenly. No woman had come on to him before, aside from Sandra, who had used her sexuality like a carrot on a stick, flaunting her curves and taunting him, practically *forcing* him to strike out at her one way or the other.

This woman, Rose, she drew out her arms and bid

him closer.

Jerry felt his mother's knife fall uselessly from his hand. The sound of its clatter on the tiles seemed far away, dulled by the pleasant thud of his own blood in his ears as he shuffled toward her, like a child taking his first steps to his mother.

Rose took him into a warm embrace. She drew his face to her bosom and cupped his head in her hand, stroking his greasy, shaggy hair. Jerry stood in her arms, pressed between her firm breasts, her heartbeat enveloping him the way his mother's once had when he was a boy. Tears welled up in his eyes, and he wept openly. She stroked his hair, shushing him, letting him weep, letting his tears smear on her breasts and drip down her belly.

"It's okay," she cooed. "It's okay."

And it *was* okay, Jerry realized. Suddenly nothing seemed to matter. The past was the past. Sandra, his father and mother were dead and buried. Her suicide and their murder, the abuses he'd suffered in the asylum in the years that followed their deaths, were nothing more than vague memories of someone else's bad dream. Jerry felt at peace, for the first time since he'd found his mother in the blossoming pool of blood on the kitchen tiles. He felt very small, a child in his mother's arms, and it was okay to be small.

It was okay.

Jerry heard a familiar sound like knives drawn across leather straps, only this was the sound of dozens simultaneously. As his mind processed this, he felt his flesh opening at his throat, his cheek, his chest, belly, arms and groin. Peeling open an eye, the one not pressed against this woman's hot flesh, he blinked away tears and got a good look at the breasts he'd been snuggling against. Only what he saw wasn't a breast at all... or, not quite. The flesh had parted, and from the nipple a long, sharp, ridged thing jutted out like a horn, slick with her blood.

Rose had grown *thorns*.

Terrified, Jerry squirmed, tearing his own flesh against her spiky protrusions. The more he wormed against her the more entangled he became. She held him close, shushing him, whispering *It's okay, it's okay*, and the thorn in his cheek popped through with a sound like the dildo springing from his father's anus, and it gouged the roof of his mouth, his tongue. The thorns in his abdomen and crotch had flayed him, his guts fell out like sauced spaghetti and his penis—just as small as Sandra had declared it—had been skewered like a cocktail weenie on a toothpick.

Jerry opened his mouth to speak, but the word gurgled out on a mouthful of blood. His heart stopped pumping, his limbs slackened, and his head dropped to the side, like a marionette on severed strings.

Rose let him go then. His lifeless body slipped from her sharp protrusions and fell to the floor in a bloody heap beside his grinder. And as her breathing slowed, Rose waited for the change to happen.

They came to her like flies to the spider, like

moths to the flame: these monsters dressed as men, rotten little boys who still feared their mothers, their sisters, daughters and wives. Unconsciously they sought her out, and Rose held them and pacified them. Often she sang to them and often they prayed, and sometimes she slapped them and sometimes she let them suck and bite her at her nipples and once or twice, they had kissed. But always, *always*, she stroked their hair and told them it was okay. Because in the end it was all these monsters wanted: someone to comfort them and tell them they were forgiven.

The thorns drew back inside her with an epileptic shuddering. Already the flesh that covered them began to heal, and she wet a bunch of paper towels in the sink and daubed away the blood before stepping back into her dress, pulling it back up over the lightening dimples on her shoulders.

Rose opened the fridge, poured herself some lemonade, and brought it to the front porch, basking in the satisfaction of having pricked another slug in the garden. It really was shaping into a beautiful day. Sun shining, birds twittering. Next door, the Anders's wind chimes rattled pleasantly, like hollowed-out bones. Mrs. Bellows from across the street stood up from weeding her lawn and threw her a big friendly wave. "Hi, Rose!"

"Morning, Mrs. Bellows," Rose shouted back. She sipped her lemonade, sitting back with a contented sigh.

A fine, fine day on Hayworth Street. Nothing

could spoil it, not even the sight of that ugly old truck and its gently rattling bell.

VIDEO NASTIES

1 – *NASTiES*

EXTERIOR. STREET. NIGHT.

In the blur of driving rain, Harlan Wallis didn't see the box of old videotapes outside the fire-blackened factory until he'd just about walked into it. As an avid collector of old movies, his eyes immediately lighted on two rare video nasties resting upon the others—*Massacre at Central High* and *Nightkill*, both films only ever available on VHS. Like a man protecting a wounded animal, he dropped to his knees to spare the soggy box from further damage. Hurrying the rest of the way home hunched over the box, soaked to the skin, Harlan just hoped the tapes beneath the first layer might still be salvageable, if not the rest.

He supposed he owed his good fortune to Vicky, who'd thrust him out into the downpour despite his fear of being struck by lightning, telling him in a flurry of words she wished it would zap him straight to Hell. The storm had died down since, leaving only the rain to worry about—along with his battered ego.

Vicky had really let him have it this time, facing him with the sad unalterable truth their relationship was definitely over.

They'd never been right for each other, he and Vicky, and it had never been more apparent than in their choice of entertainment. Harlan loved old horror movies, the cornier and nastier the better. He relished the feeling of superiority, knowing exactly what would jump out at him and when, being able to guess who would die and how within the first few minutes, and laughing derisively when his predictions came true.

Vicky, on the other hand, watched movies to be emotionally moved, and their argument tonight had related directly to this apparently irreconcilable difference. She had put on a horror movie in hope of bridging the gap, and he'd sniped about it the whole way through. After twenty minutes, Vicky had turned it off in frustration.

"You aren't even giving it a chance!" she'd cried.

"Oh, I did," he'd replied with a yawn. "It's just trying way too hard."

"And you think that's a bad thing? Maybe if you—"

She'd stopped there, but Harlan had seized on it like a piranha on a bikini-clad bimbo. "Maybe if I what? Tried harder?"

"No, that's not what I was going to say. You can't predict everything, you know."

Harlan had sputtered his objection, and Vicky,

exasperated, had thrown a handful of popcorn at him.

"I'm sick of it, Harlan! Everything needs to be self-aware and snarky, or you won't give it a second look."

"That's not true," he'd said. "I love old movies."

And that was it: the phrase that ended their relationship. Moved to tears, Vicky said, "Sometimes I think you love those old movies more than you ever loved me."

For the first time in Harlan's twenty-six years, he hadn't been able to find the words to argue.

He loved her. Of course, he loved her. The question was if he loved her as much as he loved movies, and for that, he still didn't have an answer.

At the door to his apartment, Harlan held the dripping box awkwardly on one knee, and fumbled to get the key card from his pocket. He managed to heft the box into the living room just before the cardboard split at the seams, bursting open, tapes spreading across the rug like when he was little and would dump out his Lego blocks to build an army of original monsters.

Rows upon rows of old VHS tapes already lined the walls surrounding the television, but there was always room for new acquisitions. He slipped one out of its cover (*Peeping Tom*, once banned in Finland), shook water from it, and laid it on the carpet to dry. Thinking he'd better do the same for the rest, he rushed to the bathroom closet for towels.

When they'd first started dating six years prior, Vicky had bought him a matching set of plush ones, having complained about the tattered and threadbare towels he'd scrounged from his family home after his parents had passed. The old towels were relics of his childhood—like his furniture, his posters, and much of his VHS collection.

Maybe what Vicky said is true, he thought now, looking over his newfound treasures. *Maybe I am living in the past.*

He didn't want to consider why.

Spreading the towels out on the floor and table, Harlan sat cross-legged on the rug and began removing tapes from their soggy covers, separating dry from wet. Classics like *Willlard* (the original, not the subpar remake with Crispen Glover) and Tod Browning's *Freaks*, a few Troma films, a handful of Hammer Horrors, the extremely rare *Snuff*. Looking over the vibrant, macabre, and often unintentionally humorous covers reminded him of those long-ago trips to the video store, his parents searching for what seemed like hours to find something appropriate for the three of them to watch, while he marveled at demons sprung from toilets, buxom heroines clinging to muscular warriors, half-rotted skulls, switchblade hooligans, and muscle car grilles marred by streaks of blood. He'd felt most at home there among the oddities, with some horror movie flickering on the TVs overhead, the heady smell of stale popcorn filling his nostrils.

What kind of monster would throw these out in the street during a thunderstorm? Harlan wondered. Clearly someone who couldn't see value in old things. Someone who felt the past held little worth. *Someone like Vicky,* he thought, and quickly rebuked himself for thinking it. She'd always been kind and patient, open to new experiences. If anyone had played the villain in their relationship, it had been him.

Harlan absently picked up a videotape he'd surprisingly never heard of and read the tagline aloud, "'*NASTiES* will make your life a living Hell.'" He uttered a mocking chuckle.

The painting on the cover showed a VHS tape with a pentagram burned into it, glowing red and smoking. Above this, two teenagers in hooded cloaks held black candles, apparently in the midst of some kind of dark ceremony. A swirl of tentacles and greenish mist surrounded them. He'd seen this sort of un-ironically cheesy cover dozens of times during his visits to the only retro video store in the neighborhood, and much more often when he was young, at the old Blockbuster with his parents. Harlan grinned and turned it over to read the blurb.

> *The NASTiES are just that: nasty, disgusting, rotten little tentacle demons hell-bent on nothing but destruction. High school student Troy Stark finds a possessed Betamax, and after reciting the*

ancient incantation in the accompanying instruction manual during a Halloween party at his parents' house—coinciding with a mysterious thunderstorm—he and his friends unwittingly unleash the NASTiES. One by one, they die in increasingly gruesome ways, while Troy and cheerleader Tina discover the terrible truth about his parents' involvement in the occult in their attempt to send the NASTiES back to Hell!

"Sounds fucking awful." Harlan laughed. "I love it." He nearly dropped it when he read the credits on the back cover:

CO-WRITTEN, DIRECTED & EDITED BY NICOLO FUNELLI

"Holy shit! It's a *Funelli*?"

On his list of all-time favorite B-movie directors, Nicolo Funelli had always been among the top three. He firmly believed the old studio tagline, *Funelli puts the 'Fun' in schlock horror!* He'd seen every single piece of trash the deceased Italian director had put to film, even the lost "classic" *Ragers in Space*, all except this... and the fact he'd never heard of it only increased its worth in his eyes.

Harlan cracked a beer and sat in front of his laptop. He looked up Funelli's credits, but *NASTiES* wasn't among them. He searched for *NASTiES* specifically, with Nicolo Funelli in quotations—still *niente*, as they'd often said in Funelli's early films, when he'd still been working in Italy, and the subtitles would spell out "nothing."

"An undiscovered Funelli," he muttered. "I could make a fortune off this."

The cover looked cheap, but still had the appearance of mass manufacturing, as opposed to something an industrious collector might have made for a one-off dubbed copy of a bootlegged film. The label was printed directly onto the cassette, not a sticker. Most of the names listed in the production credits had corresponding IMDB listings—Jack Emmerson, Funelli's frequent co-writer, and sometime collaborator Ham Gottlieb were among them—but Harlan found nothing about this film. Utterly baffling.

Maybe I've stumbled onto a rare one. Like, really *rare... NASTiES... wow!*

"Well, let's give 'er a run-through," he said to himself, and brought the tape to the VCR. Opening the gate, he eyed the physical tape to make sure it was free of debris and crinkles, so as not to damage the video heads. Giving it the okay, Harlan popped it into the machine. The player swallowed it with a hungry whir of machinery.

PLAY ▶ appeared on the black screen while Harlan sat on the floor amid the new tapes in his collection, eagerly waiting. The digital readout counted up:

00:00:00... 00:00:01... 00:00:02...

At **00:00:13** the VCR groaned. A horizontal line of video noise crackled down from the top of the screen. Harlan rose to his knees to adjust the tracking, or smack the top of the VCR, but the picture adjusted itself before he could do either.

00:01:32... 00:01:33...

Still nothing.

He pushed Fast Forward. The image warped, shuttling through nothing but black. His hopes sank.

"Someone must have erased it. Or left it next to a bulk eraser."

A flicker of light inside the machine caught his eye. Curious, Harlan pushed up the flap. He leaned over and peered inside. The tape dragged sluggishly over the video heads. Nothing out of the ordinary. As he closed the flap, a spark of electricity zapped his finger. Crying out in pain and surprise, he jerked his finger back. A whiff of burnt flesh and ozone stung his nostrils, the skin beneath his fingernail charred.

"Balls," he said through the finger in his mouth, hurrying to the bathroom to run it under the tap. The cold soothed his pain, but the running water made him need to urinate. *Not like there's anyone around to nag me about it,* he thought, relieving himself with the door open. The memory of his fight with Vicky made his heart hurt.

Life isn't all darkness and horror: her words from long ago echoed as he flushed the toilet. How long had it been since he'd thought of that night in her bed? Long enough he could barely remember it now. She'd helped him through that dark time, giving him six of the best years of her life, and he'd rewarded her with not-so-subtle insults, passive aggressive snarkiness, neglect. He deserved whatever fate lay in store for him.

Vicky had gotten him the job where she had worked since high school, a place much like a prison, each inmate with their own little 6'X6' laminate and fuzzy carpeted cell. But where Harlan saw only bars, Vicky saw the door, and while she rose in the ranks from Data Entry to HR Administrator, Harlan mindlessly entered data into his terminal, dreaming of one day becoming a famous movie director, each day getting one day further from realizing his dream.

ZAP!

A flash of blue flickered over his shoulder in the mirror.

ZZZZAP! ZZZAP!

A fork of lightning arced across the doorway. Harlan dried his hands quickly and hurried out, but what he saw in the living room made him launch himself back into the bathroom hall, pressing himself flat against the wall as his heart thumped. Blue flashes brightened B-movie posters on the plain white walls as he peered around the corner.

Lighting curled outward from the tape player, striking the tapes on the shelves and the ones laid out on the floor, reminding him of cheap film effects of the '80s, from *The Highlander*'s "Quickening" sequence to the clock tower scene in *Back to the Future*. Despite the very real danger of electrocution—hadn't Vicky wished he'd get struck by lightning?—Harlan scurried around to the power bar and yanked the plug with his foot before the machine could do any more damage to his collection. Surge protection would prevent errant electricity from frying his laptop, at least, but the tapes it had struck were likely toast. Dozens of them had rattled off the shelf and landed among the new tapes in his collection. Every one of them would need checking. It would take him hours. Maybe even *days*.

The VCR smoldered quietly on the shelf.

Harlan downed the rest of his beer, injured finger extended as he eyed the VCR. The tendrils of gray smoke had stopped oozing out of its mouth, but he supposed it still could catch fire.

"Better put it on the balcony, just in case."

A light mist fell. The air had cooled down considerably from the muggy, soup heat of the day. Harlan laid the VCR on a ratty old patio chair he'd salvaged from the Dumpsters, and laid a few dry newspapers from the recycle bin on top of it. He lit a cigarette butt from the ashtray, sucking the last few drags from it while gazing out at the purple bruise of sky above the apartment buildings.

He often watched miniaturized lives play out in lighted apartment windows while he smoked: people cooking dinner, having parties, playing with their children. Blue light flickered in many darkened apartment windows. After the electrical storm inside his apartment, the sight of those blue windows was vaguely sinister. He imagined arcs of lightning from cable boxes and satellite receivers zapping the zombified eyes of passive viewers, creating automatons who threw themselves down stairwells and off balconies, killing themselves to the soundtrack of some meaningless reality show.

The apocalypse will not be televised, he thought, and shuddered, crushing out the previously butted cigarette as he'd exhausted its nicotine supply.

Something clattered inside. As he peeked in through the doorway, the television came on with a high-frequency whine. He stepped in, curious and on edge despite the smoke, wondering how the TV could be on when he'd unplugged it from the wall along with the VCR.

On the TV was a dark attic, lit blue to look like moonlight. An actor meant to be high-school age—as evidenced by his letterman jacket—but clearly much older, read gibberish from an arcane tome: "*Shubish! Coitus! Interruptis!*" he cried with all the sincerity of a bad actor reading unintentionally horrible lines. Wind howled, blowing the actor's hair and flipping pages. The girl with a puffy pink sweater and teased wall of blonde bangs clung to his shoulder as cardboard boxes sprung open and dusty objects clattered off the shelves—

The image cut abruptly to the interior of a studio.

A petite brunette sat tied to what looked like a director's chair in front of a green screen. Harlan recognized her pale blue monkey pajamas seconds before she turned her wet mask of terror in his direction—but it wasn't possible. This wasn't happening. Black lines of mascara ran down Vicky's cheeks as she tried to look everywhere at once, her small frame quivering in terror. Harlan stumbled over the coffee table and kicked through the cassettes on the floor, dropping to his knees in front of the screen.

"Vicky!" Harlan called, knowing she couldn't hear him through the television but too frightened not to try. "*Vicky, where are you?*"

She turned to him, her relief short-lived as she recalled her predicament. "*Harlan?* I don't know, I don't *know*, I was watching TV. I must have fallen asleep, but I woke up, I woke up *here*, and I, I don't know how I got here. Harlan, I'm *scared...*"

Clapping came from the side speakers of his old TV. Vicky's gaze followed the sound, struggling against the ropes as a man entered the frame, dressed in black with cowboy boots and a Stetson. From his tall, slim build and the loping way he walked, Harlan recognized him immediately. He'd seen him in hours of feverishly studied documentary footage.

It was Nicolo Funelli. Or a pretty damned good lookalike.

"Hello, Harlan," the long-deceased Italian director said, and his Dali moustache curled upward as he grinned. In one hand he held a Philips VHS Movie Camera, gray with a black shell. He raised it to his right eye, aiming it at Harlan through the screen. Behind Vicky and Funelli, the green screen filled with an image of Harlan's own terrified face. When he scowled, the face on the screen behind Vicky and Funelli scowled with him.

"What is this, some kind of sick joke?" Harlan said, searching the TV for a hidden camera. "You're a lookalike, right? Somebody hired you to mess with us? Tell me this a joke, Vick. Vicky?"

She merely whimpered, shaking her head softly.

"I assure you, Harlan, this is no joke," Funelli said, his accent heavy. "We're going to have a little fun. If you play along, your lovely leading lady will be returned to you in one piece."

"If you touch her, I swear to—"

"Who? To *God*?" Funelli laughed haughtily. The green screen filled with a battle taking place in slow-motion through a spaceship's massive viewport, a scene from *Ragers in Space*. "If there is a God why am I here, talking to you, when I could be in heaven, drinking wine with Hitchcock and Kurosawa?"

For a second time, Harlan couldn't find the words to argue. This was no prank. Somehow, Nicolo Funelli had kidnapped his girlfriend.

Ex-girlfriend, Harlan reminded himself, as if the situation wasn't already bad enough.

"In here, Harlan, *I am God*."

The space battle cut to a close-up of Funelli,

grinning down at himself.

"We're going to make a film, you and I," both Funellis said calmly. "In the movies, this is what they call the 'ticking clock.' You have until midnight to discover how to release me from this videotape, so make haste, my friend. If you don't, your leading lady dies."

He removed the video camera from his eye to nod in Vicky's direction. Her gaze flicked from the director to Harlan in unbridled terror.

"As you know, I have no compunctions about killing off my main characters, and that includes you." The director showed his teeth, and made a short bow. "Adieu," he said with a slight giggle, and the screen cut to black.

"Wait!" Harlan grabbed the sides of the television, shaking it on its shelf. "Wait! *How do I let you out? How do I let you out! Vicky! VICKY!*"

The screen remained dark. He plugged the television back in, and flicked uselessly through the channels. Blue screen… blue screen… blue screen.

"You're wasting your *time*," he told himself, glancing at his watch. 8:35. Midnight deadline. He had to do something, and fast. "Okay, I can do this. I just have to work it out in my head. I've seen every damn movie that motherfucker put on film, all except this one, I should be able to   "

Inspired, Harlan leaped to his feet and hurried out onto the balcony, where the VCR still lay under dampened newspapers. He brought it back to the living room, plugged it in, and ejected the tape. Staring down at the *NASTiES* cassette on the coffee table, trying to decide what the main character of a Funelli film would do, he lit a stubbed cigarette. He wanted to smash the cassette open with a hammer, but if Funelli really had been trapped inside the tape, like a genie in a bottle, he wasn't in there anymore. He'd gotten loose when Harlan played it, gotten into the cables—once Funelli's consciousness or whatever had kept the essence of him alive hit the optical cables, the fiberwire, he could literally move at the speed of light. There would be no stopping him…

"But he needs me to get out," Harlan said. "That doesn't make sense. He can pull people *in*, oh God, Vicky—but he can't get *out*."

Think about it for a minute. Stop and think. He's got her trapped in some kind of B-movie purgatory, but he's trapped there too. There's always some kind of curse or spell or demonic incantation to solve the problem, and somebody knows it, someone who knows a lot more about what's happened. A "guide." A Yoda. Who knows more than me about Funelli? The documentarian? No. No, she lives on the other side of the country, she's probably asleep by now, even if I could find her number…

"I've got it!" Harlan slipped the movie into its case, and tucked it into his jacket as he headed out.

2 – *Funelli's Monster*

SO HIP VIDEO was dark when Harlan arrived, but he

knew the owner lived in one of the apartments upstairs. He thumbed all three buttons, hoping one of them belonged to Dave Lee. A light flicked on in the front apartment upstairs, and a slim silhouette stood by the window for a moment. A minute later, heavy soles trudged down the stairs to the paint-flecked door. With a rattle of locks and latches, it opened on Dave. He wore a black toque over his shaggy hair (dyed to a color Harlan had once heard him call "Asian orange"), and skinny pajamas tucked into Ugg boots.

"Harlan? Store's closed, bruh. Come back tomorrow," he said, already closing the door.

"Dave, wait, just listen for a minute."

"Okay, what? I just smoked a bowl, I'm trying to chill…"

"Do you know Funelli? Nicolo Funelli?"

"Funelli?" the store owner blinked sleep from his eyes. "Sure, sure, of course, he put the 'fun' in B-horror. That's a terrible tagline, by the way. Doesn't even sound the same. It's *Foon*elli not *Fun*elli, and two, Funelli's more like *D*-horror. Or *F*. Funelli puts the F in fail." He grinned proudly at the joke, scratching his sparse black goatee. "Did you wake me up just to ask me about Funelli?"

"No, Dave, I just really, really need your help. This is gonna sound crazy, but Funelli's trapped Vicky, my girlfriend. He's trapped her inside the TV or, or *something*… and I just need your help to get her out. *Please*. I'm desperate, man!"

Dave narrowed his eyes. "Are you doing a Vine?"

"This isn't a *Vine*, Dave," Harlan snapped. "This is *real life.*"

"Dead directors don't drag girlfriends into the Phantom Zone, Harlan, not in IRL. You've been watching too much Funelli, and I am way too baked to talk movies with you right now, okay?"

Dave began to close the door. Desperate to make him believe, Harlan yanked the videotape out of his pocket and waved it at him. Dave's marijuana-addled brain took a moment to register what he saw, and then his eyes widened.

"Holy Tarantino! Where did you get that, dude? Wait, don't say anything!" He opened the door all the way and tugged Harlan inside by the jacket. The cramped entrance smelled like cabbage. Junk mail littered the floor. Red bled through the black walls where paint had faded and flaked off, the stairs grimy from years of trampled-in dirt and dotted with cigarette burns. The scene reminded him of the bathroom stairwell of a goth nightclub.

Before shutting and triple-locking the door, Dave peeped up and down the street. He turned to Harlan, inches from his face in the tight hallway. "Now, tell me everything from the start."

"I found the tape, and I played it—"

"No. *Dude.*" He raised his hands to emphasize the mental stress Harlan had caused him. "Seriously, where did you find it? A garage sale? Scream Factory? The fucking *Twilight Zone?*"

00:372;00

"What are you talking about?"

Dave's eyes jittered as he tried to keep his stoned brain in focus, staring Harlan down. "This tape," he jabbed an accusatory finger at the offending object, "it was never manufactured, okay? This movie *does not exist*."

"But..." Harlan looked at the offending object. "But I'm holding it."

"No, dude, what you're holding is not *NASTiES*. It can't be *NASTiES*. You know why? Because Funelli *died* before that movie was finished, and all of the footage was lost in the fire."

"Fire? What fire?"

"You don't know about the fire? He doesn't know about the fire," Dave added to his imaginary audience. "Nicolo Funelli died in a studio fire shooting B-roll green screen footage for *NASTiES*. I mean this was some sick shit he was filming. Legend has it, he wanted this to be his version of *Hellraiser*. He'd really upped the full-frontal nudity and the gore, with just *buckets* of blood, but word is..." Dave stopped suddenly at the sound of creaking upstairs. "I'm hungry. Are you hungry?"

Harlan wasn't, but to be amiable he made a head gesture between a nod and a shake, and followed Dave up the stairs. At the top, a small landing led to three doors, each painted black, the peepholes, doorknobs and apartment numbers still rimmed with the previous sloppy red paintjob. Dave opened the door to their right, and disappeared inside.

The bachelor apartment reeked of weed. Dave had paused near the end of Dario Argento's *Suspiria* (some called Funelli a lesser Argento, but Harlan had always had a soft spot for the former, at least until very recently), and the blood-streaked woman hanging from a skylight stared at them from Dave's widescreen television. Every bit of floor space was covered in videotapes, dirty magazines, and dirty clothes, aside from a path of stained carpet leading from the door to the futon, futon to kitchenette, futon to bathroom. Harlan longed for the clean comfort of Vicky's small basement apartment. He kept his shoes on despite Dave's request to take them off at the door.

Dave walked the trail marked by '80s centerfolds and frayed tighty whities to the kitchenette, and opened a cupboard. He came back with a box of Fruit Loops and dug a hand inside, munching a handful of the sweet colorful cereal before offering the box to Harlan, who shook his head.

"Suit yourself." Dave flopped down on the futon, reclining against the arm with one foot up on the mattress, like a burnout's boudoir photograph. Considering all the skin mags on the floor, evidence of potential solo hand play on the futon, Harlan elected to gently kick some tapes out of the way and sit on a stool at the kitchen counter.

"You can sit over here, I won't bite," Dave said, his black goatee sprinkled with bright rainbow crumbs.

"Yeah, but I'm afraid your mattress might."

Dave snorted laughter. "Fair enough. Now where was I?"

"The, uh, the fire at Funelli's studio."

"Right. So…" He shoved another handful of cereal into his mouth, speaking as he chewed. "Legend has it, Funelli hired a bunch of non-union actors to shoot the cabal cutaways. If you listen to the tabloids, it was Satanists, but the word on the street is Funelli was into some really dark shit even Satanists wouldn't touch. I'm talking sex magick—that's magick with a *ck*, not with a *c*, and the extra *k* is for extra krazy. I'm talking ritualistic sacrifice. I'm talking summoning the Dark Lord Cthulhu type shit. I mean this stuff would make the Cenobites look like Jehovah's Witnesses."

In the brief silence, Harlan eyed the cassette case. "So you're saying… he was shooting some kind of ritual with these cult people when the studio burned down?"

"And Bingo was his name-o!" Dave grinned, his teeth stained purple-gray from artificial colors, BHT and God knew what else.

"Shit," Harlan said.

"Add to that the fact that the police never identified his body among the remains they found, and you've got yourself one helluva mysterious grand exit, Urban Legend-*stylee*."

Harlan considered it. Something in the story didn't follow, but he couldn't put his finger on it. The cabalists, the fire, the missing body. All of it was insane, but something felt wrong. "No, wait a second," he said, piecing it together. "I saw his funeral in those old documentaries. All of his ex-wives were there, crying and throwing themselves on the casket."

Dave shrugged. "They just buried his cowboy hat and boots."

"Jesus…"

Dave nodded. "And he's kidnapped your girlfriend."

Harlan nodded morosely.

"How?"

"I don't know. Vicky said she fell asleep in front of the TV and woke up in this studio… I saw her on the tape, tied up in front of a green screen, and Funelli was there with her. He told me I've got until—" He looked at his cell phone. The digital face read 9:04. "*Shit!* Less than three hours. He made a special point of reminding me he's not afraid to kill off main characters, and Vicky's a main character—"

"*Shit,* dude…" Dave sat up. "What does that make me? The Asian *sidekick*?" He got up from the futon and began pacing, trudging carelessly over cassette cases and magazines. "This is ridiculous, man. Just trying to smoke a bowl, watch a movie and chill, and some white dude I *barely even know*, by the way, comes knocking on *my* door and gets me caught up in a curse. I knew I shouldn't have answered the door but you're a good customer, and the customer's always right. The customer's always an *asshole* is more like it—"

Harlan stepped in front of Dave and grabbed him roughly by the shoulders. Dave snapped out of it, his gaze much more lucid than before. "Sorry, man," he said.

"No, *I'm* sorry. I shouldn't have got you caught up in all this but I'm in a lot of trouble here and you're the only person I know who knows more about bad movies than me. Also Vicky's mom is Chinese, so I don't think the 'Asian sidekick' thing really matters all that much."

"Oh, really? Where's she from?"

"Dave!"

"Sorry. Sorry."

"It's okay. Now what are we gonna do?"

"Well, okay," Dave said, gathering his thoughts. "I was thinking, Funelli's co-writer lives here in town. If anyone would know what to do in a Funelli movie, it'd be him."

"*Jack Emmerson* lives here?"

"I thought you were a Funelli *fanboy*, bro! They shot a lot of their movies here. If anyone would know how to help you, it's—" Dave paused, turning his head toward the TV in a slow motion move straight out of a demon possession film. "Wait a minute. You said Funelli zapped your half-Asian girlfriend into the television or something, right?"

"Dude, can you—?"

"What?"

"Well, what the fuck does her being half-Asian have to do with anything?"

Dave opened his mouth to reply, and seemed to think better of it. His mouth remained open, staring over Harlan's shoulder at the TV. Harlan turned to see the hanged woman break apart into digital blocks, warping and streaking across the screen, repeating the cascading motion of blocky smearing color like a digital waterfall until Funelli's face replaced her in close-up.

"*I heeeeear you!*" he said, speaking into a flopping, bloody severed ear with ragged flaps of torn flesh. Throwing the ear over his shoulder, he stepped back into a medium shot. Funelli's absence in the frame revealed Vicky tied up and unconscious on a dentist's chair. To Harlan's relief, both of her ears appeared intact. Behind them, Funelli had superimposed a room filled with scientific equipment looted from the set of some '60s sci-fi series on the green screen. Harlan recognized it as the setting for a key scene in *The Quasar Conspiracy*, where the sadistic Lead Scientist used a laser to burn the protagonist's eyeball until it split open, oozing bubbling white goo.

The scientist stepped into shot behind Funelli with the laser in one oily gray mitt. The white coat had split in places, and a dentist's face mask barely concealed the bulbous alien features and slobbering, jagged-toothed sucker mouth of Funelli's Space Rager.

"You'd better not be trying to mess with me, Harlan. You have three hours. And then, I let my creations have some *real* fun." He flashed a smile.

"Goodbye."

The screen went black.

Harlan hoped he could get to Vicky in time. He wished he'd been better to her. He wished he'd never found the box. Tears of helplessness welled in his eyes.

Dave grabbed him by his rain-dampened jacket. "Snap out of it, dude!" He dragged Harlan out of the apartment, locking the door behind them.

"We have to be careful," Dave whispered hoarsely. "Anywhere there's a TV, he can hear us. Probably even zap us from a cable connection, like that movie—" He peered around his feet, looking along the baseboards for outlets. "Okay, looks like we're safe. Here's the plan. We go to Emmerson's place, get him to help us figure out how to beat—"

CLAP!

Harlan and Dave turned to each other, both startled by the sound.

CLAP! CLAP-CLAP!

"What is that?" Harlan asked. The sound made him think of cartoon clams.

CLAPCLAPCLAPCLAPCLAPCLAPCLAP!

"It's coming from the store!" Dave bounded down the stairs. "Dammit, not again!"

"Not again what?" Harlan said, hurrying behind him.

An alarm sounded through the wall.

"I just got robbed last week, man!" Dave shouted over his shoulder, pulling his keys out of his PJs as he pushed through the front door. By the time Harlan got outside, Dave had already unlocked the door and stepped into So Hip. The alarm blared out into the street, cutting through the silence like a sawblade.

Dave cried out in anguish, swallowed by the blare of the alarm. Red light flashed over the darkened interior, throwing long shadows on the walls. Harlan thought it was all a bit much. The alarm likely did a good enough job deterring criminals on its own.

Dave snatched a baseball bat from behind the counter. Harlan barely heard him swearing at the top of his lungs for the intruder to *come out, motherfucker*. The door bumped Harlan in the ass, and he uttered a frightened little yelp, the alarm and lights making him nervous as the door swung shut behind him.

Dave crept toward the shelves, the bat slung against his shoulder. Harlan considered following, and when he'd finally made up his mind to go after his friend, a giant black limb grabbed Dave by the shoulders and picked him off his feet.

Dave's Ugg-booted feet dangled as the monstrous creature lumbered out from the shadows. Harlan saw it in red flashes: a heavy 21" television, one of the old wall monitors that would normally be playing some trashy film when the store was open, rested on the thick, clattering body of a massive humanoid beast made of plastic cassettes, wound together with shiny black sinews of magnetic videotape. The bat fell useless from Dave's hands. On the screen, Funelli's grinning face, bathed in ominous green light, stared directly into the video store owner's soul.

Harlan ducked behind the counter, breathing heavily as the alarm continued to wail. He had to help Dave, but Jack Emmerson's address was paramount. Dave could have been dead already, and Harlan wouldn't have heard his bones crack over the alarm. The little computer on the counter came to life as he reached up to grab the keyboard, bumping the mouse. Praying Funelli's Monster wouldn't notice the light from the monitor—praying the *monitor itself* had no connection to the same connection keeping Funelli alive—Harlan typed EMERSON into the search bar.

No hits.

Items on the counter and in the drawers behind him jittered as the Tape Monster shook the floor.

He tried again with two *Ss*, fingers shaking uncontrollably, then again with two *Ms*. With a sigh of relief, Harlan read the address that came up. He repeated it aloud several times before creeping up over the top of the counter.

Funelli's Monster held Dave up like a ragdoll to its flickering face, Funelli's teeth gnashing on the screen. Harlan made a decision to distract him, but he worried about Vicky. She was a pawn in all of this, a bargaining chip Funelli could use for Harlan to help him escape from his digital prison. He had to hope Funelli wouldn't harm her until midnight. He had to trust no matter how crazy being stuck in his own private Hell had made him, the director would stick to the logic of his script.

Harlan picked up the computer screen, hesitated briefly, then launched it as hard as he could. It snapped back on its cable and smashed against the front of the counter.

"Hey, Max Headroom!" Harlan shouted as he leaped out from behind the counter, waving this hands. *"C-c-c-come and g-g-g-get me, asshole!"*

The Funelli Monster's TV head twisted in his direction, Funelli's immortal rage visible on the screen.

Fear propelled Harlan toward the door. He came to an abrupt, painful halt against the frame, his conscious mind registering too late the door had opened inward. Funelli's Monster dropped Dave crumpled and unconscious to the floor, and lumbered forward like a massive practical-effect Transformer, its limbs clattering and shimmering in red flashes of black magnetic tape, rattling movies on the shelves.

Harlan fumbled with the door, his back still against it, trying to tear it open without moving closer to the creature's VHS claws. Finally, he managed to edge over far enough to get out of its way, but by then the Monster was mere feet from him. Funelli's lips twisted into a sinister grin. Harlan yanked futilely on the handle. The director snarled, mere moments from his prey, reaching out with giant black plastic fingers when the cable at the back of his TV head pulled taut, jerking it back.

Funelli uttered a startled, strangled choke before the television tore off its body, smashing on the floor tiles. His face flickered with a buzz of static before the smoldering screen winked out, and the Monster's structure broke apart in a loose twisted heap of videotapes.

Harlan laughed aloud, short of breath. "Dave?" he called over the din. "You okay?"

Dave groaned in reply, rolling over onto a heap of scattered cassettes. "Dude… that thing literally killed my buzz."

The television fell off the wall so quickly Harlan was only able to shout a choked *"Dude!"* before it came crashing down over Dave's shocked face. The screen shattered and the tube exploded. Still plugged in to the wall, electricity jolted Dave's body in a morbid dance to the smell of burning circuitry and cooking flesh.

Police sirens neared, louder than the alarm. Too late to help his friend, Harlan rushed out the door and ran. He knew the writer's address, and it wasn't very far. He just hoped he could reach him in time to end this.

3 — *The Writer*

JACK EMMERSON LIVED in a crumbling townhouse in the gentrifying warehouse district. Harlan ran the eight blocks from So Hip Video, taking breathers while streetlights changed from red to green, wishing he'd quit smoking years ago and taken up jogging. Midnight loomed like the crescent moon that had parted the clouds above the city streets, flickering in puddles and storefront windows.

Harlan thumbed the doorbell, then knocked without waiting for a response. Jack Emmerson came to the door in a plush gray robe, and blinked out at Harlan. Bald head shimmering under the front light, he scratched his salt-and-pepper beard with the backs of his fingernails and grunted, "Somebody better have died."

Harlan didn't waste time with small talk. He simply showed the man the tape.

"*Dammit,*" Jack Emmerson grumbled, his whole body seeming to sag. "I guess it's worse. Someone *came back* from the dead." He narrowed his eyes, his crinkling face giving lie to the expression *black don't crack*—though to be fair, the man was in his 70s. "Well, you might as well come in, I won't be able to sleep tonight anyway. Not knowing *he's* out there."

Jack's townhouse was neat and clean, a tastefully furnished condo if it was still the 1980s, everything smooth, shiny blacks and whites. A brown wood stereo system with a record player stood alongside retro-futuristic shelves lined with colorful record jackets in the sunken living room. Harlan noticed with surprised relief the writer had no TV.

Jack pushed on the wall near the spiral staircase. A hidden door clicked open to reveal an astonishing array of booze. "Drink?" he asked.

"No thanks, I don't drink."

Jack arched an eyebrow as he poured himself a brandy. "You might want to start."

He stepped down into the sunken area, sat on the arm of a leather sofa, and directed Harlan to the chair. Harlan sat.

"I'm guessing time is of the essence. Nick always was a fan of the ticking clock. *Too much* for my taste, but what do I know, I just wrote the shit."

"Midnight," Harlan nodded.

"And he'll, what? Kill your boyfriend?"

"Girlfriend," Harlan said with a slight frown.

"Sorry. Don't mean to imply you look gay, whatever that means, but being in the business we are I figured I'd shoot for the odds. What are you? Movie critic, wannabe director, what?"

"Just a collector."

"A collector." Jack sipped his liquor thoughtfully. "And where did you find this… invaluable collector's item?"

"I was on my way home in the rain. Vicky and me got in a fight."

"Vicky and *I*."

Harlan gave him a flustered look.

"Sorry. Continue, please."

"We got in a big fight," Harlan said, choking up at the thought of never seeing her again. "I'm pretty sure we're broken up, but anyway… I was hurrying past the old factory in the rain when I saw this box of videotapes—"

Jack held up a hand. "Wait, wait. What factory?"

"The burned-up—" Realization struck him. In all his years passing by the burned-out shell on the way home from Vicky's apartment, he'd never put the two together. Now everything made sense. Somehow, Funelli had made it so the tapes had been out in the rain when Harlan walked past, leaving them as bait for someone who loved old video nasties enough to bring them home, to dry them out and put the tape— the only tape that mattered—into his or her VCR. "On Lexington and Rebar," he finished. "That's Funelli's studio, isn't it? The one that burned down?"

"You catch on quick. So you found the tape, and what? You put it in the tape player."

"Right."

"And when you did, it started to spark. All this blue lightning went just about everywhere, is that right?"

"Right…" Confused, Harlan asked, "How do you know all this, Mr. Emmerson?"

"Jack. And like I said—" He gestured with his fingers, wriggling them on an invisible typewriter, "—I wrote the shit."

"You…" Harlan shook his head in confusion.

Jack cocked his head at an angle, displaying annoyance. "Wrote. The shit. So I guess now we're at the Old Master scene. You've come to me to ask for my help, and that's when Funelli's Tapenstein monster shows up to kill me, and you escape by the skin of your lily-white nuts."

"You wrote all of this...?" Harlan muttered, sinking to the back of the sofa. He'd felt like a man living a nightmare before but the idea of living inside one of Funelli and Emmerson's screenplays made his skin crawl. If this was a Funelli film, they were all doomed. All of them. In Funelli films, things always ended badly for its stars.

"Funelli and I wrote this script while he was filming *NASTiES*," Jack explained. "The concept was Funelli, or a somewhat comically exaggerated version of Funelli, dies in a fire during an occult ritual because he's exactly what his critics have labeled him: he worships demons, he's a maniac, etcetera. Only Funelli's not really dead, he's trapped in a kind of Videolimbo, that's what we called it, where he can control video devices through the cable, basically like that Wes Craven movie with the dude sent to the electric chair."

"*Shocker*."

"Right, *Shocker*. We called ours *Funelli's Back from the Dead*, sort of a play on the way they always put his name in front of the title because of his popularity: Funelli's *Last Stand*, Funelli's *Lake of the Damned*, Funelli's *Orgy of the Zombies*. Only, as you've probably guessed, the apostrophe wasn't possessive, it's a contraction: *Funelli IS Back from the Dead*. You dig?"

Harlan nodded. "Yeah, I... I do dig. But don't worry, that tape monster thing already showed up at the video store."

Jack chuckled dryly. "You went to a video store. That's clever, I wish I'd thought of that. Not a good idea when you're trying to escape a dead man trapped in a videotape, but as a story point…"

"So this… everything… you've already written it?"

The writer stood, shaking his head. "No. We never finished the script," he said over his shoulder as he moved toward the bar. "See, the fire happened the night we were supposed to work on the denouement, coincidentally." He shrugged. "Or not. A big climactic set piece. Main character figures out Funelli's got his girl trapped in the studio, so he sets out to find her."

"And then?"

"And then nothing, that's all we wrote. See, Nick hated to outline, and I never outlined unless I was getting *paid* to outline…" Jack spilled liquor into his glass. "You see where I'm going with this."

"The future's unwritten."

"That's a tad grandiloquent," Jack said with a shrug. He swigged from the glass, and poured more. "If this were my movie, and I suppose it is, I'd say something like…" He took another swig, lowered his voice an octave, and growled, "*Sounds like we gotta write ourselves a new ending.*" Shrugging, he added, "Or something like that."

"I think I'll take that drink," Harlan said.

"I thought you might." Jack returned to the sofa with two glasses and a smirk. Harlan took his and sipped. The alcohol scalded on the way down, and he coughed.

"Bit of a lightweight, huh? Come with me. I've got something to show you."

Harlan followed Jack up the spiral staircase to his bedroom in the loft. He stayed by the stairs while Jack opened the closet, shifted some hangered clothes aside, moved some cardboard boxes behind them, and reached up to a shelf. When Jack returned, he held a pastel turquoise suitcase. He blew dust off it, and tossed it onto the water bed. The mattress rippled as he sat beside it to open the latches. Inside was a small blue-gray typewriter.

"This here's a Smith Corona Super Sterling manual typewriter," Jack said, pitching it like a professional salesman. "Now the purists will tell you, you want a vintage typewriter, you get yourself an Underwood, the kind Hitchcock and Heinlein and Orson Welles used. But for me, it's the Smith Corona. For one thing, I don't have to punch the keys as hard. This baby's smoother than Quiet Storm."

"What's 'quiet storm'?"

"It's a type of music. Now you want my help, kid, don't interrupt me." He scowled down at the typewriter, seemingly looking for his train of thought. "The other reason I like it is, when I'm in the zone and I'm typing at 100-words a minute, I don't have time to dial back and X-out mistakes. This one self-corrects. Press a single button, it goes back and uses the correction tape to erase the previous letter.

Press it again, it gets the one before that. Etcetera. Now that may not sound special to you, with your iPhone and your intelligent TV, but when I was your age *this*..." Lovingly, he removed the typewriter from the case and pushed the carriage return. "This was a godsend."

"I'll take your word for it."

"See, that's the problem with your generation. Always gotta shoot back with some snarky comment, always gotta be smug and look down your nose at the world. *Suspend your disbelief*. It's show business, baby!"

Jack's words, echoing the argument that started all of this, shamed Harlan. He muttered an apology.

Jack brushed it off. "Forget it. Now we can make this happen, Harlan. We've got little less than two and a half hours to write the third act, and I've written entire films in less. So we bring this baby to the old studio, and we hammer out an ending where you get your girl back, you and I survive, and we send Funelli back to Hell where he belongs."

With a hoarse, triumphant laugh, Jack held out a hand.

"Right on!" Harlan said, inspired by the old writer's speech to slap him five.

Jack scowled down at his palm, and made a sour face, grasping at his lower back with his free hand. "I appreciate the sentiment but I really could use a hand getting up. Waterbeds are great for a man in his twenties, not so much when he's pushing seventy-five."

Discouraged—and even more embarrassed by his potential microaggression—Harlan helped the man to his feet.

4 – *The Acolytes of Azathoth*

JACK NEVER OUTLINED, but he and Harlan hashed out a vague plan on the way to the old studio, the typewriter under his arm. He and Funelli had continued making video nasties while small budget auteurs like Soderberg and Tarantino, Smith and Rodriguez ushered in the New Wave of indie cinema in the early-'90s. If Funelli's career hadn't ended in the fire in 1993, he would have likely still been making B-movies today. Jack had seemed fine with retirement, with his dusty old typewriter and his lack of a television, but his eagerness to jump back into writing instead of suggesting Harlan take a walk into traffic spoke of a man who'd denied his true nature far too long.

The writer's bald head shined under the streetlamps, his shoulders slumped, his back hunched with age. Nicolo Funelli, who hadn't aged a day since 1993, had been 44 when his cowboy hat and boots were buried in an otherwise empty casket. Harlan hoped Jack's aged heart could handle whatever insanity Funelli had in store for the two of them.

"Your girl," Jack said, looking back over his

shoulder. "Is she strong?"

"Strong?"

"Mentally. What I mean to say is, do you think she'll spring back from this, or will she end up in some nuthouse, blathering on and on about a 'world inside the movies'?"

Harlan thought it over. The idea had never occurred to him, but he supposed if anyone could come out of there unscathed, it was Vicky. "She's stronger than anyone I know," he said. "When my parents died, she got me back on my feet again. Got me a job, helped me settle my parents' estate. If it wasn't for her, I'd probably still be watching old movies in their basement."

"Good. That's good character motivation."

"Speaking of movies, I think we need a video camera," Harlan said, spotting the yellow sign of a pawnshop ahead. "Something to record your ending."

Jack squinted back over his shoulder, considering it briefly before shaking his head. "That's Funelli's business. I'm a writer. I don't direct."

"But if we don't record it, it's just words on paper."

"It's *all* just words on paper, Harlan." He swept an arm out, indicating the totality of creation. "All of this. Now you got a keen sense of story, kid, but as Hitchcock once told me, your pacing is shit. We don't have time to go hunting down a VHS camera, and I'm sure as hell not stepping into a pawnshop likely to be full of TVs and television equipment where our undead Eye-talian friend could easily get the drop on us."

"I'll go in then. This is my movie—my *life*," Harlan corrected himself. "Whatever. Let me take the risk."

Jack's shoulders sagged as he looked back at the yellow storefront windows. "All right. But don't take too long in there, kid, it's nigh on ten o'clock. I'll get started on the script in the interim." He squinted up and down the empty street. "There's a park bench. Meet me over there when you're done."

"Thank you, Jack."

The writer smiled thinly, and shrugged. "Hey, it's what I do."

The bell above the pawnshop door jingled as Harlan stepped in. Jack squinted in at him through the barred windows, and gave him an encouraging nod. Harlan returned it. He watched Jack head across the street before stepping up to the counter.

The proprietor of Jiffy Pawn—or Yiffy Pawn, Harlan wasn't sure, as the *J* looked somewhat like a *Y*—eyed him with suspicion through thick-lensed glasses. Above the man, a sign read **YES! WE HAVE CLASSIC ARCAID MACHINES!** An array of guns and complicated knives lay behind the counter's barred glass, holding far less potential danger than the black & white security monitor above the clerk's head.

Harlan studied it, making sure the split screen showing the store's exterior and back shelves didn't suddenly switch to Funelli and Emmerson's green-screened *Videolimbo*, as Jack had called it. He watched the old writer shrink in the exterior camera's view before Jack disappeared out of frame.

The proprietor scowled at Harlan. "Can I help you with something, or are you just gonna stand there gawking at my security monitor hoping something good'll come on?"

Harlan snapped out of it and focused on the clerk. The man stood framed by an *X-Files* **THE TRUTH IS OUT THERE** poster tacked-up alongside newspaper clippings about government conspiracies. A laptop lay opened on the counter to a website called *Society of Skeptics*, the post titled: **IS THE SPHERICAL EARTH FACT, OR DISINFORMATION?**

"Yes. Sorry," Harlan said, taking it all in. "I need a video camera."

"Uh-huh. Camcorder, SLR, security, or action?"

"No, uh, none of those. I'm looking for an old one."

"I see. Would that be Super-8 or Betamax?"

Harlan shook his head, feeling like Jack had written this man a flimsy bit part, the thankless role of an expendable character created to serve a small story point and then die a very messy death.

I live in a movie now, he thought. Once upon a time it would have been fun to imagine, but with his every move watched by a psychotic deceased director, all he wanted now was for the credits to roll so he could finish his popcorn and go home.

"VHS," he said. "Philips, specifically."

The proprietor blinked at him without expression, his blue-gray eyes magnified to twice their size. "Don't have a Philips. Got a piece of crap RCA handheld in the back, if that's okay. Hasn't worked in ages."

"Could you just check?"

Frowning, the clerk said, "I know my own stock."

"Fine. The RCA is fine."

The bespectacled man unlatched the counter flap and stepped out. He took a step toward the back, then turned and blinked his giant eyes. "You're gonna buy this thing, right? I'm not going all the way back there and rootin' through all that junk just to come back and hear you tell me you don't want it 'cause it's broke?"

Harlan nodded enthusiastically. "I'll buy it. If it works, great. If not…" He shrugged. "And if you can find a tripod for it, I'll buy that too."

Big eyes blinked. "All right then," the proprietor said, and headed into the shelves. His reflection grew in a convex mirror placed strategically in the high far corner, near the darkened storeroom doorway, until he stepped under it and out of view. Harlan looked up at the monitor to see the strange man pass through the door.

Anxious, he checked the time. 9:55. Just over two hours until Funelli had his way with Vicky, no matter what Harlan and Jack did to try and put a stop to it. He wasn't even sure what they were attempting would work. All he could do was trust in Jack's screenplay, and their vague outline.

The image on the screen switched to a room filled with heaps of old junk, where the proprietor seemed to be hunting, moving boxes aside. The other side showed Harlan looking slightly off and to his right. To the left of the monitor, the main camera pointing down at him buzzed, and the picture zoomed in to a tight close-up of his eyes.

A loud electronic *BLAM!* filled them with fear, the sound something like the blast of a Space Rager's laser. The overhead fluorescents flickered as he turned from the monitor toward the once-darkened storage room doorway, flashing now with colorful lights.

"Sir?" Harlan called out.

His gaze fell again on the sign above the counter: **YES! WE HAVE CLASSIC ARCAID MACHINES!**

On the security monitor, the proprietor moved cautiously toward the lambent screens of several old arcade games in the back. The other image cut to Jack typing up his screenplay at a park bench under a streetlight. One of the city cameras had linked to the monitor somehow—whether Funelli had done it or the proprietor had hardwired it due to his evident paranoia, Harlan didn't know, but he had a bad feeling this was the scene where he'd have to make a hard choice between saving the writer, and going back in there to find the camera.

"Shit…"

Hoping Jack could take care of himself for a few more minutes, he headed down the long, narrow aisle between shelves of broken dreams and lay-a-ways, guitars, game consoles and jewelry sold for rent and drugs and destination weddings. His reflection warped in the chipped convex mirror as he passed under it looking up, watching for movement at his back. The doorway flashed red, green and blue while the machines blared chiptune music, laser blasts, explosions and revving engines.

"Hello?" Harlan called into the otherwise darkened room.

A crackly 8-bit voice sample replied with deep booming laughter: "*MUHA-HAHA! MUHA-HAHA! MUHA-HAHA!*"

Harlan stepped through the doorway, his skin prickling at the sound. He'd never been big on video games when he was young, but he knew a bad omen when he heard it.

"Hello-ooh!"

"*MUHA-HAHA! MUHA-HAHA!*"

Dust permeated the air, the shelves jam-packed with old stock. The arcade games stood against the back wall. He recognized *Ninja Gaiden* and *Altered Beast* and *Cruisin' USA* from his infrequent visits to the arcade with friends, the one with the built-in car seat, but the fourth game was one he'd never heard of, something called *Acolytes of Azathoth*. The screen flashed **GAME OVER** again and again above three druids who stood over a man tied to a stone slab. The repetitive laughter came from its speakers: *"MUHA-HAHA!"*

Harlan approached cautiously. "Sir?" The clerk's hand slumped out from the replica car seat. "Are you okay?" he called out over the noise, even though Harlan was fairly certain he wasn't.

He peered over the headrest. The racing game displayed the same image as *Acolytes*: **GAME OVER** flashing above the three dark druids and the man fastened to the round stone altar. Adrenaline burned through his veins. *All of the screens showed the same image.* On the pixelated altar, the victim's eyes bulged behind bottle-thick glasses. Dressed in nothing but a pair of boxer shorts, the clerk's hands and feet were tied at four points of a dripping red pentagram, his head resting on the fifth.

"MUHA-HAHA!"

Each druid held a curved blade to their chests. They arced down swiftly in tandem, one blade piercing the man's heart, the second his groin, the third his throat. The middle Acolyte carved off the clerk's head with very little effort. In the driver's seat, the real clerk jittered like a man having a seizure. He uttered a strangled groan seconds before a huge red fountain splattered the screen. Drops spattered Harlan's face and shirt. He cringed at the salty copper tang, recognizing it as blood.

The clerk's severed head dropped onto the gear shift in his lap, and rolled off onto the floor, tacky blood picking up crumbs from the dirty tiles, where it stared wide-eyed and mouth agape at Harlan. On the screens, tinted a slick red, the middle druid held up his prize by the hair, blocky pixel droplets of gore spilling on the stone altar.

Harlan tripped over his own feet and fell hard on his hands and knees, his gorge rising. Before he could choke it back, he puked on the cement floor and into the drain.

"MUHA-HAHA!"

The laughter sounded closer, more human. The arcade machines had projected pixelated holograms of the three dark druids, and as Harlan crabwalked toward the door the images solidified, only their eyes visible in the shadows cast by their hoods, cackling as they raised their daggers, dripping with the pawnshop clerk's blood.

Harlan backed into something metallic and frail. It toppled with a clatter behind him. Glancing back, he found a camera already secured to a small tripod, **VHSmovie** stamped on its side. Rather than bask in his good luck, he snatched it with quivering hands and got to his feet. Steadying himself on the doorjamb, he took one last look at the evil druids before scurrying out into the aisles and running headlong toward the exit.

The bell dinged above the door as Harlan burst out into the street. He turned back, pausing to catch his breath. Jiffy Pawn stood empty, derelict, track lighting flickering. A gray ray of light burst from the security monitor, and the dark druids materialized behind the door.

"Oh, *shit...*"

The Acolytes stepped through the door. The bell dinged.

Harlan turned and ran across the street, shouting for Jack.

"Oh shit!" Jack growled, rising to his feet.

Harlan reached the sidewalk. "That's what I just said!"

"No, you don't understand, kid. Those are the Acolytes of Azathoth. They're the punks Funelli was running with on the night of the fire."

The Acolytes stood in the middle of the road. They peeled back their hoods in tandem. Despite their differences in height, all three wore Funelli's grin, his curled Dali mustache, and gleeful dark brown eyes. A chorus of voices said, "Hello, Jack. Lovely to see you."

"Can't say the feeling's mutual, Nick."

The dark druids shrugged. "You might want to scrap that draft, Jack. It's *boring.*"

Breathing heavily, Jack looked for his pages he'd written in Harlan's absence on the bench. His shoulders further slumped when he saw them in a puddle of brown water, the ink smeared and running. "*Son of a...*" he grunted.

"Midnight approaches, gentlemen," the Funelli Acolytes said playfully. "Release me..." With dramatic sweeping gestures, they added, "Or *everyone dies.*"

00:400;00

The Acolytes vanished in a swirl of mist.

"You all right?" Harlan asked.

The writer nodded a little too emphatically. "Yeah. Let's just get this over with." He lugged his typewriter up under his arm. "I see you found your camera."

"The guy didn't think he had one, either."

Jack narrowed his eyes at him.

"You don't think...?"

"Kid, if he can make *those things* appear out of nowhere, who knows what he can do that we haven't seen yet?"

Harlan nodded gravely. "Well, I guess we'd better do what he says."

"Now hold on, I didn't say that," Jack said bitterly. "This old dog's still got a few tricks up his sleeve. You just wait and see what I've got in store for you. And for *him*. Make me do a rewrite. Son of a bitch ain't even paying me."

Jack loped off down the damp street. Harlan gave one last look at Jiffy Pawn—or Yiffy Pawn—and followed.

5 — *Videolimbo*

FUNELLI'S OLD STUDIO ran with dripping rain from the gutters and still smelled charred after twenty-three years. The fire department had chained the front doors, but Jack led him down a darkened alleyway that reeked like piss and rotting vegetation.

Finally, they arrived at a low window, where Jack pointed to a cinderblock that had come free of the structure and lay broken on the ground.

"Pick that up and throw it through the window."

Harlan heaved the block at the charred window. The muted sound was more like the breakaway glass they used in the movies than the sound of real glass shattering. He supposed it would have lost much of its integrity during the fire, but the thought was cut short as Jack told him to drag a crate under the window.

"You know, for someone who doesn't direct, you're doing a pretty good job bossing me around."

"Don't get lippy, kid. Now help me up."

Jack set down his typewriter and held out a hand, opening and closing it into a fist to get Harlan's attention. Jack grabbed his shoulder, using it to leverage himself up onto the box. He slipped through the window. A clatter of wood and metal arose from the darkened interior.

"You okay in there?"

Harlan peered into the gloomy silence just as Jack rose up from the darkness, startling him. "All good, kid. Just slipped is all. Hand me my typewriter and get your ass in here."

Harlan handed the case through. He passed the camera and tripod through after it, and climbed in. The charred smell was stronger inside, reminding him of the twisted jangle of metal and glass left of the family car after his parents' accident.

"Welcome to The Funhouse," Jack said with a sardonic grin.

Harlan looked around. The second floor sagged, resting hazardously on the burnt matchsticks of support columns. Cobwebs hung in places, broken boards and heaps of crumbled concrete littered the floor, glass and broken tile lay scattered elsewhere. Thieves had torn up the walls where the fire hadn't already destroyed them, and loose pipes and the frayed ends of copper wire stuck out everywhere. He felt the dead cold of this place in his bones, the epitome of every abandoned building in every horror movie and thriller he had ever seen.

"Probably should've brought a flashlight," Jack said.

Harlan tugged his phone from his pocket and punched up the flashlight. Jack sneered at it and headed off in a seemingly random direction. Harlan followed into the darkened recesses of the building, where dripping pipes and creaking floorboards gave the atmosphere a spooky Halloween effects vibe. The beam of his flashlight caught a fat, wet rat as it squeezed into a hole in the wall.

"Try not to step on any nails," Jack warned. "Probably get tetanus just from breathing in here."

A moment later the writer stopped in a nondescript corner. He genuflected to right an old plastic school desk and chair combo. Most of the plastic had melted, but the metal frame and pressed wood tabletop remained intact. "This is where the magic happened," he grunted, and set the typewriter up on the lopsided desk. He sat down in front of it, cracking his knuckles.

Harlan set the tripod up in front of the distinctive sloped green screen wall. Now what? "Need any inspiration?" he asked.

Jack glared back over his shoulder. "I need you to be quiet. Only thing I hate more than rewrites is a producer who thinks he's creative."

Harlan shut his mouth.

The writer ran a sheet of paper through the roller and began to type. Keystrokes echoed through the dripping ruin. The old man wrote seemingly in a trance state. Harlan crept up behind him so as not to disturb him and read over his shoulder.

<u>ACT III</u>

FADE IN:

INT. FUNELLI'S STUDIO - NIGHT

The blackened interior practically drips smoke as JACK and THE KID enter. The Wordslinger swings his trusty typewriter onto a beaten-up desk.

              JACK
        This is where the
        magic happens.

JACK sits and rattles out a symphony on the old Corona. His words shake soot off

the walls and dripping pipes, scaring
rats from their nests and spiders from
their webs. JACK knows this tune by
heart. He smiles as the words flow out
of him, from FADE IN to—

Harlan stepped away from the typewriter and
began to pace like an imprisoned animal. Jack kept
on typing, tearing out sheets of paper as he finished
them, blowing on them to dry the ink, and laying
them face down on the table beside the typewriter.
He had a good four or five pages written by 11:30,
and when Harlan looked over his shoulder again,
Jack banged out the words

FADE OUT.

The old hack cracked his knuckles and leaned
back in the chair, stretching out his arms and
wriggling his fingers. "Done. *Man,* I wish I had a stiff
drink."

"Can I read it?"

"What good is a script if no one reads it?" He
tapped the pages on the desk to straighten them, and
handed them over his shoulder to Harlan.

Harlan read.

While JACK typed, he began to notice the
music of the old place. Pipes DRIPPED
at a certain pitch. Floors CREAKED at
another. The WIND howled through cracks
and splits in the exterior walls—

A fetid gust howled through the guts of the building. Harlan looked up, a chill running through him—whether from the coincidence or the howling of the wind, he wasn't sure, but anxiety leaned toward the former.

THE KID paced behind him, reading over his shoulder and checking his watch every so often.

As THE KID remembers his girl, VICKY, we see her tied to the dentist chair. Terror-stricken eyes.

FUNELLI himself paces, a caged tiger. His ACOLYTE starts up the DRILL. Its BUZZ catches her attention. The ACOLYTE grins at her from the shadow under his hood.

The CAMERA's red record light flashes, and VICKY turns her terror toward the screen.

We PULL BACK to reveal the tiny B&W SCREEN of the VHS camera.

THE KID watches the scene through the viewfinder.

Harlan put a smoke in his mouth and lit it. He wandered over to the old camera and bent to peek at the viewfinder. The screen was black. He thumbed the ON button, hoping it still had some juice in it.

The camera buzzed to life. He peered through the viewfinder. The lens struggled to focus on the wall in the gloom.

"What are you doing?"

"Testing a theory."

"Kid, I don't know what you think is gonna happen. This ain't magic. This ain't the movies. This is real life."

"Now who's cynical? Whatever happened to 'suspend your disbelief'?"

"Look, I wrote you your happy ending. That's what you wanted, isn't it?"

"I want Vicky back!" Harlan spat. "I don't need more fantasy *bullshit*. I wanted you to *end this*!"

Jack's shoulders sagged as he sighed. "Kid… I'm just a writer. And not a very good one, if you ask the critics."

"Then *quiet on set*," Harlan said, and Jack's mouth shut audibly.

The lens autofocused.

Nothing.

Harlan stepped back, disheartened. "It's not working."

"You know, I've found sometimes it helps if you read back what you wrote aloud. Get back into the flow of the story."

Harlan nodded. He picked up the script and found his place. "Pull back to reveal the tiny black and white screen. The Kid watches the scene through

the viewfinder. The tape whirs as it records—
Records," he repeated. "That's it!"

Harlan opened the tape deck. He wadded up some foil from the cigarette package and jammed it into the empty write-protection slot in the *NASTiES* cassette. He inserted the tape, and pressed **RECORD**.

00:00:00... 00:00:01... 00:00:02...

"Funelli shoots the scene over-the-shoulder," Harlan read, "prancing around like a madman. His Acolyte steps closer with the whirring drill—"

Slowly, a blurry image formed in the viewfinder. Dark, ghostly shapes moved on the tiny monitor. Harlan squinted to bring them into focus. The lens whirred, twisting and turning, attempting to focus on the imaginary images.

"It's working," Jack stage-whispered. "Jesus, kid, it's *working!*"

Harlan looked up from the screen, expecting to see vague outlines, mere ghosts. But the scene before him solidified. Vicky lay in the dental chair, eyes wide and jaw tight in terror as the Acolyte stood near with a laser blaster. Funelli, oblivious to Harlan and Jack's presence in the studio, shot the scene over her shoulder, getting her POV as the weapon reached her open mouth. It was as like watching the scene through two-way glass, a window into an alternate dimension or, he supposed, from the undamaged appearance of the green screen area, a different time.

The fear on Vicky's face physically hurt his heart. His stupid obsession with old movies had gotten her into this mess, had almost gotten her killed. He'd taken their relationship for granted. If the both of them managed to make it out alive, he promised himself he wouldn't pressure her or trick her into taking him back, like he'd done before. He would let her decide whether his actions tonight merited forgiveness.

He looked at his phone. 11:48. Still time to make things right.

"*CUT!*" Harlan yelled.

The players froze, even Funelli. Tracking lines crackled up Funelli's slim, black-clad frame as Harlan stepped around the camera and reached out to touch them.

"Be careful," Jack said, rising from the desk.

"The Kid—*Harlan*," he corrected himself, "approached the scene cautiously."

He cast the script aside, no longer needing it. He'd seen enough movies to know what happened next. Pages fluttered to the grimy floor.

"Aww, kid," Jack said glumly. "Those were decent words."

"I'm sorry, Jack, but it needs a rewrite," Harlan said, moving forward. "Harlan approached the scene cautiously," he continued, "holding out his hand toward the Acolyte. A crackle of video noise rippled outward from his touch like a splash in a pond as Harlan gripped the Acolyte's weapon..."

The tips of his fingers vibrated with static electricity as he grabbed the Acolytes pale fingers and peeled them back. Even from an arm's length away all Harlan could see of its face beneath the hood were two blazing white eyes. The Acolyte flickered, like the beam of a dying flashlight. Harlan tore the weapon from the frozen fingers and aimed.

The trigger pulled easily. A green beam sputtered from the barrel and struck the Acolyte in the blink of an eye. The hood burst into flames in the instant before its head exploded, sending microwaved chunks of skull and gray matter and boiled blood every which way.

"Jesus, kid!" Jack groaned, wiping a hot chunk of earlobe from his shirt.

"Sorry." Sucking in a deep, ragged breath, Harlan aimed the laser blaster at the director. "Harlan realized these images couldn't harm him. He stood before Funelli, his former hero, ready to send him back to Videolimbo…"

Funelli came to life with sudden ferocity, swinging the video camera at Harlan's face. It struck his jaw, snapping his head back. He dropped the blaster, tasting blood. The director cast the broken camera aside and grabbed Harlan's wrist, twisting it behind his back. Harlan reached behind himself, fingers grasping for purchase. He managed to knock Funelli's Stetson from his head, revealing the scaled, bleeding flesh beneath.

"*You should not have fucked with me, Harlan.*" Harlan felt the director's hot breath on his ear as the man shoved him toward Vicky. He struggled to raise his head from between Vicky's breasts, as much as he longed to be there, while the director scrabbled with the instruments on the table. They settled on the scraper, and grasped it in a tight fist.

"The director is always right!" Funelli snarled.

Harlan caught a blur of movement in the small mouth mirror. Funelli's grip loosened with a loud jangle of metal coils and springs. He let out a cry of anguish, and Harlan sprawled over Vicky's unmoving legs. He rolled over in time to see Funelli raise a hand to protect himself from another attack.

"Eat my words, asshole!" Jack quipped, bringing the typewriter down on Funelli's already split skull. The director dropped to his knees. Blood spilled down his face, and he blinked twice in a daze. Then he fell sideways, raising a cloud of dust on the floor.

"Untie her," Jack ordered. "Quick!"

Harlan bent behind the chair, found the knot, and began working at it.

Funelli groaned. He tried to push himself up, and Jack kicked him back down. "That's for letting actors adlib over my dialogue," he growled, and kicked the dead man in the ribs. "And that's for ruining my career!"

Harlan worked the ropes free, but his delight was short-lived. He shook Vicky. Her body slumped lifelessly in the chair, teeth clacking together. "She's not moving…"

"You're the director," Jack said, panting over the broken typewriter. "Say the magic word."

Harlan couldn't seem to think beyond fear. He shook her again. Her dead stare jumpstarted his mind.

"Action!" he cried.

Vicky sprung from the chair and threw her arms over his shoulders, kissing his cheeks and his dry, cracked lips, moistening them with her vanilla lip balm. Harlan laughed and embraced her. He'd never liked vanilla before, but now it smelled like heaven.

"I love you," she said between kisses.

"I love you, too," he said, kissing her back, not caring that it hurt his injured jaw and lip. "Now let's get out of here before—"

BEEP! BEEP! BEEP! BEEP!

The red record light flashed. Out of tape. Harlan wasn't sure what would happen, but he squeezed Vicky as tight as he could, worried she would disappear again, sucked into the void.

The scene crackled and disappeared around them. He held her, closing his eyes tight, feeling her blood pulse against his neck. The camera stopped whirring. Jack had stopped gasping for breath. Even the wind had stopped.

Harlan opened his eyes.

Funelli's scene had vanished. No more dentist's office. No more *Funelli*. Harlan spun them around. Vicky's eyes widened as she came to the same conclusion.

The camera was gone. Jack was gone. All that remained was the damaged typewriter lying in the dust and debris.

"Oh no…" He let her go, running a hand through his hair. "*Shit shit shit!*"

"What?" she said. "What happened?"

"We're *trapped* in here! He got out!"

"*Trapped?*"

Harlan stepped up to the spot where the tripod had left marks in the dust. "Jack! *Jack! Action! ACTION!*"

The echo of his voice filled the silence.

"What do you mean we're trapped, Harlan? Trapped *where*?"

Harlan slumped down on the floor. "*Videolimbo*," he panted. Frustration welled up in his throat, and he let his tears fall in the dust.

6 – *A World Inside the Movies*

HARLAN'S PARENTS DIED the year he'd headed off to film school. After hearing the terrible news of their car crash he'd dropped out, intending to take care of legal issues and clean up his childhood home to put on the market. What he'd done instead was sit in the basement his folks had converted into his bedroom and watched hours and hours of bad horror movies. He didn't bathe. He rarely ate. He'd just watched, remembering those long-ago trips to the video store, staring up in childish delight at all the exciting movie covers on the shelves.

Some good came of that time. He'd bumped into

Vicky, an old friend from high school, and she'd helped him through his grief, lifting the dark fog of depression and pessimism that had fallen over his life since a young mother paying too much attention to the kids movie playing on the dashboard DVD player had T-boned Tom and Judy Wallis's hatchback on their way home from the movies.

Life isn't all horror and darkness, she'd told him, the night she'd first brought him to her bed. *There's paradise, too, if you want it.*

Somewhere along the line he'd forgotten that. Years of frittering away the hours behind a computer instead of working at his passion had worn down the magic of that night until nothing remained of it. Instead of being appreciative, he'd grown to resent her not just for getting him the job, but for letting him keep it now that she was effectively his employer. A part of him had thought of her as his jailor.

As they looked over the vast, empty wasteland beyond the crumbling walls of Funelli's studio, Vicky said, "Remember when you wanted to be the next great director?"

The dream was a bitter reminder of his failure. There'd always been an excuse not to try: he'd never had the time, he'd never had the money, he didn't have enough connections, the gates had been closed to him. But the truth was he'd been scared to put himself out there. He'd been too scared to take a risk.

"It was a stupid dream," he said.

"No, it wasn't. You proved it here, tonight." She

left him ruminating that while she wandered back into the burned husk. When she returned, she carried Jack's typewriter with her.

"It's broken," he said.

"It's not too bad," Vicky told him, holding it up for him to see. "It just needs a little TLC."

"Don't we all."

Harlan spent the following hour working on the machine, setting coils and springs back into place, and returning the carriage to its cradle. When he'd finished, and all it missed of its former glory was the *U* key, he sat cross-legged in the dust, rolled a sheet of paper through, and began to type:

```
INT:  F NELLT'S WAREHO SE  -  PERMANENT
DARK

Harlan and Vicky stood side-by-side for
a long beat, taking one last look o t
the door at the wastelands of Jack's
Videolimbo. Finally, Vicky t rned to
him.

                 VICKY
          It's time to go.

Harlan nodded. He sat in front of Jack's
typewriter and rattled the keys.

U  tside  the  light  began  to  change,
shifting  from  deep  orange  to  bright,
s nny yellow.
```

>   VICKY
>   Hon...? It's
>   working!

Harlan typed in a fl rry. He saw a beach.
A vast, blue ocean. Palm trees. A
cabana, stocked with everything they'd
ever wanted.

"Hon...?" Vicky said. "It's *working!*"

Harlan stopped typing. He looked from the same words he'd typed to Vicky, who stood in the sun. *Coincidence*, he thought, and shook off the idea. He stood up to meet her at the door.

Outside a white sand beach stretched for miles in either direction. Vicky slipped her arm around his waist. She looked up at him and smiled.

He supposed he owed his good fortune to Funelli. The man had given them an ending he could have never predicted.

7 – *Funelli's Revenge*

HARLAN AND VICKY stayed on the beach for days, bathing themselves in the ocean, eating fruit from the trees, consuming a self-replenishing stock of cold beers and exotic food from the fridge in the small cabana. Vicky had been right. Life could be paradise, if they wanted it.

On the third perfect day, while they lay tanning

under another perfectly unblemished blue sky, a small black and white television appeared between them and the beach. All dials and rabbit ears, it rested on a rickety-looking stand.

"Vick...?"

"Mmm?" she said, rolling over from tanning her back. She sat up abruptly, covering her breasts with an arm.

The TV flickered on.

"*Oh thank God,*" Jack said, peering at them through the screen. "Dr. Saunders, I see them!"

"Jack?"

Dr. Saunders appeared beside the writer, cramming into frame. She wore her graying dark hair in a bun, and squinted through her cat's eye glasses. Harlan recognized her as the film scholar who'd done several documentaries on the video nasties craze, and Funelli in particular.

"Where are they?" she asked Jack. "Is this your 'Videolimbo'?"

"I don't know where the hell they are," Jack replied. Tiny screams rose from the speakers. "Harlan, listen to me. Funelli's gotten *loose*. He's taken over *everything*. First he made them zombies, the ones who'd been watching when his broadcast went out on all the channels, *all over the goddamn world...*"

An explosion rocked the image, followed by more screams. A fireball erupted behind Dr. Saunders and Jack, who stumbled out of view as the window shattered inward and a rain of miscellaneous body parts thudded and squelched around them.

After considerable grunting, Jack stood the camera back up with agony in his tired eyes. Behind him, blurs of terrified people scurried past the window. For a moment Harlan was sure he saw giant squirming tentacles probing the debris in the background but the picture flickered to white noise and when the image returned they were gone.

"Harlan, please… we *need* you."

"*You're wasting time,*" Dr. Saunders snapped as she moved into shot. "Mr. Wallis, we need your assistance. Millions of people are going to die if you don't help us soon."

Harlan turned to Vicky. She watched the television impassively, as if she'd seen it all before. "What do you think?" he asked her.

Vicky turned to him. "What do *I* think?" A slow smile crept onto her face. "I think it's a repeat."

Jack's face crumpled. "No, Harlan…"

Harlan stood up, feeling the hot sand between his toes as he sauntered toward the television stand.

"Harlan, please don't do this. You've got to help us, dammit!"

Dr. Saunders shook her head. "It's no use."

"*You have to help us!*" Jack cried.

"I'm sorry, Jack."

Harlan reached out and turned off the TV.

FROM THE AUTHOR

I saw John Carpenter's *In the Mouth of Madness* the year it came out—I must have been 19. To say it was a transformative experience would be a huge understatement. As far as horror goes, that and *Jacob's Ladder* are the movies that influenced my writing the most. I think the nightmarish quality of the film struck me more than a lot of people, since many of the shooting locations can be found in the area where I grew up. The asylum, the church, by the time I saw *Madness*, I hadn't seen those places in maybe five years... except in dreams. When I first watched *Madness*, I felt like the movie had been pulled directly from my nightmares.

I've spent years trying to recreate with my writing the dizzying, manic, out-of-control feeling I get every time I watch *Madness*, but I fear I've always come up short. The last of the tales in this book, the eponymous *Video Nasties*, is my most direct homage to Carpenter's much-maligned masterpiece.

When I write, I like to think of my stories as mini movies. Many of these 16 stories are homages to those films and television shows that inspired me. I hope you have enjoyed reading them as much as I enjoyed writing them.

There are many people I need to thank for this book. Firstly, I'd like to thank my wonderful and very helpful beta readers, Cindy Jensen, John Drinkall and Tracey A. Green who caught many of my mistakes. Thanks to Chad Clark, who read the first incarnation of the novella *Video Nasties* (then called *Nicolo Funelli's "Back from the Dead"*), and offered helpful advice. Thanks to all the readers who reviewed "How to Kill a Celebrity" and "Dead Men Walking" when they were standalone short stories I'd plopped up on Amazon out of various frustrations ("DMW" was originally going to be the opening chapter of a novel called Z Block, until Walking Dead went to prison; "HtKaC" was intended to be a part of a larger collection but I had to release it early when I discovered Stephen King had written a story for *Bazaar of Bad Dreams* with essentially the same concept—except his protag is, naturally, a writer).

Thanks also to those who read some of these stories within the anthologies where they were first released. And thank you to those publishers who took a chance on my little twisted imagination. Thanks to The Sinister Horror Company (including Duncan Bradshaw, who has since moved on) for asking me to be a part of the first *Black Room Manuscripts,* and letting me know that "Cuttings" was one of the nastiest stories contained within. Thanks to KnightWatch Press for printing not one but two stories of mine ("Chompers" and "Where the Monsters Live," which was later fleshed out as a standalone novella.) Thanks also to Sirens Call Publications for publishing "Sanctuary" in their eco horror anthology. And of course, a massive thank you to Matt Shaw for taking me under his wing and releasing not just a handful of my short stories, but also the wacky b-horror novella *Prick* and the extreme horror novel *Woom*.

Many thanks to Peter Frain from 77 Studios who absolutely nailed the cover art. Working with Peter on this beast was a delight every step of the way and the cover turned out far better than I could have imagined.

Lastly (but not "leastly") I'd like to thank every one of you for reading *Video Nasties*. I hope you've enjoyed what you've read and will join me again for another dark tale or two.

ABOUT THE AUTHOR

Duncan Ralston was born in Toronto and spent his teens in small-town Canada. As a "grownup," Duncan lives with his partner and their dog in Toronto, where he writes dark fiction about the things that disturb him. In addition to his twisted short stories found in *GRISTLE & BONE*, the anthologies *EASTER EGGS & BUNNY BOILERS, WHAT GOES AROUND, DEATH BY CHOCOLATE, FLASH FEAR*, and the charity anthologies *DARK DESIGNS, BAH! IIUMBUG!, VS: US vs UK HORROR*, and *THE BLACK ROOM MANUSCRIPTS Vol. 1*, he is the author of the novel *SALVAGE*, and the novellas *WILDFIRE, WHERE THE MONSTERS LIVE, WOOM*, an extreme horror Black Cover book from Matt Shaw Publications, and *THE METHOD* from Kindle Press.

For more delicious dark fiction, visit
www.duncanralston.com and
www.shadowworkpublishing.com.